COME SEPTEMBER

A Novel

Gil Merrick

MC Publishing

MC PUBLISHING
An imprint of MC Publishing, LLC

AUTHOR'S NOTE: This is a work of fiction. All characters, organizations, and events portrayed in this novel are either products of the author's imagination or are used fictitiously. Any resemblance to actual persons, living or dead, businesses, institutions, or events is coincidental. While certain real locations, historical references, and public figures may be mentioned or depicted to provide context and authenticity, the narrative remains entirely fictional. The views and actions expressed by the characters are not intended to represent those of any real individuals or entities.

Names: Merrick, Roderick Gilman, author.
Title: Come September
Description: First edition. | Delaware: MC Publishing
Paperback ISBN   978-8-9902402-3-0
eBook ISBN   979-8-9902402-4-7
Author Photo Copyright © 2025 by Mastery Concepts LLC
Cover Design Copyright © 2025 by MC Publishing

Printed in the United States of America

To Spanky...

...and my gang of incredible friends

CONTENTS

PART ONE

1997 – 2006

Thirty days hath September,
April, June, and November.

— MOTHER GOOSE

CHAPTER 1

Ryan's World

SEPTEMBER 1997

Thursday, the 25th

Mapledale, West Virginia

A shrill whistle pierced the gymnasium before the referee shouted, "Wrassle!"

At fourteen, Ryan Jackson was a lean fighting machine. Although he was shorter than most boys in his class, what he lacked in height, he made up for in brawn. Today, he was evenly matched in weight and build by his opponent, a classmate from Greenbrier Middle School who was new to the team. Ryan had won the regional championship for his weight class last year—a notable achievement in his part of Appalachia, where boys fought for dominance in their hardscrabble neighborhoods and grew up tough.

Ryan's father, Hank, paced the sidelines, barking instructions as if his son were fighting for gold. But the yelling ended after two minutes of grappling; Ryan had been pinned. The referee reached for his opponent's hand, raised it above their heads to signal the win, and the victor trotted off, fist-pumping the air. He had vanquished the reigning champ in under three minutes, leaving Ryan humiliated and Hank enraged.

The ride home in Hank's run-down '62 pickup upset Ryan more than his loss. After a tense silence, Hank said, "What the hell happened to you out there, boy—lose your nerve? You gettin' a big head and thinkin' you can't be beat? Well, you got your ass whooped. Regional champ, and now this? Maybe if you spent more time at the gym practicin' and less time in your room pickin' at that blasted guitar of yours—singin' all them silly sweet songs—you'd have more fight in ya. I'm tellin' you now, sissies don't fit in around these parts. If you can't get the better of a boy your size on a soft wrestlin' mat, how the hell you gonna get on in a world full of tough men? You wanna be a loser all your life? A loser who don't fit in?"

Ryan didn't speak for the rest of the short ride home. After pulling into the gravel driveway of their small yard, Hank slammed the truck door and stormed into the kitchen, where Ryan's mother was cleaning up after dinner. Glenda was an ordinary woman, with a sturdy build and short chestnut hair frizzled from too many home perms. As Ryan shuffled toward his room with his head hung low, Glenda looked up and said, "Sweetie, you must be starvin'. I have a plate in the oven keepin' warm for you. Come sit and eat."

"Let him go, woman," Hank growled. "He don't deserve no dinner. Sissy Boy just got his ass kicked. He can go think about how he's gonna toughen up and become a real man one day."

"Hank, what has gotten into you? Don't talk like that. Our son's a regional champion. You should be proud of him."

"I'm not proud of no losers. And that's what he was tonight—a loser. He let that other kid pin him right out of the chute. Embarrassin' as all hell."

"It was one match, dear. Just one pre-season match."

"And then it will be two, then three, and before you know it…"

Ryan had tolerated all he could. "Would you shut up already? I get it. You think I'm a loser."

"What did you say to me? You told me to shut up in my own house?" Hank stepped toward Ryan with his right fist raised, and Glenda jumped between them.

"Stop it! Don't you dare lay a hand on that boy."

"Or what?" Hank said through squinted eyes. "This is my house. I work my tail off at that damned factory to keep a roof over our heads and food on the table. Now I got to take this kind of shit from my own family? I'll do whatever the hell I want around here, and right now, I want to teach that boy a lesson about respect." With his thick red hair and matching beard, Hank resembled a Scottish lumberjack whose face was turning a matching shade of red.

Hank pushed Glenda to the side, and as he raised his fist, she grabbed him by the wrist and tried to yank him back. Hank spun away, and with an arm strengthened by a lifetime of manual labor, he smacked Glenda's face with his open hand. She saw stars and couldn't focus for several seconds, but she spotted a kitchen knife lying on the counter as her vision cleared. Repositioning himself to strike Ryan, Hank noticed Glenda eyeing the knife. He leaped toward her, snatched it away, and waved the tip, pointing from Glenda to Ryan. "If one of you *ever* crosses me again, there will be hell to pay. Now get outta this kitchen. I don't want to hear a word from either of you for the rest of the night. And there had damned well better be a six-pack of beer in that fridge."

Ryan glanced at his mother as Hank moved toward the refrigerator. Glenda waved her fingers toward Ryan's room and gently nodded, silently indicating: Go and let it be. He'll calm down.

Ryan knew better than to slam the door after walking into his room, but the anger from seeing Hank strike his mother started his blood boiling. His eyes went to his acoustic guitar—proudly standing at attention in the corner—and he thought, *Now I can't even play music without Dad gettin' on my case. The one thing I enjoy, and he's takin' that away from me, too.* His blood boiled over. Ryan lashed out, kicking his boot through the flimsy drywall beside the door. Hank reacted instantly. He barged through the closed door like a raging bull and noticed the hole. Ryan was paralyzed with fear. Hank's reddened face and bulging veins said he had reason to be. In one quick move, Hank tackled Ryan to the floor, rolled him onto his back, and pinned his arms with his knees, freeing his hands to unbuckle his belt and rip it from his waist. The last thing Ryan saw was the fury in Hank's eyes and the folded leather strap raised above his head, poised to deliver the first blow to his helpless body.

Chapter 2

Rags and Riches

September 1998

Sunday, the 6th

Pontiac and Bloomfield Hills, Michigan

By the time Ryan turned fifteen, the Jackson family's ramshackle rental in Mapledale, West Virginia, was the only home he had known. Its white clapboard exterior was long overdue for a fresh coat of paint, several boards across the front needed replacing, a broken side window had been covered with plastic sheeting and duct tape, and the asphalt roof tiles had gathered a collection of moss that could cover a small forest. The landlord insisted he would "get around" to making repairs, but since the rent was often several months overdue, Hank never raised a fuss about the work not being done. Even with three bedrooms, quarters were tight. Hank and Glenda had squeezed twin beds and a dresser into their small room, Ryan and his younger brother had a bunk bed in theirs, and Glenda's father had surrendered the closet in the largest bedroom to his granddaughter, who managed to fit in a day bed.

Hank—like most men in this region of Appalachia—had moved from job to job over the years as nearby factories and local businesses closed their doors following the shutdown of each coal mine. Glenda was busy managing a family of six and could not take on part-time work. Money was always tight, and the Jacksons lived as close to the poverty line as a family could without crossing it. Government support was scarce in a region where many families faced destitution, and Hank had to provide for the family without it.

On Memorial Day weekend, Hank's brother, Wyatt, came home for a visit. He had worked for the past two years as a bricklayer in Bloomfield Hills, Michigan, an upscale suburb of Detroit. While metropolitan Detroit was spiraling toward bankruptcy, its northern suburbs were enjoying a financial boom. Expensive homes were being built throughout the region, and Wyatt had ample work. Several homes he worked on were located on lots surrounding a large equestrian facility called The Bloomfield Riding Club. Wyatt learned that the Club was looking to hire a new property manager, so he suggested that Hank apply for the position. Hank returned to Michigan with Wyatt and was informed at the end of June that he had been hired.

The Jacksons loaded a U-Haul on Labor Day weekend and moved their well-worn furniture and modest belongings into a small house in a working-class neighborhood in Pontiac, just minutes from the Riding Club. It was a two-floor duplex, surrounded by identical units with tidy lawns and clean streets. In every regard, it was a step up from their home in Mapledale, and the family considered Hank's new job a Godsend.

"Get your ass outta bed," Hank said as he shook Ryan's shoulders. "No sleepin' in today."

"It's Sunday," Ryan mumbled, "I ain't got school until Tuesday."

"That's right, but it don't mean you got the day off. From now on, you'll be comin' with me to the Riding Club on weekends, and your mom will drop you off there after school durin' the week. I'm short of help in the stables, and you can do plenty of jobs there. Now put on a clean pair of jeans and a T-shirt with no holes. We're leavin' in twenty minutes."

It was a fifteen-minute drive along Woodward Avenue from Pontiac to the Bloomfield Riding Club, and they arrived a few minutes before eight. The Club was established in the early nineteen hundreds on forty acres primarily used for fox hunting. In the 1960s, the open landscape, which was well-suited to fox hunting, was gradually sold off to developers, and the hunt was later disbanded. The Club then focused on providing top-quality boarding facilities for local horse owners, most of whom were accomplished physicians, lawyers, and business executives. In addition to the stables and riding areas, the Club had a large outdoor pool, numerous courts for racquet sports, and a clubhouse for dining and social events. The property was surrounded by dozens of newly constructed McMansions built for families who fancied living in an equestrian-themed community, with many of the homes showcasing brickwork installed by Hank's brother.

Ryan's jaw dropped as they rolled through the gated front entrance, elegantly flanked on both sides by white brick walls adorned with neatly trimmed hedges and vibrant flower beds. All the buildings shared the same style—New England farmhouse with gleaming white siding—and the stables extended the length of a football field. The paddocks were enclosed with white four-board fencing and stretched back a hundred feet to two sand riding arenas. Attached to the stables was an indoor riding arena with three rooftop cupolas and sliding windows on its sides to protect it from the weather. It was a playground for the wealthy, and Ryan sensed immediately that he might not fit in with its members.

As Hank parked the truck, Ryan noticed a young man cycling to the stables' entrance. The man dismounted and leaned his bike against the wall. As he walked inside, Hank gestured toward him and said to Ryan, "Over there is the tack room, where the saddles and bridles are kept. I'll show you where the brooms are, and you can start by sweepin' out that room. When you finish, you can sweep the barn aisles."

The barn had forty stalls—twenty on each side of the aisle leading to the riding arena. Ryan had finished sweeping one end of the stables and paused in the middle to shovel loose hay into a wheelbarrow. In front of him were four wash stalls—open areas where horses could be tied for showers and grooming. He stepped aside when he saw a rider leading his saddled horse toward him. It was the young man with the bike.

Kip Reynolds was the same age as Ryan but looked older than his fifteen years. With a lean and athletic build, Kip was at that growth stage where he resembled a man more than a boy. He had the classic good looks of a preppy WASP, with a strong chin, high cheekbones, and dark blue eyes. His wavy brown hair was highlighted with honey-blonde streaks from a summer spent by the pool. Although he had just finished riding under the hot sun, he looked ready to step onto the set of a Ralph Lauren shoot.

Noticing the broom in Ryan's hand, Kip guessed he worked there and said, "Could I ask a favor? Would you hold my horse while I head to the loo and wait for one of the wash stalls to free up? Adler here had a good workout and could use a shower before I turn him out in the paddock."

Although uncertain what a "loo" was, Ryan was sure he knew nothing about handling horses. His father had emphasized the importance of being polite and helpful to the members, so he hesitated to say, "I'm afraid I'm new here, and I don't know nothin' about handlin' horses."

"Well, welcome aboard. My name's Kip, Kip Reynolds, and I'd be happy to show you what to do. This guy is pretty tired, and he won't give you any trouble. What's your name?"

"Ryan."

"Nice to meet you, Ryan. Let me show you how to slip the bridle off and put on his halter." Kip picked up Adler's halter from a hook in front of a wash stall and buckled the longest strap around Adler's neck. He undid the bridle's throat latch beneath Adler's chin, unbuckled the leather band around his nose, reached for the bridle atop his crown, and slid it forward and toward his nose as the metal bit dropped from his mouth. "There. Now unbuckle the halter and place it here." Ryan undid the strap and cautiously positioned the halter around Adler's nose. "That's it. Now, take the long strap in your right hand and reach up to throw it over his neck." As Ryan lifted the strap, Adler raised his head, and the halter slipped off.

"Oh, shit," Ryan said under his breath.

"No worries. Just put it back on and try again. Give Adler a little scratch on his right cheek before you raise your hand to move the strap. That will soothe him, and he'll drop his head down. And talk to him. Horses like to be talked to." Ryan did as instructed, and Adler dropped his head down, softly pushing his muzzle into Ryan's abdomen, and wiggled his lips across his navel. "Well, what do you know? You're a horse whisperer. Adler likes you. It looks like you have the touch. Now, hold on to this lead rope and stand by his neck, behind his head, so he doesn't get fussy looking for treats in your pocket. If he tries to walk forward, give a couple of quick tugs on the rope and say, 'Whoa.' I'll be right back."

A minute later, a rider led her horse out of a wash stall and walked away. Several other riders were around, so Ryan moved Adler into the open stall before anyone got there. He clicked his tongue and stepped forward. Adler stayed by his side and followed him in. Ryan faced him forward and then attached the ropes like the other horses were tied.

Kip returned and saw that Ryan had removed the saddle from Adler's back and was massaging the area where the saddle had lain. "So much for not knowing how to handle a horse," Kip said. "You'll fit in well around here. Give him this peppermint, and he'll be your friend forever."

Ryan unwrapped the mint and placed it in his palm, holding it an inch below Adler's mouth. He felt the tickle of Adler's whiskers and the velvety softness of his lips as the horse gently mouthed the mint. A calming sensation coursed through Ryan, reminiscent of those moments he spent alone with his guitar, immersed in a song. It was a feeling he rarely experienced, one he longed to stay and bask in.

But the tranquility was shattered when his father bellowed from across the aisle, "Ryan! If you're finished helpin' Kip there, come with me. I got hay bales to move and need a hand."

Ryan turned to Kip and said, "Thanks for the help. I enjoyed meetin' Adler. I'm happy to help anytime. Just ask." Ryan walked away, leaving behind the joy of the moment and stepping back into the reality of living in Hank's world.

Tuesday, the 8th

Pontiac, Michigan

Glenda and Ryan's appointment with the principal of Pontiac Middle School was at ten-thirty, and Glenda made sure they arrived early. Although the summer heat had not yet passed, Glenda insisted that Ryan wear his newest trousers and a long-sleeved collared shirt. As they walked toward the office, she fussed to tame his scruffy hair and reminded him to sit up straight for the meeting. She had managed to find the only sleeved dress she owned, which she had carefully ironed after digging it out of a moving carton. She believed they both looked about as upstanding as they ever would.

The principal's assistant collected them from the foyer and introduced them to Simon Buchanan, a heavyset man with balding gray hair and a bulbous nose, whose redness suggested he enjoyed a drink or two in the evenings.

"Please, take a seat," he said, gesturing to the folding chairs across from his metal desk. With an overflowing inbox and piles of folders spread across the desk, Glenda supposed Mr. Buchanan was either very busy or remarkably disorganized. After several minutes of welcoming the Jacksons to Pontiac and expressing how pleased the school was to have Ryan as a new student, Buchanan got down to the business at hand.

"We've reviewed young Ryan's records from Greenbrier Middle School and see that he struggled a bit with his grades during the past academic year. He also had twenty-six full-day absences, which might explain his C-minus average. Mrs. Jackson, has Ryan been ill this past year?"

Glenda had to walk a fine line to avoid lying. As Ryan progressed through eighth grade, he began withdrawing from the family, going for days without speaking, and regularly missing meals. She received calls from the school informing her that he had not shown up for his morning classes and was talking back to teachers, becoming highly agitated when asked about his tardy arrivals. Ryan rarely submitted homework assignments on time and would storm out of the classroom when pressed to explain why.

He was developing a hair-trigger temper, causing him to lash out at the slightest provocation. However, much of his anger was directed toward opponents on the wrestling mats, and despite his father's misgivings, Ryan had become regional champion again that year. Only through the coach's efforts to prevent his suspension did Ryan complete the winter semester. But he had become sullen and lethargic when away from the gym, and Glenda had grown increasingly concerned. She knew Ryan was struggling emotionally and attributed his problems to her husband's abusive behavior toward him. She intervened when possible and went out of her way to counter Hank's aggression by showing Ryan her love, but it frustrated her to feel so helpless.

"Mrs. Jackson, how has Ryan's health been?" Buchanan probed.

Glenda forced a smile and, with her best diction, said, "Actually quite good, never really sick. I think Ryan has just been suffering from exhaustion. As you know, teenagers burn a lot of energy, and between going to classes, wrestling practice, and helping out a good bit at home, he's feeling a little burned out. Burning the candle at both ends, you might say. With our move behind us now, I'm sure he'll settle in and do just fine here."

Buchanan continued, "We are committed to every student's success, and it's my job to ensure that we set every student up for that. I've reviewed the curriculum from Ryan's first two years in middle school, seventh and eighth grades, and we believe that Ryan will have the greatest chance of success if he starts in the eighth grade here. There will be some courses he didn't take last year, and he mustn't feel left behind. He will always struggle to catch up with the other students if he doesn't get off to the right start. We certainly don't want to impose that hardship on him."

"You want to hold him back a grade?"

"Let's just call it an adjustment to account for the differences in school curricula." Turning to Ryan, he said, "Does that sound like a good plan for you, young man? We want to ensure you have the best possible experience here, and our teachers will take great care to make that happen. Come to this office tomorrow at eight, and I'll introduce you to your homeroom teacher."

Ryan stared at him blankly and nodded slightly.

"Ryan, dear, please answer Mr. Buchanan's question. Do you understand his plan?"

Ryan looked at Glenda as he stood and said, "Yeah, I understand. I ain't even started yet, and I've already been flunked a grade."

Ryan slammed the door as he left the room, leaving Glenda to assure the principal that Ryan would be fine once he had time to digest the news and understand that holding him back was in his best interest.

Glenda crossed the parking lot and saw Ryan standing by their pickup. When he noticed the passenger door was locked, he kicked the running board violently, making Glenda fear it might come loose. As they turned onto the road, Ryan began pounding his right fist against the door and his other hand on the banked seat between them.

Glenda pulled over and stopped. "Ryan, dear, I know this is upsetting, but…"

"Damn right it is! Might as well give me a T-shirt to wear tomorrow that says, 'Big Fuckin' Loser' on it."

"No one needs to know the particulars. You're new here, and nobody will know you're getting a fresh start."

"They'll find out. The first kid who gets in my face about it will regret opening his yap. I'll beat the crap outta him."

Glenda was at a loss for how to calm Ryan down and became agitated. "Well, if you do, you can look forward to being suspended, and they might even expel you. Then where will that leave you?"

"No worse off than I'm gonna be now, once Dad finds out. He'll go ape shit on me tonight."

"You can take your brother and sister to the Dairy Queen after dinner, and I'll explain things to him then. By the time you get home, his temper will have calmed down. I'll make sure of it."

"Good luck with that," Ryan said sarcastically, "and we can both hope he ain't wearin' a belt."

CHAPTER 3

Roy and the Wrestler

SEPTEMBER 1999

Friday, the 24th

Pontiac, Michigan

Ryan felt he would never get used to his parents' fighting. Today was no different. Hank walked into the living room and caught the end of Ryan's rant to his mother.

"How long do I got to put up with this? Those kids at school never let up: 'hillbilly, hill-jack, redneck, lug-head, po-boy, retard.' I swear I'm gonna lose it one day and knock the shit out of someone. That'll put an end to it. And if it don't, I'll just keep poundin' on 'em until it do."

Glenda stood from the sofa and walked over to give Ryan a hug. As she opened her arms, Hank said, "Sounds like the right idea to me. Show them boys you ain't no sissy. A couple of bloody noses and some bruised ribs, and those boys will change their tune. Time to be a man and stand up to them bullies."

Glenda stopped and said, "Hank, we've discussed this before. If Ryan lets his temper take hold and hurts someone, he'll sure as hell get himself expelled. Then what? He'll go through life without a high school diploma. What kind of future would that be?"

"You think the school would expel our boy just because he beat up a bully? What kind of *life lesson* does that teach a kid? Maybe I'll trot in there and give 'em a piece of my mind—let 'em know they don't mess with the Jacksons."

"You'll do no such thing," Glenda said. "Ryan is handlin' things just fine." Turning to Ryan, she said, "Just keep ignorin' them, sweetheart. As hard as it is, it's for the best."

Hank looked to the kitchen and said, "How come I don't smell no supper cookin'?"

With a sigh, Glenda said, "Because it's Friday, pizza Friday. I'll phone for it now. The kids will be home from the park soon, and they'll be starved."

With a high-pitched, mocking tone meant to imitate Glenda, Hank said, "Ryan is doin' great. The kids will be starved and need to eat. Dad's as dumb as a rock and don't know what he's doin'." Resuming his normal voice, he said, "Seems the only one in this house who's a problem is the one who pays the bills and keeps a roof over our heads. Keep it up, woman, and one mornin' Mr. Breadwinner here might walk out that door and not come back."

If only, Ryan thought.

Sunday, the 26th

Bloomfield Hills, Michigan

It was two-thirty, and Ryan had completed his afternoon barn chores. He sat on a trunk in the tack room, enjoying a cold Coke when Kip walked in to clean his saddle and bridle.

"It's quiet around here for a Sunday," Kip said. "You done for the day?"

"Nah. I gotta hang around until five to throw the horses their evenin' hay."

Kip thought for a moment and said, "Does your father still keep those fishing poles in the shed by the pool house? It would be a perfect day to head over to the pond and catch some bass." A five-acre plot of undeveloped land adjacent to the Club's property had a stocked pond. It was where Ryan's grandpa went to hunt turtles, shoot squirrels, and gig frogs for his mother to cook up in dishes that reminded the family of home.

Ryan smiled and said, "Yeah, they're still there, and a tackle box my grandpa uses when he comes to fish. Sounds good, as long as I'm back by five. My mom's comin' at six to bring me home."

Throughout the past year, Kip had sought opportunities to spend time with Ryan at the stables and help him adjust to his new environment. Kip taught him all the basic skills needed to handle and care for horses: grooming and tacking up, leading them out to the pastures, catching them and putting them back in their stalls, holding them steady while being worked on by blacksmiths or veterinarians, putting on their sheets and blankets, and leading them around after a good workout while they cooled down and recovered their breathing. Ryan picked up on everything quickly and had a natural rapport with horses, even those somewhat difficult to handle. He had a calming presence, and they took an instant liking to him. Ryan felt at home with horses, and many of their owners sought him out for help. When a rider needed to leave right after a workout, Ryan was quick to offer his assistance and put the horses away for them. It was rewarding for Kip to see Ryan, a young man who had arrived at the Club shy and withdrawn, growing in confidence and taking pride in his work. Kip's nature was to reach out and help the underdog. In this case, it was leading to what he felt would become a lasting friendship.

Kip and Ryan spent a quiet hour at the end of the dock without so much as a nibble, but it gave Kip the opportunity to ask questions and get to know Ryan better. After Kip got a conversation going, he learned that Ryan loved playing acoustic guitar. He owned a 1960 Gibson SJ-200 given to him by his grandpa, along with enough basic instruction to teach himself to play by ear. He could get through pieces by John Denver, Glen Campbell, and James Taylor, but Elvis became his inspiration after discovering that he had taken up the guitar at the age of eleven. Ryan understood that Elvis never excelled at playing, but owning a guitar became part of the Elvis legend, which appealed to Ryan. Elvis was the undisputed King, and everybody adored him—an experience Ryan could only fantasize about.

Kip asked Ryan how school was going and how he liked living in Michigan. Ryan seemed uncomfortable sharing details, but he revealed enough for Kip to understand that fitting in at school remained challenging. The average yearly income for a student's family in Pontiac was greater than what many workers in Ryan's part of West Virginia would earn in three years, and Ryan knew he was viewed as "the poor country boy" at school. His distinct Appalachian dialect marked him as a target for bullies who were determined to make his time there a living hell. Ryan said he counted the hours each day until he could leave school and head to the Club. That was where his friends were.

Shortly after 4:30, the tip of Ryan's fishing rod dipped toward the water, and it's quick bobbing signaled that he had a catch. Within seconds, he was reeling in a fifteen-inch bass weighing several pounds.

When Kip asked if he planned to bring it home, Ryan replied, "Nah. My old man can't stand the smell of fish fryin', and my mom says it tastes too strong to cook up good. So, this guy can go back to his pond."

As they broke from the woods and walked across the field

toward the stables, Kip said, "Your dad does a great job around here. The horse owners always comment about how well their staff keeps the barns, and other members say how nicely he maintains the tennis courts and pool area. He seems like a nice guy."

"Well, maybe around here he is. At home is somethin' else. He can be a real asshole sometimes. It's his way or the highway, and we've all learned the hard way not to cross him."

"What do you mean, 'the hard way'?"

Happy to end the conversation, Ryan stopped and pointed toward the barn's side door. "Did you see that?"

"See what?"

"Somethin' just ran into the barn, a small animal, brown and white, I think it was a dog."

Kip said, "A few of the horse owners have dogs. As a rule, they're not supposed to run loose, but people are pretty lax about it. Horse people are dog people. Nobody seems to mind."

"I never seen that one before. It looked scared. Let's check it out."

They laid the fishing gear by the paddock gate and walked through the side entrance into the barn. "Shh," Ryan whispered. "Hear that? That whimper? It's comin' from behind them hay bales."

Ryan and Kip each slid a bale away from the wall and saw a chestnut brown puppy curled up against it. He had a white patch on his chest and black tips on his ears. His short hair was damp and matted, and his eyes were nearly caked shut. It looked like he had been dragged through a mud puddle.

Ryan picked the puppy up and began wiping the dirt from his eyes with the bottom of his T-shirt. "Poor little guy. Looks like somebody dumped him off. I bet he ain't had nothin' to eat in days."

Kip said, "I don't think we have any dog food here, but I can go get some."

"I still got some of my ham sandwich from lunch. He can have that."

Ryan finished cleaning the puppy's eyes and held him up to his face to see if they were clear. He paused for a moment and said, "I got an idea. How 'bout you keep an eye on him while I throw hay to the horses? Then we can give him a bath and feed him. My mom will be here in about an hour, and I'll ask if I can take him home. Don't look like he belongs to anybody here. If nobody comes 'round for him, I could, you know, adopt him." Right on cue, the puppy poked his head forward and gave Ryan a series of quick licks on his nose. Their bond was sealed.

Kip beamed and said, "Now, *that* is a great idea. Sold."

By the time Glenda arrived, the puppy had been bathed with horse shampoo, dried off, and brushed. Aside from his protruding ribs, he was as good as new. His short tail wagged relentlessly as he was introduced to Glenda, who said, "Looks to me like this little guy is the product of a tryst between a German shepherd and a beagle. He's adorable."

Ryan said, "I was hopin' I could bring him home with us. I promise he won't be no trouble. I'll look after him real good. But I s'pose Dad won't let me keep him. He's got some kind of bug up his ass these days and will prob'ly say no."

"Over my dead body you ain't keepin' this sweet thing. We could use some happiness around that house. This little bundle of joy is just the ticket. What are you gonna name him?"

Ryan thought for a moment and said, "Roy."

Glenda smiled knowingly. "Roy? Like Roy Rogers from all them cowboy movies you watched as a kid?"

"Yeah. He used to sing and play guitar with the Hollywood Hillbillies. Roy here ought to fit right in with our family."

Rolling her eyes at Kip, she said, "Well, it's time we head home and face the music. We'll let you know how it goes."

"My money's on you," Kip said. "Good luck."

CHAPTER 4

Swiss Miss

SEPTEMBER 2000

Thursday, the 14th

Bloomfield Hills, Michigan

Adam Kinzler's uncontrolled chortle was the opening salvo in the ensuing battle.

It was Dr. Gerald Greene's last year teaching world history, and he had lost all patience for students like Adam and the petulance they brought into his classroom.

Sitting behind a stately oak desk and peering over his half-glasses, he said, "Is there something you would like to add to the conversation, Mr. Kinzler?"

"Nope," Adam said.

"I assumed from the animal sound you emitted that there is. Please share your thoughts on the topic with us. You seem to take issue with my point." Dr. Greene had been down this path with Adam before and did not welcome another debate.

"Just that Napoleon Bonaparte wasn't actually that short," Adam said with a smug grin.

"And I presume that in your infinite wisdom, you are familiar with the phrase, 'Napoleon complex'?"

"Yes, but that is based on a common misconception. Napoleon measured around five feet seven inches tall using modern measurements, which was the average height for a Frenchman of his time. The confusion arises from the difference between French and British inches in historical records. The term 'Napoleon complex' stems from the myth that he was unusually short."

"So, are you suggesting that after teaching about the Napoleonic Wars for 35 years, I have been misleading my students by sharing a myth?"

"Not misleading, misinforming. It is well-documented in texts from that period."

"Then I look forward to you sharing your sources with me at another time. Now, if you don't mind, I would like to continue. And please try to refrain from making any more unwelcome outbursts, whether verbal or otherwise."

"No, I don't mind at all. Please, continue."

Adam always sat in the back row, where he could critically observe the students' exchanges as if watching a show staged solely for his entertainment. Everyone knew Adam had an IQ well above 145 and respected his reputation as a science and math genius. Although in his junior year, he typically attended advanced placement courses with the upper school seniors. Since world history was required for graduation and offered only to juniors, Adam acquiesced to joining the average students' ranks and endured the boredom of Dr. Greene's lectures.

Kip needed to turn sideways in his customary front-row seat to see the whole exchange. He had never crossed paths with Adam when they attended middle school together, but like everyone else, he knew who Adam Kinzler was. While Kip respected Adam's intellect, swarthy good looks, and role as ice hockey team captain, he considered him arrogant and conceited. After watching this exchange with Dr. Greene, he decided his opinion was justified and did not need to know Adam any better.

Aside from the entertainment factor, another advantage for Adam in sitting in the back row was the opportunity to escape from the room immediately after a lesson. That was part of his strategy for keeping to himself and avoiding interaction with other students. He didn't consider himself anti-social, he just didn't like most people. They annoyed him. Adam slipped out when Dr. Greene dismissed the class while his classmates lingered to avoid him. They were either intimidated by his good looks and confident demeanor or feared being stung by his sharp wit if they dared to engage.

It was Kip's last class of the day, and since he did not live on campus like many upper school students, he began his stroll to the parking lot. The Cranbrook School was an 80-year-old preparatory school in Bloomfield Hills. Established in 1922 by a wealthy publishing mogul, the campus covered over 300 acres. Its lush gardens surrounded stone archways and distinguished brick buildings in the Tudor style. The sprawling campus resembled Oxford, Cambridge, and Harvard, and its reputation was equally storied. Kip savored the familiar scent of the greenery and noticed that the leaves on the maples and oaks were changing color, signaling autumn's arrival. Autumn was the best time of year to enjoy his favorite outdoor sport: polo.

At 17, Kip was starting his junior year in upper school, and upon turning 16, his parents gave him the burgundy Audi cabriolet that his mother drove. Given the wealth many students at the school enjoyed, Kip's car was not seen as a status symbol in comparison to their BMWs and Porsches, but it was well-suited to fulfill its primary purpose: getting him to the stables every day for training sessions. Today, he would stop at home to change and grab something to eat before heading to the stables.

Kip pulled out of the school lot and drove through the quiet suburban streets to his home on Vaughan Road, an Italian Renaissance mansion clad in a yellow limestone façade and capped with a tiled Mission roof. It was built in 1932 by his grandfather, Grayson Reynolds, who made his fortune manufacturing components for Detroit's Big Three automakers in the heyday of the early twentieth century. Kip had lived there since he was six, when his grandfather passed away from a heart attack at 78. Kip's father inherited the grand home and moved their family in before the grass had sprouted on Grandpa Reynolds' grave.

Sitting 500 feet back from the road, Kip's slow drive past the small lake with its elegant fountain allowed him to turn off thoughts of school and focus on planning the day's training sessions. Kip changed into his riding clothes and prepared a sandwich for his three-mile drive to the Bloomfield Riding Club. Kip's father had played polo when summering with his family in Pinehurst, North Carolina, and was delighted when Kip expressed an interest in playing. At age 10, Kip had already demonstrated his athleticism running track, but after watching a polo match while vacationing in Palm Beach, he was bitten by the horse bug and declared polo his passion. It was now his only sport, and consumed all his free time. The team's riders practiced their basic skills in the Club's riding arenas and open fields, traveling to venues throughout Michigan and Ohio to compete in monthly matches.

Kip pulled into the cobblestone courtyard in front of the stables and found his usual spot by the tack room entrance. He inhaled the rich scents of leather and lanolin as he walked into the saddle room, savoring the familiar smells that never failed to intoxicate him with excitement. He tucked his navy polo jersey into his riding pants and pulled on his knee-high leather boots before collecting his saddle and bridle.

Walking into the long barn aisle, he noticed a dark bay horse standing in a grooming stall with a young girl preparing him for her ride. She placed her brush into a bucket and removed the saddle from its rack on the wall. A stirrup leather caught on the rack and almost yanked the saddle from her arms as she turned to walk toward the horse. After a slight stumble, she wiggled the saddle loose, turned, and stood on her tiptoes beside the horse, unable to reach the top of his back.

Flashing a smile with perfect white teeth, Kip approached and said, "Would you like some help? Without a ladder, I doubt you'll get that saddle on him anytime soon."

She turned to look at Kip and was taken in by his charming demeanor. "Thanks, but I think I can get it," she said, feeling a flush of embarrassment rise in her face.

"Well, not if you want to join the others for your five o'clock lesson. Here, let me help."

Standing four inches taller than her five-foot-six frame, Kip effortlessly placed the saddle on her horse's back and adjusted the saddle pad before tightening the girth.

"I can do that," she said, "but thanks for the help. You're right, he's a bit taller than I realized. Even so, I can get the bridle on just fine. He likes me and always lowers his head when I ask him to. We've already bonded, and I've only ridden him twice!"

The girl possessed an uncommon assertiveness for a 15-year-old, but given her striking and somewhat exotic appearance, Kip wasn't surprised. Her dark auburn hair was pulled back in a ponytail, glistening like silk in the afternoon sun that filled the stables. Her wide-set eyes were an unusual shade of nomad green, accentuated by her olive-brown complexion.

"My name's Kip. Kip Reynolds. I keep two horses here and play on the junior polo team. I haven't seen you here before. Is this your horse?"

"My name is Claudia, and no, I just started riding here last week. I had been taking lessons at Oakmont Farms, but they sold out to a developer and closed the stables, so I'm taking lessons here until my parents let me buy my own horse."

"Are they at the Club now?" Kip asked.

"No. My brother dropped me off and will be back at 6:30 to take me home. Thanks for your help, looks like I'm going to be on time for my lesson."

"No problem. Have a great ride."

Kip set to work grooming both his horses. Although technically larger than ponies—standing just over sixteen hands—they were experienced polo ponies that his father had purchased from a friend in Pinehurst. After playing an aggressive match on Sunday, Kip took them on an easy hack around the property instead of having a rigorous training session. They were hosed off and blanketed when Kip set off for home shortly after 6:30. He opened the door to the tack room and saw Claudia sitting on a trunk, flipping through *The Chronicle of the Horse*.

"Hi there," Kip said. "How was your ride?"

"It was great. I love that horse. I feel like Chester would do anything for me, which is more than I can say for my brother."

"Yeah, where is he? You said he was picking you up at 6:30."

"It's not the first time he's been late picking me up somewhere. He's a computer geek and loses track of time when he gets absorbed in his projects. I just phoned, and he didn't answer."

"I'm guessing you don't live too far away. Can I give you a ride home?"

"I live in Birmingham, just a few minutes' drive away. It's only a forty-five-minute walk, but my parents would have a fit if I walked, and I'm not sure how they'd feel about me getting a ride home from someone they don't know."

"Did you try calling them?"

"My mother is at her studio working late with a client, and my father is out of town on business. But I guess they'd prefer someone from the stables to drive me home rather than find out I walked alone on Woodward Avenue at sunset. Besides, you don't seem like someone who would abduct me." Claudia instantly regretted her last comment, but when Kip flashed another bright smile, she forgot her embarrassment and said, "So, yes. I'd love a ride. I have a ton of homework after dinner and want to finish up before my dad gets home from his trip. If my brother does show up, that's too bad. It will serve him right."

During the short drive to Birmingham, Kip learned that Claudia was beginning eighth grade at Cranbrook's middle school. She was born in Geneva, and her family moved from Switzerland to Birmingham four years ago when her father was transferred to manage his bank's private investment office. Her native languages were French and German. Her English skills were not yet well-honed, so she had been held back a year in school when they arrived. Claudia's mother was born in Barcelona and met her father while vacationing in the Costa Brava with her family. Kip surmised the Spanish bloodline gave Claudia her dark complexion and luxuriant hair. He also understood why she spoke with a hint of an accent—something that added a special flair.

Claudia's family lived in a spacious Tudor home along Lakeside Drive on the east side of Quarton Lake, an eight-acre body of water fed by the Rouge River and bordered by city parks. Birmingham and Bloomfield Hills ranked among the most desirable areas for Detroit's affluent residents. Its beautifully landscaped properties and proximity to the town center made Quarton Lake the perfect location for their newly immigrated family.

As Kip drove around the semi-circular driveway to drop Claudia at the front door, an older model black BMW 528i came down from the garage. "Well, if it isn't my brother Adam, finally breaking away from his computer long enough to pick me up. Guess this will teach him a lesson," Claudia said.

Kip's heart skipped a beat before he glanced away from the driver and said, "Adam Kinzler is your brother?"

"Yeah. Do you know him?"

"Not really. He's in my history class at Cranbrook, but we've never actually met."

"I'm not surprised. He keeps to himself unless he thinks someone is being stupid and feels he needs to point it out. I ignore him when he's like that, which is fairly often."

Adam rolled down his window as he brought his car to a stop and took a moment to check out the unfamiliar car in his driveway. Having an infallible memory, he recognized Kip as one of the eighteen students in his history class—the pretty boy who always sat in the front row.

Claudia stepped out of the car and said to Adam, "I thought you had forgotten about me, so I let Kip give me a ride. I guess you know each other from school?"

"Nope," Adam said, casting a glance at Kip. "But thanks for bringing sis home. You didn't have to, I was already on my way."

"Better late than never, right?" The smile on Claudia's face indicated her remark was meant jokingly, but Adam's expression remained blank.

"You take what you get with free chauffeur service," Adam said. "I'll still head out, but I'll be back by nine when Dad gets home. I'll be at the rink shooting some pucks." This time, Kip noted a slight accent he hadn't detected at school. Kip assumed that with the name

Kinzler, his father might be of German heritage, but the accent sounded more British than German.

Kip called to Claudia across his open convertible and said, "I'm glad we met. Good luck getting your homework done, and hopefully, I'll see you at the Club this weekend."

"You will if you're there on Saturday or Sunday morning, that's when I have my next lessons. Thanks again for the ride."

Kip made a mental note to make sure he scheduled his weekend accordingly.

Saturday, the 16th

The Bloomfield Riding Club buzzed with activity on weekends. Kip was in the grooming area, saddling up his older horse, Champs, a black gelding with white markings on his legs, and wondered if he might see Claudia before riding out to the fields for some galloping work. He glanced down the aisle toward the tack room, hoping to spot her, and saw Ryan's silhouetted figure approaching him. Ryan stepped into the sunlight streaming through the barn window, and Kip noticed how much Ryan had matured since they met two years ago.

Ryan was still a few inches shorter than Kip but weighed about the same. Kip was lean and lithe, while Ryan was well-muscled and stocky. His mop of loosely curled light brown hair had almost a reddish hue, and his green eyes were in a perpetual squint. His light complexion did little to hide a persistent mild acne outbreak, and his mouth was slightly too big for his face. Ryan was not unattractive, but he also wasn't handsome. He was *almost* handsome, in a rugged way.

When Kip realized it was Ryan, he called, "Hey, how's it going? Do you know if Claudia is scheduled for a lesson this morning?"

Before he could answer, Ryan whistled and yelled, "Roy! Git over here. Leave that cat alone before you git your nose swiped again."

Looking over at Kip, Ryan said, "Nah, I ain't seen her. But she'll be here. She's scheduled for an eleven o'clock lesson with Terry."

Kip noticed Ryan's expression brighten when he mentioned Claudia's upcoming arrival. Ryan had revealed to Kip that he was mesmerized by Claudia's green eyes and exotic features, and said he considered her the most attractive girl he had ever seen. Although Ryan didn't seem book smart, he demonstrated good intuition and a sense of street savvy. When he confessed his attraction to Claudia, he acknowledged that becoming friends with a 15-year-old of her caliber was unlikely, but he figured there was no harm in enjoying her company.

A moment later, Kip saw two figures walking in from the barn's side entrance. One of them was Claudia, accompanied by a man who was at least half a foot taller. Ryan could see they were approaching Kip and Champs, and said, "There you go—see ya later," as he shuffled off in the opposite direction.

"Good morning, Kip," said Claudia. "Thanks again for the ride home on Thursday. This is my father, and he's come out to watch my lesson on Chester. Dad, this is Kip Reynolds."

"Nice to meet you, Mr. Kinzler. We're glad to have Claudia at the Club, and I'm sure Chester is happy to have her riding him. Claudia says they fit together like a hand in a glove. I'll swing by the ring on my way out with ole Champs here and watch some of her lesson."

"It's a pleasure to meet you, young man. My name is Conrad, and I appreciate your efforts to make Claudia feel welcome and for giving her a ride home yesterday." Turning to Claudia, he added, "I don't want you ever to consider walking home from this Club, regardless of the time of day."

Without missing a beat, Kip said, "Well, Mr. Kinzler, I mean, Conrad, I'd be more than happy to give Claudia a lift on any day she has a riding lesson. I live on Vaughan Road, just fifteen minutes from your home, and attend Cranbrook, so bringing her here would never be a problem. I'd be glad to do it. After three years of riding my bike every day, I understand what a luxury getting a ride can be."

"That's a very kind offer, Kip. If you don't have plans, why not come to the house tomorrow night for dinner and meet the family? Claudia's mother doesn't open her studio on Sundays, and I know her brother Adam will be home. He's a junior at Cranbrook. Do you two know each other?"

"We haven't really met, but yes, he's in my history class. And thanks for the invitation. I'd love to join you."

"Wonderful. Dinner is at six."

What a great opportunity to get to know Claudia better and find out if Adam is as arrogant as he appears, Kip thought, before letting out a chortle he hoped was not a prelude to a match of wits with Adam the following evening.

Sunday, the 17*th*

Entering the foyer of the Kinzler home felt like stepping into a photo spread in *Architectural Digest*. Sophia Serrano, Claudia's mother, and owner of The Serrano Design Studio in downtown Birmingham, designed many of the elegant interiors in Birmingham and Bloomfield Hills, with the Kinzler home serving as a showcase for her talent. Regular features in the local *Hour Magazine* and occasional TV coverage of her parties ensured a steady stream of clients. Sophia had a keen eye for the latest trends in contemporary design and infused a European flair into all her projects. Clients appreciated her outgoing personality and caring nature, often waiting months to join her waiting list. While touring the house's manicured gardens, Kip discovered that Conrad was born in Tutzing, just outside of Munich in the Bavarian Alps. After earning his bachelor's degree from the University of Munich, he pursued an MBA in Global Banking at the EU Business School in Geneva. He advanced through the ranks at UBS Bank Group in Geneva, and after six years, he was transferred to manage their branch in Birmingham. Conrad carried his six-foot frame with perfect posture and walked with a precise stride that suggested military training. His facial features were classically Aryan, and rectangular rimless glasses framed his steel blue eyes. Although only 42, his short hair had more salt than pepper, and his Italian designer clothes reflected fashion trends that a younger man might wear. Kip suspected Sophia had a hand in selecting Conrad's wardrobe.

Sophia accompanied Kip and Claudia on Conrad's tour of the gardens, and it was clear to Kip that they were a loving family who cherished one another's company. The gentle touches Conrad placed on Sophia's waist and the playful way he brushed Claudia's hair from her face revealed a tenderness that one might not immediately detect from his otherwise stoic demeanor. After 18 years of marriage, Conrad still appeared enamored with his bride's ebony hair, deep olive complexion, and lean, wispy build. Sophia's flowing dress was splashed with a colorful floral design and cut with just enough flounces to be playful while still conveying an air of elegance. Kip could see where Claudia got her good taste, sophistication, and plucky attitude. She was every bit her mother's daughter.

Adam, however, was not at all like his father. Although he had Conrad's tall frame, broad shoulders, and handsome face, Adam had inherited his mother's black hair, dark complexion, and thick eyelashes that gave him a look the girls on campus called "dreamy." Adam seemed to take his good looks for granted, with an attitude that said, "Isn't everybody this handsome?" What he took the most pride in was his intellect. On that count, he knew he was exceptional. He was 13 when his family moved to the States, and he had already become fluent in German and French. He had picked up some Spanish on visits to his mother's family in Barcelona and began learning English at school in Geneva. Languages came easily to Adam, but his true forte was mathematics and science, especially computer science. Thanks to a generous endowment, the Cranbrook School had a state-of-the-art computer lab to which Adam had access. Having deemed all commercially sold PCs too limited in their capabilities, he had successfully built a machine at home that met his needs. When Adam wasn't perched in front of his computer monitors, he could often be found at the local ice rink. He had never been on a pair of skates before coming to Michigan, but after one season of practice, he had become a star player on Cranbrook's varsity ice hockey team. It was a sport that used his natural athleticism, quick reflexes, and ability to outmaneuver any opponent. Although Adam was respected and liked by his teammates, he was the first to leave after practice and made no effort to socialize with the other boys. He preferred retreating to his secluded world and uncovering answers to his endless questions about the hidden workings of the vast new internet.

Kip had already taken his seat next to Claudia in the formal dining room when he heard Adam padding down the stairs. Adam burst into the room wearing a snug cashmere sweater that perfectly matched his eyes. He wore a white T-shirt, leaving it untucked over his black Levi 501s, creating a look that intentionally showcased his athletic physique.

He surveyed the room and said to Claudia, "Hey, *Liebchen*, your friend is sitting in my chair."

"My friend is Kip Reynolds, and you know him from school. Don't be a jerk. I'm sure it won't be too disorienting for you to move your seat for one meal." Claudia's delivery came with a generous smile that told Kip they had a loving relationship, expressed through teasing banter. "And how about saying hello? You may have forgotten that we live in a civilized home."

"Hey," Adam said without looking at Kip.

Conrad and Sophia entered the room carrying two casserole dishes fragrant with rosemary and oregano. "I hope you're all hungry," Sophia said. "I've prepared a Mediterranean stew with orzo. As always, I made too much. And don't fill up on the bread, I've made a tiramisu for dessert."

"It smells wonderful, Mrs. Kinzler. Thank you so much for inviting me," Kip said. He realized how strange it felt to sit with a family at a properly set table. At the Reynolds' home, everyone ate at different times. Dinner wasn't an event, and meals were always some variations of a prepared entrée from the gourmet market.

"You're quite welcome, dear, but please, call me Sophia. Besides, I go by my maiden name, Serrano. It's better branding for my business. I own the interior design studio on Old Woodward Avenue. You must have seen it, it's next to the movie theater."

Kip had been by the studio hundreds of times—located on the main shopping street in Birmingham—but as a teenager, he had no interest in the home décor items she sold or the design services for which she was so well-known. "Oh yes. I'm quite familiar with it— from the outside—and I believe my mother might stop in from time to time. Patty Reynolds, do you know her?"

"I know her name. She's quite active in the local fundraising community, but I don't believe we've met," Sophia said.

"I'll tell her to stop in and introduce herself."

"How long have you been playing polo, Kip? Claudia says you are quite good and spend all your free time at the stables."

At that moment, a loud chortle erupted, and Kip recognized it as the one he had heard in history class. *Here we go*, he thought. *This should be entertaining.*

Conrad looked at Adam and said, "What's so funny? You spend all *your* free time tapping on a keyboard and staring at computer monitors. Everyone has their own passion."

"Yeah, but mine doesn't involve abusing innocent animals."

"Adam! We've had this discussion before," Claudia said. "There is nothing abusive about riding horses. If you treat them right, they will bond with you and do anything you ask, as long as they understand what you want and are physically able to do it. I have already bonded with the horse I'm riding at the Club, and he loves me."

Adam had been looking forward to having this conversation with Claudia again. The last time she said that her horse loved her, he decided to do some research, and now he was armed with new information for the debate.

"No," Adam said, "That horse does not love you. He sees you as a vehicle for delivering peppermints and carrots and nothing more. I guarantee that if you turned a few horses out in a pasture full of grass and opened the door to your horse's stall, he would trot himself right out to join his herd and never look back. You're foolish if you think a horse would rather be bound in leather straps and carrying you around than going out and grazing with his herd."

"There's nothing abusive about putting a saddle and bridle on a horse and giving him some exercise. It only makes him stronger and healthier," Claudia said. "They're like people. They enjoy having something to do. Every horse wants a job and is happier when they have one."

"Let me find a draught horse who's been plowing a field for eight hours in the hot sun and see how much he loves his job," Adam said.

"I'm not talking about workhorses. I mean sport horses. Men have been riding horses in many forms of sport for centuries, and horses have proven to be incredible partners in all of them. They wouldn't be if they didn't feel bonded to their riders and enjoy what they were asked to do. A courageous horse will give you its heart."

"And it's life," Adam said. "Last year, in the sport of racing, 33 horses in this country died on the track. During the previous five years, over 150 courageous horses were euthanized at tracks throughout America. And that's just one country. Those animals begin racing when they are as young as two, and at that age, their ligaments and tendons are not fully developed, and their bones are still growing. I'm going to say that is abusive."

"Okay, I agree. Racing needs to make some major changes to how the sport is run. The problem is that money and greed have taken over the sport, and yes, that's wrong. But for centuries, we treated our horses as companions in sport, and that hasn't changed."

"You might fantasize about knights in shining armor when you say that. In the sixteenth and seventeenth centuries, the sport of jousting was used to prepare soldiers and nobility for war. A man's armor and weapon could weigh as much as 150 pounds, and the horses' armor weighed about 60. Men averaged five feet four and weighed as much as their armor. Add a 15-pound saddle, and you have a horse carrying about 375 pounds. Horses were smaller then and weighed about 800 pounds. Since a horse can comfortably carry about one-third of its weight, it was overburdened by about 100 pounds. I'm going to guess the horse did not enjoy that sport too much, especially when a jousting festival was only practice for charging into battles where more horses died than soldiers."

Sophia interrupted. "Adam, darling, you make some valid points, but I'm sure Kip didn't come here to listen to a debate about the ethics of riding sport horses."

"There's no debate, Mother—and *all* my points are valid—because there is nothing ethical or humane about abusing a helpless animal."

"Well, let's leave it at that," Sophia said. "And please don't be shy about seconds, there's plenty."

Kip's good nature prevented him from taking offense at Adam's comments, and oddly enough, he found something likable about Adam's integrity and compassion toward what he viewed as innocent and somewhat helpless animals. Kip was surprised by this reaction and pleased that there was a side to Adam he could respect. Kip thought, *Maybe I could become friends with this guy and, as a bonus, spend time with Claudia away from the stables. Not bad. Not bad at all.*

Tuesday, the 19th

After thirty minutes of practicing in the field, Kip walked Champs back to the barn and lamented his lack of progress in improving his near-side forward swing. Of the many swing variations used in the game of polo, this was the one Kip found hardest to execute consistently. Frustrated, he resolved to focus on it for the remainder of the week in preparation for Sunday's match. As he passed the outdoor ring, he saw Claudia walking Chester on a loose rein while the other girls took turns jumping a small course.

Claudia waved to Kip and said, "Did you see our last round? It was awesome. Chester and I have finally clicked, and I think he's loving it, despite what Adam might say."

Kip walked his horse toward her and said, "I know Adam is a

genius, but he's out of his league when it comes to horses. I'm with you on this one. You and Chester look great together."

Claudia started gathering her reins and was turning away when Kip said, "Sunday afternoon, we're having a birthday party for my brother at the house, and I'd love for you to come by. Some of Bradley's friends from Cranbrook will be there, and I'd bet you'll know a few. It's totally casual and will kick off around two."

"I'd love to. Bradley and I are in the same economics class, and we've gotten to know each other pretty well, so I'll be there."

Pleased that Claudia had accepted the invitation so quickly, Kip made his way to the wash stall to give Champs his well-deserved shower. While putting away his riding gear, he noticed Ryan climbing down the ladder from the hay loft. "Hey, Ryan. The hose nozzle in the wash stall keeps popping off and probably needs to be replaced. Thought you might want to let your dad know."

Ryan turned from Kip and walked away without answering. Kip knew Ryan had heard him and said, "You okay, buddy?" Ryan kept walking, confirming to Kip that something was wrong. After three long strides, Kip caught up and put his hand on Ryan's shoulder, prompting him to whirl around and confront Kip with an angry look.

"Whoa there, pal. I'm just letting you know about the hose before one of the prissy stable queens gets their knickers in a knot and kicks up a fuss about it," Kip said while Ryan continued walking away.

Suspecting his comment about the hose nozzle was not the source of Ryan's anger, Kip said, "Come on, man, we're friends. What's up? It's not like you to blow me off like this."

"I don't need you jumpin' my case on top of everythin' else. That son of a bitch coach kicked me off the team Friday. I've a mind to go back and bust the lights outta his car." Ryan was beginning his sophomore year at Pontiac High School and had already secured his spot on the varsity wrestling team.

After Kip calmed Ryan down enough to tell him what had happened, Kip learned that Ryan had been wrestling a teammate at practice, who was one of his regular tormentors at school. When Ryan hit the mat after an illegal takedown, he rolled over and seized his opponent's right leg with both hands. Fueled by his rage, Ryan yanked the leg back at an unnatural angle and then threw his body, professional wrestling style, onto his opponent. After a prolonged cry of agony, Ryan heard a loud crack. It was his opponent's right femur.

"Coach said I used 'unnecessary aggression' and 'illegal moves,' and that, 'til I could show I'm a better sportsman, I'm off the team. It was the other asshole who was bein' illegal. Far as I care, they can all go to hell. Don't need that shit."

Kip wondered when Ryan's aggression would finally lead to something like this. Feeling compassion for his friend, Kip said, "That really sucks. Maybe just lay low for a while, and the coach will come to his senses and put you back on the team. Your school has a big season coming up, and this may be the year Pontiac High makes the finals. They need you."

"Who cares? I hate that school anyways."

Looking for a way to lift Ryan's spirits, Kip said, "Well, you'll graduate in a couple of years, and then you can get away from it all. Maybe it would be good for you to have a change of scenery. My brother's turning 14 on Sunday, and we're having a party at my house. A bunch of friends from Cranbrook will be there, and I know Claudia is coming. It should be fun."

Ryan's face lit up when he heard Claudia's name, but it quickly fell when he replied, "Thanks, but my dad's workin' Sunday and I don't got no way to get there. Club's got a wedding in the afternoon, and my dad will be stuck here 'til late."

"No problem. I'll wrap up with my horses by two, and you can ride to the party with me. I'm happy to drive you home afterward."

Ryan stared at the ground for a moment, contemplating whether going to the party with a bunch of rich kids was a good idea. However, hoping to talk with Claudia and see her dressed up for the party, he lifted his eyes and said, "Um, sure. Thanks. I'll ask my dad for the afternoon off."

Sunday, the 24th

The morning polo match in nearby Lansing had gone into overtime, so when the trailer pulled into the Club to unload the horses, Kip knew he would be an hour late for his brother's party. While leading his second horse off the ramp and walking toward the barn, he saw Ryan working under the hood of his father's pickup and walked over. "Sorry, we're running late. I need a half-hour to put the horses up, then I'll be ready to go."

"No problem," Ryan said. "Dad asked me to change his oil while I waited, and I'm just finishin' up."

Kip tended to his horses and signaled to Ryan he was ready to go. As Ryan walked over to the Audi, Kip noticed a three-inch oil stain on the front of Ryan's long-sleeve Henley and said, "Bad luck with your shirt, mate. I'll wait here while you change."

Ryan looked down and said, "I don't got another shirt, and it pisses me off my dad made me change his oil. I just bought this. Cost me twenty bucks at the Gap."

"Well, you can change into one of my shirts when we get to the house. It might be a little long, but it should fit your shoulders and chest just fine. You're big on top."

At the end of their long driveway, Kip pulled up behind his house and parked in front of the six-car garage. Halfway down the trellised walkway to the house, Ryan stopped and said, "Shit. You never said you lived in a friggin' mansion. This thing is huge. How big is your family?"

"Only me, my parents, and my brother. We moved in after my grandfather passed away. My mother complained it was too big for our small family and would be a pain to maintain, but my father insisted. You'll see when you meet him, he's an odd duck."

A stairway led from the back door to the second floor, and they went straight to Kip's room. Kip found a button-down shirt with a conservative plaid pattern and handed it to Ryan. "This should fit you. My mom bought it for me, and I've never worn it. I'm going to pop down and let her know we're here. There's a bathroom over there if you need it. Just come down the stairs we came up, and turn left into the kitchen. I'll see you there."

Kip's mother was at the refrigerator filling a glass with ice when Kip walked in. "Oh, there you are. How was the match, dear? I assume it ran late." Patricia Reynolds was half a foot shorter than Kip, but her ramrod posture and regal stance made her look much taller. She was known at the country club and throughout the area's social circles as Patty, a high-bred debutante from Park Avenue who was accustomed to only the finest things. Her platinum blonde hair was pulled back tightly and secured in a ponytail with a tastefully bejeweled four-inch clip—her signature hairstyle. Her clothes were impeccably tailored and made from expensive cashmere, silk, or linen, and she eschewed anything with frills or lace. She exuded conservative elegance, no matter the occasion. On her right arm, she wore a double-strand diamond and sapphire tennis bracelet her husband, Dudley, had given her on their tenth anniversary, the only item that betrayed her look of understated wealth.

"The match was good," Kip said. "Champs wasn't really on his game, but Adler rose to the occasion, and we won. Sorry we're late. My friend Ryan is upstairs and will be down in a minute."

Seconds later, Ryan appeared in the doorway, and the sight of him startled Patty. With his shirt untucked and only half-buttoned, his tousled hair hanging over his forehead, and a smudge of something black on his hands, he looked to be what she typically referred to as a "ragamuffin."

"You got scissors?" Ryan asked. "There's a tag on the neck, and I don't want to tear it off. Might rip somethin'."

Patty watched Kip remove the tag while Ryan unzipped his jeans, lowering them over his hips before buttoning his shirt and tucking in the tails.

"Kip! Could your friend perhaps finish dressing upstairs? We have guests."

Ryan looked up and said, "That's OK, ma'am. I'm almost finished. Nice shirt."

Kip knew that in his mother's world, everything was done discreetly and properly. Arriving to meet the lady of the house in a half-dressed state certainly did not meet her standards. He feared Ryan's introduction had made a bad first impression when Patty turned on her heel and swept out of the kitchen without saying a word.

"Can we git somethin' to eat? I'm starved," Ryan said, unaware there was anything untoward about his entrance and that he hadn't been introduced to the hostess.

"Sure. We'll head out front and see what the caterers brought. Mom doesn't cook."

Ryan's eyes went to the crystal chandelier hanging 20 feet above as they walked past the mahogany dining table with its fourteen chairs. The adjacent sitting room was elegantly appointed with a hunter-green suede sofa, matching wingback chairs, bookshelves stacked with leather-bound books, tables holding ceramic urns, and the far wall decorated with a floor-to-ceiling Medieval tapestry. Leading up from the foyer was a grand staircase that branched left and right at the first landing, above which hung a six-foot portrait of the Reynolds family.

Gazing at the 40-foot ceiling adorned with stained-glass panels, Ryan said, "Man, this is like something out of a friggin' movie. If I were in it, I guess I'd be the servant who cleans the fireplaces. You could park a car in those things."

Kip playfully slapped the back of Ryan's head and said, "Nah, you'd be the pool boy my mother flirts with all day. I think she secretly enjoyed your little show in the kitchen. She's not the prude she likes to pretend she is."

Ryan smirked as they walked out the front door and descended the flagstone steps to the front lawn. Every ten feet, there was a terraced bed of flowering bushes, with many roses still in bloom. At the bottom of the steps, an arched wooden bridge flanked by four-foot stone walls spanned the small stream flowing into the lake. The path ended at an open lawn the size of a soccer field that stretched along the water's edge. A single spout of water rose twenty feet from a fountain in the lake's center, creating a steady and tranquil splash that could still be heard above the voices on the lawn.

Walking toward the bridge was Kip's father, Dudley Reynolds, and at first glance, Ryan could tell Kip was right: Dudley appeared to be an odd duck. Besides the actual duck images on his light-yellow golf pants, he sported a bright blue sailor's cap wrapped in gold braid and a red polo shirt with the Bloomfield Hills Country Club emblem monogrammed on the pocket. The light brown hair spilling over his ears suggested he was overdue for a haircut, and his tortoise-rim glasses gave him an owlish look. Dudley walked with slightly drooped shoulders, creating the impression of a man beginning to deflate.

With a raspy voice hoarse from many years of scotch and cigarettes, Dudley said, "Hello, boys. Glad you could join us. Better late than never, I guess."

"It looks like the party is getting on fine without us," Kip said. "Dad, this is my friend Ryan Jackson from the stables."

"Nice to meet you, young man. Now, if you'll excuse me, I need to pee before I go up and say a few words."

As Dudley walked away, Kip said, "What Dad really needs is to refresh his drink. He's a bit of a snob when it comes to scotch, and he keeps the good stuff in his den. He's too cheap to serve it to everyone else. His friends can really drink and will have been at it all afternoon. I'm guessing Dad got started during brunch at the country club. He'll be tanked and in bed by eight o'clock."

Ryan and Kip continued onto the lawn and saw a dozen friends of Bradley—the birthday boy—along with some of their parents, family friends, and Kip's cousins from his father's side, standing in clusters and enjoying the DJ's selections from the eighties and nineties.

Ryan spotted the food and drinks under the pitched white canopy and said to Kip, "There's the food over there. Is it okay to walk over and take somethin', or do we gotta wait?"

"No, it's an open buffet. All you can eat," Kip said. "And look who's walking over: Claudia and two friends from her lacrosse team she brought along."

The small group had already caught Ryan's eye, and upon seeing Claudia, he stopped to take a deep breath. Her hair was pulled forward over her right shoulder, its natural waves rippling down the front. The top three buttons of her Oxford blue dress shirt were undone, revealing a delicate gold necklace with a dangling horseshoe, and a lavender sweater was draped over her shoulders and extended halfway down her back. Ryan had seen Claudia only a few times since she began riding at the Club, and he had always found her looks breathtaking. Today, she was a vision. He knew he had never seen such a beautiful young woman.

Kip could see how Claudia had captured Ryan's attention, and he was equally enchanted. Claudia's friends were beautiful young women in their own right—each sporting a version of "young, wealthy, and chic" attire—but Claudia was the showstopper. Her Iberian heritage gave her a look that distinguished her from the other girls, and with her lean physique, there was no mistaking that she was an accomplished athlete. Kip felt certain that if she didn't already have a cluster of boyfriends, she most certainly would when she moved to the upper school next year.

Kip and Ryan deviated from their straight line to the buffet and drifted over to Claudia and her friends. Kip welcomed them while Claudia made introductions and thanked Kip for the invitation. Ryan's eyes never left Claudia. He either wasn't aware he was staring, or he didn't care. Never prone to long conversations, he said "Hey," when introduced and never broke his gaze.

Kip said that he and Ryan had not eaten since breakfast and excused themselves to head for the catering tent.

After their second plate of food, Ryan said to Kip, "You think Claudia knows the barn is closed tomorrow? We're repavin' the aisles. She's 'sposed to have a lesson on Mondays, but they've all been canceled."

"I don't know. Why don't you go over and tell her? You could chat her up a bit, you know, if you wanted to get to know her better."

Ryan looked down as if searching the ground for ants, and after a long pause, said, "Okay," and began his stroll back to the group. He approached tentatively, stopping at one point to reconsider his bold move, and then sidled up to the group. Hardly able to look Claudia in the eye, he abruptly broke into the group's conversation and said, "Hey, Claudia. Was you plannin' on havin' a ridin' lesson tomorrow?"

Claudia flashed Ryan a smile and said, "Yes, Ryan, I was. Will you be at the stables as well? It's nice to know you'll be at the barn when I'm there. You understand how everything works, and being new, it's great that I can come to you if I need anything. You're always such a doll."

If Ryan could have melted on the spot, he would have. A combination of embarrassment from being the center of attention and the pride he felt hearing Claudia's compliments left him speechless. Seeing that Ryan was at a loss for words, Claudia said, "Why do you ask? Has there been a change to the schedule?"

With great difficulty, Ryan was able to make eye contact and said, "They's fixin' the barn aisles tomorrow, and the stables are closed. They'll be open again Tuesday, but everythin' Monday is shut. My dad and me are gonna have a long day."

"Well, it is very thoughtful of you to let me know. I was going to ask Kip if he could give me a ride tomorrow, but now it looks like I won't need to. Thanks!"

Claudia felt guilty as she watched Ryan walk away, as it was not her custom to lie. She knew the barn would be closed, but she was so charmed by the courage Ryan mustered to approach her that she didn't have the heart to tell him she knew. Kip had told her that Ryan was struggling with school and fitting in, so she looked for any opportunity to show him kindness. Although Ryan came across as awkward, Claudia suspected he was a good guy just trying to find his way in life. Anyone who showed the kind of affection Ryan did toward his cute little dog Roy was a kindred soul to Claudia.

As Ryan was making his way back to Kip, Dudley began his

walk up the steps to the small platform in front of the DJ booth to wish his son a happy birthday. Feeling the effects of his third scotch, Dudley's right foot caught the edge of the second step, hurling him forward onto his hands and knees. Struggling to get up, he pushed himself to the left and tumbled off the second step onto the ground, lying on his back. Kip ran to Dudley, and what he saw as he approached stopped him in his tracks. A wet spot was growing on the inside of Dudley's trouser leg. Apparently, Dudley had neglected to pee when he went to the den for his last scotch. This was the kind of embarrassing moment Kip had experienced in front of friends and family too many times, the kind of thing that made Kip ashamed of his father and fueled his vow to never become like him. He was mortified that Claudia had witnessed the fall.

The DJ stopped the music, and everything quieted as the guests tried to figure out what was happening. Then Ryan heard, as clear as a bell, one of Claudia's friends finish her sentence with, "…but I feel sorry for him. If that poor little redneck thinks he stands a chance of dating a Cranbrook girl, he's going to have a rude awakening. He's kind of cute, but he's out of his league."

The blood froze in Ryan's veins. He suspected the rich girls who came to the Club thought he was low class and "cut from a different cloth," as his mother had reminded him. However, he had never heard one of them say it out loud. He was humiliated and angry. He knew from experience that when he felt rage, he might explode like a cannon, and his instincts told him to control himself. So, clenching his teeth and fists, he turned away from Kip and began to walk up the steps to the house.

Ryan sat on a bench beside the garage, waiting for Kip, pounding his fists onto his thighs while suppressing his screams. After several minutes, he dropped his chin and closed his eyes, retreating to a dark place in his mind he knew all too well. It was his inner cave, the place where the demons lived, that lured him in and forced him to do things he would later regret. It was a place that was beginning to feel like his second home.

Kip found Ryan asleep in the Audi shortly after Dudley had been escorted back to the house. Once Kip realized that Ryan had not just slipped away for a few minutes, he went in search of him and had to shake him briskly until he awoke.

"Hey, Rip van Winkle, wake up. I was waiting for you to come back. Looks like you're whipped. Are you ready to go home so soon?"

"I don't care. Whatever. At least sittin' in the car, I won't embarrass you. I'd hate for Claudia's friends to think your hick friend was hittin' on her."

Kip didn't understand where Ryan's tone of resignation was coming from and said, "I don't know what you're on about. Did something happen?"

"Forget it. Don't matter anyways. I don't want to ruin your day, too. I'll wait here 'til you're ready to split."

"If there's something wrong and I can help, just tell me what it is." Ryan's silence told him the conversation was over and that he wanted to leave. "I'll just run down and say goodbye to everyone—be back in a bit."

When Kip returned, Ryan was not in the car. As he turned to leave, Ryan came walking from the side of the garage, zipping his pants. "Had to pee," he said.

"Well, you'd be surprised to know we have about fifteen bathrooms in that house over there."

"Wouldn't want to shock your mother again with my hillbilly behavior. I seen the look on her face before."

"I told you, she's a little stuck on formalities and everything being proper. I'm sure she likes you just fine. So, are you ready to go home?"

"Yeah, I guess."

Fifteen minutes later, Kip turned off Arlington Avenue into the small community where Ryan and his family lived. The Jacksons occupied one side of a two-floor duplex, a red brick structure showing its age after 50 years of weathering. The wooden window frames needed a fresh coat of paint, and several asphalt shingles were missing from the roof. The aluminum gutters appeared as if they might come down during the next winter storm, and the numerous cracks in the cement driveway resembled a large spider's web.

"If you don't mind the noise, come on in. I'll change my shirt and give yours back," Ryan said. "I ain't no charity case."

There were no signs of life in the adjacent duplex, but as Kip and Ryan walked up the short driveway, the commotion inside the open front door grew louder with each step. "Guess my mom's still at work. She don't get off 'til 7 on weekends. If she were home, them kids would be sittin' all quiet and watchin' TV, but when she ain't home, they fight like cats and dogs."

Given their size difference, Kip pegged Ryan's 11-year-old sister, Brittany, as the cat. She was considerably smaller than her 14-year-old brother, Joshua, but based on the shouting match Kip was witnessing, the cat was louder than the dog. Her curly red hair, long blonde lashes, and sweet, round face were deceptive. She appeared fiercer than her brother, the spitting image of Ryan, just smaller. As far as Kip could tell, the battle in the living room had something to do with the car chase unfolding in the *Grand Theft Auto* game on the TV's PlayStation.

Brittany shrieked, "You've been hoggin' the TV all day. Mom said I could watch *Gilmore Girls*, and it's already started."

"I told you—just record it. Geez, you're a pain," Joshua screamed over the screeching tires on the screen.

"Okay, rug rats, knock it off! Josh, turn off the damned game and let Brittany watch her show. There ain't no more tapes, so she can't record it," Ryan said.

"Then let her record over somethin' else. I don't got anywhere else I can play," Joshua said without looking away from the TV.

"Well, work it out and quit the yellin', or I'll start bustin' heads. You two is a royal pain in the ass sometimes," Ryan said as he turned to Kip and pointed toward the stairs. "Let's go to my room and get away from their damned bickerin'."

As they headed toward the stairs, Ryan's sidekick, Roy, bounded from the kitchen and made a beeline for Ryan. Although Ryan had trained Roy not to jump up, Roy's excitement overcame him, and as he attempted to pounce on Ryan's thighs, Ryan gently pushed against Roy's white chest and said, "Now, git down. You know better, bud." Ryan's gloomy disposition suddenly shifted, and a small smile crossed his face.

Kip glanced left as they started up the stairs and saw a kitchen in even greater disarray than the living room. Dishes stacked in the sink and on the counter suggested that cleaning up after meals was a low priority in the Jackson household. The newspapers, empty Diet Coke cans, and various chip bags strewn about the kitchen table appeared to be a permanent fixture. As Kip walked down the hall to Ryan's bedroom, he caught a glimpse of the bedroom his siblings shared and thought he might be looking at the aftermath of a small explosion. The kind of battle playing out in the living room was apparently a reenactment of one the bedroom had recently seen.

With Roy leading the way, they stepped into Ryan's bedroom, and Kip felt as if he had been transported to a different world. Aside from a neatly made bed, a nightstand, and a small dresser, the room was devoid of other furniture and was as immaculate as a military barracks. The sliding door to the closet was half-open, revealing a row of clothing—long-sleeve jerseys, T-shirts, and jeans—neatly hung on plastic hangers and carefully arranged equidistantly from one another. The walls were bare except for a single poster of Elvis, clad in his classic white jumpsuit—knees bent, arms extended to the side—with an acoustic guitar strapped around his neck and the word "Elvis" emblazoned in lights above him. Besides three wrestling trophies on the dresser, the only other item that added a personal touch to the room was a framed Polaroid on the nightstand. It showed Ryan sitting on the bed with his arms cradling Roy, who was in his lap, reaching up to give Ryan a lick under the chin. Having been there for Roy's rescue, the photo brought a smile to Kip's face, and he understood why having Roy as his loyal friend was so important to Ryan.

But the item that took prominence was the Gibson guitar, propped on its cradle in the corner. There was no chair beside it, no music stand or sheet music, only the highly polished guitar with its sparkling pearl inlay, resembling an exhibit in a museum.

As Kip walked to the window, Ryan shut the door and said, "Sorry about the racket downstairs. They're good kids, but when my folks ain't home, they get kinda rowdy. I'll change my shirt, and you can head out."

"No hurry," Kip said, "I don't have anywhere I need to be. Besides, I'd love to hear you play something on that guitar. I know you like to play, and I'll bet you're pretty good." After seeing Ryan come to life with Roy's warm welcome, Kip thought that getting Ryan to do something he enjoyed might help take his mind off whatever transpired at the party.

"Nah. You don't want to hear me play. I'm sure you got better stuff to do."

"Nope. I don't. Come on, choose something you like playing, and let me hear it."

After changing shirts, Ryan slowly picked up the guitar and sat at the end of the bed, while Roy jumped up and lay behind him. Kip leaned onto his arms on the windowsill, waiting as Ryan carefully positioned his guitar on his thigh and settled his fingers onto the strings. In the moment before Ryan began playing, Kip noticed the noise from downstairs had stopped, and all he could hear was a woman's quiet voice. He presumed Glenda had come home and was bringing order to the house.

The silence was broken when Ryan began strumming the first bars of the Beatles' ballad, "Here Comes the Sun." Kip could not believe his ears. The notes came through with a clarity he had never heard in any recordings of the popular song. Ryan floated through the melodies as if the instrument were a part of him, and Kip was fascinated by the way Ryan seemed to disappear into another world where nothing existed but him and the music.

After two minutes of playing, Ryan stopped abruptly and began standing. Kip said, "Hey, keep playing, man! That's incredible, and I love the song."

"I don't normally play for nobody."

"Well, you should. You are really good. You learned by yourself and play by ear?"

"Yeah. My grandpa showed me the basic stuff when he gifted me the guitar, but he was never too good at it. I think that's why he gave it to me. But he always asks me to play for him 'cause he likes some of the bluegrass stuff I learned. Him, I'll play for."

"Go ahead, finish the song."

"Sorry. My mom just got home, and I need to go down and help put the groceries away. She's always complainin' she's got to work full-time at the freight terminal and still take care of everything at home. I feel sorry for her. My dad don't do too much around here to help out. Says the job at the Club is wearin' him out, and when he gets home, he just wants to chill on the couch and drink his beer."

With no place on the table or counter to set the grocery bags, Glenda bent over and pulled out a box of Captain Crunch as Ryan and Kip walked by. Within seconds, Brittany and Joshua were rifling through the grocery bags and arguing about who would get which snacks. Ryan could tell an eruption was brewing and ushered Kip out of the house.

"Well, now you've met the rest of my family, 'cept Grandpa. He's down in Mapledale visitin' with my uncle. My family's not all fancy like yours, but we're doin' okay now that we're out of hillbilly country."

Kip sensed a closeness between Ryan and his family. He noticed what seemed to be an appreciation for their newfound financial security and the comforts that come with it. Now that Kip realized Ryan could retreat into his private world of music and escape the discomforts of being around wealthier families, he felt somewhat reassured that his friend Ryan might be okay after all. He had no idea how wrong he was.

CHAPTER 5

The Day the World Burned

SEPTEMBER 2001

Monday, the 10th

Birmingham, Michigan

Serrano Design Studios was closed on Mondays. Sophia customarily met with clients throughout the weekend, and Mondays were reserved for running errands and catching up on things at home. She spent the afternoons cooking her family's favorite dishes, ensuring there was always a home-cooked meal in the refrigerator on the days she worked late into the evening. Growing up with a large extended family in Barcelona, where meals took center stage every day, she could not bear the thought of her family eating food prepared in a commercial kitchen.

Adam had retreated to his room after dinner, and Claudia was helping her mother load the dishwasher when the phone rang. It was their father.

After asking how meetings at Conrad's Boston office had gone, Sophia said, "Claudia, dear, would you please run upstairs and ask Adam to pick up the phone? Your *papá* wants to talk to him."

"Hello, son. I thought I would be flying out to Los Angeles tonight, but our regional vice president joined us late, and we're all going out to dinner. Looks like I'll be staying overnight and flying out tomorrow instead. My secretary got me on an early flight, but I can't get into LA in time for the morning meetings. That means my whole itinerary has to shift, and I won't make it home until Friday night. I'm afraid I will miss afternoon practice and was hoping you could run it for me. Put them through the basic drills and have them work on their skating and fundamentals." Conrad coached Cranbrook's varsity ice hockey team, and despite his heavy travel schedule, he could usually get home by Friday afternoon for their practices.

"No problem," Adam said. "I'm happy to fill in. It will be fun to drill everyone until they drop."

Sophia was still on the line and said, "Have a safe trip, *mi vida.* I love you."

"See you Friday, *mi trésor*," Conrad said.

"See you Friday, *Papá.*"

"Thanks again, Adam. And show the team some mercy. I don't want to hear about any crippled bodies when I get home."

Tuesday, the 11ᵗʰ

Adam was eating breakfast when Sophia walked in from the garage. "Your sister is so excited to be starting at the upper school. Now that she's 16, we'll have to think about letting her use your father's car when he's out of town so she can drive herself. It will be a good way for her to learn on quiet streets. That, and driving to the stables."

"Too bad her first class starts at nine, otherwise I'd drive her. I don't want to wait around every day for an hour until mine starts," Adam said. "But I guess I could have taken her today. I booked time in the computer lab before class, so I'm going there now. Sorry I didn't say anything."

"*No problemo, mi cielo,*" Sophia said, softly kissing Adam on the head. "I'm not opening the studio until ten today, so I have some extra time. Have a good day."

Adam's BMW rolled out of the driveway a few minutes after nine. It was early September, and with the mild morning temperatures, he had his window open and the radio tuned to NPR. Adam had a keen interest in international politics, and since he took his computer projects far too seriously to call them a hobby, studying foreign affairs was what counted as one. The complex strategies countries employed to address global threats were like a giant game of chess to Adam, who fancied himself someone who could always see one step ahead of where things were heading on the world stage. NPR was his go-to radio station.

As he was turning into the school grounds, the voice of *Morning Edition's* host, Bob Edwards, interrupted a pre-recorded piece from a colleague and said, "We're breaking into Susan's report to give you breaking news from New York City where planes—two planes—have hit both towers of the World Trade Center in Lower Manhattan. On the upper floors of the World Trade Center— each tower, one-hundred-ten stories high—television networks were showing pictures of the first crash, which occurred shortly before nine o'clock this morning, so that everyone watching that picture saw a second plane hit the second tower moments after, maybe five or 10 minutes past nine o'clock Eastern Time this morning. Carrie Nolan, a reporter for WNYC, our member station in New York City, is with me now. Carrie?"

As Adam listened to the details, he surmised that these plane crashes were not accidental and that a world-changing disaster was unfolding. His first instinct was to find Claudia. He had no way of knowing what would transpire, but he was sure they needed to be home with their mother. Before he could reach the side entrance to the main classroom building, he spotted Claudia sitting on a bench in the front courtyard, talking to Kip.

"Sis, get your stuff, we're going home," Adam said. "There's a tragedy playing out in New York City, two planes have crashed into the World Trade Center. There's no way it was an accident, the odds don't support that theory. I don't know what's going down, but we need to be home."

Claudia turned to Kip and said, "Are your parents still out of town?"

"Yeah, they have another week at Cape Cod. I'm looking after Bradley. Let me run over to the middle school and find him."

"Well, when you do, come over to our house while we find out what's going on. No sense being alone in that big house of yours if something bad is happening," Claudia said.

"Trust me," Adam said, "Something very bad is happening."

At 9:37, while pulling into their driveway, Adam and Claudia learned that another commercial plane had crashed into the Pentagon. By the time they joined Sophia in the kitchen, CNN was broadcasting live images of the burning Twin Towers, and at 9:57, they stood in horror as they watched the South Tower collapse upon itself, as if in slow motion. It was almost impossible to view the images without believing they were watching a fictional disaster movie, that this was happening in the real world, in front of their eyes.

"*Oh, mi querido Dios,*" was all Sophia could say as she thought about the victims of the crash and the terror afflicting anyone still trying to escape the burning towers. So devastating were the scenes that none of them could form words or express emotions.

Thirty minutes later, Kip and Bradley knocked on the kitchen door and walked in to see the images of the North Tower beginning its collapse.

"I'm glad you guys are here," Claudia said, "This is no time to be alone."

And then it hit him. Adam's thoughts turned to his father and his plans to travel from Boston to Los Angeles that morning. The FBI had just confirmed that all the planes had been hijacked, with two departing from Boston's Logan Airport. Adam's blood ran cold as he made the connection. The flights had not yet been identified on the news, but Adam understood enough about statistical odds to know there was a chance his father could have been on one of those planes. It was a thought too distressing to entertain, but Adam's instincts told him he needed to follow through on his horrifying suspicion. Remembering that Conrad's secretary had made a last-minute change to his flight, Adam slipped away from the kitchen and called his father's office.

Conrad's secretary Rita picked up on the first ring and whispered, "Yes?"

"Rita, this is Adam Kinzler. I'm calling to…"

"Oh, dear God, Adam. I booked your father on a United Airlines flight that left Logan around 8:15. I can't get through to the airline—the phones seem to be cutting off—but I just heard on the news that all flights have been grounded, and I haven't heard from him. Have you?"

"No. No word. Can you tell me the flight number you booked him on?"

"Hold on, I wrote it down. The flight wasn't very full, so getting him a seat in first class was easy. Here it is, flight 175."

Holding on to the faint hope that their father was not on the United Airlines flight that had crashed into the South Tower, Adam did not share what he feared as he rejoined the group in the kitchen. But when the CNN anchor confirmed the flight numbers of the hijacked planes, Adam, just 18 and barely a grown man, had the daunting task of telling his mother and sister that they had witnessed their father's horrific death in real-time.

Sophia's face turned to stone for an instant, and then she exploded with screams of disbelief through a chant of: "No! No! No!" Unable to move from the barstool, Sophia's shoulders crumpled onto the marble countertop as she cupped her head into her folded arms. Adam and Claudia went to their mother and embraced her. With Adam on one side and Claudia on the other, they wrapped their arms around Sophia's shoulders, pressed their heads into her neck, and sobbed quietly. No words could comfort their mother, and at that moment, there was no one to comfort her children. The shock was setting in, and they each felt disoriented and numb.

As Kip and Bradley looked on in disbelief, Kip stepped over to Bradley and put his arm around his shoulder. Their eyes moved from the TV and what seemed like a non-stop loop of horrific images to the scene unfolding in the room. Claudia burrowed her head into Sophia's chest as Adam embraced them from behind.

After what felt like an eternity, the discomfort of not knowing how to respond was more than Kip could bear, and he broke the silence, saying, "I have no words. I'm...I'm...."

"It's OK," Adam said, looking Kip straight in the eye, "There are no words. But I'm glad you're here. *We're* glad you're here. None of us should be alone right now." In that instant, Kip sensed his relationship with Adam was forever changed. Kip saw the look of compassion and bravery in Adam's eyes, and he realized that behind the bravado and feigned arrogance, there was an incredibly kind and caring man, someone he wanted to have as a friend.

"You're right," Kip said. "But my parents will be worried sick about Bradley and me. I need to run home and phone them at their friends' in Cape Cod. I don't have the number with me." Kip could see Bradley's look of discomfort, knowing he would be alone with the Kinzlers, unable to process his own feelings, let alone take care of theirs. "Brad, why don't you come with me? We can call Mom and Dad, change out of our school clothes, and head right back."

When Kip and Bradley returned, Sophia, Adam, and Claudia had moved into the living room and were huddled on the couch. Kip told them his parents would return the next day, borrowing their friends' Volvo for the 12-hour drive.

In a slow whisper, Sophia spoke the first words Kip and Bradley had heard since the tragedy began. "Why don't you boys spend the night here? We have plenty of room." If Kip had known the onslaught of activity about to overtake the house, he would have taken Bradley home and endured being alone until his parents returned.

News of Conrad's death had not reached the Kinzlers' extended family or circle of friends. Only Conrad's secretary was aware. After Adam called, she felt profound guilt about booking Conrad on that United Airlines flight. She collapsed in the office after calling her family to say she was too ill to drive, and her husband had taken her to the emergency room.

The commotion started with the arrival of Sophia's friend, Francesca, who was worried when she could not get a call through to Sophia. Francesca knew that Conrad's bank had an office in Boston and that he regularly traveled there. She only needed to step into the foyer to understand what had happened. Francesca approached Sophia and Claudia, doing her best to console them, learning, as everyone else had, that there were no sufficient words. Without asking Sophia, Francesca went to the phone and informed Sophia's business partner, Rhonda, of the shocking news. Rhonda arrived within the hour, accompanied by two mutual friends. As the afternoon turned into early evening, the doorbell rang, and Adam saw a black sedan parked in front of the house. Three people in dark suits emerged—two men and a woman—who identified themselves as FBI agents from the Detroit office. The tragedy would now be confirmed.

Adam knew that nothing would ever be the same for his family. Despite his young age, he understood that when a family member or close friend dies, either from an illness or a familiar type of accident, people have an emotional capacity to deal with their loss. Feelings of sorrow, disbelief, and even anger are somehow accessible to grieving loved ones. However, Adam could see that nobody could possess the strength or fortitude needed to cope with a senseless death caused by an act of unfathomable terror.

September 11, 2001, was the day the world changed forever. Adam vowed to find a way to bring restitution to his family and the families of the other 2,753 people who died in the Twin Towers, the 343 first responders who gave their lives in service to others, the 184 people in the Pentagon who perished at work, and the 40 brave souls who crashed in the field in Shanksville, Pennsylvania. But right now, it was Adam's job to take over as the man of the house. He stoically jumped in with both feet as he began the slow process of rebuilding a shattered family.

Chapter 6

The Aftermath

September 2002

Wednesday, the 18th

Bloomfield Hills, Michigan

One of Adam's first decisions after his father's death was to request early graduation from Cranbrook. Although he was just beginning his senior year at the time of the tragedy, he already had the requisite number of credit hours. Given the unusual circumstances, the school awarded Adam his diploma. He was confident that his advanced skills with computers would ensure a lucrative career, one well-tailored to satisfy his insatiable quest to stay at the bleeding edge of technology, and Adam had never intended to attend college. Being at home and looking after his mother and sister was his number one priority, and there was a lot of looking after to do.

Sophia's business partner had tried to keep the Serrano Design Studio open, hoping the prospect of returning to work would help Sophia regain a sense of normality in her life. Rhonda discovered that Sophia's effusive personality—along with her unique execution of European-inspired design—was what the customers really wanted, and business soon waned. When the lease expired last spring, Rhonda closed the studio at Sophia's request.

Freed from the demands of running a business, Sophia was able to commit to three weekly sessions with a therapist who specialized in family trauma. Claudia and Adam joined the sessions on Monday afternoons, allowing the Kinzler family to work together through their healing process.

In the twelve months after 9/11, Adam transitioned from a cocky young man with an arrogant attitude to an emotionally mature 19 year old with a serious outlook on life. In addition to running the household and ensuring Claudia completed her sophomore year, Adam began navigating the legal maze that would eventually lead to a financial settlement for the families of the 9/11 victims. He had no idea how long and complicated that process would be, but he was determined to spare his mother the stresses of handling it alone.

For the first few months after the tragedy, Claudia had been unable to cope with being in a social environment, and she could not bring herself to leave the house and attend classes. Cranbrook had been diligent about providing educational materials to her, and a weekly tutoring session kept Claudia engaged with her studies. Still, she was not ready to interact with the other students. She had stopped going to the stables and had given up any thought of one day owning her own horse. Disconnecting from her life at the Club and missing the joy of being with horses, Claudia had fallen into a depression her therapist believed would be best treated with an antidepressant. As far as Claudia could tell, it did not help. There was an ache in her heart that burrowed so deep she was sure it would never subside.

Kip came by often to check on the family, and Claudia welcomed his company. When Claudia mentioned that she would enjoy reading something other than school texts, she asked Kip if he could bring her crime novels and mysteries to challenge her mind. She especially liked stories by Michael Connelly and Dan Brown, and Kip worked hard to keep her supplied with new books to satisfy what had become a voracious appetite for reading. Kip learned that he and Claudia shared a passion for literature and writing. When Kip told Claudia he had been accepted at Georgetown University to study journalism—and would be leaving for Washington after the summer—her depression deepened. Kip had become Claudia's closest friend, and she could not imagine how she would get along without him nearby. Kip had been a reliable presence at the Kinzler home, and he had even developed a bond with Adam, built around their shared responsibility to be a source of stability for Claudia and Sophia.

Kip knew he would miss seeing the Kinzler family regularly. Yet, he relished studying journalism and building a career from the passion he had developed as editor of *The Crane-Clarion,* Cranbrook's student newspaper. He had declared a double major at Georgetown, combining a degree in journalism with one in international affairs, alongside a minor in Mandarin Chinese. Like Adam, Kip had a keen interest in global politics. He was particularly interested in the events unfolding in Southeast Asia following Hong Kong's handover to China in 1997 and the world's growing concerns about a potential Chinese takeover of Taiwan. He found it challenging to reconcile his excitement for his upcoming studies with his sadness about seeing the Kinzlers only during semester breaks. Still, he believed obtaining his university degree was essential for his future. He remained steadfast in his commitment to become his own man and make a difference in the world, and he was certain this was the path to achieving that.

After settling into life on campus and completing his first few days of classes, Kip returned home for the long Labor Day weekend to take care of a job he had been dreading. His five-year stint as a polo player had come to an end, and he needed to say goodbye to his equine companions. Kip's father had arranged for both horses to return to their original home with his friend in Pinehurst. Champs had faithfully served out his long career as a polo pony and would enjoy the rest of his years grazing in pastures. Kip's younger horse, Adler, was still in his prime and would continue playing with a team down south.

Kip was melancholic as he parked in front of the tack room and was flooded with memories of all the good times he had enjoyed at the stables, especially during the year Claudia had been coming for lessons. He realized that although Claudia was two years younger, they had bonded as equals, and he knew his feelings for her went deeper than those for a casual friend. Knowing he was leaving for Washington, he had made a concentrated effort during the past year to keep enough emotional distance from Claudia that he did not lead her to think he wanted to be anything other than friends. The year had called for an enormous amount of empathy from Kip, and it wasn't easy when offering a hug of support not to let it linger so long that it felt like anything else. It had proven to be more difficult than he expected. He thought leaving for school might be a good way to escape those challenges for a while.

It was Saturday morning, and Kip had already packed two large trunks with the horses' equipment. All that was left to do in the barn was to secure the felt-lined shipping boots onto the horses' lower legs to protect them from injury on their twelve-hour van ride to North Carolina. His eyes teared up as he led each horse up the ramp into the van and backed them into their shipping stalls. After ensuring they each had a large net of hay, full water buckets, and windows open wide for ventilation, he wrapped his arms around Champs' and Adler's necks for a final hug and then quickly descended the ramp, unable to look back at his departing friends. The tightness in his chest signaled the sad end to a five-year love affair with his two incredible equines and the sport he had shared with them.

Before he reached the barn door, Kip heard yelling across the parking lot. It was coming from an animated argument between Ryan and his father. Hank was a bit shorter than Ryan and built like a middleweight boxer. He always wore a neatly pressed button-down navy shirt provided by the Club, a matching baseball cap with its monogram embroidered in gold, and khaki cargo pants that the Club sent out for dry cleaning each week. They were the nicest clothes Hank owned. Hank's face bore the rugged look from a lifetime of working outdoors, with wrinkles from years of worry, living paycheck to paycheck, and supporting a large family. He was a conscientious man with a strong work ethic, but a life of hard knocks had toughened him, and he took no guff, especially from his 19-year-old son, who was still living under his roof.

Ryan started walking away from Hank when he saw Kip, but he turned to his dad and shouted, "Then just go ahead and kick me out. I'm not goin' back to that school!"

When Ryan learned about the death of Conrad Kinzler, he stopped coming to the stables for several months. Thanks to the horsemanship skills Kip had taught him, Ryan often helped Claudia get her horse ready before a lesson and offered to put Chester away afterward if she was running late and needed to leave. Claudia always went out of her way to show kindness to Ryan, and he appreciated it. The days that Claudia was in the stables with him were among the only times he felt inspired to do his best work and be his best self. He always wore a clean shirt and kept it tucked in, he even combed his unruly hair when he arrived for work. She never talked down to him and always smiled warmly when they spoke.

The compassion Ryan felt for Claudia rendered him unable to be in the only environment he associated her with. Being there brought a sadness he had never experienced, and he did not know how to deal with those emotions. Ryan's absence from the barns left Hank shorthanded, especially on weekends, and he had been burdened with extra work. When an Arctic Clipper swept down from Canada in January, the water pipes in the barns froze, and the walkways and parking lots were covered in two feet of snow. Hank demanded Ryan return to work, and from then on, there was a tension that never subsided.

Before Ryan returned to working at the Club, Kip had reached out to him occasionally and picked him up from home to get a pizza or go for a drive. Since Ryan was never one for long conversations, Kip had to work hard to figure out how Ryan was faring emotionally. Kip could tell Ryan's feelings for Claudia ran deep and that he was working through his own grieving process. The last time Kip picked him up, Ryan's brother and sister had left with their mother for an event at school, and Ryan was alone in his room. The window was open as Kip walked to the front door, and he could hear music coming from the room. For the first time, Kip learned that Ryan had a beautiful singing voice. He was an alto with a light vibrato, and Kip stood in silence as he listened to the wistful lyrics from Simon and Garfunkel's 1970 hit, *Bridge Over Troubled Water*.

Kip could not help but think Ryan was singing that song for Claudia. He had waited to knock until Ryan was finished and then decided not to say anything about the singing. He knew Ryan was shy about his musical talent, and Kip did not want to embarrass him or make him uncomfortable.

Kip approached Ryan as he stomped away from Hank and said, "Hey, pal. What was that all about?"

"My old man's gonna kick me out of the house if I don't go back to school. I got suspended after the first day back."

"What happened at school?"

"It was my little brother's first day startin' at the high school, and I went by his locker after sixth period to see how it was goin'. I turned the corner and that asshole Ricky—the kid whose leg I busted up at wrestlin' practice—was messin' with Josh. He says to him, 'Well look at that, Redneck Ryan has a baby brother. Now we got two Hill-Jacks to deal with.' I got in his face, and he shoved me into the wall. I pinned him to the floor in a minute, but two teachers pulled me off before I could lay into him. We both got suspended until next week and I told my dad I ain't goin' back. Who cares if I graduate? Won't make no difference to me."

"Seems like you might want to go back and just suffer through the rest of the year. I mean, you're only nine months away from graduating."

"I got other plans."

"Like what?"

"I was at the mall, and a guy from the Army was there at a booth. He gave me some brochures and said I'd make a great soldier, that I could sign up and go over to them countries where the people who killed Claudia's dad are from and help take them out. That sounds a hell of a lot better than livin' with my folks and puttin' up with the shit at school."

"Have you called the guy?"

"Yeah. He's comin' by the house on Friday to talk to my folks. He says I'm old enough to sign up on my own, but if I drop out of school, I need to take the test for a 'G and D,' or somethin' like that."

"He probably said GED. It's a graduate equivalence degree, a test that says you know as much as you would have if you had graduated from high school. Your grades have been okay, so I guess you would pass."

"He said there's a testin' place in Pontiac and I can make an appointment for next week. If I do pass, I'm outta here. I already know how to shoot good, and I can't think of nothin' I'd like more than to take out some of those terrorists who killed Claudia's dad and all them other people."

"Wow, that's a big change of direction. But that might be just right for you, the Army."

"Gotta be better than what's here, now that you're gone to school and all." Ryan looked over to see the driver closing up the ramp to the horse van and said, "Well, it looks like Champs and Adler are all set for their trip south. You gonna miss 'em?"

"Hell yes. I'm going to miss seeing you every day as well. You've become a fixture around here, and I've gotten used to seeing your mug," Kip said as he slugged Ryan's shoulder. "I'm flying back to DC on Monday night, so let's go for a pizza on Sunday. I'll swing by your house around six and pick you up."

"Sure, if my dad hasn't kicked me out by then."

As Kip left for his car, he pictured Ryan in combat fatigues, packing a weapon and riding in a Humvee through Afghanistan, patrolling for terrorists. He thought: *Maybe the Army will be a perfect fit for old Ryan. It seems like a good place for him to act out his aggression, all for a good cause, and nobody will care where he's from. It might be somewhere he can feel he belongs. Yeah, this might be a really good thing for my friend.*

CHAPTER 7

Boots on the Ground

SEPTEMBER 2003

Tuesday, the 9th

Washington, DC

Patty Reynolds had an extensive network of friends from New York scattered throughout the country. Her closest friend was Amelia, who had settled in Washington, DC, after marrying her college boyfriend. Before Kip started at Georgetown University, Patty convinced Dudley that purchasing a 1400-square-foot townhouse on 33rd Street, walking distance to the campus, would be a wise real estate investment. The property would increase in value during Kip's four years in school, and there would always be a strong demand for homes in that neighborhood. Dudley knew that in addition to sparing Kip from the sparse living conditions of a campus dormitory, it would provide Patty with a convenient way to escape from home to visit Kip and spend time with Amelia. After 22 years of marriage, Dudley understood how Patty's mind worked, and he saw no downside to her plan and made the purchase.

Kip quickly developed a routine after moving in. He spent a few hours in the university's library each day after classes and arrived home shortly before seven. Today, he turned on the TV to watch *The*

PBS Newshour, and the opening story covered two suicide bombings in Israel. Both terrorists were members of Hamas and detonated their devices within six hours of each other, one outside an army base and hospital near Rishon LeZion, the other outside a café in Jerusalem. Sixteen people were killed, and over 80 people were wounded. Reporters from multiple news agencies provided footage of the carnage to PBS, with visuals of the bloody aftermath and audio dominated by the sound of sirens. The first 20 minutes of the program focused on coverage of Middle East terrorism and the Iraqi war, now entering its sixth month. While watching the report, his mind filled with disturbing images from two years ago and the live coverage of the 9/11 attacks. He realized how raw the emotions from that horrific morning still were. Watching the Kinzlers' lives ripped apart on that day ignited an intense desire to come to Claudia's rescue and alleviate the pain inflicted on her and her family. His feelings of love and compassion forged a bond with Claudia that he knew would last forever.

Kip turned off the TV before the program ended and sat in silence as the sun slowly dipped below the horizon. Two blocks away, the sirens from a police car and ambulance blared in dissonant harmony, unnerving Kip to the point that he thought a stiff vodka and tonic might help settle him down. As soon as he entertained that thought, his voice of reason weighed in. *So, what happens now?* Kip thought. *Every time you are triggered by sirens or thoughts of the devastation Claudia has been through, are you going to head for the bottle? Before you know it, you'll become like your father, relying on alcohol to numb your pain and get you through the day. You have lost all respect for your father; do you want to also lose respect for yourself?*

Kip was thinking clearly enough to realize that, in his case, having a drink or not was a matter of choice, which did not appear to be the case for his father. Dudley was suffering from the disease of alcoholism, and without treatment, the disease was in control. Kip resolved to take control and do whatever he could to make his contribution, large or small, to the global effort combating terrorism. His desire to seek retribution for the destruction in Claudia's life was his driving force. He was certain a career in investigative journalism was the right vehicle to provide him with that opportunity. Earning his degree at Georgetown University would be the launchpad for his career, and right now, it was the most important thing he could do. He was in Washington, DC, away from Claudia, by choice, and he reconfirmed his commitment to helping her however he could.

Sunday, the 14th

Fort Benning, Georgia

Ryan had worked the early morning shift every Sunday for the past eight weeks and was frustrated. He had no doubt his commanding officer took a personal dislike to him, one reflected in the work roster's scheduling. After Ryan's second altercation with soldiers in his barracks and a month of disciplinary leave, he knew he was under scrutiny. He had been warned that another fight could lead to his discharge from the Army.

Ryan had come through 10 weeks of Basic Combat Training with flying colors. He excelled in exercises that required a combination of physical strength and agility, like hand-to-hand combat, while obstacle courses were like a playground for adults. After finishing BCT, Ryan was assigned to the Ordnance Corps to learn basic maintenance on the Army's wheeled vehicles. Six months later, his application to rent a furnished apartment on-post was accepted. Only one two-bedroom unit was available, and Ryan was told he would have to share it with a fellow soldier, Benny Lipcolm. When Ryan walked in the front door and met his roommate, it was like pouring kerosene on a fire.

Benny was from a small town in Louisiana and was the youngest of nine children. He had four sisters and four brothers, who delighted in picking on what they called "the runt of the litter." Benny was short, with a wide, flat nose, protruding ears, and beady black eyes that gave him the look of an oddly assembled Mr. Potato Head—his siblings' go-to nickname for him. Their bullying had been relentless, driving Benny out of the house and into the Army on the day he turned 17. An hour before Ryan showed up at his new home, Benny discovered for the first time what a luxury it was to have an entire living space to himself. When Benny arrived, he dropped his duffle bags on the living room floor, removed his shoes, socks, and trousers, and flopped onto the sofa to enjoy a bag of Cool Ranch Doritos and a Mountain Dew. The cable TV had not been connected, so Benny plugged in his boom box and turned up the volume to enjoy his new CD by the Red Hot Chili Peppers.

Ryan eagerly anticipated seeing his new living space. After a particularly stressful day at work, struggling with a stubborn water pump, he was ready to settle in and enjoy the six-pack of Michelob he had bought at the 7-Eleven on his walk home. The music from the boom box blared louder as Ryan approached the front door, and when he stepped into the living room, it further jangled his already frayed nerves.

"Hey, can you turn that thing down?" Ryan said, without saying hello.

Benny looked at Ryan coolly and, without adjusting the volume, said, "What's the problem, don't like music?"

"I like music just fine, but not *that* music. To me, it's just a lot of noise and it's too friggin' loud. Turn it down, man."

"Jesus Christ, no need to be an asshole about it."

"Hey! Rule number one: we don't take the Lord's name in vain in this house. Hear me? Or is the music too dang loud?"

Benny stood and walked up to Ryan, jutting his awkward face within six inches of Ryan's. "Let's get something straight around here: I'll be paying rent the same as you, which means I do like I want, and you can just do you, Jesus Boy."

That was the spark that ignited Ryan's fire. Thanks to ten weeks in boot camp, Ryan was stronger than ever. Employing the well-honed skills from his wrestling career, he had Benny on the ground and pinned before he could land his second punch, the first of which had broken his opponent's nose.

Benny went to the infirmary and then promptly filed a complaint against Ryan with the housing office. Ryan was reprimanded for disorderly conduct and given a warning. From that day on, the roommates lived their separate lives in their shared space and made no effort to become friends.

It took every ounce of self-discipline to contain his anger when Benny inevitably got on his nerves. Ryan's greatest fear was being discharged from the military, and he knew that his hair-trigger temper could lead to his downfall. What he wanted most was to serve on a deployment to the Middle East and make good on his pledge to pursue and kill terrorists before they could attack innocent people like Claudia's father. Ryan's life had been filled with struggles, but he knew they were nothing compared to Claudia's after Conrad's death. In the recesses of his mind, Ryan harbored the fantasy that by proving his competency as a soldier and avenging her father's death, Claudia might one day recognize him as a man worthy of her love. He knew it was a far-fetched fantasy, but it was one worth fighting for, as long as the fighting took place on a battlefield and not in his own home. Benny would not become the reason he failed Claudia.

CHAPTER 8

State of Mind

SEPTEMBER 2004

Wednesday, the 1st

Birmingham, Michigan

Dr. Rachel Patterson began seeing the Kinzler family for psychotherapy sessions immediately after the events of 9/11. The Detroit FBI office had made the referral, and Sophia had diligently attended her three weekly sessions. Sophia knew Adam and Claudia found their sessions helpful, and she was pleased they had continued with them for three years. With Claudia focused on graduating from Cranbrook and Adam starting his career as a self-employed tech entrepreneur, Sophia could see they were concentrating on the future while progressing in their grieving process. For Sophia, moving on was not as easy.

"Have you given more thought to selling your home?" Dr. Patterson asked.

"Yes, and I think I'm finally ready," Sophia said. "I still haven't been able to discard any of Conrad's clothes or remove anything from his study, but I know it's time. The financial settlement from the Victim Compensation Fund is now complete, and Price Waterhouse confirmed to Adam that it will be the full amount they applied for in our claim. I have no financial reasons not to sell the house, it's the emotional ones that have been holding me back. Now that Adam has worked us through that process, I realize how dependent I've become on him. My God, that young man is only 21 and has taken on responsibilities a man twice his age would struggle with. I'm afraid that selling the house and downsizing to a condominium might have Adam thinking about moving out on his own. That thought terrifies me. Claudia has already begun looking at colleges, and with her straight-A average, she can probably pick any school in the country. At least I'm certain now that paying for her education will not be a problem. I guess that's something to be thankful for. But I still don't know how I could face being alone if Adam moved out after she left for college."

"Did you make it into the two classes you were on the waiting list for?"

Wayne State University's College of Education in downtown Detroit offered a concentration in Clinical Mental Health Counseling. Sophia had looked into attending the program with the hope of one day providing mental health support to families navigating their own trauma. She believed her studies might help her better understand the psychology of trauma and its impact on her and her children, while also preparing her for a career where she could help others.

"Only one of them, but I'm going to go ahead and get started. My first class is next week," Sophia said.

"I believe it's a good idea. Let's focus our work on how to begin the difficult process of selling your home and processing the memories you have there. Joining a new community at the university and being around other students might benefit you while creating this new path forward. You are making significant progress in accepting the loss of Conrad, so I think we're ready to examine your feelings about bringing closure to raising Adam and Claudia in that home. Moving on from that will also feel like a loss, and we will need to consider how you navigate that grieving process."

"Thank you. Yes, I think I'm ready for that. Adam has already started looking at townhouses in Birmingham. A new block of buildings is being built on Brown Street, and two homes are still available. He says we should meet with the sales agent soon, since they have been selling quickly. Now that I know it's affordable, I think I'll bite the bullet and go, as long as Adam is with me. I can't imagine what I'm going to do without him."

"Well, he *is* still with you, so let's focus on the issues in front of you right now."

Easier said than done, Sophia thought.

Friday, the 3rd

Bloomfield Hills, Michigan

Kip flew home on the Friday before Labor Day and walked into an empty house. His father had spent the morning playing golf at the country club, and his mother was hosting a fundraising luncheon for the Humane Society. Bradley had begun his first week as a senior at Cranbrook's upper school and was enjoying the afternoon in his hand-me-down Audi with his friends. When Kip announced that he was attending Georgetown University and had no need for a car in Washington, his parents happily gifted the Audi to Bradley, thrilled to be released from any future chauffeur duties.

Kip walked through the kitchen and dining room before stopping at the bottom of the grand staircase. He looked around the vast rooms and realized the house felt empty even when his family was home. There was always something missing, that something that makes a house a home: the outward demonstration of love that transforms the people living there into a family. He had felt it when he first met Claudia and her family, and he fully understood it after their father died. Strangely, despite the tension between Ryan and his father, he also sensed it when he visited the Jackson home. *How sad*, he thought, for his family to possess all their wealth yet still lack something as invaluable as showing love to one another. Kip knew that this had a lot to do with the joy he received from helping others, it provided him a way to feel close to the people he cared for. After settling into his room, Kip phoned Claudia and asked if she wanted to go for a drive. Sophia had given Conrad's car to Claudia the year after he died, and Claudia felt a strong connection to her father whenever she drove it. Kip enjoyed being seen with her in the silver Mercedes SL 500—rolling through the shady streets of the suburbs with the top down.

At 19, Claudia had matured into a stunning young woman, but due to her humble nature, Kip suspected Claudia was unaware of just how striking she was. Any boy at school would have jumped at the chance to date her, but after her father's death, Claudia retreated into herself and did not participate in any sports or social activities at school. Instead, she had become engrossed in her study of computer science, eager to have her older brother teach her at home about the intricacies of the online world and everything underneath the surface of the internet.

Claudia treasured every minute with Kip during his visits home from school and gladly accepted his invitation to go for a drive. Kip stepped out of the back door onto the cobblestone driveway as she arrived to pick him up and saw his mother getting out of her midnight blue Jaguar.

"Kip, darling, I had no idea you would be home so early. I thought your flight got in this evening," Patty said.

"I got to the airport early, and the line through TSA moved fast for once, so Delta put me on their earlier flight. Claudia and I are heading out for a drive."

"Your father stayed at the club after his golf game and is playing backgammon in the lounge. I will head over around 5:30 to join him for dinner. Would you like to come along? I know your father would love to see Claudia."

Kip caught the almost invisible shake of Claudia's head and said, "Thanks, Mom, but Claudia and I made plans to eat at our favorite place in Royal Oak tonight. Claudia hopes to attend MIT next year, and I'm going to help with her application prep." Although Kip thought that was a great idea once he had said it, he and Claudia had no plans other than to drive around.

"Well, then maybe Claudia could join us for brunch at the club on Sunday," Patty said.

"Thanks, Mom. I'll let you know."

As they rolled down the drive, Kip said, "Sorry for the made-up excuse, but I saw you didn't want to go."

"It was perfect. Besides, dinner at The Tavern sounds great, and I would love to pick your brain about the whole application process. Date?"

"Date. And I thought we might drive by the Riding Club to see if your old buddy Chester is still there. He was a great lesson horse, so I doubt they've let him go."

"You know, I think I'd like that. I haven't been back since things changed, and I'd love to give him a hug and say a proper 'thank you.' He and I really bonded, and although I think riding is part of my past, I'd like to have some closure. Let's go."

They found Chester quietly munching hay in the stall he had occupied four years earlier. Kip left Claudia alone to spend time with Chester and strolled through the barn aisle, reminiscing about the good times they had shared. It was hard to believe how much had changed over the past years, but recalling the day he met Claudia struggling to get her saddle on Chester's back, rekindled the spark he felt when he first laid eyes on her. They were now young adults, and what might have been a teenage crush on Claudia back then had blossomed into a romantic attraction. However, his compassionate nature and innate sensitivity urged him to respect Claudia's need to heal from losing her father in her own time. He sensed her pain was still too raw to invite her into a relationship that would have an uncertain future. He would graduate from Georgetown in two years, while Claudia would start her first year at whichever college she got into. Anything could change during those years, and he did not want to be the reason Claudia might have to face another loss if the relationship did not work out. Kip believed he should wait until their plans for the future were more settled before attempting to take their relationship to the next level. It seemed best to shield her from any more hurt.

As Kip approached the end of the barn aisle, Ryan's father, Hank, walked in, pushing a wheelbarrow with three feed sacks.

"Well, look what the wind blew in!" Hank said. "I thought you'd moved away without sayin' goodbye. After that girl's daddy got killed, she stopped comin' for lessons, and you disappeared right along with her."

"I graduated from school that year and moved to Washington, DC. I'm in my junior year at Georgetown University and returning on Monday. The girl whose father died is Claudia Kinzler, and she's here with me now, down in Chester's stall."

"Nice girl. That was just horrible what happened. Horrible," Hank said, shaking his head.

"Well, it's good to know there are people like Ryan who will put their lives at risk to protect our country from ever having another attack. Has he been deployed to Iraq or Afghanistan? I saw him right after he enlisted, and he was leaving for Fort Benning and basic training, but I haven't heard from him since. Is he still in Georgia?"

"Not anymore," Hank said. "His unit didn't get deployed right away, and then our boy Ryan started gettin' himself into a heap of trouble, fightin' with the other soldiers and then bustin' up a bar in town. I don't understand why that boy is always so angry and gettin' into trouble like that. Anyways, they kept him in Georgia when his unit went to Iraq and had him workin' on equipment maintenance and such. But then he got all depressed and quit showin' up for duty. They put him in their treatment facility last month to see if they could figure out what was goin' on in his head. Second day there he got into it with an orderly and nearly busted the guy's head open with a fire extinguisher. The docs said he has some kind of disorder, you know, in his brain, so they discharged him. Now they have him in their VA hospital in DC tryin' to figure out if there are some drugs or somethin' that can help when he comes home. He can't be far from you there. You ain't heard from him?"

"No, I just got a new cell phone, and he wouldn't have the number. But jot down where he is, and I'll look him up when I'm back."

"Well, he's gettin' out in a couple weeks and comin' home to us. Glenda and me decided to move back home to Mapledale at the end of the month. I gave my notice, and the twentieth is my last day. Geez, I've been workin' here 'bout six years, if you can believe it. But Glenda's dad ain't doin' too good and he misses the family in West Virginia. Now that I got all this experience takin' care of a fancy club like this, my brother thinks I should apply for a job at the Greenbrier Resort in White Sulphur Springs. It's only a piece down the road and they's always lookin' for good people, long as they got experience. And now I do."

"I wish you and your family all the best, it sounds like a good move. I'm sure they'll miss you here, you've always done a great job. The place has never looked better. I'll be back in DC on Monday and see if I can meet up with Ryan over the weekend. I'll bet he could use a friendly face right about now."

"I think he'd like that. You two got along real good, and Ryan said you always treated him like an equal, not like those kids at his school did. Even some of the folks around here weren't so nice to him. He's a good boy. Just strugglin', I guess. Hopefully, he'll get sorted out when he's back home and more comfortable with things. I'll get his number and give it to you before y'all go."

Kip shared with Claudia the details about Ryan's struggles during their drive to dinner, and Claudia wondered whether he was being treated with drugs for a mental disorder. She told Kip presciently that if he was, Kip should expect to see a different version of his friend than the one he had last seen.

Saturday, the 11ᵗʰ

Washington, DC

Kip returned to Georgetown after the Labor Day weekend and jumped back into his new routine: attending classes during the week and spending afternoons with his friends at the student newspaper, *The Hoya*. Kip planned to apply for a summer internship next year at *The Washington Post* and intended to start working on his application on his first weekend back. However, his conversation with Hank about Ryan's problems had concerned him, so he decided the application could wait a week. Seeing Ryan before he was discharged from the VA hospital was more pressing.

It was a quick Metro ride from Georgetown to Brookland Station near the VA Medical Center. Hank had provided him with the nursing station's phone number on Ryan's floor, which made it easy to locate the wing where Ryan was being treated.

When Kip arrived, he was taken to a visiting room with two armchairs and a couch—no tables, lamps, or decorative objects. The small windows facing the hallway were single-paned with embedded wire mesh. The fabric on the walls yielded slightly to the touch, and the floors had a thick foam mat beneath the wall-to-wall carpets. It was a padded room. Twenty minutes later, Kip heard the door handle click, and a hospital attendant walked Ryan into the room. He wore a drab green hospital shirt, matching trousers with an elastic waistband, white slip-on shoes, and a medical bracelet. Everything reminded Kip of a prisoner being led in for interrogation. After studying Kip with a stone-faced glare, Ryan went to the couch and sat, directing his attention to his feet. The attendant left the room, and Kip sat next to Ryan. Breaking the silence, Kip said, "It's great to see you, bud. How are you getting along here?"

Without making eye contact, Ryan whispered, "I found Jesus."

Being caught off-guard, Kip paused momentarily and said, "Oh. That's...great." As Kip closed his mouth, Ryan sprang from the couch, dropped to the floor on his hands and knees, then leaped from the floor to the couch, back to the floor, and onto a chair, barking like a dog. Kip looked at him, speechless. Ryan jumped from the chair and stood before Kip, locking his gaze.

In a low voice laced with menace, Ryan said, "I'm a dog—not a fuckin' hillbilly. You and your fancy friends can all go to hell. Jesus is taking *me* to heaven." Before Kip could respond, Ryan turned away and started banging on the window, yelling for the attendant to retrieve him.

On his way out, Kip stopped at the nursing station and asked if he could speak with a doctor about Ryan's condition and their intended treatment plan. After determining that Kip was not a family member, the attendant sent him on his way and said, "We're sorry. I'm sure you understand that HIPAA regulations restrict the sharing of patient information. Rest assured, he is getting the best care possible. The VA has a lot of experience with patients like your friend. He's in good hands."

Based on what Kip had just experienced, he was not sure he was.

CHAPTER 9

Say Goodbye

SEPTEMBER 2005

Wednesday, the 21st

Birmingham, Michigan

Sophia's heels tapping the bare parquet floor echoed through the empty dining room. As she approached the leaded glass windows and looked out at Quarton Lake, she saw the moving truck's taillights illuminate as it turned out of the driveway on its way to their new home. The sun had set, and the reflection from the streetlights around the lake twinkled on its still waters. It was a scene that Sophia might have otherwise found tranquil, but it made her reflective and melancholy. She had been working with her therapist for a full year to prepare for this day, and she thought she was emotionally ready to say goodbye to their home of 10 years. She was not. The five years before Conrad's death had been filled with nothing but joy here. When they arrived in Birmingham, Adam was 13 and Claudia was 11. Life was filled with new adventures for all of them. Conrad would thrive with his big promotion at the bank. The children would get to explore a new country, learn its language and customs, make new friends, and enjoy their teenage years at an elite private school. Sophia would turn their new house into a warm and nurturing home while she prepared to fulfill her lifelong dream of owning an interior design studio. This was to be their Camelot.

After Conrad was ripped from their lives, this is where the healing process began, where shared memories of their times together lived, the place that connected them to him and each other. Preparing to walk out the door for the last time was one of the hardest things Sophia ever had to do. It was time to say goodbye to all that had been good.

Adam wore running shoes, and Sophia did not hear him come up behind her. She jumped when he said, "*Mamá*, I've checked all the rooms, and they got everything. It's time to go."

Sophia turned and put her arms around Adam, resting her head on his chest. "This is harder than I ever imagined, *mi cielo*. I don't want walking out that door to mean I am leaving all my beautiful memories behind. I want to hold on to them forever. Leaving here almost feels like a betrayal of your *papá*."

"You don't have to leave anything behind. Those memories live in your heart and will hold them forever for you to cherish. That's *papá's* gift to you."

"You and Claudia are his true gifts. I cherish you more than you know."

"We know, *Mamá*. We know."

Tuesday, the 27th

Mapledale, West Virginia

"Thanks for the beers, Jason. My turn on Friday." Ryan's friend drove off in his old Honda Civic, leaving Ryan on the front lawn of his parents' new home. They had saved enough from their two jobs in Michigan to afford a down payment on a modest two-floor home at the edge of Mapledale, two streets away from where they had rented before. The house was built in the fifties, and although it was an upgrade from their previous home, it needed work. Several white clapboards were askew, and the house badly needed new vinyl siding and gutters. Hank's job at the Greenbrier was paying well, and Glenda had recently applied for a job there, but any significant upgrades to the house would have to wait. The light over the front door was burned out, and with no streetlights to help, the outside of the house was dark and unwelcoming. Ryan stopped before crossing the lawn and realized he was slightly drunk from the six-pack he and Jason had shared. The front door was left open, and Ryan could see the mosquitoes clinging to the screen door, waiting for him to come through and let them in.

My life sucks, Ryan thought. *Twenty-two years old and livin' in this shack with my family. No car, no job, no girlfriend, no future.* He reluctantly shuffled into the house and hoped to slip past the living room without having to talk to his parents. He could hear Steve Carell's familiar voice and knew they were watching *The Office*, a show he also enjoyed. But Ryan wanted to get to his room, hoping to find enough vodka left in his hidden bottle to put him to sleep so he could say goodbye to another rotten day.

Hank heard the front door close and said, "Ryan, that you? You missed dinner again. Where you been?"

"With Jason. I'm goin' to bed, got a headache."

"Well, liquor does that to a man. You been drinkin' again?"

Ryan looked at the empty beer cans on the floor beside Hank's La-Z-Boy and said, "Like you? Nothin' wrong with a drink now and then."

"Well, the difference between you and me, boy, is that I don't go bustin' up furniture and smashin' guys' heads in when I drink."

Glenda and her father were on the couch, and Glenda was hoping this exchange would not end up in another shouting match. She said, "Ryan, dear, there's brisket from the weekend in the fridge if you want me to fix you a plate."

Hank said, "Let him git his own damned food, looks like he could use somethin' to soak up the liquor."

Grandpa was usually quiet, but he could tell that without an intervention, things were going to explode. "If y'uns don't mind too much, I'm tryin' to enjoy my story here. Maybe the boy just needs to lie down a spell."

Ryan took two steps into the living room, bent down, kissed his grandpa on his balding crown, and said, "Thanks, Grandpa. You're the best." He went upstairs to find that his hidden bottle was half full. He drank it empty and collapsed on the bed, fully clothed, passing out before he had a chance to bid his day goodbye.

Wednesday, the 28th

After multiple attempts to wake him, Glenda finally shook Ryan out of his deep sleep. He blinked, squinted to see through his haze, and heard his mother say, "Honey, wake up. It's almost noon. I have somethin' sad to tell you, somethin' real sad."

Ryan could make out his mother's swollen eyes and knew she had been crying. He struggled to sit up, so he lay on his side, propped on his elbow, and said, "What's up?"

"It's Grandpa. He's died. We just got back from the hospital."

"Died? How? He was here last night, watchin' TV."

"He went to bed normal time and looked fine. But 'round about three this mornin' we heard a crash in his room. He had gotten out of bed and collapsed on the floor. I come runnin' in and he was holdin' on to his chest, sayin' it felt like an elephant was standin' on him. Your father and I carried him to the truck and got him to the emergency room, but an hour later, his heart stopped. We was both with him."

Ryan dropped onto his side and deflated. "Just like that. Dead."

"Sometimes, that's how it happens, son, just like that. He asked me to tell you somethin'."

"What's that?"

"He said to tell you that he loves you and knows you'll end up doin' just fine."

Glenda left the room and went to the kitchen to join the rest of the family. Ryan rolled onto his back and stared at the ceiling, trying to imagine life without Grandpa. They had formed a special bond when Ryan was very young. Fishing, hunting, gigging frogs, and catching turtles had given them hundreds of hours together, just the two of them, and being with Grandpa felt like a breath of fresh air after feeling stifled by his oppressive father. Ryan recalled the day he sat in the backyard, listening to Grandpa play a favorite bluegrass ballad on his Gibson and being invited to hold the guitar while learning where to place his tiny fingers. He only produced one distinguishable chord, but Grandpa assured him he had a bright future as a musician, as long as he practiced hard. Ryan did practice, and when he turned 12, Grandpa gifted him the Gibson as a reward for his tenacity and discipline.

The movie playing in his mind ended abruptly when he heard Hank yell from the bottom of the stairs, "Get your ass down here, now. We got family comin' over, and this place is a mess. Time you pulled your weight around here. Move it!"

Ryan swung his legs over the side of the bed and sat up, looking straight into the corner where the Gibson stood. He snatched the pillow, shoved it into his face, and sobbed, tuning out the sound of his angry father and praying to God that one day his torment would end.

CHAPTER 10

Broken

SEPTEMBER 2006

Thursday, the 7th

Birmingham, Michigan

Four years after closing the Serrano Design Studio, Sophia sat at her kitchen table, drinking tea with her friend and ex-business partner, Rhonda. They had become friends almost 10 years ago, shortly after the Kinzlers emigrated from Geneva to Birmingham. Sophia had gone to Rhonda's upscale boutique on Maple Street to buy linens for their new beds, having discovered that bed frame sizes were not the only thing different in America. Rhonda recognized Sophia's European sophistication as soon as she stepped through the door and began a conversation that quickly led to their friendship. Now in her mid-forties, Rhonda had finally grown accustomed to being alone after 10 years of divorce and a childless marriage. Her broad face, wavy brown hair, and light blue eyes were a tribute to her Irish heritage and contrasted sharply with Sophia's Iberian looks.

"It's amazing what you've done with this townhome in just 12 months," Rhonda said. "You still have that magic touch. And how wonderful you could buy it before the interiors were built out. Your floors are stunning, and this kitchen is worthy of a spread in any magazine. You must be thrilled with it."

"Yes, I am, thanks to Adam," Sophia said. "I was hesitant to go ahead with the purchase—I wasn't sure I was emotionally prepared for a move—but he convinced me that by closing the sale when we did, I could work with the architect on all the interior build-out. That young man is amazing, Rhonda."

"He is just one of your blessings, my dear. The other is your creativity and design talent. I came to tell you that space is opening up on the second floor of the Merrillwood Building, just across from where we were before, and if you would be interested in bringing Serrano Designs back to life, I'd be happy to partner with you again. This time, maybe on a smaller scale, without the large retail store. You know, working only with private clients on interior design projects. An incredible number of new homes are being built in Birmingham and Bloomfield Hills, and we could be as busy as we wanted."

"You are a sweetheart, Rhonda, and thank you for offering to partner with me again. But I only have 50 hours left in my internship and then I will sit for my National Counselor Exam. I enjoyed my studies at Wayne State, and now that I have my degree, all I need to do is pass the exam, and I can begin working as an LCP. I think that's where my passion lies. I can always dabble in the design world by working for close friends."

Sophia and Rhonda turned their heads when they heard the back door open. Adam stepped into the kitchen, wearing black cycling shorts and a white Lycra tee.

"Hello, *mi cielo*. How was your ride?" Sophia asked.

"It was good. I drove to the Kensington Metroparks and did the ten-mile loop around the lake. It was pretty crowded for a Thursday, but I made good time. I've got to run upstairs and shower. Coach and I are getting together this afternoon to lay out the schedule for this year's hockey practices, and I told him I'd be there by four. Nice to see you, Ms. Cantrell."

As Adam trotted up the stairs, Rhonda said, "He was always a good-looking teenager, and so well-mannered, but he has grown into an exceptionally handsome young man. I'm sure you are very proud."

"You have no idea. I used to think Adam was too handsome and intelligent for his own good. Claudia once said the kids at school had labeled him 'wicked smart,' which I think is a left-handed compliment, and now he is turning his computer savvy into a lucrative business he runs from his room. Don't ask me what he does, I've never understood his technology world, but whatever it is, he's incredibly good at it. It will only be a matter of time before he moves out to pursue bigger things, so I want to have something meaningful to do, like helping families process their trauma during times of loss. I learned that there is a real need for that, and now I want to give back. I hope you understand."

Before Rhonda could answer, Sophia's phone rang. "Do you mind, Rhonda? It's Claudia calling from school. She's starting her sophomore year at MIT and has moved into a new dorm."

"You bet, hon. I'll be on my way. Give me a call when you're free for dinner one night. *Chiao.*"

"Hello, sweetie. How is it going?" Sophia asked.

Claudia updated Sophia on the details of her move into a new dormitory, her first impressions of her roommate, and her class schedule for the fall semester. "My classes end at noon on Fridays, and I'm catching a flight down to DC to spend the weekend with Kip. He's started his new job at *The Washington Post* and been assigned to the Southeast Asia desk. He'll only be doing background research at this point, no actual writing, but it's exactly where he hoped to be. He says he is fluent in Mandarin Chinese now and can use it for his research work. I can't wait to see him."

Sophia had hoped that Claudia's casual friendship with Kip might blossom into something more serious, and she was pleased that even if they were living so far apart, they still traveled to see each other. Although it was less than a two-hour flight from Logan Airport to Reagan National, Sophia believed she would never overcome the fear that gripped her whenever one of her children got on a plane. At least Sophia knew where to send her prayers that night.

Friday, the 15th

Georgetown, Washington, DC

Kip and Claudia enjoyed a leisurely walk along the Potomac River, relishing in the cooler autumn temperatures settling in after an especially hot summer. They left the Georgetown Waterfront Park and walked up the hill to the Four Seasons Hotel to enjoy a bottle of wine and tapas on the outdoor terrace. Kip shared with Claudia the little he knew about his new job at *The Post* and said he was sure it would eventually lead to assignments in Asia. All he had to do was put in the long hours required of every new journalist and prove what he could do. Over the past two summers, his internship had been a great training ground, and he knew he was ready for the challenges ahead. In the meantime, he would be kept busy writing short articles for the paper's website and assisting the seasoned journalists with background research.

Claudia told Kip how pleased she was that Adam's training at home had given her a leg up in preparing for the advanced computer science classes she would be taking this year. Claudia had declared mathematics as her major, and her curriculum would include cryptography and number theory courses. She had a special interest in the evolving GPS technologies, especially as they related to intelligence gathering. The insights Adam had shared about that field would serve her well in her upcoming studies.

Claudia met with her academic advisor at the end of her first year and learned about the National Security Agency's Cooperative Education Program. The NSA was based in Fort Meade, Maryland, about an hour's drive northeast of Georgetown, and was accepting applications for the program that would begin in the fall semester next year. If accepted, Claudia would attend alternate semesters at MIT and the NSA program at their headquarters. The semesters at NSA would include work on live projects using their labs, equipment, and advanced technologies. Graduates of the Co-op Program would be prime candidates for a career with the NSA, something that appealed to Claudia on many levels. Besides being work she would find interesting and engaging, it felt like a way to help her country in its ongoing battle against terrorists and other groups planning to harm the USA. Kip had agreed to work with her this weekend on her application forms, and she was eager to get started.

"Thanks for agreeing to help with my résumé tomorrow. I have a good feeling about this. I had no idea just how valuable a mathematics degree from MIT could be," Claudia said. They raised their glasses to toast the future, and Claudia became subdued.

"Is something wrong?" Kip asked.

"My thoughts suddenly went to Ryan. What happened after you visited him at the VA hospital? Did you stay in touch?"

"I lost track of him when he was released. His dad said the family was moving back to West Virginia and that Ryan would be moving down with them. I stopped by the Riding Club when I was home for spring break. They gave me Hank's phone number, but when I called, Hank said Ryan had been away for a few days and didn't know when he'd be back. I left my number with him, but never heard from Ryan."

"We should give him a call this weekend. I guess I'm feeling guilty about how well things are going for us, while Ryan seems to be struggling so badly. I hope he's getting the kind of treatment he needs. Mental illnesses are complicated, and if his meds aren't right, he could be worse off than if he didn't have any at all. I have to wonder what kind of facilities are available to him in Appalachia. It scares me."

The sun was setting as they walked up the steps to the front door of Kip's townhouse, built in the classic red brick style with black shutters on the windows and two gabled dormers on the roof. They had left for their walk when Claudia arrived and dropped off her bags. Now it was time for Kip to get Claudia settled in. He had thought about where she should sleep and decided that the guest room on the main floor would provide her with the most privacy. The larger bedroom on the second floor was Kip's, while the smaller room was the one his mother used on her frequent visits. Kip felt that if Claudia stayed in the room adjacent to his, where they would share a bathroom, there would be too many opportunities for awkward encounters. He wanted to keep things uncomplicated until he knew where his relationship with Claudia was headed.

After a homemade brunch the next morning, Kip said to Claudia, "I was thinking about what you suggested last night, and I agree, we should try to reach Ryan. I'll call him now before we head to the Mall." Kip and Claudia planned to spend the day in DC, taking in the sights along the National Mall and finishing with a visit to the International Spy Museum. After only a year at MIT, Claudia had developed a special fascination for surveillance and intelligence gathering, an interest sparked during her time learning about the hidden workings of the internet from Adam. Although the museum was geared toward curious tourists rather than serious investigators, a trip there felt like going to a tech-geek's version of Disneyland.

Kip called the number Hank had given him, and Glenda answered. After hearing it was Kip, she handed the phone to Hank. Claudia could not make out what Hank was saying, and the call continued for ten minutes. Kip interjected occasionally with comments like, "Oh, I see. Do you know what medications he's been on? Any recreational drugs, like pot? Had he been drinking often? Yeah, that doesn't sound good. How long will he be in the hospital? I'd appreciate it if you could let me know once he's home. Sure thing. Glad I called. Please give my best to Glenda."

Kip hung up and shared the details of Hank's story as they visualized the tragic accident that had befallen Ryan.

One Month Earlier

Mapledale, West Virginia

> *Ryan's brother married his high school sweetheart at nineteen. He moved to Charleston, leaving Ryan at home with his 17-year-old sister, Brittany, and the ongoing challenges of maintaining peace with his parents. Although his mother found small ways to express her love for Ryan, she struggled between helping him and upsetting Hank. He was losing patience with Ryan's ongoing unemployment, which he viewed as freeloading. Ryan's only reliable source of joy in their home came from being with his faithful dog, Roy, now seven and happy to be back at Ryan's side.*

Ryan would often ask to use the truck when Hank had a day off from work. Ryan would drive as far as the state capital, Charleston, just over two hours from home, but never shared details about his trip upon returning. Hank couldn't understand why Ryan always seemed to have plenty of spending money, he didn't have a steady job, but guessed he was doing odd jobs at some local businesses. Otherwise, Ryan seemed to spend most of his afternoons and evenings at The Rusty Nail, the local dive bar where nothing good ever happened.

When Ryan learned that Willie Nelson was playing with John Fogerty on August 16th in Cincinnati, he told his family he was riding to Ohio with his friend Jason in hopes of scoring some scalper tickets for the concert. They had no luck getting in, and on the drive home, Ryan and Jason got into a heated argument. Hank later learned that Ryan had been drinking beer throughout the day, and combined with whatever mood stabilizers, antidepressants, and antipsychotics he was taking, he had an adverse reaction to the drugs. It was not the first time Ryan and Jason had come to loggerheads, and Jason had had enough. He put Ryan out just south of Charleston and left him on his own to get home.

A CSX freight train was stopped across Ryan's path toward town. Disoriented and in a manic state of mind, Ryan climbed onto an empty flatbed car. He sat against the back wall, trying to clear his head and figure out what to do next. The train began to crawl, and within minutes, they were traveling east at 45 miles per hour. The strong wind jolted Ryan back to his senses, and he realized he was in trouble. He stood up, bracing himself against the wall as he sidestepped to the edge and grabbed hold of a post. Coming from the opposite direction was a freight train slowing down as it approached the crossing.

A combination of sensations overtook Ryan: standing untethered in an open space with the roar of wind rushing past his ears, unsteadied equilibrium due to the rocking movement of the accelerating train, the rush of adrenaline pumping through his veins, and the mind-altering effects from the drugs. The oncoming train's carriages were passing by in a hypnotizing rhythm. As each car passed, Ryan saw a flash of light in the gap between the cars, emanating from the low-hanging half-moon. In his disoriented state, Ryan began hallucinating the image of Jesus Christ floating behind the oncoming train, arms outstretched, beckoning Ryan to join him. A series of empty flatbed carriages raced by when Ryan leaped toward what he thought were the open arms of his Lord. As soon as his feet hit the floor, he was catapulted backward and slammed into the wall at the back of the carriage. The force of the impact threw Ryan onto his side and sent him sliding across the bed of the car, destined to be hurled from the edge of the train onto the tracks below. His survival instinct took over, and as he was ejected from the train, he reached out with both hands for one of the vertical posts mounted on the side of the carriage. The train's momentum swung him over the edge, and while still holding on to the post, his body pivoted as both legs dropped to the gravel track bed, shattering the bones in his feet upon impact. His legs bounced momentarily, and feeling the pain radiate through them, Ryan let go of the post and flew eight feet onto the gravel, landing on his side and rolling down the bank into a ditch.

This happened close enough to a residential area where someone had witnessed the accident and had called 911. Ryan was admitted to the emergency room at Saint Francis Hospital in Charleston with all the bones in his feet shattered, multiple breaks in both legs, a fractured pelvis, broken ribs, a dislocated shoulder, and two torn rotator cuffs. It would take months before Hank could bring Ryan home and begin the long recovery process. Ryan's life would never be the same.

END PART 1

PART TWO

2007 – 2012

Eeny, meeny, miney, mo,
Catch a tiger by the toe.
If he hollers, let him go,
Eeny, meeny, miney, mo.

— Mother Goose

CHAPTER 11

Moving Forward

September 2007

Thursday, the 6th

Birmingham, Michigan

Adam's career as a self-employed entrepreneur began in 2002 when he formed a company and registered it in Delaware as Custom Solutions Group LLC (CSG). Shortly after receiving his diploma from the Cranbrook School, Adam started building his home computer systems to accommodate his need for fast internet searches in areas of the net that most people did not access. Some parts were referred to as the Dark Web, where nefarious activities involving illegal trade, child pornography, and malicious hacking occurred. However, Adam had no interest in participating in any of those activities. His interest was in looking behind the curtain to understand how those perpetrators operated and to find opportunities to capitalize on his advanced knowledge of TCP/IP: Transmission Control Protocol/Internet Protocol.

In the year Adam was born, 1983, the Defense Advanced Research Projects Agency (DARPA) completed the fourth version of a network protocol that would drive the internet. Developed by the U.S. Department of Defense, this protocol aimed to connect government computer systems through a global, fault-tolerant network. The Defense Department network was eventually opened to research institutions and the general public, which expanded the foundation for today's internet. Two years after emigrating with his family to the U.S., Adam began his first year at Cranbrook's upper school and gained access to their state-of-the-art computer lab. There, he started researching the technology that drives the internet and all that occurs away from the general public's eye.

By 2004, Adam had developed a business model generating significant revenues. He identified a half-dozen U.S.-based corporations that were prime contractors to the Defense Department, companies fulfilling multi-billion-dollar orders and receiving top-secret information from the Pentagon regarding future technology requirements. Their data systems housed some of the most sensitive defense information in the world, and Adam understood that every system, regardless of sophistication, was vulnerable to hacking. Adversary countries such as Russia, Iran, North Korea, and China had either stolen or independently developed the means to infiltrate the world's most sophisticated systems, often using software engineers trained at U.S. universities. Cybercrime and cyber hacking became the new weapons in international warfare, leaving everyone at risk of an attack.

Adam had spent two years investigating the vulnerabilities of A.S. Gilman Systems (ASG), a satellite communications and telecom provider receiving billions of dollars in defense contracts. After completing a benign hack into their most sensitive databases, he waited a month to see if their software engineers would identify the breach and construct a firewall to prevent future attacks. Adam had ensured the hack could not be traced back to his computer, and he knew that if he could hack into ASG's system a second time using the same methods, it meant the original hack had gone undetected and their vulnerability remained. He accessed the same databases using the same techniques, and there were no additional firewalls to circumvent. ASG was unaware they had been hacked. Adam understood it would be invaluable for them to know they had been hacked, as it made their data vulnerable to corruption and theft. They would pay a lot of money to learn exactly how the hack had been executed so they could build the appropriate firewalls to prevent future break-ins.

Adam emailed the CEO and the Chief Technology Officer at ASG late Wednesday, reporting his accomplishments. Today, he returned from his morning run and booted up his laptop at the kitchen counter while drinking a protein shake. Among the roster of incoming emails was one from Darryl Long, CTO at A.S. Gilman Systems.

> *Thursday, September 6, 2007 at 01:24*
> *dplong@asgilman.com*
> *To: Adam Kinzler*
> *Cc: Brian Sampson*
>
> *Mr. Kinzler, we would like to meet with you at our*
> *Cleveland headquarters. Given the nature of your*
> *email, we consider the need for a meeting urgent.*
> *Please advise your earliest availability.*
>
> *Regards,*
> *Darryl P. Long, CTO*
> *A.S. Gilman Systems, Inc.*
> *859 Superior Ave.*
> *Cleveland, OH 44114*

Most of the three-hour drive from Cleveland back to Birmingham was on interstate highways and the Ohio Turnpike, allowing Adam to open up the old BMW and let her go. The roads were usually dotted with speed traps, but he felt lucky today. If things went the way Adam suspected they would, he would be driving a 2007 BMW 750Li before long.

ASG's CEO had joined their meeting that afternoon and instructed Darryl to obtain the necessary government security clearances to allow Adam to begin work on his new contract. Once received, Adam would be given access to all of ASG's computer systems. He would then identify the source of their vulnerabilities and, more importantly, provide technical training to dismantle them. It was a six-figure contract for five months of work, and Adam knew he had started a valuable business. Once he had a successful project with a principal defense contractor like ASG, the sky was the limit for obtaining new work. Adam had never been more confident that he was on his way to success as CEO of his own company.

Tuesday, the 25th

Mapledale, West Virginia

Ryan's physical rehabilitation took longer than expected. He was released from the hospital three weeks after his accident and spent the next four months at a rehabilitation facility in Charleston. When he finally came home, Glenda had set up a bed in the living room so he would not have to walk up the stairs while he fully recovered. The downstairs bathroom had only a commode and sink, but since Ryan would be restricted to sponge baths for the coming months, he had everything he needed until he could move back to his room. Glenda left Ryan a sandwich and snacks before she left for her job each morning as a housekeeping supervisor at the Greenbrier Resort. Ryan could manage, with great difficulty, to get to the bathroom on his own. Otherwise, the TV remote provided access to the only activity he engaged in each day. His sister, Brittany, was starting her senior year at high school and had no interest in sitting with her brother after school. She and her friends found plenty of ways to keep themselves busy in town.

Ryan spent 10 hours a day in his La-Z-Boy, watching TV and nibbling snacks, with his loyal friend Roy at his feet. He was still in a lot of pain and had been given a prescription for oxycodone when he was discharged from the rehabilitation facility. He had been taking the prescribed dosage and enjoyed the pain relief, but boredom had set in, and he began craving more of a high from the drugs. After two months, Glenda drove him to the VA Medical Center in Beckley, about an hour away, where he declared his pain level to be a seven when three would probably have been the correct number. The physician approved an increase in the dosage and made several changes to the medications for his mental health disorders to accommodate the increased oxycodone. Ryan was also prescribed a course of home physical rehabilitation that would begin as soon as a therapist could be found who served his region.

Jenny Windsome was a licensed physical therapist with an office in nearby White Sulphur Springs. At 25, she was a year older than Ryan and had been a therapist for three years. She was of medium height with streaked blond hair, a baby doll face, and a sturdy build. Her dimpled smile was warm and welcoming, and she had a caring personality well-suited to her healing profession. Her affiliation with the Beckley VA Medical Center provided a steady flow of patients, and she had been assigned to work with Ryan four days a week until he could walk unassisted. Now that he could walk up the stairs without crutches, Jenny treated him twice a week.

"Just two more," Jenny said while Ryan struggled to part his knees with an elastic band around his thighs. "That's it, breathe in when you bring your knees together and breathe out when the band is fully stretched."

Ryan grunted as his knees collapsed before completing the stretch. "Why does it still hurt so bad? It's been almost a year, and I'm weak as a baby. Damn, hard to believe I was a wrestlin' champ back in the day. Will I ever be right?"

"Of course, you will, you'll be stronger than ever. But Ryan, it takes time, and we've only started. You've got at least another year of this before everything is back to normal."

"Well, that sucks. Not that I don't want to see you every week, that's the only thing I look forward to. It just sucks feelin' like a cripple. And if I don't get out of this house soon, my dad might turn me into a right invalid. He's got one hell of a temper."

"Like father, like son? Sorry, but you've shared enough stories over the last few months that I'm aware of your anger issues. If I'm not mistaken, that's what got you into this situation in the first place. Your pent-up anger is like a bomb waiting for the fuse to be lit, and let's be honest, when you mix alcohol with the medications you're taking, that fuse spontaneously combusts."

"Does what?"

"Lights real fast. Can we have another conversation about getting you back to the clinic so the docs can reevaluate your meds? And maybe see what it would take for you to cut back on the drinking?"

Ryan understood that Jenny cared deeply about his well-being, both physical and mental, but he could not perceive the drugs and alcohol as a problem. They were his coping mechanisms and the only way he could envision numbing the physical pain and quelling the frustration of living under his father's roof. "Not today, Jen. I'm whipped. Maybe Monday."

"Okay. Just one more try with the band, then we'll wrap up." Jenny pursed her lips and smiled, noticing her feelings toward Ryan were more than empathy and compassion for his struggles. She was falling in love.

CHAPTER 12

Deadly Threats

SEPTEMBER 2008

Monday, the 1ˢᵗ

Georgetown, Washington, DC

Claudia had been looking forward to Adam's arrival all week. She had just begun another work-study semester at the NSA campus in Fort Meade. She had grown accustomed to staying in the two-bedroom apartment they provided in the nearby town of Laurel, just off the Baltimore-Washington Parkway. Her roommate was away for the Labor Day weekend, so the apartment would have been hers to enjoy, but she had decided to stay at Kip's townhouse in Georgetown. She could hardly believe it when Adam accepted Kip's invitation to stay there. She had assumed the privacy of a hotel might be more to his liking.

Adam had a job interview in the DC area that would run throughout the Labor Day week. In typical fashion, Adam had not revealed any details about the job he was interviewing for, he was not known for graciously offering information about things he was involved in. Although most people who spent time around Adam found that trait to be a sign of arrogance, Claudia had learned that withholding information from others was his way of avoiding unnecessary chit-chat. If information were needed, Adam would share exactly as much as required and no more. His communication was efficient and pragmatic, something Claudia had learned was common to intellectual geniuses like Adam.

This would be Claudia's final semester in the NSA Co-op Program, and she had set her hopes on landing a full-time job at the NSA when she graduated from MIT. Kip was in his third year working at *The Washington Post,* but he had become frustrated with the limited scope of his work assignments. Kip's editor was pleased with his research work and the short articles he had written for the newspaper's online edition, but he had yet to give any assignments that Kip felt he could dig his teeth into. Kip wanted to delve deeper into the geopolitical issues in Southeast Asia and begin writing from an investigative viewpoint rather than simply reporting on past events. Kip believed that with his fluency in Mandarin Chinese and his eagerness to relocate overseas, he would be happier working as a freelance journalist, a job that came with no guarantee of a reliable income. Thanks to the money he had saved over the past three years and the quarterly stipend his trust was paying, he could afford to make the move if it could lead to a more fulfilling career. He was beginning the 12-month-long application process for a visa allowing him to reside and work in Hong Kong. Claudia knew this might be one of the last times they would spend time together before their careers sent them in different directions.

Adam's flight arrived mid-morning at Reagan National Airport, and the taxi dropped him off at Kip's townhouse before noon. Claudia was already there and ran down the front steps to greet him. "Hello, *Liebchen.* I am so glad you're here," she said. "And I love the three-day beard—it suits you."

Adam grinned and said, "Two—it's a two-day beard. Glad you

like it."

"And the aviators, very 'international man of mystery.' Kip is getting his friend's bike up the street, I brought mine with me. Not only does the NSA provide an apartment, but they also give me a monthly stipend and the use of a car. It's a really sweet deal. I sure hope it leads to a full-time job there."

Kip rode down the hill as Claudia and Adam walked toward the house. "Glad your flight was on time," Kip said. "We loved your idea about going for a bike ride, and I thought you could ride mine. This belongs to a friend and is probably not up to your standards, but it will be fine for me."

Adam looked at Claudia's bike and said, "Why do you have a shopping basket on your handlebars? Doesn't that make steering awkward? This will be a long ride. You might do better without it."

"I meant to remove it, but it's attached with zip ties, and I couldn't get it off. Kip, do you have scissors in the house?"

"No worries, I've got it." Adam reached into his pocket and pulled out a Swiss Army knife.

Claudia watched as Adam cut the ties and said, "Are you ever without that thing?"

"Nope. As you can see, it comes in handy." With a mischievous grin, he added, "You never know when you'll need a good knife."

Kip ignored the implication of Adam's comment and said, "And how long will the ride be?"

"According to MapQuest, it's just over eight miles. Most of it is along the canal towpath, so it should be a fairly easy ride. Let me change clothes and get some energy bars, then we can head out."

Kip showed Adam to his room on the ground floor. He had decided Adam would appreciate its privacy, so for the first time, he invited Claudia to use the guest bedroom across from his. When Claudia was studying nearby in Fort Meade, they were able to get together often, but only for the day. Claudia had only stayed at Kip's twice, on her visits from MIT. He was having a hard time reading Claudia's signals. There were several instances where a heartfelt story from their past was shared, or they had soul-searching talks about the future and the careers they would pursue. Still, despite the intimacy of those moments, neither of them moved to embrace or demonstrate any sign of a romantic attraction yet, it was there, and they both felt it. Kip wondered if and when he would act on his feelings. *Everything in good time*, he thought. *There is still a lot of change on the horizon.*

They filled their water bottles, packed some nuts and dried fruit into their backpacks, checked the tire pressure on all three bikes, and took off for a day on the trails. It was perfect September weather, with clear skies and temperatures in the low seventies.

As they pedaled along the path to the Potomac waterfront, Kip said, "Adam, are you going to tell us our destination today, or is it going to be a mystery?"

"We're headed to the Chesapeake and Ohio towpath, about three miles northwest, and then we'll get onto the Route 50 bike trail. That will take us to Langley. We'll take a break and come back the same way. All up, it will be about three hours of riding."

"Sounds good," Kip said. "Any special reason we're going to Langley?"

"Nope. It's just a nice ride along the Potomac, and the trails are mostly wooded, so it should be a pretty easy ride for you and Claudia."

Kip didn't know Adam to be one who proposed an activity simply because it was 'nice,' so his choice of a destination was suspicious. However, Kip knew the area well and agreed it would be a great way to spend the afternoon.

Kip had made dinner reservations that evening at his favorite waterfront restaurant in Georgetown, Sequoia DC, and had reserved a corner table with sweeping views of Arlington across the river and the Kennedy Center around the bend. Adam never drank alcohol, so Kip and Claudia shared a bottle of pinot grigio as he enjoyed his freshly squeezed orange juice. Unsurprisingly, Adam did not have much to say during the meal, but Kip and Claudia were having a lively conversation about what lay ahead in the coming year.

Claudia said, "Adam, I've been telling Kip how helpful your advice was when I started high school. You said that studying mathematics could open many doors after college, but I never suspected I would enjoy the subject so much. It makes sense, given my love for solving mysteries and puzzles. Mathematics is the key to explaining how pretty much everything works."

"I knew you had a head for it," Adam said. "You were smart to declare it as a major and then focus on the science of cryptology. Leave it to you, sis, to find your way to the NSA."

"I'm fascinated now by the world of encryption. The way we convert information into scrambled code with our algorithms and secret keys, enabling us to protect our networks from cyberattacks, is a new frontier. The intelligence the NSA collects is secure even if the system is compromised, and now the programs we've developed are used throughout the government. I get a real sense of satisfaction knowing I'm doing my small part to help protect us. But I'm determined to land a full-time job there, and when I do, watch out!"

"The world will never be the same," Adam said lovingly, reaching his glass across the table to toast her.

"Cheers to that," said Kip, joining the toast.

"Adam," Claudia said, "You haven't said a word about your job interview, except that you have meetings throughout the week. No surprise, we're used to your brevity, but you could at least share a *few* details."

"There's nothing much to share until I know I have the job. They emailed me when they learned about a project I had been working on. They were impressed with my work and said I fit the bill for a position opening up, so I'm meeting with a bunch of people in different departments to make sure I'm the right fit. I know I am, but I need to get a good look at them and their operations before committing. If I am going to leave Mom alone in Birmingham, I need to be certain this is the right job."

Claudia was hit with a pang of guilt. It had been a hard decision when it came time to select a college. She felt her choices in Michigan were limited if she stayed home to be with their mother. Michigan State University was world-class, but the commute to Lansing would have been almost an hour and a half, in good traffic, and she would have needed to live on campus. Claudia figured that if she flew home on school breaks from MIT to visit Sophia, she would see her about as often as if she had attended MSU.

"*Mamitá* always puts on a brave face when I'm there, and she says working as a mental health counselor is helping with her healing, but I still worry about her," Claudia said. "She became so fragile after Dad was taken from us. You have been a Godsend to her, Adam, and I worry less with you there all the time."

"Mom is going to be okay, sis. It's taking her more time to heal than you and me. We're young, inventing our futures. She thought she knew what hers was, and then those dreams were shattered. Reinventing her life has been tough, but so is she. She wants more than anything for you and me to be happy. That's the best way to support her now, to show her we're creating brilliant futures that will make us happy."

Kip's mouth almost gaped as he listened. It was the first time he had heard Adam express genuine compassion. Kip had just seen a part of Adam he always knew was there, the part that lived beneath a curated veneer of stoicism, the part that had Kip believe he and Adam could one day become good friends. Tonight, he finally felt like they were.

Resuming the levity from toasting Claudia, Kip said, "I have no question you will make your mom proud. And I believe you will do your part to keep our country safe. If anyone can help change the world, my money is on you."

"Well then, we can be partners in that," Claudia said. "You are paying your dues at *The Post,* and if you receive your visa and can establish yourself as a freelancer in Hong Kong, that will be your chance to do meaningful reporting and help readers understand what's transpiring in that part of the world. The thought of North Korea developing a nuclear weapon that could reach our shores terrifies me as much as the thought of another terrorist attack. People need to understand the complexities of the diplomacy going on now and what might happen after this election. Whether Obama or McCain gets into office, the Japanese need to be assured we will continue our strong alliance with them and work to mitigate the tensions on the Korean peninsula."

Kip said, "I'm enjoying delving into those complexities and making sense of them. China has become hopeful that with our attention over the past five years focused on our wars in Afghanistan and Iraq, we might be ignoring our interests in Asia. If the Chinese see us looking away, they will take advantage of that."

Claudia said, "I read from time to time about a looming takeover of Taiwan by China, but I'll be honest, I don't understand why that should concern the U.S. as much as it does."

Kip looked to Adam and, realizing he had the floor, continued. "The U.S. has a treaty in place to come to Taiwan's defense if China ever attacks it, and there is reason to believe it is only a matter of time before China decides to retake what it has always claimed belongs to the mainland. It seems like our government has been so focused on its Middle East wars on terrorism that we're not giving enough attention to our foreign policy in Asia. Don't get me wrong, we need to be at work eliminating terrorist threats to our country, but we also need to worry about China and its alliance with North Korea."

Adam decided to weigh in. "Good points, Kip, but don't underestimate the importance of what's happening in Syria and Iraq. We're successfully dismembering al-Qaeda, but that is creating a vacuum being filled by other terrorist groups. A group called 'al-Qa'ida in Iraq' is an offshoot of al-Qaeda. It was founded in 2004 by a man named Abu Musab al-Zarqawi. He died two years ago, and they've gone underground while they rebuild their leadership. Still, our government's intelligence says they are quietly building their ranks and will emerge if they see the U.S. pulling back its efforts in Iraq and Afghanistan. I can see why our foreign policy has taken the direction it has."

"You've really taken a close look at these things," Kip said. "I thought I was up on everything through my work at *The Post*, but you seem to have information not everyone has."

"I do my research," Adam said.

They finished dinner as the sun was setting, and their walk home was quiet, each reflecting on their conversations at dinner. Adam was mainly focused on his interview the next day and thinking through the questions he planned to ask. His choice of Langley as their biking destination was not accidental. He was exploring what might become his future commuting route to the George Bush Center for Intelligence, the CIA's headquarters in Langley. Named after the current president's father, George H.W. Bush, its 258-acre campus was the largest intelligence headquarters in the world. Adam was confident it would be his new training ground in short order. He had been through a preliminary interview via phone and the internet and received a conditional offer to join the CIA's ranks as an independent contractor. The agency worked with hundreds of contractors worldwide, and Adam's company was a perfect fit for their profile.

Adam had completed his project with the A.S. Gilman company in June, and they were obligated through their contracts with the Defense Department to disclose any potential security risks to their systems, so in due course, the Pentagon had been made aware of Adam's work for ASG. That information made its way to a cybersecurity expert at the CIA and resulted in the offer Adam was there to entertain. Adam had vowed after his father's death to dedicate himself to two things: taking care of his family and seeking retribution for the evil acts that had claimed their father's life. This was Adam's next step in those efforts. He would be subjected to a barrage of tests throughout the week, including the CIA's infamous polygraph tests. After the week, he would receive an offer to engage his company's services. After a three-month orientation in Langley, he would be given his first contract and formally partnered with the world's largest intelligence agency in a battle to take down terrorists.

Thursday, the 4th

White Sulphur Springs, West Virginia

Kip had not used his vacation days during the three years he worked at *The Washington Post*. After Tuesday's election, Kip knew if he did not take some vacation now, he would not have an opportunity until well after President Obama had been inaugurated and the dust had settled.

Kip was flying this morning from Reagan National Airport to Roanoke, Virginia, where he was meeting his parents' flight from Detroit. From there, they would make the 90-minute drive to the Greenbrier Resort in White Sulphur Springs. Dudley's best friend from Pinehurst and a married couple who had become mutual friends were making the five-hour drive to enjoy three days of golf with the Reynolds. Kip's mother, Patty, did not play golf and had invited Kip to join them so she would have company while the others were on the links. It wasn't Kip's idea of an exciting vacation, but he had enjoyed his mother's visits in DC and felt he had neglected his father over the past few years. He agreed to join them for the long weekend out of a sense of duty to his parents.

Kip had kept in touch with Ryan by phone after his accident, and Kip always said he would come for a visit. Ryan's birthday was the next day, so this seemed like the perfect opportunity to kill two birds with one stone. After two years, he hesitated to see Ryan again. He had not seemed like himself on their calls. Kip had noticed him drifting off in the middle of sentences and remaining silent until he could jar him back into the conversation. Ryan sometimes slurred, jumbling words and sentences, and often babbled incoherently. Ryan said he was taking medications for pain, as well as for treating his "condition," a condition he never elaborated on. Kip did not think Ryan was keeping anything from him. He believed Ryan did not understand what his mental health condition was and that a diagnosis had never been explained to him in a way he could understand. Kip was concerned for Ryan and hoped he had the full support of Glenda and Hank as he tried to recover, both physically and mentally.

Kip's flight arrived an hour before his parents', so he sat at the Starbucks across from baggage claim and read the latest *Foreign*

Affairs issue. Their flight had been delayed by half an hour, and as they approached their belt at baggage claim, Kip heard his father's raspy voice and inhaled deeply as he prepared himself for the days ahead.

"I still don't understand why we had to change planes in Atlanta," Dudley said to Patty. "Flights out of Atlanta are always delayed. You can't get anywhere on Delta without going through that blasted airport. They say when you die, you have to go through Atlanta to get to heaven. I'm sure Saint Peter has gotten used to the late arrivals."

"Yes, dear," Patty said, "I'm sure he has. And look, there's Kip."

Kip had grown accustomed to his father's eccentricities. Today's outfit was a bright green blazer over a yellow polo, navy cotton shorts, and Dockers without socks. His persistent slouch and unkempt hair made him appear older than his years, and a fisherman's bucket hat punctuated his odd duck persona. Kip's mother was perfectly attired in a white Chanel suit with capped sleeves and a pleated skirt. Her shoes and handbag were also by Chanel.

Dudley rejected the first three cars that the Herz's lot attendant offered them. The first was too small, the second too large, and the third had a strange odor. He settled for the silver Volkswagen SUV but became irritated as he struggled to load the luggage, dropping a bag on its side as he snatched the glasses falling from his nose. Kip's offer to help provoked a small outburst from Dudley, "Oh, for heaven's sake, I can do this. I may have turned 50 last month, but I'm not over the hill yet. Just get in the car, and we'll be on our way."

"Yes," said Patty, "And please sit in the backseat, Kip. Your father is having one of his meltdowns and is obviously in a state. I'll be driving. Dudley, you can relax and enjoy the beautiful drive through the mountains."

"I'm perfectly-"

Patty cut him off. "You're perfectly flustered and highly agitated. Plus, you had several Bloody Marys on the flights down. I'm driving. End of discussion."

While Dudley decompressed, Kip shared the details about Claudia and Adam's Monday visit. After 20 minutes, Dudley said, "Well, it sounds like everyone is working very hard. Adam is a bright young man. Wherever he plans to work, they will certainly want to take advantage of his intellect. I always knew his sister was a go-getter, and working for a government agency like the NSA is quite a thing. I suspect it is challenging and grueling."

Kip knew his father had never worked an actual job, so having one seemed daunting. After Dudley's father passed away and his financial assets had been placed in trust, their financial manager at Merrill Lynch allocated the money between several accounts. One provided short-term income from stocks and bonds for the Reynolds family's living expenses. Another account was for long-term assets that would appreciate over time, and one was for the trusts held for Kip and his brother, Bradley. They began receiving a modest quarterly disbursement from their trusts on their twenty-first birthdays. All the assets would be released to them upon their father's death. Grandpa Reynolds had seen his error in not requiring Dudley to embark on a career and work for a living. He could see Dudley had grown accustomed to his leisurely life at the country club and vacationing in Pinehurst, Hilton Head, and Cape Cod. He did not want his grandsons to grow up without a work ethic and a proper sense of responsibility for their finances. Dudley's only "job" was to meet monthly at the club with his financial advisor, play a round of golf, and discuss any "open matters" over drinks at the 19th hole. Dudley felt that earned him the right to say he worked as an investment manager.

"I would imagine the folks at the newspaper are taking advantage of your youthful ambition and working you more hours than you signed up for," Dudley continued. "Are you fed up yet and ready to move home and relax a bit? I know your mother misses you, not that she hasn't burned a path between Detroit and DC these past years, and with Bradley living in California, it's awfully quiet around the house."

"All the more reason to sell that monstrosity," Patty said. "We could be quite happy with a townhouse in Birmingham, like the one Claudia's mother purchased, and a winter home in Palm Beach. I've always wanted a place there, and I'm sick and tired of the Michigan winters."

"Well, that's not happening," Dudley said.

"We'll just see about that, won't we?"

Kip could envision his mother sipping drinks with friends on the terrace at the Breakers Hotel in Palm Beach. He wondered how long it would take before a membership opened at The Everglades Club on Worth Avenue, perhaps the most exclusive private club in the country. Kip had no doubt his mother would one day get her way. Dudley was a pushover when it came to Patty.

"I might as well tell you both while we're together," Kip said. "I will be leaving my job at *The Post* next month and striking out to establish myself as a freelance journalist based in Hong Kong. Living there will allow me to cover political developments in Asia and provide insight into what they mean for U.S. policy. My editors aren't ready to give me assignments like that, but I believe I could do a fantastic job as an investigative reporter if I lived in Asia. *The Post* isn't planning to open an office there, and I'm willing to go it on my own. It is the best way to propel my career forward, and I need a big challenge like this. No offense, Dad, but I'm not going to live my life as an entitled nepo baby."

"Like me?" Dudley snapped. "Just say it: *like your father*."

At a very young age, Kip had promised himself he would never use his family's wealth to avoid taking responsibility for his future. As he matured, he noticed how his friends at school spoke admirably about their fathers, their careers, their promotions and successes, and how proud they were to spend time in their presence. Their fathers were their heroes. Kip looked with disdain at his father's lack of ambition. Playing a good round of golf or adeptly booking a vacation did not count as successes to Kip, and it required no ambition to spend every afternoon and evening raising tumblers of scotch and falling into bed before nine. Kip had always been embarrassed to have friends visit their home and see his father drinking his way through the day. In Kip's mind, Dudley was the anti-hero in his life story.

"That's right, Dad. I want to be my own man. I *need* to be my own man. That's what's important to me and what this career will do for me."

"I've seen how hard you studied at Georgetown," Patty said. "And you gave up two summers for your internship at *The Post*, so I have no question that your hard work will pay off. We're very proud of you, Kip. Aren't we, Dudley?"

The Bloody Marys had caught up with Dudley, and he had nodded off. Thirty minutes later, they arrived at the grand entrance to the Greenbrier.

It had been a beautiful drive through the Blue Ridge Mountains in Virginia, and the final stretch along Route 64, winding through a region of the Allegheny Mountains void of any towns, portended the solitude and grandeur of what lay ahead. Nestled among the hills at an elevation of two thousand feet, the Greenbrier's eleven thousand acres were surrounded by spectacular mountain views. The resort had been constructed in 1913 to serve as a luxury getaway for wealthy East Coast businessmen and their families, members of society, and politicians from across the country. It belonged to the rarefied group of Grand Hotels built after the turn of the nineteenth century and had played host to 28 U.S. presidents. The Greenbrier boasted over seven hundred guest rooms and private cottages—decorated in the fashion of the early twentieth century—and housed over 50 restaurants and shops. It had three golf courses, including one designed by Jack Nicklaus, and was the only resort course in the world to have hosted both the Ryder Cup and the Solheim Cup.

The quarter-mile drive from the entrance wound through a wooded area before opening to an oval driveway surrounding a manicured garden the size of a football field. Behind it stood the main building in its full splendor. The brilliant white structure was home to seven floors of rooms built atop a ground level hosting dozens of boutique shops, each fronted with a red Bostonian awning. The grand portico in front of the main entrance was 50 feet wide and supported six round, 50-foot-tall Grecian columns.

As Patty pulled up to the valet station, she said, "Your father and I love coming here. I'm sure you can see why. I think we'll have a grand time. It's the perfect season for your father's golf, and I'm sure you and I can fit in some tennis. There are over a dozen courts, and half are indoors, so bad weather won't keep us from playing. Dudley, have you looked at a weather forecast?"

At that point, Dudley awakened, ignoring Patty's question about the weather. He left the check-in process to Patty and went to the bar to await his friends' arrival. As Kip observed his father, he knew it might be a challenge to enjoy his stay here, and he was nervous about seeing Ryan. He had a premonition that something bad would happen and was about to be proven right.

Friday, the 5th

Numerous emotional setbacks had complicated Ryan's recovery. Jenny's agency had authorized her to treat Ryan twice weekly over the past year. Still, his frustration from being stuck at home, along with the growing tension between him and his father, had led to debilitating bouts of depression. Ryan began canceling many rehab appointments and confined himself to his room, only emerging in the evenings to hang out with friends at The Rusty Nail.

Jenny came as often as Ryan allowed and tried her best to ensure Ryan was taking his medications as directed. She could tell by his erratic behavior that he was not managing his medications well. When he struggled with exercises, he would have fits of rage followed by a slew of apologies when he calmed down. She realized his painkillers were running out long before the prescriptions were due for refills, but somehow, Ryan was still treating his pain with pills. She had no idea where he was getting them, but in their part of the world, drugs like oxycodone could be found pretty much anywhere the locals gathered, and the use of methamphetamines was rampant.

The VA determined by the spring of 2008 that Ryan's rehabilitation was complete, and because he was unemployed, there was no basis upon which to approve follow-up occupational therapy. Jenny's assignment to Ryan's rehabilitation was terminated in May. But during the 18 months she had worked with Ryan, Jenny discovered the part of him that almost no one saw: the sensitive and caring side. It was most apparent when she watched Ryan and Roy together, each enjoying companionship built on years of mutual trust. Although she could never entice Ryan to play his guitar for her, she saw how immaculately he cared for it and the special place it claimed in his room. Ryan had an evident love for music, and Jenny wondered when and where he could express himself through it. Jenny noticed that his three wrestling trophies had been won over ten years ago, but they were displayed proudly atop his dresser as if he had stood on the winner's platform only weeks prior. Ryan's sensitivity lay deep beneath his rugged exterior, and Jenny hoped he would eventually become comfortable sharing it with her.

During her many visits to the Jackson home, Jenny had got to know Ryan and his family well. She could see the warmth between Glenda and her children and how they looked out for each other. Jenny saw that even at 17, Brittany knew her older brother needed help dealing with his frustrations and anger, and she was moved by the empathy Brittany showed toward Ryan when he became aggressive. Ryan fussed over Brittany, complimented her outfits, and praised her school achievements at every opportunity. Jenny knew Hank could be tricky to deal with, but Glenda seemed to have found a way to cope with her husband's outbursts. He also had anger issues, and they were exacerbated by the six-pack of beer he drank each night. When Hank and Ryan had simultaneous fits of rage, Jenny watched as Glenda intervened to ensure they would not come to fisticuffs. Glenda showed compassion for Ryan and the challenges of living at home with Hank, and Jenny encouraged him to find a job that would get him away from the house and allow him to live independently.

Glenda was perceptive about her children and harbored the hope that Ryan and Jenny might eventually develop a romantic relationship. It appeared to Glenda that Jenny's caring for Ryan went deeper than what was required as a therapist. She detected what women from her generation called a "spark" between them, and it was evident that Ryan appreciated the kindness and nurturing that Jenny had shown him over the months. In Glenda's world, hope was sometimes the only thing that gave her strength, and Glenda had plenty of both.

Ryan got out of bed that morning without remembering it was his birthday. Roy followed him downstairs, and they were greeted in the kitchen by his mother, busily scrambling eggs for Brittany's breakfast. "Good morning, birthday boy. How does it feel to be alive for a quarter century? It ought to feel pretty good after what you've come through."

"I feel like crap," Ryan said. "These pills ain't workin' like they should. Jenny says I gotta do my exercises every day, and the pain will start leavin' after a while. I hope she's right. I don't want another 25 years like this."

"Well, be glad you got Jenny to help look after you. Is she comin' by today?"

"When she gets off work at five. She's takin' me to dinner at Shelby's. My van's still in the shop, damn piece of shit."

The phone in the living room rang, and Ryan said, "I'll get it. Might be Jenny."

Before Ryan could answer, Roy began barking at the kids walking by the house. "It's ok, Roy. Same kids you see every mornin,'" Ryan said affectionately.

As he lifted the receiver, Brittany snapped at Glenda, "I know! Geez. Every Friday, the same thing. Yes, I will remember to bring my books home. Quit naggin'."

Kip knew the phone had been answered, he could hear the commotion in the background, but no one spoke. Then he heard Ryan say, "Dang it, Roy. Kock it off. You ain't goin' out." Then Ryan said, "H'lo?"

"Hi, Ryan. Is that you? Kip here. It's been a while."

There was a long pause as Ryan processed the voice on the other end. "Oh, hey. Yeah, been a while."

"Well, happy birthday, buddy. The big two-five. How are things going?"

"Been better," Ryan said.

"I'm not surprised, after all that's happened. Last time we talked, the casts had been removed, and you were starting to get around okay. Did you end up buying that old Econoline van you were looking at?"

"Yeah, but I think I got ripped off. It's always got somethin' breakin' down. It's in the shop again, and I ain't got the money to pay the repairs."

"Sorry to hear that. I'm calling to see if you have any plans for tonight. I'm staying here at the Greenbrier with my parents and won't leave until Sunday. I'd love to come by to see the family, and then you and I could go out and have some fun on your big day. I've got my folks' rental car, they're having dinner tonight with friends at the resort."

"Remember the girl Jenny I was tellin' you about—my therapist? Well, we're friends now, good friends, and she's takin' me to dinner."

"Sure, I remember her. It's great that you've become friends. I know you were kind of sweet on her. I'd love to meet Jenny, she sounds like a special person. Any chance we could hook up somewhere for a drink after dinner?"

There was another pause, and then Ryan said, "Okay, I guess. If Jenny don't mind."

"That's great. Just let me know where to go and when to be there."

"It's called The Rusty Nail. You head out the resort and turn left on Main Street. Once you pass Pocahontas Trail, keep goin' straight and it's about a mile on the right. You can't miss it. It's a local dive bar for rednecks like me."

Kip chuckled and said, "Alright then. What time?"

"Dunno. Eight, I guess."

"Great. Eight it is. If anything comes up, give me a call at the resort. I'm in room 624 and will get back from a tennis game with my mom by four. I'll get something to eat at the café here and hang out in my room."

"'K. See ya."

Jenny arrived at the Jackson home shortly before six, and Ryan got up from the living room sofa to let her in. She welcomed Ryan with a birthday hug and a peck on the cheek and turned to greet Hank and Brittany, who were watching the local news.

"What's that under your arm? It looks like somethin' you found layin' around a construction site and put a big ole bow around," Brittany said with a giggle.

"A present for your brother. It's called a foam roller, and it will help his back feel better once I teach him how to use it."

Ryan eyed the two-foot-long tubular block and raised his eyebrows. "That's gonna help me feel better? I gotta see this."

"You will. I'll come by after the weekend and show you how to use it. You're gonna love it. Trust me."

Hank swallowed a large gulp of beer and said, "I'm a trustin' man, but I can't get my head around how that could be good for anythin', 'cept maybe hittin' that boy upside his head if he don't hurry up and get a job."

That was Ryan's cue to usher Jenny out of the living room. He knew an argument was ensuing, and with Hank on his third beer, it would probably get ugly. "Mom's in the kitchen icin' a cake. She thought we could stop back after dinner and do the whole cake and singin' thing. Why don't you say hello, and I'll run upstairs and fetch my wallet."

As Jenny left the room, Hank said to Ryan, "Don't know why you need your wallet, ain't nothin' in it, far as I can tell. Seems to me a man of 25 ought to be out workin' a job somewhere and payin' rent. My union is still threatenin' to strike, and if they do, that Greenbrier could go belly up, and then we'll all be out of a job. Even if the union settles, we're on thin ice there. Your freeloadin' days are over, boy. I need to see some rent money. Looks like you have money to hang out and drink with your friends at that bar, and God knows how much you paid for that rattle-trap van, so you're getting' it somewhere. Better be legal, is all I can say, 'cause I ain't payin' to get your ass outta any trouble."

Glenda and Jenny heard Hank and suspected tempers were about to flare. "Maybe you can get Ryan out of there and be on your way. This won't end well," Glenda said. "This ain't the first time they've had this argument. Last time, I thought Ryan was gonna throw a punch. If that boy ever hits his father, it will turn into a dog fight, and I don't know who I'd put my money on. I don't understand where all Ryan's anger comes from. Those meds just seem to mess him up. He ain't been himself since his accident."

"I worry about him, too, Mrs. J. Ryan's not good about taking his meds when he's supposed to, and I think we both know he's taking way too many pain pills. They don't mix well with the scripts for his other issues and he really shouldn't be drinking any alcohol. But I know he does when he's with his buds."

"Honey, he keeps a bottle of vodka in his bedroom and just sips away while playin' his guitar. He plays real sad songs sometimes, just him and little Roy hunkered in that room together for hours. But when he comes out and his father's in a mood after a bad day at the resort, it's like settin' a match to kindlin'. It scares me sometimes. It would be best if Ryan moved out, much as I hate to say it, but I'm not sure he can look after himself. You are a true blessing to that boy, and I know he appreciates all you do for him. So am I, sweetheart. You're a good egg."

Ryan was the first to raise his voice. "It ain't none of your business where I get my money!"

"The hell it ain't. Long as you live under my roof, everything you do is my business. So, here's your damned birthday present: one more month of freeloadin'. From then on, if you can't pay somethin' for rent, you're out on your ass."

"To hell with you then. I'll move out now and just live in my van until I find my own place."

"Yeah? And how you gonna pay to get it out of the shop, rob an ATM?"

"Never you mind. I got a plan."

Glenda and Jenny walked into the hallway, and Glenda said, "Thanks for stopping by, Jenny. Now, you kids, be on your way and enjoy your dinner. Come by after for some German chocolate cake and ice cream. I got the Breyer's vanilla bean with cinnamon bits."

As Ryan walked upstairs, Hank said to Glenda, "I got a bad feelin' about what that boy's up to. Don't make sense to me. He's got no job, but he always has money to hang out and buy booze. Whatever it is, I'm tired of the whole thing. Time he grow up and live on his own."

"He right near got killed, and now that he's healed, you're ready to put him out? His body may be fixed, but those docs still don't have him actin' right." Glenda turned to Jenny and said, "Sometimes they got to experiment with them drugs until they get 'em right. Isn't that so?"

"That's right, Mrs. J. We're just not there yet. Close, but not there."

Ryan came downstairs and walked past Glenda and Jenny without looking into the living room. "Come on, Jenny. Let's go before my old man blows his gasket. See you later, Mom, unless Dad's locked me out."

"Well, if he does, he'll be sleepin' in that chair."

Kip had no problem finding the bar. It was the only building on the dark stretch of road leading out of town, and the illuminated Bud Light and Michelob signs in the windows identified it as a bar. "The Rusty Nail—Where Friends Meet" was painted on a rickety billboard behind the gravel parking lot, its overhead lamp burned out. The dozen or so pickup trucks and old sedans were scattered like puzzle pieces waiting to be assembled. The building was a long rectangle with red clapboard siding and a flat roof. The humming of the air conditioning units promised a cool inside, signaling to Kip he would get some relief from the unusually hot September weather. He could hear men talking behind the building in what he suspected was a smoking area, along with loud voices and a jukebox as he approached the entrance.

Kip's senses were assaulted as he stepped through the narrow, windowless door. It was a well-worn room that smelled of stale beer, old wood, and the hint of someone's cheap, sweet perfume. Through the dim lighting, he saw a bar that ran along the room's length, wrapped with corrugated tin. The wall behind it was cluttered with neon signs a local beer distributor had provided to advertise its wares—some flashing, some sparkling, and some burned out. To the left was a pool table underneath a faux Tiffany lamp, surrounded by paunchy men with unkempt beards and leather jackets. Kip figured they belonged to the bikes he had seen out front. To the right of the bar were two pinball machines butted against a wall with the head of a six-point deer mounted above. There was a narrow hallway to the right of the bar that Kip assumed went back to the restrooms and the outdoor smoking area. A couple dozen patrons were scattered about in groups of three and four, some sitting at old wooden tables with mismatched chairs and others standing in clusters. Three men and a woman had taken up residence at the bar, each with a bottle of beer, staring intently at the TV and watching the first game of the college season between the Yellow Jackets and the Golden Bears. The jukebox along the windowless back wall was playing at full volume, and the lyrics from John Mayer's song, *Waiting on the World to Change*, struck Kip as ironic. It seemed to him that this world would not change anytime soon.

The floor was sticky under Kip's loafers, and he knew he should not have tucked his light blue polo shirt into his beige linen pants if he had intended to look casual. It was the most understated outfit he had brought for his stay at the five-star resort, but he realized after taking in the room that he could not fit in, regardless of his clothes. Kip grinned and thought, *Gee, one of these things is not like the others.*

He spotted Ryan standing by the bar with a woman he presumed to be Jenny. Ryan's light brown hair was shorter than he had last seen, a grown-out buzz cut with tight curls, and he was about 15 pounds thinner. He had retained his muscular build but had developed a slight stoop, like Kip's father. His face looked a bit weathered and drawn, not surprising after the stress from his lengthy rehabilitation, and his sleeveless t-shirt revealed light skin that had not seen much of the outdoors. Despite the changes, Ryan was still a man women could find attractive, and Jenny was hands-down the prettiest woman in the bar. She touched his arm and shoulder as she talked to him, and they both seemed enamored with each other.

Kip approached and was unsure whether to offer a handshake or a hug to his friend of ten years, but Ryan solved the dilemma by grabbing his beer with one hand and raising the other to say, "Hey, you made it."

"You bet," Kip said. "I wasn't going to miss the chance to wish you a happy birthday. And I'm guessing this is your own Florence Nightingale—Jenny?"

Ryan's look told Kip that he did not understand his reference to the acclaimed nineteenth-century founder of modern nursing. Jenny reached for Kip's hand and said, "Yes, that's me. And you are the renowned Kip Reynolds. It is so nice to meet you finally."

"The pleasure is all mine," Kip said, mockingly bowing six inches. "How was dinner?"

The three engaged in casual conversation for 20 minutes, straining to be heard over the cacophony of voices and the amped jukebox. Ryan then excused himself to go to the restroom and started down the corridor leading to the back of the building. After a few minutes of pleasantries, Kip said, "Jenny, if you don't mind me saying, my pal Ryan doesn't seem to be in great shape mentally. You've done a spectacular job with his physical rehabilitation, he walks like a champ. But I've noticed when I phone, and I can see it now, he's kind of out of it, like he's half-stoned or even drunk. Is that normal for him now? It worries me."

Jenny's eyes softened, and she said, "We all worry about him, Kip. He is on some strong meds to treat what the doctors say is bipolar disorder, but he forgets to take them, or doesn't want to take them, and I know he's drinking a lot, even during the day. He spends most of his time alone at home, and the only place he sees people other than his family is here. I've been with him on nights when he disappears out back and comes in a few minutes later, stoned. I don't know if it's pot or meth, but he's definitely out of it. He always resists when I suggest I drive him home, and he's stubborn, so he won't let me. He's been lucky so far, but at some point, the luck will run out. I can't imagine him getting through another accident. He still has a script for oxy, but he takes more than he should, and when he runs out, he always finds more to tide him over until a refill is due. I'm afraid, at this point, Ryan is addicted to the drugs and alcohol, and he needs help. There are several AA meetings nearby, but unsurprisingly, he refuses to admit he has a problem. I don't think his parents will intervene because Hank has his own issues with alcohol, and Glenda doesn't know how to deal with him either. I care so much for Ryan, I just don't know how to help him."

"You are an angel, Jenny. I hope Ryan appreciates all you do for him."

"Oh God, he is always so thoughtful and kind toward me. A good man is hidden beneath that rough demeanor but struggles with his demons. I've grown to love him and trust he will find his way if we all stick by him." Jenny's eyes were tearing.

Kip put down his drink and hugged her. "You are both good people, and I'm sure you will be able to help him find the support he needs. Have faith."

At that moment, they heard a voice rise above all the others, and it was Ryan's. "Get your goddamned hands off my girlfriend, you mother fucker! You may think you can have whatever you want with all your damned money, but you sure as hell can't have what's mine!"

As Kip and Jenny separated, Ryan bounded forward and pushed Kip backward, almost knocking him off his feet. "Whoa! Calm down, buddy," Kip said. "It's not what you think. I was-"

"You was hittin' on Jenny, and I ought to smash that pretty face of yours to a pulp," Ryan said, giving Kip another push. "Maybe I can't have what you have in your ritzy world, but down here with the hicks, what's mine is mine. You can't come in here and take what ain't yours, you son of a bitch." Ryan took another step toward Kip, this time with a clenched fist.

Two men sitting at a table beside them stood and stepped behind

Ryan, each one grabbing an arm. Two others came over from the pool table to intervene, and the rest of the bar went silent as they waited for an entertaining brawl to commence. They were in luck. Ryan swung to the left and escaped one of the men's hold, years of wrestling had taught him the moves, and as he reached for the man's arm, he kicked out and hit the other man in the groin. His victim let go of Ryan and crouched to the ground while Ryan cracked the neck of his beer bottle on the edge of the bar. His arm was cocked and ready to lunge at the first man's face when both bikers jumped into the fracas and wrestled Ryan's arms behind his back.

Kip was trying to move Jenny behind the bar when another man shouted, "Let the pussies duke it out, assholes. Somebody has somethin' comin' to 'em, and it ain't up to us to figure out what. Nothin' like a good cock fight. My money's on the tough guy, pretty boy don't stand a chance."

The two men considered releasing Ryan and letting the chips fall where they may when they heard sirens. The police station was a half mile from town, and the bartender had seen what was unfolding. The Rusty Nail saw frequent visits by the police, and the two officers entering the bar knew what to expect. All the men backed away from Ryan, and seeing the one man lying on the floor, moaning, and Ryan standing above him with a broken beer bottle in his hand, the officers went directly to Ryan. The patrons returned to their places and looked on as the officers handcuffed Ryan and walked him toward the door.

Jenny turned to Kip and said, "This will not go well. Ryan is stoned and drunk, and it's anybody's guess what is going to happen at the station if his rage lets loose. They have no way to know he has a mental disorder. I need to go with them."

"Then I'll come with you," Kip said. "He's not the only one who is going to need support. I'll drive us there, and we can come back for your car once he's out and his dad's taken him home."

Kip and Jenny came from behind the bar and walked toward Ryan and the officers. Ryan looked back and said, "So, what? Now you're gonna take Jenny to your fancy room at the Greenbrier and do her? I'll kill you, you mother fucker! I'll *kill* you."

Jenny looked Kip in the eye and said, "It's best if you leave. I'll drive to the station and make sure he's okay. Then I'll take him home. His father will go ballistic and probably throw him out, even on his birthday. If he does, I'll be there for him. He can stay with me. I won't abandon Ryan, I love him."

"I can tell," Kip said. "Please call me tomorrow morning at the Greenbrier and let me know how things go. Room 624. Good luck."

CHAPTER 13

False Flags

SEPTEMBER 2009

Sunday, the 6th

Birmingham, Michigan

The walking paths around Quarton Lake were filled with pedestrians and cyclists enjoying the warm morning temperatures on a beautiful Labor Day weekend. Sophia and Claudia followed their familiar route, circling the lake on their way into town to pick up lattés from Starbucks. As they passed their former home on Lakeside Drive, Sophia said, "I know I'm like a broken record, but it bothers me every time I see what those buyers have done to our beautiful home. Tudor stucco is meant to be white, and yellow is just plain gaudy. And why would they have removed the weeping cherry by the front door? Some people have no taste."

"Well, certainly not good taste like yours," Claudia said. "Our new home is a testament to that. I've missed living here with you and Adam, but my time away at school is paying off now. I'm excited to have you come to Fort Meade and help decorate my apartment. It will feel like a home away from home. And the NSA gave me a generous moving allowance that I'm putting toward future air tickets home. I promise I'll visit so much you'll get tired of seeing me."

"Silly girl, that would never happen. You are one of my two most precious treasures, and with Adam leaving for Baghdad, I will cherish your visits even more."

"I know, *Mamá*. You must feel very lonely, but you are not alone. You will always have us."

"Of course I will, and I thank God every day for that blessing, but with your father gone, I have a hole in my heart that can never be filled. That's something I must learn to live with, I counsel my clients in that every day, but it's easier said than done."

"I know that hole can never be filled, but have you thought about one day finding a man who would cherish and adore you for the woman you are now? Not a replacement for *papá's* love, but an enrichment to your life today, a steadfast friend and companion who partners with you for the rest of your life. It seems that might be what's missing, the piece that could replace some of the loneliness."

"I think about it all the time, but I don't feel I'm ready. I'm working through this with my therapist, and I've realized that what I can't let go of is the fear of having someone I love taken away from me again. The loneliness seems easier to deal with than the sorrow of losing another life partner. My world has already been shattered once, another lost love would destroy me for good. I can't face that."

"I understand. I'm glad you're working through it. I've never seen you give up on anything, so I can't imagine you starting now."

Their walk around the lake took them to West Maple Road, and they continued a few blocks east into the town center. The Starbucks was next to the movie theater with its grand 1920s-style marquis, and as they left the store, Claudia took her mother's arm and waited to cross the street. She looked past the movie theater to the shop next door and said, "Do you miss having your business, *Mamá*? People still talk about the Serrano Design Studio and all the beautiful homes you decorated."

"I do, *mi cielo*, but closing the business was the right thing to do. I'm enjoying my work as a counselor and feel I contribute as much there as I did when bringing beauty to people's homes. It's been an important part of my healing process, and I'm content with that."

"I can tell. Every time I visit, I can see you getting better. You seem lighter, like some of the burden is being lifted from your shoulders. And you smile more, that big, bright, beautiful smile."

"I have some good days, especially when I think about the bright futures you and Adam are building. So, yes, I am slowly healing. I've also noticed the same kind of changes in you. Is the wellness program you designed with your therapist working out as you envisioned?"

"It's been amazing. I practice yoga at home every morning, followed by 25 minutes of meditation before getting ready for work. I'm attending a Bikram class one evening each week and another on the weekend. When the weather is nice, I go for a run, and I've even joined the local Y, they have a fantastic lap pool. I've been off antidepressants for two years, and although I feel sad sometimes, I never fall back into a prolonged depression. Everything is going well."

"It's amazing how powerful a tool the mind is for helping us heal. I'm glad you've found the right formula."

"It looks like we both have," Claudia said as she squeezed Sophia's hand and they sprinted through the crosswalk.

They made their way to Shain Park in the center of town and sat at a table across from the fountain, lulled by the steady squeaking of the children's swings at the adjacent playground. Sophia had been quiet while sipping her latté, still thinking about their talk at the lake, and then said, "I know you worry about me being alone, but honestly,

I worry about you as well. I know you can make new friends at your job, and any man who did not fall for you would be crazy, but I have always sensed that Kip is the man you truly want. How are you feeling about him leaving for Hong Kong on Friday?"

"You're right, *Mamá*. I fell for Kip the day I met him, and it didn't take long before I knew I was in love. I believe he loves me as well. We've both tried to be realistic and come to terms with the fact that we are on different career paths and that unless one of us makes a change, we can't be together as a couple. Waiting for Kip and hoping to be together one day is less painful than if we had started a serious relationship and then found out I was standing in the way of him becoming an international journalist. I would never deprive him of that, I love him too much."

"Have you ever talked about trying? You know, to have a long-distance relationship, as more than just friends?"

"No. I'm too afraid."

"Too afraid to talk to him about it?"

"No. Too afraid he will say yes, find out it doesn't work, and then end up losing him. Like you, I can't face losing another man I love. I just can't."

"And here we sit," Sophia said, "Two peas in a pod, afraid to place our full faith in God and trust that taking the risk of being in love again could have a happy ending. But I guess all good things are worth waiting for. Our time will come."

Thursday, the 10th

Kip turned onto West Brown Street and parked his mother's new Jaguar XF in front of the Kinzlers' townhouse. He was meeting Claudia for lunch at the nearby Lebanese restaurant and was looking forward to spending time together before they took off in different directions the next day. Kip rang the doorbell, and Adam answered.

"Claudia's not home, she's gone out for a yoga class," Adam said.

"Guess I'm a bit early. I told her I'd come by at noon."

"Right. She wanted to go to the earlier class but got caught talking with Mom before leaving. Claudia's class ended at 11:45, so she should be home any minute." Kip noticed Adam looking at him as if he were being scrutinized, his eyes slightly squinted and peering into Kip's as if trying to discover some hidden thought. "Claudia says you leave tomorrow for Hong Kong, that you're off to launch your career as an independent journalist."

"That's right. It's time to leave the nest, if that's what you can call *The Post's* newsroom, and fly on my own."

"Cute," Adam said without breaking eye contact. "And why Hong Kong? Why not fly back to your little nest in Michigan and work from here?"

Kip wondered where the conversation was leading and, with the slightest tone of irritation, said, "Because that's where the stories are. I'll be covering Southeast Asian geopolitics."

Adam couldn't withhold his sarcasm and said, "I'm guessing they taught you at Georgetown about a new thing called 'the internet' and that you had a chance to use it at *The Post.* Takes away the need for travel—pretty much everything a person needs to know can be found there."

Kip felt his patience running thin. "If I were only interested in regurgitating the news about what had already happened, or in researching subjects my readers may not know about, this newfangled internet thingy is probably useful. I'd have to look into it more carefully to be sure, it's still pretty new." It was hard to tell by Adam's glare if he knew Kip was also being sarcastic. "But if someone wants to do true investigative journalism, it's kind of important to have access to the people they want to investigate in the places where they work and live. In my case, that would be Hong Kong." It took every ounce of self-control not to finish the sentence with, "Jerk." Kip took a deep breath and said, "Why all the concern about me going to Hong Kong?"

"Because I care about my sister. She begins her new career in Fort Meade next week, which is a huge life change for her. She decided to work at the NSA when she thought, or hoped, that you would be living in DC and working for *The Post*. You may have told her you would move overseas at some point, but I don't think she expected it right now. In the four years Claudia has been at school, she hasn't reached out to make friends, most likely because she knew you would be there for her. Only a fool couldn't see that she cares for you as more than just a friend. I'll be honest and say it: I think you are being selfish by moving away at a time when your best friend could use you nearby."

Kip broke eye contact and took a moment to compose himself. He had considered this dilemma at great length. He could stay at *The Post* to be near Claudia, remaining unfulfilled in his job, and gamble that one day she might be ready for a romantic, long-term relationship. Or he could move to Hong Kong now, stay in close contact while she settled into her new job, and be ready to jump ship and come home if she let him know she was ready for that kind of relationship. He trusted he was making the right decision and was furious he was being challenged this way by Adam.

Kip looked him in the eye again and said, "Selfish? I'm being selfish by advancing my career and building a successful future that I might be able to share with Claudia one day? Who are you to judge that?"

"I'm her brother, the person who has always been there for her, no matter what."

Without missing a beat, Kip said, "Unless I've gotten bad information, you are leaving next month for an assignment in Baghdad and will be gone for at least a year. So, I'm not so sure you are *always* there for your sister."

Ignoring Kip's comment, Adam said, "Honestly, I don't care about you and your future unless what you do hurts my sister." And then Adam shot the silver bullet through Kip's heart. "You can go anywhere you want, do anything you choose, and you are choosing to do the thing that may end up hurting Claudia. I guess when someone lives off the generosity of a family trust, it is easy to pick up and move halfway around the world without considering how that might affect others."

"You arrogant son of a bitch. How long? How long have you been holding that grudge against me, against my family? What, you think I'm some selfish nepo baby who can only think about himself? I've tried very hard to like you, Adam, but liking you is no easy job. Maybe one day, you'll come down off your high horse and realize that people are not defined by their IQs. We don't all have to be geniuses to count for something in this world, and I can assure you, having a lot of money has nothing to do with someone's worth."

Claudia came in through the kitchen and stopped in her tracks. "What's all the shouting about? Is something wrong?"

Kip knew it was time to leave, there was no chance he would win a war of words with Adam. "I'll meet you over at the restaurant, Claude. Take your time changing. I'll leave it to your brother to recap our discussion. You can share with me his version of things over lunch."

Kip left through the front door, and Claudia waited for it to close before she said, "Well, what was that all about?"

"It was about Kip moving to Hong Kong right when you're

beginning a challenging career and could use the support of a friend who lives an hour away, not halfway around the world. He got his knickers in a knot when I told him he was being selfish and that with all his family's money, he could afford to work wherever he wanted."

"You said that? You said he was being selfish because his family is rich? My God, Adam, that is so wrong. Kip is moving to Hong Kong to advance his career. Can't you understand that?"

"Sure, but honestly, he doesn't need to make the move right now. Wouldn't you rather have Kip in Georgetown for the next year, where you can get together on weekends and holidays, rather than being eight thousand miles and twelve time zones apart? If you ask me, Kip's being foolish. One day, some brilliant and handsome guy will come along and sweep you off your feet, and from then on, Kip will be 'someone you used to be friends with.' Is that what you want?"

"Of course not. I want to think we'll end up spending the rest of our lives together, but I've decided to accept his making this move now and trust that we'll join paths when the time's right."

"I hope you're right, sis. I hope you're right."

Friday, the 11th

Detroit, Michigan

Morning rush hour at the Detroit Metropolitan Airport fizzled out shortly before noon on most weekdays, but this morning was especially busy with travelers ending their long Labor Day vacations. Claudia dropped Kip off at Delta's international departures terminal and drove around the massive garage to find a parking spot. When she returned to the terminal, Kip had finished checking in and was waiting in front of the line snaking into the TSA checkpoint.

"Sorry that took so long," Claudia said. "This place is a madhouse today."

Kip waited for the overhead paging to stop so he could be heard over the shouting of TSA agents reminding passengers of the items they could not carry through security. "It's nice of you to come in. Parking here is always a mess, but this beats hopping out of the car and sneaking a quick hug before the airport traffic police shoo you away. But given this long line, I should probably move along. I'm going to miss you, Claude. I'm going to miss you a lot."

Their eyes began tearing up before Claudia could answer. She wrapped her arms around him and pushed her forehead into his chest, forcing herself not to sob. Kip was starting an exciting adventure. She reminded herself that she was there to celebrate its beginning, not to mourn her loss. Kip held her close and dropped his head to hers, also fighting to hold back his tears. Words were not needed, the warmth of their embrace said everything they were feeling. It was the first time they had experienced such physical intimacy, and they both realized it was what they had been longing for over the past years. Neither was willing to say what they were thinking: *Why did we wait until today?* They had come dangerously close to having that discussion at yesterday's lunch, but neither could find the courage to start it. Their choices were made, and their plans were in place. It was time to move forward.

They leaned back from their embrace, giggled at the sight of each other's moist eyes, and found themselves resisting an almost overpowering urge to kiss.

"You'd better get going," Claudia said. "This looks like the line for Splash Mountain at Disney World. But don't worry, you're taller than the little man's outstretched arm." Injecting humor was

Claudia's way of supplanting her sadness, she had underestimated how hard saying goodbye would be.

"Right. Looks like there's no Lightning Lane Pass here. You take care of yourself, Claude. We'll Skype every week."

"Yes. Every week." Claudia stayed where she was for the 20 minutes it took Kip to wind through the line, waving and smiling each time he looked over. Holding back her tears for 20 minutes felt like an eternity, and after Kip made it past the podium and joined the line at the scanners, Claudia turned to leave and sobbed the whole way back to her car. *Things will never be the same, and not telling Kip how much I love him may have been the biggest mistake of my life.*

Kip had an hour's wait before boarding his flight to Hong Kong. He left security, stopped to buy water and snacks, and walked to the Delta Lounge, where he found the quietest section near the back. He was still moved by the feelings of intimacy his goodbye hug with Claudia had aroused. He convinced himself that moving to Hong Kong was the right decision, despite the niggling thought that he might be making a mistake and losing any chance of being with her for the rest of his life. Someone would surely come along to steal her heart. His rational mind told him the move was not permanent and that he could keep their connection strong if he Skyped with Claudia weekly and came home often for visits. He reminded himself that this move was the first step on his journey to do his part in combating terrorism, a mission he could fortify with his love for Claudia. Right now, his rational mind was acquiescing to his emotions, and like Claudia, he prayed he had not made the wrong decision.

The lounge began to empty as the last morning flights boarded, and Kip had the room to himself. He had put on his headphones to drown out the noise, and he had been looking at his copy of *The*

Economist, unable to concentrate. When he finally looked up, his eyes went to the TV monitor above the coffee station. He froze when he saw the images on CNN: United Airlines Flight 175 barreling into the South Tower of the World Trade Center. Kip became nauseous and gasped. It was September 11, and the nation was remembering the events from that day in 2001. Kip had noted the date when he booked his flight, but he was not concerned about any travel risk. He had put it out of his mind as soon as the reservation was complete and focused on his plan to establish himself in Hong Kong and on how to prepare for the inevitable separation from Claudia today.

Kip was glad the lounge had emptied. Although he had no shame about crying in public, he wanted these last moments to himself to register the gravity of what lay ahead. Although he had told himself he was on a mission to help the greater good, he knew now it was more than that. It was a crusade to carry out retribution on behalf of the woman he loved, and he would stop at nothing to succeed.

CHAPTER 14

Blueprint for Terror

SEPTEMBER 2010

Wednesday, the 1ˢᵗ

Baghdad, Iraq

After a rigorous workout, Adam stepped out of the Olympic-sized pool, thankful for the air-conditioned indoor structure. It was only nine a.m., and temperatures outside had already reached one hundred degrees. It would be another month before some relief from the desert heat would come, but if everything went according to plan, he would be wrapping up his contract with the CIA and returning to Michigan for Christmas.

The U.S. Embassy in Baghdad had been his home for the past 11 months, and although he could see the tops of palm trees from his apartment, it was impossible to think of his base as an oasis in a desert. Despite its marbled interiors, crystal chandeliers, and grand archways, it still served as his government's base in the middle of a war-torn country.

The Embassy opened in January 2009, and Adam moved in eight months later. The U.S. diplomatic mission's largest compound was built on one hundred and four acres. Close to 12,000 people worked there when Adam arrived. Two thousand were diplomats, and the rest were contractors like Adam. There were six apartment complexes for employees, two diplomatic office buildings, water and waste treatment facilities, a power station, and amenities to help its residents feel somewhat at home: a gym, a cinema, a shopping mall, tennis courts, and the pool Adam enjoyed every morning before beginning his workday. His routine included a weekly trip to the shooting range, where he was quickly honing his skills as a marksman. He was becoming one with his Sig Sauer P226 Luger and considered it his new best friend.

U.S. forces, along with those from five allied countries, had launched Operation Iraqi Freedom in March 2003 to oust Iraq's president, Saddam Hussein, and eliminate the threat of what was believed to be his stockpiled weapons of mass destruction. On April 9 of that year, the city of Baghdad fell to U.S. soldiers, and with the help of his two sons, Hussein, along with the bulk of Iraq's national treasury, fled the city. U.S. troops killed his sons on July 22, and Hussein was finally captured on December 13. Six months later, in June 2004, the U.S. prepared to open its original Embassy within Baghdad's Green Zone in a former presidential palace. Adam had heard stories from his colleagues about life at the old Embassy and living in constant fear of attack. The U.S. Embassy in Jeddah, Saudi Arabia, had been raided by al-Qaeda gunmen three months before the old Embassy's opening, and the war in Iraq was in full force. The old Embassy in Baghdad was a fortress, and working there was hardly viewed as a plush diplomatic assignment.

But living in this new complex posed its own risks. Eight weeks ago, an unknown group fired a rocket that struck one of its firing ranges, killing three Embassy guards and injuring 15 others, including two Embassy contractors. Adam had known one of the contractors well, and his colleague's death brought home the reality of their dangerous situation. However, change was on the horizon, which is what today's meeting with his department head was about.

After seven years of war and forty-four hundred U.S. casualties, along with the deaths of tens of thousands of Iraqi citizens, combat operations had come to an end on August 31. About 50 thousand U.S. troops would remain to train and partner with Iraqi forces, but they were scheduled to leave by the end of next year. Adam would be completing his contract with the CIA in December. It was time for him to return home from Iraq along with the U.S. troops.

Andrew Dickinson's office was at the end of a long, carpeted hallway. It was on the other side of the building from Adam's office: a small but comfortable room with no outward-facing views, only a floor-to-ceiling window and a glass door looking out to the bullpen filled with administrative staff. Adam finished training at CIA headquarters in February 2009 and was assigned to Dickenson's department. Adam never learned what Dickinson was responsible for other than to ensure that Adam had access to the computer systems and equipment that enabled him to do his work. Adam's contract had been issued by the CIA's Engineering Development Group in Langley. He was one of a dozen contractors hired for advanced hacking assignments, most of whom worked out of a facility in Chantilly, Virginia, about twenty miles from Langley. Given the scope of Adam's assignment, the CIA believed he would be most effective if he had direct access to the satellite and communications networks that supported the Embassy in Baghdad. Adam had an office equipped as a virtual extension of one in Langley, and he could use countless resources that were only available here. His work had been a success.

Non-governmental organizations (NGOs) and charitable organizations were increasingly being used as fundraising vehicles for terrorist organizations such as al-Qaeda. These large organizations appeared to work in war-torn and destitute areas throughout the Middle East to support the poor by providing food, clothing, shelter, and medical care. However, behind the façade of humanitarian work was a network of logistical support for terrorists in the form of cover employment, false documentation, travel facilitation, and training. Some of the NGOs were doing legitimate work in their local branch offices, but they unknowingly housed employees sympathetic to terrorist causes. Adam was hired to identify those branches that were supporting terrorist activities and to track the online financial transactions related to them. He had identified a handful of NGOs that constituted most of the terrorist support network. Although more branches remained, Adam was confident he had built systems, protocols, and procedures that could be handed off to his local team. He could assure Dickinson, that after three months of training, his team would be well-equipped to continue the work on their own. He was here to sell Dickinson on his proposal for the next contract.

Dickinson waved Adam in as he approached the door. Adam entered a well-appointed office decorated in the style of a British gentleman's study. As he settled into the hobnailed leather armchair, Adam glanced at the wall of certificates, awards, and photos, the most prominent item being a photo of Dickenson shaking hands with President George H.W. Bush in the Oval Office.

"Thanks for taking the time to see me," Adam said. "I want to talk about my plans for wrapping up my contract and, hopefully, moving on to the next one."

"I'll be interested to hear your thoughts. You've done a stellar job here, and I'm certain our relationship will be ongoing. What did you have in mind?"

"I have more than thoughts, sir. I have a plan. My current

assignment's systems and protocols are fully developed and implemented. You've assigned me an extremely competent team of associates, and with three months of training from me, the team will be able to carry on with the project independently. They will not require supervision, only direction."

"That sounds excellent. The upcoming troop withdrawal will change the in-country dynamics considerably, and my time will be at a premium. Your team is doing important work, and I would not want it to be neglected."

"I have no concern that it would be, sir. Regarding my proposal for a follow-on project, our work has identified a trend among these terrorist activities within the local NGOs. Our tracking shows that funds are being raised outside this region and then funneled through the U.S. and into the Middle East. The amounts are significant and are finding their way to groups that support Amir Abu Bakr al-Baghdadi. Since taking over Zarqawi's group, he has been aggressively funding al-Qaeda in Iraq with a plan to expand its operations into eastern Syria. We know this could be the beginning of an attempt to establish an Islamic State throughout the Middle East and, eventually, the world. I propose that I work from a base in the U.S. to identify those overseas groups routing funds through the U.S. and those working with them on our home turf. I believe I can be most effective if I am based there. My company will establish an office in Birmingham, Michigan, as my domestic headquarters. I will assemble a small team there with the appropriate agency clearances and continue to report to my director in Langley. I could be available at any time to meet with him in person once I relocate. I plan to return to the States on December 20, which gives me 90 days to finish my team's training."

"Well, that is a very clear plan. I appreciate your commitment to progressing this project, the goals are well-identified. Let me take this up with Langley, and I'll get back to you as soon as possible."

"I appreciate that, sir, but I will need an answer by the end of this week."

Adam had his answer 24 hours later and was ready to head home. He had not seen his family in person over the past 11 months, but before leaving, he had opened a Skype account for Sophia on her home computer. Working for the NSA, Claudia was already set up for online video calls. Adam decided this was the perfect day to Skype with his family and share his good news.

"Hi, *Mamá*, hello, Little Sis, it's great to see you again. A month seems like a year around here, but I have great news. My project is wrapping up, and I'll be coming home right before Christmas. I leave here on the 20th, and depending on which flights I can get, I should land in Detroit late afternoon on the 21st and be home for dinner."

"Adam, that is the best news anyone could give me! How long will you be able to stay?" Sophia said.

"For as long as I want. I am coming back for good. I'll be opening an office for Custom Solutions Group in Birmingham, where I'll be permanently based while continuing to work with the Department of State as my main client." As part of Adam's security clearance, he was instructed never to reveal the CIA as his client and, if asked, say he worked for the State Department, a large organization of countless anonymous entities. As an independent agency within the executive branch of government, the CIA was not even part of the State Department. "Any chance you'd have room for a boarder until I find my own place?" he asked mischievously.

"As if you need to ask?" Sophia said.

"Oh, Adam, that is fabulous news," Claudia said. "It means you've done a great job for your client, and now you can continue building your business. Congratulations. There was never any question you would hit a home run with them, but it's nice to see it confirmed. Who knows, maybe you could hire me to be on your team someday. I can't think of anything I'd enjoy more than moving back home and working with you."

"Let's get you a couple more years' experience with the NSA, then we can talk. In the meantime, keep learning all you can about key management, data integrity, and cryptographic authentication. I'll want someone on my team to have those skills. I already know all that stuff, but I'll be busy and need someone to do it."

"Of course, you already know all that, silly me," Claudia teased. "In that case, you'd just have to settle for second best."

"Nothing could make me happier than if my children ended up at home. I would be truly blessed." Sophia made no effort to hold back her tears, and her children knew they were tears of joy. After nine years of grieving, they were giving their mother the most cherished gift of her life.

Friday, the 3ʳᵈ

Hong Kong Special Administrative Region of the People's Republic of China

Kip stepped outside the entrance to his apartment complex and gazed at the sparkling lights scattered across the mountains of Victoria Peak, known to the locals as The Peak. It was where Hong Kong's wealthiest residents lived, and their luxurious homes were a far cry from the utilitarian 695 square foot apartment Kip rented in the Skyview Court. His building was in the Mid-Levels section of the city, a middle-class neighborhood close to any place Kip needed to be, and it was affordable. Twenty thousand Hong Kong dollars a month for rent was a lot for a local citizen, but when converted to

U.S. currency, twenty-eight hundred dollars seemed a fair price to Kip, even though he was funding his stay in the city himself. He saved most of his salary during his three years at *The Washington Post*. His parents had not charged rent for living in their townhouse and had paid his college tuition. He was confident he would soon write articles he could sell, but the income would be minimal even then, journalists were never in it for the money. Kip had decided that if he needed to spend some of the quarterly income from his grandfather's trust fund to survive, he would. He could say it was an investment in his future, not an excuse to freeload. He would never be like his father.

Kip took a moment to take in his surroundings and inhaled deeply. He studied the clusters of lights atop The Peak as he dissected the many aromas unique to Hong Kong, a pungent fragrance visitors say they can almost taste. There were smells from the South China Sea's waters, the lush tropical vegetation blanketing the city, and diesel exhaust from the trucks, cars, and double-decker buses that ferried about the city's inhabitants. Typhoon Lionrock had just weakened to a tropical storm, but thunderstorms continued day and night, adding the heavy scent of rain and wet pavement to the mix. The name Hong Kong translates in English to "Fragrant Harbor," and Kip understood why.

He was excited to go out that night for another small adventure in this mysterious metropolis. Being here was better than he had anticipated when he submitted his visa application at the end of 2008. A quota-based system called the Quality Migrant Admission Scheme was implemented in 2006, and the application process usually took one year. There was no requirement for a job offer in Hong Kong. Still, applicants were required to take a General Points Test that included six scoring factors relating to age, academic and professional qualifications, work experience, language proficiency, professional sector, and family background. Kip had scored one hundred and sixty-five out of two hundred and twenty-five maximum points, and with relatively few applicants that year, he was awarded a visa. With it, he received residency approval, multiple entries into Hong Kong, and permission to seek employment. The visa became Kip's key to the city, an ideal location for his Southeast Asian base.

Kip's research work and small writing assignments for *The Washington Post* had given him an expert understanding of the tensions that had been building over the past four years on the Korean peninsula, and there were plenty of events for Kip to cover. He hoped this evening's affair would give him an inside perspective to share with a prospective audience. He was to be a dinner guest of Terrance Ackerman, a resident representative at the U.S. Consulate in Hong Kong. Ackerman had lectured the previous week at Hong Kong University on the Obama administration's strategic pivot toward Asia, and he had been impressed by the insightful points Kip made during the Q&A about the U.S.'s stance on the Korean conflict. Kip sought Ackerman out after the event for a private conversation, and having combined his natural charm with his journalistic intellect, Kip impressed Ackerman and was invited to join his guests from the diplomatic corps for dinner.

Due to the proximity of Kip's apartment block to the university, plenty of taxis were lined up at the nearby stand. Fifteen minutes after getting into his cab, Kip was speeding up the narrow roads leading to The Peak, hoping his driver was sufficiently skilled to navigate the many hairpin turns. After each bend in the road, Kip's view of the city expanded until he looked down upon a vast sea of brightly lit skyscrapers, home to the seven million people who lived and worked around the Fragrant Harbor. It was the largest expanse of neon he had ever seen. Dozens of cargo ships were anchored in and around the harbor, and the overhead cranes in the ports resembled the arms of gigantic octopuses hovering above the vessels. Like New York, Hong Kong is a city that never sleeps, and the loading and unloading of the freighters was in full swing. A well-oiled machine, working frenetically with no "off" switch.

The front of his host's single-floor home was mainly glass, and before Kip stepped in, he could see through the living room window its sweeping view of the city below. He was greeted by the Filipino houseman, wearing a starched white linen jacket and black bowtie. He ushered him into the living room, where Terrance Ackerman and his wife, Alicia, were talking with the first guests.

"Good evening, Mr. Reynolds. We're so glad you could join us. Let me introduce my wife, Alicia, my colleague from the consulate, Brian Foldstrom, and his wife, Rose. Our other guests should arrive shortly."

"It's nice to meet you all," Kip said, extending his hand to each. "Thank you for the invitation, and please, call me Kip."

"The pleasure is all ours," Terrance said, turning to his guests. "Kip is the journalist I was telling you about. We met during my lecture at the university."

Brian said, "Ah, yes. Terry says you have interesting views on President Obama's pivot toward Asia. I'm looking forward to picking your brain over dinner. I'm always interested in hearing the thoughts of our citizens who live outside the Beltway."

Kip said modestly, "Actually, I lived in DC for seven years: four while studying journalism and international affairs at Georgetown University, followed by three working for *The Washington Post*. I moved to Hong Kong a year ago and am researching articles to publish as a freelance journalist."

The doorbell rang, and the houseman appeared from the kitchen to answer it. The smells emanating from there were tantalizing, a combination of pungent vegetables, local spices, and roasting meat. Kip suddenly realized he had skipped lunch and was ravenous.

Terrance introduced the new guests, and Kip learned they were both professors at the university: Susan Wang, who arrived unescorted, and Peter Chung, accompanied by his wife, Karen. The houseman passed glasses of sherry as everyone remarked on the spectacular views of the city below. Susan appeared to be in her late 30s and had skin like a porcelain doll. She was the picture of elegance, her hair cut in a short bob and wearing a loose-fitting crimson silk dress. Peter looked like a man well past retirement age and wore a striped linen suit badly in need of an iron.

"I was born in this magnificent city almost 80 years ago, in 1930, and in many ways, it is sad to see what it has become," Peter said. "Its unbridled growth through the second half of the last century was exciting for us here, but we knew 1997 was on the horizon and that everything would change once the British handed the territory back to the Chinese. We had no idea just how much. Seeing so much political unrest now and all the pro-democracy demonstrations in our streets concerns me. I feel it's only a matter of time before Hong Kong experiences its own Tiananmen Square incident with the Chinese government. However, the discord China is wreaking throughout the rest of the world is my biggest concern. I doubt I'll be around to see whether they are ultimately successful with their strategy. I believe they need another 20 years to bring it to fruition."

"Are you referring to their predicament with North Korea?" Kip asked. "They are playing a balancing act: supporting North Korea's nuclear weapons program and being its largest purchaser of exports, while denying to the West that it is formally allied with them."

"No. That is simply a geopolitical game they are playing in plain sight of world leaders," Peter said. "I am referring to their strategy of fostering discord throughout and between democratic nations, the most important of which is the United States. Suppose they can bring Western society into a state of chaos and stoke the fears of its populace that the elite class has taken over, and the average citizen will be left destitute. In that case, the fabric of democracy can be torn apart. That is their strategy. Never forget, the Chinese think in terms of centuries, not years, and they have had the goal of becoming the world's only superpower since the Cultural Revolution ended with Mao Zedong's death in 1976. This is still a part of recent history for Beijing and its leaders."

The houseman approached Terrance and signaled that dinner was ready. With the Ackermans seated at the heads of the elegantly carved teak table and Kip to his left, the other guests found their places. The houseman's petite wife was the family's chef, and together, they served the first of six courses: a delicate soup that smelled of flowers and shrimp.

As Kip put down his spoon, he restarted the conversation. "Professor Chung, can you give a specific example of how China sows chaos in the U.S.?"

"No, I cannot give you *a* specific example. By its very nature, chaos is a seemingly random distribution of erratic and dissonant activities that, in combination, create disruption and disorientation. The Chinese are at work in many areas, all under your noses, with their tactics being executed in a steady, drip-like fashion. Something like Chinese water torture. They are hacking into your universities, research centers, and defense contractors to extract technology they can use. They are using all the new social media platforms to influence public opinion. There are half a billion people on Facebook right now, and they have access to all of them. And for the past decade, they have been killing your social underclass at an accelerating pace. When the Reagan administration expanded the globalization of your manufacturing industries, much of the production of steel, automobiles, and most other consumer goods was transferred to China. The areas of your Midwest, which you call the Rust Belt, along with cities and towns throughout the Appalachian Mountains, were abandoned by the manufacturers, and millions were left jobless and in poverty. Just look at West Virginia as a prime example." Images of Ryan's hometown filled Kip's mind.

"People there have been unemployed for two generations," Peter continued. "In their desperation, they turn to any source of relief from their suffering. The Chinese have cunningly provided that relief in the form of illegal drugs, specifically methamphetamine. The key ingredients for the manufacture of methamphetamine are ephedrine and pseudoephedrine. Both substances are legally produced in China and sold to the pharmaceutical industry there. They are derived from the *Ephedra vulgaris* plant, abundant in China. It is used in traditional Chinese medicine, such as *Ma Huang*, making it quite easy to obtain in large quantities and export to methamphetamine manufacturers in regions like South America. Colombia stands out as a particularly popular destination. Their drug cartels have been establishing extensive networks for decades to distribute thousands of tons of cocaine within the U. S. They create the methamphetamine in liquid or powder form and transport it through Mexico and Venezuela to conversion labs in South America, where it is transformed into crystal meth, its street version. The Chinese government knows that Colombian manufacturers often enhance the volume and potency of their drugs by mixing them with other substances. It seems fentanyl is becoming more widely used. Of course, both methamphetamines and fentanyl are highly addictive and can lead to deadly overdoses. This situation creates a perfect formula for chaos in the lower echelons of your society and fuels the political conflict between the impoverished underclass and the elites."

Terrance signaled to the houseman to clear the soup bowls and said, "This adds a dimension of complexity to our U.S. diplomatic efforts. The Chinese government is fully aware that we know about their strategy to inflict chaos and weaken the democracies of Western nations. This is just one tactic they are employing. The more success they achieve, the more powerful China becomes."

Peter spooned the remaining broth from his bowl and said, "This beautiful harbor we are gazing upon is a primary channel for the Chinese to transport their precursor drugs through your California ports and onward to Colombia. They are playing a game of odds. Everyone knows how the Chinese enjoy gambling. Your Drug Enforcement Administration is not equipped to inspect every one of the hundreds of thousands of containers arriving each year from Asia into the Long Beach and Oakland ports. If even five percent of their shipments are detected, ninety-five percent go unnoticed. The odds favor their gamble, so in this instance, the house always wins."

Kip processed this for a moment and said, "The U.S. intelligence community considers the Sinaloa cartel in Mexico to be the largest and most powerful drug trafficking organization in the world. I knew Colombian cartels dominated cocaine trafficking, but I didn't realize they were involved with other drugs."

Professor Susan Wang was seated across from Kip and said, "Yes, the Sinaloa Cartel is still the largest, but the Colombian cartels cooperate with it, and they have found new clients who can benefit from their distribution networks. Iran and its Lebanese proxy, Hizbullah, are two of its most important. Iran has been erratic in its financial support of Hizbullah over the past years, mostly due to a shortage of funding after the 2006 war in Lebanon, and its leadership is looking for a more reliable way to finance its operations. Trafficking cocaine from Colombia through the Netherlands and Turkey has been especially lucrative, and they intend to dominate those routes. Daniel Barrera, known to most as *El Loco*, is a major player in Colombia, and he has been partnered with agents from Hizbullah for over a decade. The only way the Colombian cartels can reliably supply their expanding networks with drugs like methamphetamine is if they have a consistent flow of the source ingredients, which come from China via Hong Kong's ports. If you want to investigate a story that will motivate your government to dedicate more resources to this problem, *this* is the story."

"Well, on that note," Alicia said, "Let's move on to the next course."

After their five-course dinner and a brandy in the den, Kip bid his goodbyes and stepped out of the air-conditioned foyer back into the night's stifling humidity. The Ackermans had arranged for a private car to take him home, and the temperature dropped 30 degrees as he settled into the backseat. The night skies had cleared, and the harbor below was illuminated like a high-definition mural. Kip looked at the hub of activity and saw it in a new light, knowing that some of the containers stacked on those docks were transporting crucial ingredients for synthetic drugs, ones that would end up in the hands of desperate people struggling to survive in a world that seemed to have given up on them. Ryan's world.

Kip had walked through the Ackermans' front door intent on learning more about how his reporting could highlight the dangers that China's geopolitical ambitions in Southeast Asia posed to the world if they were not constrained. But now, walking out that door, his mission had changed. He would dedicate himself to investigating how these drugs were being smuggled from China through the Hong Kong ports for distribution to impoverished areas like Appalachia. He would expose the governments and cartels that were collaborating to destroy the lives of people like Ryan. He would find a way to disrupt the financing of terrorist groups that had destroyed Claudia's family. And he would help take down the cartels that were fueling the destruction of the friend he left behind in Mapledale almost two years ago to the day. This would be a way to make a difference in the world and become his own man.

Sunday, the 5th

Mapledale, West Virginia

Jenny pulled up behind the old machine shop and carried a bag of takeaway food to the door of Ryan's apartment. It was his 27th birthday, and Jenny knew he was in no shape to go out for dinner. The past week had been especially rough, the pain pills, meth, and alcohol were tearing him down, and Jenny thought he might rally with one of his favorite meals from The Tavern: chicken fried steak with mashed potatoes and gravy. Ryan had stopped eating regular meals, and he was losing weight at an alarming rate. Jenny was grateful he had not yet done any damage to his teeth. They were not showing any of the blackening and rotting that accompanies repeated meth use. She stopped by each day to dole out his medications, hunt for illicit drugs, and remove them, under protest from Ryan, while continuing her pleas for him to seek professional counseling. She was doing everything she could to help him, but she was trained in physical therapy, not psychotherapy. Ryan was in trouble, and treating his addictions was beyond her scope of competence.

She was greeted every day by Roy, who remained Ryan's constant companion. His wagging tail and expectant eyes told her Roy needed more attention than he was getting. Ryan slept most days and only left the apartment to drive down the street and run errands for friends at The Rusty Nail. Some days, he would be gone for six hours. When she asked what he was doing, he said he was picking up supplies in Charleston for the bar, but that made no sense to her. It was a two-hour drive to Charleston, and any supplies a bar would need were delivered by the local distributors of alcohol and snacks. Although never aggressive with Jenny, Ryan became agitated when she asked too many questions, and she settled for having to guess where he was going and why. Jenny suspected he was engaged in something illegal. He seemed to have an ample supply of oxycodone, even though his prescription had expired a year ago, and she knew his friends at the bar always bought him beers and shared their marijuana and meth with him. Jenny thought that one day she would follow him on his drive and see what he was up to. Maybe if she knew what he was doing, she could somehow help.

Jenny was a daily visitor and did not need to knock before coming in. Ryan's two-room apartment was a wooden shed attached to the back of a large metal building that housed a machine shop. The owner rented the space to tenants like Ryan: people down on their luck with hardly the means to pay the $250 monthly rent. Jenny made sure Ryan never went into arrears and paid the rent for him when he was short, but inevitably, within a few weeks, Ryan appeared to be flush with cash, for a while.

Jenny walked into the kitchen, picked up the empty bags of Cheetos and pork rinds littering the floor, and took the empty beer cans from the linoleum table to the trash can outside the door. It often smelled of spoiled take-out food from the rare times Ryan ate a hot meal at home, and she had decided it should not be kept indoors. The living room and kitchen were connected, and Ryan's bedroom was through a door on the side.

After tidying up and setting two plates for dinner, Jenny called to the other room, "Ryan, it's me. I brought your favorite dinner. Come on out, and we'll celebrate." There was silence. Jenny called again, and there was no answer. Roy was especially needy for her attention and appeared unsettled. Jenny had a bad feeling as she walked across the room to the half-open bedroom door. Inside was Ryan, curled in a fetal position on the floor, gurgling through the sound of shallow breaths. His purple lips and fingernails told her he was having an adverse reaction to drugs. She suspected it was the combination of oxycodone, alcohol, and his anti-anxiety medications. She left him on his side so he would not choke if he began vomiting, pulled the comforter off his bed, wrapped it around him, and put a pillow under his head. "It's me, honey. You're going to be alright. Just breathe. I'll call for help."

In a tense and croaky voice, Ryan shouted, "No! I'll be fine. Just get me into bed. I got some bad food or somethin'."

Jenny pulled the cell phone from her purse and dialed 911. Roy lay by Ryan's head and slowly licked his face.

It will be okay, she told herself. *Please, God, don't let him die.*

CHAPTER 15

Requiems

SEPTEMBER 2011

Sunday, the 11th

New York City, New York

It took the Kinzler family less than ten minutes to walk from the Beekman Hotel on Nassau Street to the corner of West Broadway and Murray. The sun was rising as they approached their destination's entrance, but the overcast skies forecasted a gloom that would saturate the day. The memorial service organizers had sent packets to the 9/11 victims' families, instructing them to check in before 6:30 a.m. After the group assembled, their short walk to the Memorial Museum was orchestrated to have them in their seats by 8:00, well before the moment of silence at 8:48, marking the time the first plane hit the North Tower ten years ago on this day.

Sophia had decided she would not wear black to the ceremony. She was not there to bury her husband, she was there to honor him. She chose instead to wear a navy pantsuit Conrad had always said made him proud to have her by his side. He never missed an opportunity to tell her how beautiful she was. Claudia had suggested to Sophia several times over the past few years that coming to New York might help bring closure to their grieving process. Sophia told herself that if she ever went with her children to visit Ground Zero, it would only be if she had the strength to help them through the ordeal. Only now, in the company of the other surviving families and friends, with the eyes of the world upon them, did she believe she had that strength.

This morning was the opening of the National September 11 Memorial. Two beams of light, titled "Tribute in Light," were projected from the Memorial grounds into the sky throughout the previous night. The Kinzler family had stood on the rooftop terrace of their hotel, absorbing the powerful statement of resurrection from those beams, with Sophia, Claudia, and Adam mourning privately. Adam was the glue holding the family together on this trip, and whatever emotions he harbored inside, he held in a private vault only he had access to. Claudia had never felt closer to her mother and brother than she did now, and she longed to be back in Birmingham and live near them. She sensed today would be a turning point.

She was beholden to Kip for accepting her invitation to join them on the trip. She had invited him at Christmas when he was home with his family, and he had booked his flights from Hong Kong to New York before leaving town. Kip had promised he would always be there for her when she needed him, and this was one of those times.

A perfectly orchestrated succession of songs followed the moment of silence that began the ceremony. There were words of remembrance from George W. Bush, President Barack Obama, and several survivors of the attacks. Sophia's resolve to remain stoic that day was extinguished as she listened to the angelic voices of the children's choir singing *A Place for Us* from West Side Story and a heartfelt rendition of *Amazing Grace* from a victim's wife. But the floodgate of tears opened at the end of the ceremony when the orchestra played the solemn yet majestic piece by America's legendary composer, Aaron Copland: *Fanfare for the Common Man.*

After the indoor ceremony, attendees were escorted outdoors to the Memorial Plaza: two reflecting pools, each covering almost an acre, constructed atop the Twin Towers' footprints. Thirty-foot waterfalls cascade down from their perimeters to a flat basin, and from there, the water in each pool drops another twenty feet and disappears into a smaller, central void. They are encircled by a waist-high granite wall with bronze parapets, bearing the names of the 2,983 victims. The raised dais in front of the pools held a podium with two microphones, and the organizers seated the victims' families so they could ascend the platform in alphabetical order and speak the names of the loved ones they had lost. The family had decided Adam and Claudia would walk together to the microphone, and Claudia would say their father's name in remembrance. Sophia remained seated and watched, grateful that Kip would be by her side. She did not expect to hold back her emotions when she saw her children together and heard Claudia say Conrad's name. Sophia closed her eyes and said a silent prayer as Adam and Claudia walked the steps, holding her breath as they approached the microphone.

Claudia had promised herself that in honor of her father, she would speak his name clearly and proudly and not make the world's audience struggle to hear her voice through sobs and tears. And she fulfilled that promise.

"Conrad Otto Kinzler. Our beloved father, an immigrant who was honored to call the United States of America his home. We will always love you, *Papá*."

Sophia released her held breath, along with a painful moan, and as Kip took her hand and put his arm around her shoulder, he felt her grief as if it were his own. Adam and Claudia returned to their seats, one on each side of Sophia, and Kip moved back to his own seat beside Claudia. He reached over to hold hands and was overcome by his love for her. That is what finally moved him to tears.

The formal ceremony ended at 1:00 p.m. with the playing of taps by a local firefighter, cementing the emotions of the day into the memories of everyone who attended. It was a pleasant 65 degrees as they began their walk from the seating area to the granite wall surrounding the south reflecting pool. Sophia and Claudia read the parapet numbers as they turned the first corner and found themselves before their plaque. They stood shoulder to shoulder, holding hands, listening to the tranquil sound of falling water, and staring in disbelief at the engraved name of Conrad O. Kinzler. Adam stood behind the two women, arms around them both, with Kip at their side, watching a reenactment of what he had experienced ten years ago in the Kinzlers' kitchen.

Sophia and Claudia eased away and started their walk back to the hotel, with Adam and Kip following behind. They walked silently for several minutes before Adam said to Kip, "Thanks for making the trip and being here for the family. It's a great help to them." Adam paused momentarily and added, "I'm sure you remember the last conversation you and I had, two years ago in my kitchen, when I accused you of being selfish for moving to Hong Kong."

"Actually, I haven't stopped thinking about it."

"I said what I meant that day, and I haven't changed my mind about any of it, but I can see you will always do the right thing by Claudia. I respect you for that. Despite the eight thousand miles between you, it looks like you are making your friendship work. I believe you will both get this right, eventually."

"Thanks, Adam. Now that I'm all squared away in Hong Kong, I'd like to start making more frequent trips home. I have an idea about how I might be able to do that and have the best of both worlds, a base in Hong Kong and a reason to travel home regularly. I'm flying back this Friday evening. Could I come by your office around lunchtime on Friday and run my plan by you and Claudia?"

"Sure, as long as you bring the sandwiches. Turkey and Swiss for me, on rye. No mayo."

"Glad you're not fussy," Kip joked and landed a friendly punch on his arm. It seemed to Kip that their friendship was resurrected, and he was looking forward to their meeting on Friday.

Monday, the 12th

They had made plans to take the Liberty Island Ferry this morning to see the symbol of what most European immigrants associated with their opportunity to live in America: The Statue of Liberty. Fair skies and warm temperatures made for a pleasant 25-minute trip from Battery Park. On their approach to Liberty Island, Sophia turned to her children and said, "I've seen photos of Lady Liberty a thousand times, and I've always been moved by what she stands for, but I never expected it to overwhelm me with its grandeur as it is now. I can't find the right words."

"You just did," Claudia said.

They disembarked at Liberty Island, walked the perimeter of the Statue, and climbed to the Pedestal's observation deck with its unobstructed views of the new One World Trade Center. Eighty of its planned 94 floors were already complete, and it was easy to see the magnificent testament it would be to America's ability to renew itself in the aftermath of a tragedy. They stepped into the lobby of The Statue of Liberty Museum while waiting for their return ferry and sat on a bench next to windows with views of the Statue.

"This was the right thing to do," Sophia said. "Thank you, Claudia, for suggesting we make this trip and for all your support in getting me here. It was harder than I had imagined, but much more rewarding than I believed possible. And Adam, I guess I always feel stronger when I have you by my side. Nothing could make me happier than I am now, with you back home. Nothing, except having Claudia back as well. But everything in good time."

Claudia was quiet for a moment and then said, "Well, *Mamá*, I've been thinking, and I feel it is the right time, now, to wrap up with the NSA and move from Fort Meade back to Birmingham. Adam doesn't know it yet, but I will be hitting him up for a job at his company."

"You've only been at the NSA for two years," Adam said. "I thought we planned on you being there for three to maximize your training and gain experience."

"Guess what? Plans can change."

"Not unless I say they will." Adam smiled and said, "Are you asking for a job interview at Custom Solutions Group?"

"Yes. I'm free on the 14th before I head back to Fort Meade at the end of the week. Any time that works for your schedule that day will work for me," Claudia said haughtily.

"I'll check my calendar and have my girl call your girl." Adam was thrilled at the prospect of Claudia returning home and working by his side. For all its sadness, this had been a joyful trip for Adam, the end of a ten-year transition period for his family and the dawn of a new era.

Looking over the ferry's bow on the return to Battery Park, the Kinzlers and Kip were lost in their thoughts.

Sophia was overjoyed that Claudia was planning to come home after six years. Sophia had spent the first couple of years worried about Claudia's struggle to come to terms with the loss of her father. During each visit home, Sophia watched Claudia stop in a room to stare at a photo of Conrad or pick up a memento he had collected on a trip and hold it to her chest. In the following hours, Claudia would stay in her room and only emerge for a meal, during which she was quiet and distant. Claudia continued to see her psychiatrist when in Birmingham, and Sophia saw it as a sign of progress two years back when the doctor felt Claudia could stop taking antidepressants. Adding yoga and meditation to her wellness program was helping with the healing process. They enabled her to become more aware of the subconscious thoughts troubling her, and she could shut them down by being aware of them. It was a huge step forward and enabled Claudia to progress on her own. Sophia knew that without the support of her own therapist, she would not be able to function normally. But the counseling work she was doing with mothers grieving their losses and coming to terms with the traumatic experiences that brought them about was helping Sophia heal. That had been her hope when she began her studies at the university. She looked forward to sharing this newfound strength with Claudia when she moved back home. Sophia realized that nothing in her life was more important than contributing to her children's happiness. She believed it was her greatest gift to Conrad.

Looking back at all her progress over the past two years, Claudia knew that keeping herself busy was an essential part of her coping mechanism. Attending MIT and working at the NSA had kept her from being pulled down and immobilized by her sadness, and Claudia was not yet ready to abandon that tactic. She resolved today to spend her time partnered with Adam to seek retribution for their father's death. If they could make even a small dent in the ability of terrorists to destroy families like theirs, it would give her a sense of fulfillment, a reason for getting up each day, and a way to keep her thoughts from dragging her back into depression.

Adam had spent the past 48 hours pondering questions he knew he would eventually answer. Did the U.S. government or any of its allies have any advanced knowledge of the 9/11 attacks, and if so, why was that information not shared between agencies? What part of the interagency communication structure was broken, and how could it be fixed? Osama bin Laden was from a wealthy Saudi family; he had the intellect and resources to plan and carry out the most sophisticated terrorist attack the world had ever seen. How many groups were out there now—four months after bin Laden had been killed—equally capable of repeating that kind of attack, and how were the CIA and FBI tracking them? Adam believed the most effective way to uncover covert operations was to follow the money, and his work for the CIA showed him that was an area where they needed help. He knew Claudia would be an asset to his company, even though she had only two years of experience with the NSA. He smiled as he told himself that their two minds would be exponentially more effective at uncovering terrorist activities than his one. He welcomed the chance to work with his sister on something as crucial as thwarting terrorists. He was looking forward to conducting her interview on Wednesday—big brothers never missed an opportunity to mess with their younger sisters.

The image of the Kinzlers standing in front of Conrad's memorial plaque stuck in Kip's mind. They took him back to that horrific moment in their kitchen when they realized the images they were seeing, over and over, of United Airlines Flight 175 slicing into the South Tower, were not part of Hollywood's most terrifying disaster movie, but a real-time broadcast of their father's death. Kip had never known what it was to lose a family member, but the closeness he felt to the Kinzler family after a decade of friendship had him believe he understood their grief. He knew he could use his talents and energy to disrupt the way terrorists fund themselves, with the hope that no family would have to go through what the Kinzlers were. His resolve doubled when he thought about the devastation being wrought on millions of American families from the growing drug epidemic, fueled by chemicals exported from countries like China. Kip had seen how Ryan and his family were tinkering on the edge of destruction, and he knew if he joined forces with Adam and Claudia, they would be a formidable team that could help stop the decimation. It was time to plan for his return home.

Bloomfield Hills, Michigan

Kip's flight from LaGuardia landed at four p.m., and he arrived at his parents' home in time for cocktails. His father usually had his first drink at lunch after a round of golf, but it comforted Dudley to believe the evening cocktail hour was the day's official start of his daily love affair with scotch. In the evenings when Patty was home, she joined him in the sitting room off the foyer, but today, they were on the back terrace enjoying the warm summer evening. Kip poured a vodka and tonic in the kitchen and stepped outside to join them. It took a moment to realize what he was looking at.

"Bradley? Hey, little brother, I wasn't expecting to see you here," Kip said. "It looks like California living has gotten to you. Is that a ponytail you're sporting?"

Bradley turned his head and said, "Yeah. No preppy crew cut for this surfer dude. And look at you. All decked out in your khakis, polo shirt, and loafers. Nice to know some things never change. Good to see you, bro, it's been a while."

"I know. You've missed the past two Christmases. I thought you had found someone crazy enough to marry you and that you just didn't tell us. Foolish me. No such luck, huh?"

"Nah. No such luck. You can't get rid of me that easily. So, how's life in Hong Kong with all those geisha girls?"

"That's Japan, ding-a-ling. And life in Hong Kong is exciting."

After 20 minutes of catching up and refreshing their drinks, Patty cleared her throat and looked at Dudley. "Darling, do you want to start?" Dudley stared silently at the drink resting on his knee. Patty continued, "Boys, I have some disturbing news."

"It's not disturbing," Dudley interrupted. "It's terrifying."

"Well, it is bad. Three years ago, when I turned 50, I began getting annual mammograms. Last year, we extended our stay with the Mitchells in Cape Cod, and I forgot to reschedule my mammogram appointment for August. I got busy organizing the upcoming Red Cross gala and kept putting it off. I finally went for the test last month, and they've found a lump. They did a biopsy and told me last week that the tumor was malignant. I went on Friday for an MRI, and they said it is growing quickly, by almost one percent a day. I have what is called triple-negative breast cancer, and I will need surgery. At this point, they suspect the cancer cells may have invaded my lymph nodes. They say it is 'locally advanced,' meaning I am in stage three, and they are going to begin treating it with a combination of immuno- and chemotherapy to try and shrink the tumor before doing surgery. The bottom line is that I am on a rough journey in the coming months. If the cancer metastasizes and advances to stage four, it's anybody's guess how many more birthdays we'll celebrate together. I don't mean to sound dramatic, I'm just being realistic."

Dudley got up and poured another drink for himself. He turned and said, "Anybody want something?"

"Yeah. Vodka on the rocks," Kip said. There was no need to ask for a double. With his father bartending, it would come automatically.

"It looks like *my* drinking days are over," Patty said.

Bradley stood, stopped as if about to speak, and left to go upstairs. He was 25 but had never seemed to outgrow his teenage ways. It was clear he was about to grow up quickly, the realities of adult life had just come knocking on his door.

Kip said, "Mother, if it helps, I decided while in New York to finish up the project I'm working on in Hong Kong and then come home, probably for good. I may need a month to wrap things up there, but I promise I will be here for you. I won't let you and Father go through this alone."

"I can't think of anything that would help me more. I suspect this will be a bigger challenge for your brother to deal with than it will be for you, so please find a chance to talk with him before you leave and see how you can support him. I can understand if he doesn't want to move home. He seems happy with his new life in Huntington Beach. But wherever he is, he will need you to lean on."

"Count on it," Kip said.

Patty shared what few details she had about her near-term treatment plan and explained that it would unfold in steps as they learned more about the growth and spreading of the cancer cells. She confirmed what her family already knew about the side effects of each treatment protocol, and although Patty felt a need to put on a brave face, in truth, she was terrified.

Dudley was visibly shaken and seemed unable to bear any more details. "Are we going over to the club for dinner tonight?" he said.

"I don't think so, dear. I picked up some chicken piccata from Mandy's Kitchen. There's plenty for all of us. We'll just eat here."

Kip finished his drink in two gulps and started up the grand staircase to his room. With the experience in New York still fresh in his mind, he thought, *Mom has to come through this okay, or our family will also be destroyed. I've seen how the loss of a parent tears a family apart, and I pray it is not our turn.*

Tuesday, the 13th

Birmingham, Michigan

Kip decided to ride his bike rather than drive to Shain Park. He had lain awake all night trying to come to terms with the turmoil his family was about to go through. *How long would it take before the chemo treatments begin? How often will Mom need to go to the Mayo Clinic? When will they know it's time to schedule the surgery? How long will the recovery take, and when will they know all the cancer has been removed?* Kip hoped the half-hour ride in the morning air would calm his mind.

Claudia was waiting with two lattés when Kip pulled up and sat on the fountain's marble ledge. After Kip's call last night, she had also been consumed by thoughts about Patty's illness, but her concerns were primarily about his well-being.

"Thanks for coming over," Kip said as Claudia handed him his latté. "Breakfast with my parents was awkward. Brad didn't even come downstairs. I went up to talk to him, but he sent me away when I knocked on his door. He said he was sleeping in. Neither he nor my dad knows how to handle this. It worries me; Mom will need them to be strong until I return from Hong Kong. After that, I can take care of her and Dad."

"And who is going to take care of you? Your mom's prognosis is uncertain, and although I have every confidence that the team at the Mayo Clinic can get her through this, living with the fear of losing her will be incredibly hard. I want you to know, Kip, I understand. I'm your best friend and will do everything I can to support you. I'm here for you, no matter what."

"Thanks for that, Claude. You mean the world to me."

"And you to me."

Friday, the 16th

Delta's flight from Detroit to Hong Kong departed at eight p.m., so Kip had the afternoon free to meet with Adam and Claudia. He arrived at Adam's home shortly after noon with a bag of sandwiches from Panera, and they sat at the kitchen island to eat. Adam had purchased a two-bedroom condominium on the fifth floor of a building on Woodward Avenue, the primary route connecting Birmingham to downtown Detroit. Located at the north edge of town where Bloomfield Hills began, it was only a ten-minute walk to Sophia's home. His unit was ideally suited to his needs. The kitchen opened into the dining and living room areas, which he had set up as his office. With no expectation of having overnight guests, one bedroom had been converted to a TV and music room, and the other was for his king-size bed and dresser. Kip noted that the office area would easily accommodate three workers.

Since Kip had told Claudia about Patty's diagnosis, he knew Adam was aware of what he was dealing with. Kip did not want his mother's illness to be a part of the conversation. His agenda was to lay the groundwork for his move back to Birmingham and to establish a formal working relationship with Adam and Custom Solutions Group. They finished lunch and stayed seated at the island until Kip opened the conversation.

"I'd like to talk about how I could partner with you and Claudia in taking down some of the groups in Asia who are contributing to the drug epidemic here. I've made some important contacts during my time in Hong Kong, and I've learned a lot about how these drug dealers operate. Let me tell you what I've learned, and then I'll suggest a plan for working together."

"Have at it, the floor's yours," Adam said.

"I've spent the past six months working with my friend from

Hong Kong University, Susan Wang, to better understand the role Iran and Hizbullah are playing in Latin America. She has a relationship with a senior fellow at the International Assessment and Strategy Center in Alexandria, and he testified to a House subcommittee this past July. He said Hizbullah's presence in Latin America is growing. A former U.S. ambassador to the Organization of American States testified before Congress in March that Iran has more than 80 operatives in at least 12 Latin American nations."

Adam lifted his hand and said sarcastically, "I know it might be ancient history, but you might recall that I just returned from working for the State Department in Iraq for ten months. This is not news."

"Adam, don't be a jerk," Claudia said. "I need to learn more about this. Keep going, Kip."

"Right. Susan's contact in Alexandria testified that there is no question Hizbullah has become more heavily involved in the drug trade recently, primarily through the Revolutionary Armed Forces of Colombia, a Marxist rebel group known as the FARC. If the drug manufacturers in Colombia can't get the primary drugs they need, the whole financing apparatus could fail, so it's critical that the supplies from China are not interrupted."

"So, the key to reducing the amount of synthetic opioids coming through South America to the U.S. lies in disrupting the Chinese deliveries?" Claudia said.

"Yes. Susan believes that through her access to proprietary databases, she has identified three Chinese companies that may be the key players in getting their drugs through the Hong Kong ports. But her investigation is stuck, and she can't confirm which company, or companies, are actually involved. They are all based near Guangzhou and transport their shipments by ferry along the Pearl River and through its delta to the ports in Hong Kong. The smugglers have more control over those shipping routes than they do if shipping on land, fewer officials to bribe. Susan doesn't have access to the bills of lading from the freight companies that transport goods out of Hong Kong and into the California ports. Those documents will have been altered to show that harmless consumer products are being shipped, the drugs would be hidden within those products. She believes the clue to identifying the actual criminals lies in tracking the finances associated with the shipments. She would need to see invoices paid by the Hong Kong importer of goods from China, invoices paid to the Hong Kong exporter by the U.S. importer, and invoices paid to the freight companies. Susan's area of study is trade relations and commerce between China and the U.S. That information lies outside her reach. From what little you've shared, Adam," Kip said with a grin, "This seems to be where you come in."

"I'm going to need more information, but yes, I'm an expert at this," Adam said. "Keep going."

"All you need to do is map out the details about what you need, and I'll work through my contacts in Hong Kong to get whatever information I can," Kip said.

"I don't need *whatever* information you can get, I'll need specific information. In two weeks, when I finish the outline of my plan, I can email you the questions."

"Perfect," Kip said. "I have a pretty good network established already, and I know where to go for help in areas outside my current contacts."

"Pretty good isn't going to cut it if you want to identify the players in this game. Are you sure you're up to this?"

Kip realized that working with Adam would not be the usual fare. Adam was a legitimate genius, and near enough would not be good enough. Kip welcomed the challenge and said, "Yes, I am up to this. Disrupting these drug cartels, to whatever degree we can, is what I'm committed to. I'm giving this one hundred and ten percent. So, does that mean you'll partner with me?"

"Yes, but I can't pay you until we show results. Then I can go to my client and ask to expand the scope of my contract."

"No problem. As you know-" With a wry smile, Kip said, "I am self-sufficient, financially."

Pulling back the corners of his lips and nodding slightly, Adam said, "Yes, I know."

Claudia said, "So it's settled? Kip's on board? That's fantastic. CSG has its first unpaid intern!"

Adam's demeanor became more serious. "Once we identify which of those companies is the major player, we will need to hone in on a specific shipment from them and track it. As soon as you are back in Hong Kong, you will register an import-export business, call it Sunny Luck Trading Co., and use your local address as the business address. Half the businesses registered in that city are shell companies, so nothing about yours will look untoward."

"Piece of cake," Kip said.

"Not if you don't dot your I's and cross your T's. Research the registration process carefully. You don't want there to be any questions because something is missing from a form. This operation must be completely above board and stay under the radar. I will set up a wholesale import company here in Detroit. I can sublet space for a small office in nearby Troy, so it isn't associated with this home address. After Kmart closed its headquarters there, many local businesses left, and plenty of cheap space is available. As soon as we identify the Chinese company, Sunny Luck will begin placing small orders with them for whatever it is they sell. Over six months, you will slowly increase your order size until you have one large enough to fill an entire twenty-foot shipping container. Claudia, is Mom's friend, Francesca, still married to the guy who owns that metalworking business in Dearborn?"

"Keep talking," Claudia said. "I'll text Mom now and find out."

"If he does," Adam continued, "We will have the crates, and eventually, the container, drop-shipped to that business. It has a large outdoor yard for steel storage and would easily hold our container. All invoicing and payments will go through our two businesses so that it will be legit. Depending on what our target company manufactures, other than the drugs, we might even make some money selling that."

"Let's hope it's not something obscure, like sex toys," Kip said.

"There's plenty of profit to be made there," Adam said without a smile.

"I'll need the next month in Hong Kong to set up the business and extend the lease on my apartment for a year. Then I'll want to come home to be with my family. I'm sure Claudia told you why. My friend from the university, Susan, can come by my building every week and collect any mail from my box in the lobby. I'll give her pre-addressed envelopes so she can drop them off at DHL, I'll have the mail in three days. But there is no reason I can't begin ordering goods from here once we are set up."

Claudia's phone pinged with a reply from Sophia. "Here we go. Yes, on both counts. Francesca is still married, and her husband still owns the business in Dearborn."

"Great," Adam said. "Now, this is where you come in, sis."

"Hit me."

"Once we have proven to this Chinese manufacturer that we are a legitimate business and can eventually order enough goods to fill a container, it will get ferried to a Hong Kong port for shipment to the U.S. Hopefully, it will be sent along with other containers from the company that have drugs hidden in them. These people are smart, so not every container has the drugs. If they ship six containers with normal products, and the drugs are concealed among them in just one, they minimize the risk of being detected upon entry into the U.S. However, there is a good chance they have bribed inspectors in Long Beach and Oakland, and there will be no one to initiate a spot inspection. Kip, you will need to return to Hong Kong right before the shipment leaves China to figure out which docks that company uses. It won't be easy because they probably change with each shipment. It won't matter at that point which ship the containers are loaded on. What matters is that all the containers remain together and are held at the port for at least 24 hours before shipping. And that's where you come in, Claude."

"I'm all ears."

"Kip will need to find a way to access his Sunny Luck container on the dock. He will not be allowed to open it, it will be secured with a padlock, but he can invent a reason he needs to check the outside. Figuring this out will be your biggest challenge, Kip, but you have close to a year to work on it. When you return, you can observe activities at all the docks and find a loophole to get you access. You only need a few minutes by the container."

"So far, my ears aren't hearing anything that involves me," Claudia said.

"The whole point of this exercise is to enable Kip to get an electronic tracking device secured to the container with GPS technology that lets us know where the container is at every point of its journey. Claude, we need you to assemble a GPS device that will attach, I'm guessing with magnets, to the container where it won't be spotted. Then, we will activate it throughout the journey to determine its locations and notify the Drug Enforcement Administration where the containers will arrive and when. After the DEA seizes our shipment, we share the Chinese manufacturer's identity with them. The State Department can take it from there and apply diplomatic pressure to shut them down, and the Department of Commerce can apply sanctions."

"Got it," Claudia said.

Claudia and Kip did not know how this whole operation tied into Adam's work as a contractor to the CIA. Once the incoming shipment was seized and the DEA knew the identity of the Chinese manufacturer, all relevant information would be entered into the DEA's database. That information would include the names of the companies the shipment was consigned to in the U.S. Adam could link those names to the extensive database he had already built, containing information on organizations he suspected were helping fund the terrorists working for Hizbullah. He had identified several NGOs based in the U.S. who had apparent links to Iran and the terrorists. Being able to identify a specific drug shipment, with knowledge of who the Chinese manufacturer was, who they were working with in Hong Kong, and who was receiving the shipments, would allow Adam to identify financial links between the organizations and confirm the intended destination of the drugs in South America. His investigation had pointed to *El Loco's* cartel in Bogotá, Colombia, but the success of this operation would rule out any role played by the Sinaloa group in Mexico. With that, Adam could expand the scope of his project with the CIA. Claudia's security clearance from the NSA would allow him to hire her, and Kip could continue to work as an outsider, uninhibited by government restrictions.

Adam continued, "Kip, you'll open a business bank account with Wells Fargo in Hong Kong, and I'll open one at a branch here. I will set up a VPN for emailing, and Claudia can develop some encryption tools to ensure privacy. I can take on everything else regarding database access at the DEA and other government agencies."

"It's all yours," Kip said.

"Nope, it's all *ours*. From now on, we operate like The Three Musketeers, however, I won't be wearing one of their frilly hats with a feather. But I am looking forward to seeing you both in yours. All for one, and one for all. Let's get started."

It was the first time Kip had seen Adam demonstrate the combination of excitement and humor. It was gratifying to know the man he was about to join forces with possessed all the qualities he believed a good friend should have, and he welcomed the chance to deepen their friendship.

Friday, the 23rd

White Sulphur Springs, West Virginia

Jenny rented a two-bedroom cottage off Main Street on the east edge of town. It was a simple brick structure nestled among old pines, with a white porch and a small front yard. Decorated with quilted fabrics and cheerful colors, it was nothing fancy, but she had made it a warm and welcoming home. The physical therapy clinic where she worked was in a strip mall on Main Street, and her parents lived five minutes from there. Jenny was born and raised in Charleston and moved to White Sulphur Springs when she was ten, and her father began working as a physician at the Greenbrier Valley Medical Center. Given that her mother was a registered nurse, Jenny was naturally drawn to a career in caregiving. She had completed a bachelor's degree in physical therapy at the University of West Virginia and earned her accreditation right after graduation. She considered her job at the clinic to be low stress with its regular work hours, caring atmosphere, and good pay. She enjoyed working there, and with her family nearby, Jenny had felt she had everything she needed to be content, except a man to share it with. And now that had changed.

The day Jenny met Ryan for his first therapy appointment, his body was wrapped like a mummy in casts and bandages, and when she entered his parents' modest home and saw him bedridden in the living room, her heart went out to him. Roy leaped up as soon as Jenny walked into the room and came bounding toward her, with his tail wagging and a big smile. She thought it sweet how Roy stopped in his tracks and quietly walked back to Ryan's bed when he whistled for him. This broken man had a close bond with his canine friend, and Jenny knew it had been earned through years of kindness. She instantly saw Ryan's compassionate side.

The first four months of treatment went well, and Ryan was healing quickly. But when he began canceling appointments and appeared sullen and withdrawn when she could see him, Jenny knew his challenges were not just physical. He had emotional issues to work through that she guessed were there before the trauma of his train accident. Although not trained in psychotherapy, her compassion for his struggles enabled her to provide some of the emotional support she knew Ryan needed.

After Ryan's overdose last year, his landlord told him he needed to move out. He had been looking for an excuse to evict Ryan, and an ambulance pulling onto the property with its lights flashing and siren blaring was the one he needed. That's when Jenny invited Ryan to move into her house. They had not become intimate at that point, Ryan's regular use of drugs and alcohol had rendered him incapable, so they kept separate bedrooms. They were living together like a married couple, with Jenny looking after Ryan as she would a husband, and she had adopted Roy as if he were her own. No one would call it a happy family, but they were living the best life they could given the circumstances.

By summer, with Jenny's support, Ryan was able to stop his daily use of oxycodone, and he had stopped meeting up with his friends at the bar who were sharing their meth pipes with him. After being treated for his drug overdose, Jenny had suggested Ryan be taken off his anti-anxiety medications, and the physicians agreed he would be better off without them until he could see a psychiatrist to help treat his drug addiction. She had doubted for some time that Ryan was suffering from what the VA had diagnosed as bipolar disorder. His symptoms appeared to be more consistent with those from past trauma than with a person experiencing long-term psychosis.

Jenny felt she was making progress in helping him manage his addictions, but she knew he was engaged in some nefarious activities that were going to land him in serious trouble. He drove his van to Charleston weekly to pick up what he called "supplies" and deliver them to The Rusty Nail. After each trip, Ryan had a bit of extra cash to help toward rent, and for the next few days, he would sneak behind Jenny's back to smoke pot, drink beer, and pop pills. Jenny felt the key to breaking this cycle was to figure out what he was doing in Charleston and find a way to stop it. She did not mind supporting Ryan financially, so having to wait while he found a legitimate source of income would not be a problem. Her real challenge was to find a way to disconnect him from this destructive pattern of behavior.

"I'll be goin' out tonight," Ryan said when Jenny entered their kitchen. "Gotta make a run to Charleston. Probably won't get back before midnight."

Jenny had her plan in place. "Okay. And hey, my mom isn't feeling well. I think she needs to see a specialist for her migraines. My dad doesn't seem to know what to do for her. He's away at a medical conference this weekend, so I told Mom I'd stay with her tonight. She's so dizzy she can hardly get out of bed on her own. But I'll be home in the morning to change. I'm working a half-day at the clinic tomorrow." Jenny's mother was in on the plan and knew to say that Jenny had just stepped out for a minute if Ryan phoned. She would text Jenny and have her call him back. "What time are you heading out?"

"In a couple of hours. I need to lie down before I go."

"Let's eat something, then I'll head over to Mom's when you lie down."

Jenny hated lying to Ryan but rationalized that she was doing it to help him get well. Her father was home, and Jenny had arranged to borrow his new blue Prius for her drive that evening. She would park her car in her parents' driveway, where it could be seen, and head out on I-64 toward Charleston, the only direct way to get there from Mapledale. She would leave an hour before Ryan and stop about 25 minutes south of Charleston at the roadside rest area in Eskdale, where she would park on the ramp and watch for him. His white van was 15 years old with no windows in the rear, so it would be easy to spot. Knowing Ryan would not recognize her vehicle, she would follow behind until he reached his destination. She did not know what she would do once they arrived, she would have to figure that out on the fly. But she was certain she would know more after this trip than now, and any information about what he was doing could help her find a way to stop it. This was one of those times Jenny put her faith in God and trusted He would help them both in their time of need.

Ryan filled a bowl of kibble for Roy, topped his water bowl, and got in his van. He drove for an hour and a half along I-64, cursing the mountains for obstructing the reception from any of his favorite radio stations. He never understood why all the southern Baptist preachers could break through with their foreboding sermons, but popular tunes that might lift his spirits could not. Just part of the curse that seemed to have cast itself upon his life, he thought.

Jenny's plan proved solid. She was parked at the head of the on-ramp going back to the interstate when she spotted Ryan's van approaching. At that time of night, there was little traffic, and it was easy to keep a quarter-mile distance from Ryan's van with his taillights in view. Low clouds drifted through the mountains, leaving a heavy blanket of mist in their path. The roads were wet and winding, and Jenny hoped Ryan would not drive any faster, she was already nervous.

Twenty-five minutes later, he exited onto the Kanawha Turnpike about three miles from downtown Charleston. He took an exit ramp that appeared to head toward the rail yards, and Jenny prayed that there would be other cars on the quiet side streets that offered little light. Within minutes, Ryan turned into an empty parking lot between a large factory building and the rail yard. He killed the van's lights as he parked beside a metal building with four overhead garage doors. Jenny found a spot at the entrance to the lot where she could park beside a large truck and trailer that looked as if it had been left for the night. She had shut off her headlights before leaving the road and was thankful the hybrid engine in her Prius ran silently. Her window was lowered halfway to keep the windshield from fogging, and the sulfurous smell of damp coal permeated the air. The only sounds were the clanking of metal and the hissing of air brakes from the trains slinking through the yards. She had a direct line of sight to Ryan and his van.

Ryan stayed in his van for five minutes before the garage door nearest him was opened by a large man wearing a plain black windbreaker and matching baseball cap. The man nodded at Ryan as he turned to go back into the darkened garage, indicating that Ryan should open the back of the van. At that moment, the engine in the truck she had parked beside roared to life, and its headlights shone directly on Ryan's van. Her instincts told her to get out before she was spotted. Without turning on the headlights, she threw the Prius into reverse, backed up ten feet, and made a hundred-and-eighty-degree turn away from the parking lot. As she swung around, she could see the man in black inside the garage, illuminated by the lights from the truck. Her blood ran cold when she realized what she was looking at: the hulk of a man, dressed entirely in black, pointing an AK-47 directly at the cab of the semi. In an instant, Ryan jumped into his van and sped toward the road, his tires spitting gravel as he made his escape.

Before Ryan reached the end of the driveway, Jenny rolled to a stop alongside the railyard without touching the brakes. She could feel her heart pounding, and she realized she was holding her breath. *Breathe, Jenny. Keep your foot off the brakes. And don't move. You haven't been spotted yet. Don't drive on until the coast is clear. Ryan is safe for now.*

Then she heard the rapid-fire shots from a high-powered rifle and saw the white flares exploding from the weapon of the man inside the garage. Jenny's heart raced as the next round of shots rang out from the passenger side of the semi's cab, louder and faster than the first. And then she saw the man in the garage drop his rifle as he crumpled to the ground like a deflating balloon. Everything went eerily silent for a moment, and then the driver got out of the cab and walked behind the truck to open its rear door. The other man walked to the body lying on the ground, picked up his weapon, and rolled the body over with his foot to make sure it was dead.

Both men entered the garage and had their backs to the parking lot. Jenny saw her opportunity to escape without being seen and got onto the road, driving toward the turnpike. It took almost an hour before she stopped shaking and recovered her nerve. Of all the thoughts running through her mind, the one that kept circling back confirmed her greatest fear: Ryan was running drugs, and he was part of an operation that had just turned deadly.

CHAPTER 16

The Trail of Shadows

SEPTEMBER 2012

Monday, the 3rd

Hong Kong Special Administrative Region of the People's Republic of China

Dr. Susan Wang's office was typical of most university professors: small, with a single outward-facing window, overstuffed bookshelves along one wall, framed diplomas and certificates behind the wooden desk, and several orchids apropos of the room's proximity to the tropics. Kip was visiting Dr. Wang's office for the third time since meeting her two years prior at Terrance Ackerman's home on The Peak. His last visit had been just before Christmas, after which he returned to Michigan to be with his family and support his mother through the first stages of her cancer treatment. He had spent the following eight months at home and only returned to Hong Kong two weeks ago. After a few minutes of casual conversation, Kip got down to business.

"My associate has researched the three companies you identified last year, and after tracking dozens of online financial transactions between them, their transport agents, and their customers, he has identified one, Guangzhou Manufacturing Ltd., that we believe is the largest supplier of precursor drugs. They are a sports equipment manufacturer with customers worldwide, but they ship between six and eight 20-foot containers every few weeks from here. They arrive in California through Long Beach or Oakland and are picked up by agents who deliver them by truck to destinations in Arizona, Nevada, Texas, and Tennessee. We have been placing orders with them each month for one of their more popular products. Our orders have grown from several cartons to a dozen pallets, and we are ready to order a quantity sufficient to fill an entire 20-foot container. We suspect the company has an insider working for Menzer Hong Kong Ltd, as all shipments to the California ports have been loaded onto their ships. The containers arrive at the Hong Kong port from Guangzhou. They are transported there by ferry through the Pearl River Delta. They are stored on the docks for several days before being assigned to a vessel, usually a few hours before it departs. The insider would be the one who makes the assignment. The drugs would be hidden within the products in some of the containers destined for the U.S. The other containers would appear to be normal shipments, like ours. I want to access the dock area where our container will be stored. I was hoping you might be able to help."

"I guess that depends on what kind of help you need," Susan said.

"I would like to get into Menzer's container facility on the pretense of interviewing their logistics manager for an article I'll be writing to showcase modern port efficiencies. I have an idea how I can get him to bring me to the containers arriving from Guangzhou Manufacturing, including ours, but I need a way to get that interview."

Susan bit the tip of her pen and swiveled her chair to look out the window. After a few moments' thought, she turned and said, "Do you think you could grow a short beard, you know, one of those trendy three-day numbers?"

"Ah, well, I guess I could. I've never tried, but I have to shave every day if I don't want stubble. Why?"

"I know a man named Steve Norris at the Hong Kong Trade Development Council. He's about your age, and his parents are British expats. We're close friends. He was born here and went to the American School, so he has no British accent. His hair is about your color, but with much less gel, and he has a very short beard. He also wears wire-rim glasses. With a beard and glasses, you could pass for him. I could ask Steve to phone Menzer and request an interview for himself, saying the Council wants to showcase Menzer as an ideal shipping partner for companies getting started in Hong Kong. He works in the department focused on SMEs, small and medium enterprises, and it would make sense that he'd be interested in highlighting Menzer as a resource for its members. The Council puts on numerous exhibitions and conferences, and Menzer is probably already a participant, so it would not seem odd that he was contacting them."

"So, if Steve agreed, I would go to the interview using his alias?"

"That's right. He publishes many articles for the Council, and his picture is on their website. If anyone runs background on him, they'll see he's legitimate."

"And why would he do that for me, for us? If I'm successful and we can track the containers to the U.S. port, they will be seized upon arrival. Wouldn't there be a risk his role in this could be uncovered?"

"He would do it because I asked him to. He is my boyfriend. We've been together for six years, and he has partnered with me to expose corruption here, especially regarding drug trafficking. He developed a cocaine addiction after leaving high school, and his parents eventually kicked him out of their home on The Peak. He started attending one of my classes, and I saw him struggling. I helped him get sober, and now he is on a personal mission to do what he can to disrupt the drug trafficking rings operating here. The interview request will seem completely above board. Since Menzer ships thousands of containers each week, it would be unlikely someone working in logistics would link your container to the seizure in California unless you gave them a reason to be suspicious."

"No worries about that. I'll be very careful."

"Just remember that you can't be too careful. You could be heading into dangerous waters."

"I understand. Just one question, though. If you believe you know which companies are manufacturing and shipping these drugs, and that they are finding their way through the South American cartels into European and U.S. cities, why aren't you notifying the officials in Beijing, or going directly to our Drug Enforcement Administration? I recently found a website for the Independent Commission Against Corruption in Hong Kong. Wouldn't they be an ally to your cause?"

"The ICAC was established in 1974 with excellent intentions. Its primary objective was to combat corruption in the public and private sectors. However, after Hong Kong was handed back to China in 1997, the commission itself was mired in controversy. Because it reports directly to the Chief Executive of Hong Kong, it is essentially another arm of the Chinese government. Many ICAC officers and directors have been found guilty of accepting bribes, as have judges adjudicating cases against government officials. I believe that to rid our government of corruption, we cannot rely on its own agency to be an honest partner in that. So, I look for ways to combat corruption through other channels. That is why I want to help you."

"I appreciate the risk you're taking. Your dedication is

admirable. If you don't mind me asking another personal question, of all the areas you could be devoting your time and energies to, why this one? Why is anti-corruption so important to you?"

"The year before I began studying here, 1999, my father was a judge in the Sha Tin district, where the horse racing track is based. Two government officials were being prosecuted for siphoning off money from tax payments the racetrack was making to the treasury. The racing business is the largest source of tax revenue for Hong Kong, so the amounts were in the millions. My father had told a close friend about being offered a bribe to dismiss the cases for lack of evidence. It would have been a lie, so my father declined. Several days later, my father celebrated the Chinese New Year with this friend at a local restaurant. They left the restaurant and went their separate ways. His friend told us a black sedan pulled up beside my father and shoved him into the backseat. They sped off, and that was the last time anyone saw him. This is personal, a way to seek retribution and feel that I have some agency in my healing process."

"My God, Susan. I am so sorry. If I had known, I wouldn't have asked for your help. I apologize."

"No need to apologize. You had no way to know. So, what's the next step?"

"I'll place our order this morning with Guangzhou Manufacturing for a container load of basketballs and let you know when they'll be delivered to the dock. Based on our past orders, they should arrive next week."

"Great. Let me know the date, and I'll have Steve schedule the interview. I can't wait to see how you pull this off. Locating your container among the thousands waiting dockside will be like finding a needle in a haystack."

"I love a challenge, and I already have a plan for that. I'm looking forward to meeting my new container face-to-face," Kip said flippantly, masking his realization of how serious this game was about to become.

Friday, the 14th

Susan had delivered on her promise, and Kip's meeting with Menzer's senior logistics manager at the Kwai Tsing Chung Terminal was set for four o'clock this afternoon. It was a quick taxi ride from Kip's apartment through the tunnel connecting Hong Kong Island to Kowloon. Minutes after exiting the tunnel, the taxi turned off the Kowloon Highway at Mai Ching Road and dropped Kip at the visitor's entrance to the terminal. Kip let the receptionist know that he, Steve Norris, had an appointment with Kenny Shiu and was invited to take a seat. Through the large Plexiglas window, he could see the tops of a dozen Panamax cranes crawling and lifting in a slow, methodical rhythm. At 120 feet tall, they could hoist a single container atop eight others and were the 24/7 heartbeat of Hong Kong's ports. Even with the loud hum from the window air conditioners, Kip could hear the buzz of machinery outside, and as always, he could smell the unmistakable fragrance of the harbor.

Ten minutes later, a plump Chinese man in his fifties welcomed Kip, wearing an orange reflective vest and a white construction helmet.

"Good morning, Mr. Norris," Kenny said. "Sorry, I'm running late. It's been a busy afternoon."

"No problem. It's nice of you to take the time."

"Please, put on this vest and helmet, and we'll drive over to my office," Kenny said, gesturing to his white flatbed truck with a spinning yellow light on the roof.

They started their drive across a sprawling expanse of cement that housed the thousands of containers awaiting transfer to their designated ships. Kenny kept his eyes fixed on the pathways as he navigated between the dozens of semis transporting containers and the utility vehicles moving personnel and supplies. He shared some statistics with Kip about the volume of cargo the terminals handled. He said he had worked for Menzer since he was 19, starting as a forklift operator and earning his way to senior logistics manager. Kip could see that Kenny was a proud, if not arrogant, man. He suspected this was going to be a short meeting.

They pulled up to a building resembling a white shipping container with windows along one side and an air conditioner on the roof. Stepping inside, the temperature dropped 20 degrees, a shock after being in the hot and humid air hanging over the port. One wall was covered with ocean maps and a half-dozen clocks set to international time zones. Mounted on the wall behind Kenny's desk were over a dozen framed award certificates, each with the Menzer logo and an embossed blue ribbon—a proud display of his achievements.

Kenny offered Kip a chair across from him at his desk. "So, I understand your article will focus on the state-of-the-art logistics system Menzer has developed here. Do you know anything about logistics?" Kenny asked sarcastically.

"I've done as much online research as possible about the sea freight industry, but I couldn't determine how a company like Menzer can track every container's exact location as it moves through the terminal. I was hoping you could show me how it all works." Kip could tell by Kenny's frequent looks out the window, glances at his computer screen, and checks of his watch that he wanted to give a quick demonstration and send Kip on his way.

"Well, the key lies in our barcode tracking system. Each container has a barcode on its rear door identification card. It is read by a handheld scanner at every iteration of its journey and includes information about which storage area it will be held in, how long before transport to its assigned berth, and the vessel it is to be loaded on. Our central computer tracks everything in real-time and will update the data immediately if anything changes. An incoming ship may be delayed, the loading order might be rearranged, the dock could be reassigned due to equipment maintenance, and so on. Next year, we are implementing a new system based on the latest GPS technology that will allow us to track containers at every point of their overseas journey, and we will receive read-outs of internal and external temperatures, air pressure, etc. It's all quite complex."

"And fascinating. I would love to see it in action, so I've prepared something I think would allow you to show me everything I need for my article. We have a member of our council who joined a few months ago. They are growing rapidly and have just received their first full container of product for export to the U.S. They are exactly the kind of company we want to help succeed, and they make a great case study for us to profile. They gave me the bill of lading and manufacturer's invoice for the container delivered to Menzer yesterday. I would like you to show me how you locate the container in your system and then take me to it so I can get a few photos of us in front of it. It would make everything come to life for the reader. The company is Sunny Luck Trading. Here is the paperwork."

Kenny hesitated before reaching for the document, and Kip could see he did not like the idea. "Hold on," Kenny said. "Let me see if these documents have all the necessary information."

"It should all be there."

Kenny stared blankly at the screen after entering a few numbers into his computer. The container he had been asked to locate was one in a group of eight they had received from Guangzhou Manufacturing. This company was secretly paying Kenny to let their containers slip through Menzer's docks without inspections. There was no reason anyone should be asking to see this particular container, and Kenny was suspicious.

Kip tried to read Kenny's expression but could not tell if it was one of confusion because the container's location did not come up, or one of concern. Either way, Kip sensed Kenny was disturbed, and he decided to play upon his sense of pride by asking, "Is there something wrong with the system?"

"No. There is nothing wrong. The system works perfectly. Of course, I've located the container."

"That's incredible. It took less than a minute. Let's head over, I'll snap some photos, and then I'll get out of your hair."

"Go out to the truck, and I'll be right with you. I have to make a quick call."

Kip got into the truck, reached into his shoulder bag, and switched on the tracking device Claudia had given him. It was ingenious in its simplicity: a battery-powered satellite transceiver module made by Iridium, the size of a credit card, only one inch thick, and weighing less than a pound. Adam had embedded a GPS application connecting to Iridium's network of low-orbit satellites along with a software script that activates the device every six hours throughout its journey. Once activated, a radio signal is sent to the nearest satellite, and the location data is relayed to Adam. The device then goes to sleep for another six hours to conserve battery power, after which it is activated again. Ships arriving at their port are held offshore for at least ten hours before docking, so the container's location would be confirmed before it is unloaded. The transponder and battery pack were enclosed in a waterproof container the size of a cigar box with a magnetic strip covering the back side. The entire device weighed less than three pounds and would be easy to slap onto the container.

Kenny hopped into the cab and said, "Who did you say owns

Sunny Luck Trading Co.?"

"I didn't say. It's the subsidiary of a company based in the state of Delaware, in the U.S."

"And what do they export?" Kenny asked skeptically.

"Sports equipment, in this case, basketballs. They have a handful of clients in Europe, but most are in the U.S. This one is located in Dearborn, in the state of Michigan." Kip suspected this line of questioning was not random, that Kenny was trying to figure out some puzzle.

"No customers in South America?"

"I don't believe so, but I'm not certain. They sell mostly to philanthropic organizations. This is an order for a dozen gross of basketballs being donated to Boys Clubs in low-income areas of major cities throughout the U.S. They do great work there, and the council is proud to have them as a member."

"Well, here we are." Kenny parked in the lane running between a long row of containers stacked four high. He stepped out and signaled Kip to follow, walking beside a block of eight containers. They reached the back, and Kenny pointed up. "That's your container, top right. Scheduled to ship with this block the day after tomorrow."

"All right then, I'll just move back and get a few photos."

Within seconds, a three-wheeled flatbed cart drove up, and a wiry man about Kenny's age parked beside his truck. Kenny turned to Kip, said, "Help yourself. I'll be right back," and walked toward his colleague.

Kip knew something was wrong. Kenny's demeanor changed as soon as he saw the identification of Kip's shipment come up on his screen, and his line of questioning seemed more like an interrogation than a casual conversation. He decided to capture a few photos of the eight stacked containers and, with no other choice, removed the magnetized box from his shoulder bag and mounted it onto the lower left corner of the container directly in front of him. The containers had similar markings, and Kip could see the Chinese characters for 'Guangzhou Manufacturing Ltd.' on each one, so he deduced that his was part of a larger shipment from the drug manufacturer and that Adam's assumptions were correct: their container would be tracked along with those containing the illegal drugs.

Kenny and his associate were in front of the container and could not see Kip as he walked toward the front. He stopped ten feet short of the driveway and could hear the conversation in their native Chinese.

Kenny's associate said, "I found it, and Sunny Luck Trading is only a year old. It's registered to an American named Kilpatrick Reynolds, and its business address is a residential apartment in the Mid-Levels neighborhood. There's no office or warehouse, but I have a phone number."

"No surprise there. Did you talk to your man at Foster & Young?" Kenny asked.

"Yes. They have a vessel departing tonight and have room for all eight containers. He'll squeeze them in at the end of loading, so they'll have to travel on top. But the ship is not going to Long Beach. Its destination is Oakland."

"Not a problem," Kenny said. "I'll have ten days to reorganize the pickup. Make sure the containers make it onto that ship. I'll make it worth your while." Kenny saw Kip approaching, leaned closer to his associate, and said something Kip could not hear.

As the man stepped away, Kip noticed something odd about the outline of his head: his left ear was missing. There was only a puckered hole and a scar that ran from there to the middle of his neck, and Kip thought, *This is a man who has seen some trouble*. Kip looked away, walked in front of the container, and said to Kenny,

"Thanks very much. It looks like I have everything I need."

Kenny paused briefly and said, "Right. I'll drive you back to the reception area, and they can get you a taxi, Steve."

Kip's phone rang as the flatbed truck approached the reception area. Before he could answer, the ringing stopped, and Kip saw a local phone number on the screen without a name. He turned to Kenny before stepping out, saw the grin disappear from his face, and knew who had called.

Kip phoned Adam as soon as he arrived at his apartment. It was seven a.m. in Birmingham, and he knew Adam would be back from his daily run. "I have good news and bad news. Which do you want first?"

"I want a full update. I don't care what kind of news it is," Adam said with his usual matter-of-fact tone.

"I found our container among a group of eight and attached the device to one of them. Our container was on top of three others, so I couldn't get to it, but I confirmed with photos I took that all of them are going to California as a group. But they won't be going to Long Beach on the Menzer vessel, which we were assigned on the shipping confirmation. I overheard my guide telling a colleague to load the containers tonight on a ship belonging to Foster & Young, and they're going to Oakland. Adam, they're on to us. Everything was going well until my guy looked up the shipping information on his computer. He phoned a colleague and had him research Sunny Luck Trading. They learned it was registered in my name and got the phone number I had provided when it was registered. As I was leaving, his colleague rang my phone, and my guide saw me go to answer it. He knows I'm not Steve Norris."

"That means you have identified the drug manufacturer's inside man at the port. He could only know that ours is part of an illicit shipment if he's involved. That's why he got the shipment diverted at the last minute. If our container stays with the others, we have a chance of tracking it. A risk is that the container gets loaded into the ship's center or has some obstacle that interferes with the radio signal. It needs a direct line to the satellite."

"Then I think we're in luck. I heard them say the containers will be the last ones loaded onto the ship. That would put them on top, right?"

"Probably. I'll run the first activation test tonight and see what comes back. In the meantime, you need to get on the next plane and come home, for good. If they're on to you, being there is no longer safe. Don't bother notifying your landlord. You wouldn't be the first to walk out on a lease in that city. When you don't renew your business license, it will be canceled, so don't contact anyone there. Just pack your things and get home. You can transfer any funds you hold at the bank there when you get back."

"Right. Flights to Detroit go out in the early afternoon, so I'll pack up tonight. Would it be okay to stop by Susan's and say goodbye? This wouldn't have been possible without her help."

"That's not a good idea. She shouldn't know more right now than she already does. You can phone her when you get home. Does Susan know why you wanted to get to the container?"

"Yes."

"Well, that's a problem. Stop at Susan's office in the morning on your way to the airport and tell her your cover was blown and that her friend should not disclose that they know each other. Make sure she knows how important that is. On your flight back, write a short article about Menzer that Steve can publish on his organization's website. That should give him some immediate cover with Menzer. I'll get the article to him when you get home."

"Got it. I'll text my flight information to you once I've booked a ticket."

"Nope. There will be no more communication until you get home, no emails, texts, or calls to anyone. I will have deleted your email account and phone service by tomorrow morning. It will be as if they never existed. You'll have new ones when you arrive home."

Adam stopped short of telling Kip what he was thinking. *Susan and Steve's lives are in danger. If the Chinese drug manufacturer learns about their roles in identifying this shipment, they may do anything necessary to silence them, and there is nothing we can do to protect them.*

Monday, the 17th

Birmingham, Michigan

When Kip returned from Hong Kong last January, Adam had finished converting his rectangular living room into an office to accommodate three people. A corner at the far end was flanked by Adam's stand-up desk and a workstation with three computer monitors arrayed in an arc. Along the short wall was a stack of data servers, and in the opposite corner was his black leather Eames chair and a portable laptop stand. In the center of the room were two large desks touching front to front where Claudia and Kip could sit, with a rolling chair at the end for Adam when he joined them for a team conference. The glass sliding doors leading to the balcony on the other long wall brought in plenty of daylight, and Claudia decided the addition of a few green plants would be her contribution to the room's aesthetic. Adam's three-foot painting with the straight-on portrait of an elephant's head was the only item that added any character to the room. When asked why an elephant was in the room, Adam replied, "Because I like elephants."

Kip and Claudia had been told they would do all their work from laptops and that their office is a paperless one. Adam insisted that he never see paper on anyone's desk. It was 2012, after all, and they were a tech-driven company. The exception was their planning work on the large whiteboard mounted on the wall behind their desks. If they created anything there whose content needed to be saved, they would snap a photo with an iPhone and distribute it through Slack, the messaging app he had selected.

This morning, Kip walked into the office carrying a small tub of coffee from the nearby Tim Horton's and a box of donuts. The first thing he saw was Claudia standing at the kitchen sink, washing a cup. She was dressed in snug jeans and a simple white collared shirt, her long hair pulled back in a loose braid. Every time Kip looked at her, he reacted as if noticing her beauty for the first time. She was becoming the center of his world, and he was looking forward to the day he could secure her place there with a ring on her finger.

Adam turned from his standing desk and asked Kip, "Why did you bring coffee? Did you forget we have a kitchen here? There's a new modern appliance called a coffee maker, and we got our hands on one of the first prototypes. We also found a source in Colombia for coffee beans, roasted ones, so we can brew our own. And if those are donuts, you can take them home with you. We don't eat that kind of crap around here."

"Good to see you too, pal," Kip said.

"We missed you," Claudia said with a welcoming smile. "It sounds like you had quite a trip. It's great to see you, but it would be better to see you without that beard. I'm not sure what's up with that, but may I suggest you lose it? Doesn't go with the whole preppy WASP image."

Kip scratched his chin and said, "Oh, right, this. Yes, I'll shave it off tonight, long story."

They gathered at the desks, and Adam took his place at the whiteboard. "I've activated the transponder every six hours since Kip attached it to the container, and it's working perfectly. Kip, your guess was right. Being the last containers loaded onto the ship, they must have been placed on top, and most likely, they were placed near an outward-facing side. The ship left port at 11:39 p.m. that day, and Claudia confirmed what you overheard on the dock: they were loaded onto a Foster & Young vessel. She has found the transit map for its route, and it is headed for Oakland. Once it's parked and waiting to be assigned a berth, I'll notify my contact at the DEA, and they will take it from there."

"I love it when a plan comes together," Kip said. "I still don't understand how this is going to disrupt the operations of the cartel Hizbullah and Iran are working with in any meaningful way. Susan said once this shipment is seized, the Chinese manufacturer will shut down this operation and open another with a different name. The government authorities in Guangzhou will give it all a wink and a nod, and it will be business as usual."

Adam explained, "Our intent was never to shut down the manufacturing in China. That industry is too large, and the Chinese government would never allow it to happen. This is not like David and Goliath, our tiny company versus China. It's more like King Kong versus Godzilla, the U.S. and China. Our client hired us to identify the NGOs in the U.S. who are helping the terrorists facilitate the sale of precursor chemicals to the drug cartels in Bogotá. After our shipment is seized, the DEA will enter the data for all eight containers into their system. At that point, I can access it and see who was scheduled to pick up the containers and where they were destined for."

"Aren't the DEA agents already suspicious of containers coming in from China via Hong Kong?" Claudia asked. "The smugglers have been doing this for years."

Adam began mapping out a diagram on the whiteboard. "Thousands of containers come in from Hong Kong every month, but these cartels are sophisticated. They know that if a large group of containers were picked up at the dock and then loaded onto trucks traveling to Mexico, that shipment would be flagged as suspicious, and those containers would most likely be inspected. However, if each container goes to a different destination in the U.S., the incoming shipment will most likely escape any attention."

"Got it," Claudia said.

"Once we know where these containers are being delivered, we can identify the groups working with Hizbullah. Our client wants us to identify the kingpin in the U.S. coordinating the shipments, who most likely works for *El Loco's* cartel in Colombia. Bringing in our one container is just a mechanism for doing that. Once I know where the containers are going, I can take it from there and identify the kingpin. Then our client will work to apprehend him and extract the information they need to shut down the entire cartel."

"I don't suppose you're ever going to disclose who our client is," Kip said.

Adam smirked and said, "Nope."

Wednesday, the 26th

Mapledale, West Virginia

One year ago, Jenny discovered the reason for Ryan's trips to Charleston. Tobias Furth was a drug wholesaler who worked out of the basement at The Rusty Nail, supplying oxycodone, marijuana, and crystal meth to local small-time dealers. A tall man built like a football player with a nose that may have been on the receiving end of many punches, Tobias looked the part. The narrow hallway leading from the bar area to the back door and restrooms also had an unmarked door that led down a wooden staircase to a basement originally intended for coal storage. When a modern HVAC system was installed on the roof, the bar's owner converted the storage area into a small office, and Tobias established a lucrative business there. The key to running it was Ryan's ability to drive his van to Charleston and pick up parcels of drugs. They were brought in from Mexico by a local cartel and hidden within boxes of paper goods like toilet tissue and hand towels. After the night of Ryan's last pickup, when he narrowly escaped being caught in the gunfire between Tobias's supplier and the Colombian cartel whose turf he had encroached upon, Ryan was told it would be his last pickup for a while. Ryan explained to Jenny that he needed the job to get the pain pills he wanted. Tobias paid him $500 for each run, so she offered to help him find a job if he promised to stop working with him. Ryan promised he would, and Jenny found him a job.

It took Jenny a lot of convincing to get Ryan's father to agree. Still, Hank put Ryan in contact with the grounds supervisor at the Greenbrier, and Ryan landed a full-time job doing light landscaping work around the outdoor recreation facilities and the private guest cottages, about five acres in total. Due to his past injuries and inexperience in landscaping, his jobs consisted mostly of lighter work: raking flower beds, picking up leaves, cleaning walkways, and delivering plant material in his utility golf cart. Jenny ensured he got to work on time each day and drove him back and forth on the way to her physical therapy clinic when Ryan's van was in for repairs.

July and August had been especially hot in the mountains, with temperatures in the high 80s most days. Ryan enjoyed the cooler September afternoons and the relief they brought from working outdoors. The upcoming weekend was fully booked at the resort, and the past few days had been stressful. He was glad to be going home and looked forward to relaxing in his La-Z-Boy and enjoying a few cold beers. Ryan had kept his promise to Jenny and no longer worked for Tobias, but he still could not do as she asked and stop taking oxycodone and drinking alcohol. He no longer drank vodka at home and was able to cut back to a six-pack of beer in the evenings, but he often took small amounts of oxy to allow him to sleep. He knew Jenny was running out of patience, but could not imagine how he would ever quit completely. For now, cutting back was the best he could do.

Ryan pulled into their driveway and saw he had arrived before Jenny. As he shut his car door, his eye caught something moving high above the porch steps. The sun was low and shining directly in his eyes, so he had to walk closer to determine what it was. Through the glare, he saw the outline of a hanging figure swaying in the light evening breeze, something resembling a piñata. As he reached the first step, the sun dropped behind the roof, and the object came into focus. It was the strangled body of Roy, dangling from a rope tied around his back legs and attached to the overhead beam, blood dripping from his gaped mouth into a black pool on the step.

Birmingham, Michigan

Adam had activated the transponder yesterday afternoon and saw that the Foster & Young vessel was being ferried through the outer channel entrance into berth 26 at the Oakland harbor. It was time to activate the plan he had put in place with the DEA.

This morning, shortly after Kip and Claudia arrived at the office and settled in with their first cup of freshly brewed coffee, Adam clapped his hands and yelled, "Yes!" He spun around and stood up with a fist bump above his head. "We did it, Musketeers, they've seized the containers, all eight of them, and five were loaded with pallets of ephedrine and pseudoephedrine. Those are enough chemicals to produce-" Adam did some quick math in his head. "Close to $200 million worth of crystal meth on the street. Our friends at Hizbullah are going to feel the hit. I guess their colleagues in Lebanon will be running a bit short on bombs and firearms for a while. And it looks like we will own a dozen gross of basketballs if our container is ever released. Now I need to watch the DEA database and wait for the shipping manifests to be entered."

"Score one for the team," Claudia said, walking toward Adam to give him a hug.

"No hugs, Claude. This is all business. It's what we do here, and there's more work to do before we can call the project a complete success. But great work, everyone. Really great work."

"Thanks, Adam," Kip said. "I don't suppose I can share the good news with Susan. This wouldn't have happened without her help."

"Not yet. I need to monitor our servers and make sure nobody is trying to hack in. Remember, we have one big fly in the ointment. You had no way to predict that of all the people working at Menzer's shipping terminal, the guy you met with would be Guangzhou Manufacturing's insider. It's bad luck, but something like that is always a risk of doing business in our game. As Susan said, the people in China will likely shut down operations briefly and then do business as usual under a different name. They will probably stop using Menzer for a while, which will put, what's his name, Kenny? temporarily out of commission. He would be smart to lie low until things return to normal. There's no benefit to him in raising his hand and calling attention to this."

"I agree," Kip said. "I guess in the meantime, we should head over to Dick's Sporting Goods and buy ourselves a basketball hoop to set up out back." Claudia imitated shooting an imaginary ball through a hoop, and Adam rolled his eyes as he returned to his screen.

As Kip gathered his shoulder bag to head home for the day, Adam began tapping furiously on his keyboard. Claudia noticed his sudden burst of activity and turned toward Kip, shrugging her shoulders with a look that said, *I wonder what's up?* Kip sat on a kitchen barstool and looked on.

After five minutes, Adam said quietly, "Well, there we go. Bingo." He turned to face the others and said, "It looks like Guangzhou Manufacturing Company has some very philanthropic customers just outside five major cities: Phoenix, Tucson, Reno, Las Vegas, and Knoxville. They all have similar names. Community Youth Services of Scottsdale, Boys and Girls Club of Tucson, Metropolitan Youth Center, Las Vegas, and so on. I guess each of those could use a container full of basketballs, inflatable rafts, gym mats, and camping tents, which the bills of lading said were inside the containers. Each location is ideal for receiving the Chinese chemicals and transferring them to trucks traveling through Mexico to Colombia. They may also keep some of the chemicals at facilities near those cities and manufacture street drugs for sale here in the U.S. The other three containers were consigned to legitimate customers: one in Santa Fe, one in Salt Lake City, and the third to us. Our wholesale distribution company in Troy, which I named Pachyderm Imports, has already received an email from Foster & Young advising that our shipment has been delayed and that we will be informed of a new delivery date. This explains why our order was not shipped with the customary FOB terms."

"You'll have to remind me what that means," Claudia said, trying not to sound too uninformed.

Adam gave her a brotherly smile and said, "FOB means 'Free on Board.' The seller is responsible for delivering the goods to the port of departure, Hong Kong, clearing them for export, and loading them onto the ship. After that, the buyer is responsible for unloading the container when it arrives in California and having it shipped to its final destination."

"And what were our terms?"

"CPT—'Carriage Paid To.' The seller is responsible for the costs of transporting the goods to a named destination, in our case, the factory lot in Dearborn belonging to Francesca's husband. Those are extremely unusual terms for this kind of shipment. They usually go FOB. Using these terms, Guangzhou Manufacturing controls who picks up the containers at the portside, allowing them to change the original pickup from the Menzer vessel, originally scheduled to arrive in Long Beach, to the new pickup from Foster & Young in Oakland. They didn't need to alert their customers about the change of vessels and ports. They only advised the change in delivery date, since it wasn't up to us to schedule the pickup at the port."

"Got it."

"So, what's next?" Kip asked.

"Now the real work begins. It's time to find out who is behind the companies that were supposed to receive those five containers and uncover their link to our terrorist friends in the Middle East."

"Oh," Kip said, stroking his beardless chin. "Good to know that up to now, we haven't been doing any real work. I can't wait to see what's next."

Hong Kong Special Administrative Region of the People's Republic of China

Kenny Shiu had just finished his takeout dinner of fish and chips when he saw a call coming in from *Lǎobǎn*, his boss at Guangzhou Manufacturing, Li Chen.

"We have a problem, Mr. Shiu," Chen began. "Our last shipment of eight containers was detained upon its arrival in Oakland by the American Customs and Border Patrol agency and the DEA. Can you tell me why the shipment did not go to Long Beach as planned and why it arrived two days early?"

The color drained from Kenny's face, and his throat tightened. This confirmed his greatest fear: that the visit from Kilpatrick Reynolds, under the alias of Steve Norris, was, in fact, an intelligence-gathering operation. Somehow, even with the diversion of the containers to Foster & Young's ship, Reynolds had been able to track the containers, and he had fallen for the ploy. He looked up at the many certificates of achievement on the wall and knew his storied career was now in danger of coming to an end. He could not admit that his visitor had duped him and lose face. This required some quick thinking, and the weather chart mounted on the wall gave him an idea.

"Tropical depression Sanba was forming off the Philippine islands and was predicted to become a severe tropical storm. I wanted to get the containers on their way as soon as possible to avoid weather delays. I got them out two days early and thought I had made the right decision. This typhoon has been one of the worst of the decade. Shipments out of our port experienced significant delays throughout the week."

"I see," Chen said. "We should have been informed of the change. As you can imagine, we do not like surprises. By the end of today, Guangzhou Manufacturing will no longer exist. You will not hear from us until we are established under a new name, and then we expect to continue operations as before. If anyone from Menzer asks you about our containers, tell them you made the changes at our request. You were only following instructions from the customer. Anyone's efforts to contact us for confirmation will be in vain, there will be no company to contact. This won't be the first time our friends at Menzer will have seen a customer disappear. They know how things work in Hong Kong."

Kenny hung up and called his associate at the docks. He briefed him on his call with *Lǎobǎn*, and they coordinated their stories. Now, all there was to do was wait and pray this would pass without anyone finding out he had been duped.

Mapledale, West Virginia

Ryan sprinkled the last shovel of dirt over the grave as Jenny watched on. The sun had set, and a waning full moon rose above the mountain. With temperatures in the low 70s and a light breeze, it would have been a beautiful night had Ryan not just buried his best friend. *Such a horrible death, and all because of me*, Ryan thought. He couldn't bear to think of how much Roy would have suffered. For the past 12 years, Ryan could count on him to be there. Waiting at the back door after school, coming to the Riding Club, greeting him like a long-lost friend when he returned from the Army, and staying by his side while recovering from the train accident. Ryan stared at the grave and made no effort to hold back his tears. Jenny wrapped her arms around him and swayed softly as she stroked his hair.

"Why, Ryan? Why did they do this? You said you had stopped making runs for Tobias and weren't making any more trips to Charleston. I thought you had finished all that and were free from him and his gang. I know you would never lie to me. I've always trusted you to be honest. So, please tell me why you think they did this. And why did they leave that note on the door saying it would be a shame if anything were to happen to *me*? I'm frightened, Ryan. For both of us."

"I didn't want to scare you, so I didn't tell you. Tobias said the guy who got killed that night at the railyards was part of a Mexican cartel bringin' in the drugs from South America. The guy who shot him was from a Colombian cartel who said Charleston was their turf and that he was crouching on it. I guess he'd been warned before to stay out. Anyhow, Tobias couldn't get no more drugs from these people, so he laid low for a while, and I stopped makin' the pickups. Some other guy over in Covington stepped in to sell to Tobias's customers and the owner at The Rusty Nail told Tobias he couldn't work there no more. You know the metal recycling shop on Pocahontas Road? Well, they got a couple dozen storage garages there, and Tobias rents two of 'em. That's where he works from now."

"Sure, I know it. The garages are right beside the factory." The look on Jenny's face was becoming increasingly fraught.

"Couple weeks ago, Tobias found me at the bar and took me out back. He said I still owed him money for drugs I bought before he shut down. Says it was over a thousand dollars. I didn't remember, 'cause I was doin' so many back then, before you got me the job and helped me get better. Tobias said he has a new business now. He says instead of just sellin' to small customers, like people going to a store for a few things, he is now selling to the stores. And he don't sell weed no more. The guy in Covington does that. Tobias says it's easier, like they have an understanding. He sells the oxy and meth, and the other guy does the weed."

"I got it, honey. He's taken over the business that his friends in Charleston were doing. He's now supplying the major local dealers. He's going for the big leagues."

Ryan reflected a moment and said, "I guess. Anyways, he said since I owe him money, I needed to drive my van over to Knoxville and make a pickup from a fruit and vegetable dealer there. But I promised you I wouldn't do that shit no more, so I told Tobias no. He got real pissed off and threatened to mess me up. I said I would get the money somehow, but he said he didn't want the money. He wanted me to work with him like before, makin' the pickups. He told me to go away and think about things real hard, that he knew I'd make the right decision. He said he hoped nothin' bad would happen to you or Roy if I didn't. Son of a bitch. If I had a way to kill him for what he done to Roy, I would."

Jenny pulled Ryan in a bear hug and held him for a minute before saying, "Sweetie, you did the right thing. You kept your promise to me, and that means everything. You are a good man, but you have gotten involved with some very bad people. You got tied up in all this back when you were really sick. You did what you thought was right. I'm proud of you for standing up for yourself. Let's go inside and get something to eat. We'll need to think this through and figure out what to do. We're in this together. I'm not sure if we have any good options, but if there is one, we'll find it. I pray to God we'll be okay."

"Don't seem like God cares too much about what happens to me, but that don't mean bad things have to happen to you too. This is all my fault, and now I gone and screwed up your life. It's okay if you want to hate me, I'd understand. I'd understand if you didn't want nothin' more to do with me."

"Ryan, I love you. I truly do. I want to spend the rest of my life with you. Maybe we just need to find a way to get out of here before that man Tobias does something to hurt us more. If we were to leave here and move somewhere safe, then we could get you to the right kind of doctors who could help you, you know, figure out why you sometimes get so angry you can't control yourself, and then do things you regret. If we could understand what has made you so angry, we might be able to help fix things."

"One thing is for sure, if I could get away from my old man once and for all, I might someday forget all the bad stuff he done to us and not be so angry."

"It's not unusual for kids to have disagreements with their parents, that's normal." Jenny considered this for a moment and said, "Did something happen, Ryan? Did something really bad ever happen?"

Ryan had never heard anyone besides his mother say, "I love you," and even that had been years back. It took a moment for those words to set in, and then he said, "Yeah. About 15 years ago, when I was in the eighth grade."

"Please, honey, tell me about it. It might help me understand how to help you. I would never share your story with anyone."

Ryan knew he could trust Jenny, so for the first time, he shared the details of that night. It was an event that he had kept secret since he was 14, the source of endless nightmares and the fuel for a volcano buried inside, forever on the verge of erupting.

September, 1997

> *The back of Ryan's head hit the hardwood floor with a thud as Hank flipped him on his back, straddled his two-hundred-pound hulk atop Ryan's light frame, and pinned his arms to the floor with his knees. With his hands freed up, Hank unbuckled his belt, ripped it from his waist, and raised the leather strap above his head. Ryan saw the rage in his father's face, and the only defense available was to close his eyes and jerk his head right to avoid a direct strike to his face. He heard the swoosh of the folded belt whizzing past his ear before it cracked*

on his left shoulder. Ryan's body stiffened, and his fingernails dug into his palms in anticipation of the next blow. He had bitten his tongue when he hit the floor, and blood was trickling from the corner of his mouth. Ryan could taste the iron and, for a moment, wondered if that was what death tasted like. The next strike came rapidly and landed on the exposed skin of his neck. The intense sting told him the belt's edge had lacerated his clavicle. His body went limp as he surrendered to what he was sure would be a prolonged beating, when his father suddenly sat up and rotated to the right, hurling his arm backward. Ryan opened his eyes when he felt Hank's weight shift and saw that Glenda had come up from behind and was yanking on his collar with all her might to pull him off. The belt struck Glenda across the right side of her head, causing her to let go as she staggered back, blood beginning to pool in her ear. Before Hank could react, Ryan saw his grandpa's figure appear at the door. A second later, he heard the loud 'chk-chk' as Grandpa cocked his Remington shotgun and pointed it at Hank's head. Ryan only knew Glenda's father to be soft-spoken and reserved, so it shocked him when Grandpa bellowed, "Hank Jackson, you stand up right now, or I'm puttin' a bullet straight through that thick skull of yours."

Hank rose slowly, contemplating whether to lunge for the gun, when Grandpa dropped his voice an octave and growled, "I'm an old man and have lived a full life. I'm happy to spend the rest of it in prison for murderin' your evil ass if you even think about raisin' a hand to my daughter or my grandbabies again. Now pack a bag and get out. You can stay with your brother, or sleep under a bridge for all I care, but you are leavin' this house tonight and not comin' back 'till you learn to control that temper of yours. From now on, I'm the new sheriff around here, and I will die before I let you hurt anyone in this family. Now get!"

Hank shifted his gaze from Grandpa to Glenda and gave her a defiant look as he shuffled out of the room. Glenda knelt to help Ryan up and stood holding him while Grandpa followed Hank to the front door and made sure he left. Glenda felt Ryan shaking and said, "I know, dear. It's all been frightenin'. But don't worry, you have me and Grandpa here to protect you, Brittany, and Josh. Daddy will calm down in a few days, and we'll try to get him some help. I'm sure he loves you all, he just don't know how to control his temper, and when he loses it, he gets ugly. We'll get his head right, and things will be fine. No need to be afraid."

Glenda left to get the first aid kit, and Ryan sat on the bed, his adrenaline pumping. He thought, I'm not shakin' because I'm scared. I'm shakin' because I'm mad. If my dad ever raises a hand to my ma again, I'll find a way to kill him—with Grandpa's gun, a huntin' knife, the garden hoe, or Dad's own pistol. I'll show him who the loser is.

END PART 2

PART THREE

2013

I see a shiny nose and two eyes.
It's a bear!
Run out of the cave.
Run, run, run!
Climb up the mountain.
Climb down the tree.
Run, run, run!
Swim through the river.
Run, run, run!
Run through the grass.
Run, run, run!
Open the door.
Shut the door.
Run upstairs and
Jump in bed.
We're safe!

— MOTHER GOOSE

CHAPTER 17

Retribution

SEPTEMBER 2013

Tuesday, the 3rd

Birmingham, Michigan

"How will we know that the raid has gone down?" Kip asked after settling in at his desk that morning.

After twelve months of intensive work by Custom Solutions Group, today was the day the FBI was to launch its raid at the home of the Colombian drug cartel's kingpin in Hunting Valley, Ohio. This man had been importing drugs to social charities in Phoenix, Tucson, Reno, Las Vegas, and Knoxville. Community Youth Services of Scottsdale, Boys and Girls Club of Tucson, and all the others were fronts for purchasing sporting goods that were supposedly being delivered for use in their charity programs. The containers were destined for small warehouses in nearby industrial parks. After retaining a small amount of the drugs to convert into crystal meth for sale in local markets, they would transfer the bulk of the Chinese drugs to trucks destined for Colombia. The street drugs were routed to nearby distributors of wholesale goods like fruits and vegetables, where a cartel insider would facilitate their delivery to dealers like Tobias Furth.

CSG had been hired to uncover the name and location of the man running the organization: Ahmed Karam, a 50-year-old Lebanese expat from Beirut who had been a part of the Hizbullah organization since its inception in 1982. He was one of their masterminds for money laundering. Karam had developed a sophisticated network for buying used cars in the U.S., shipping them to Africa for sale in local markets, and routing the money through offshore banks back to the U.S. to purchase more cars. All profits were delivered to Hizbullah using a new online currency run through the Dark Web called Bitcoin. It made the transactions invisible to all but the most experienced online detectives, one of whom was Adam, thanks to the specialized training he had received from the CIA in Baghdad. Over the past decade, Karam had been expanding his operations to include the routing of precursor drugs from China to Colombia and the trafficking of street drugs from Bogotá to the eastern United States.

Claudia had spent the past year tracking emails, texts, and phone calls between the registered owners of the charities and Karam, which was the information Adam needed to identify him. She now understood why passing the Patriot Act in the aftermath of the 9/11 attacks had been so important. It had empowered the NSA to develop new surveillance techniques for mining information that could prevent future attacks against the U.S. In this case, the methods Claudia had learned there served their intended purpose of infiltrating terrorist networks, and she hoped her father might be smiling down on her.

Kip had spent most of his time over the past six months helping his parents get through Patty's breast cancer treatments. Sitting with Patty during chemotherapy sessions, traveling to the Mayo Clinic in Minnesota for her surgeries, playing nurse at home, and helping manage the household provided Kip the opportunity to grow close to his parents for the first time. Although his father continued to go to the country club each day, he would not leave home until he knew Patty's needs were attended to in the morning, and most afternoons, he came home after lunch without having played a round of golf. Getting out each day relieved him from the stresses at home, a luxury afforded him by Kip's constant presence, and he was usually sober enough when he returned home that the three of them could spend quality time together before he got too far into his bottle of scotch.

When he could get away from the house, Kip spent time with Claudia and Adam in their office. It was a welcome relief from his duties at home, and he enjoyed the work assignments Adam had given him. He had been responsible for drafting briefing documents and writing updates for their client, which Adam passed along at the end of each month. Kip knew the FBI had the information they needed to raid Karam's home.

Adam had continued typing after Kip asked his question and, without looking away from his screen, said, "We'll know that the raid has gone down when our client tells us."

Without hiding his sarcasm, Kip said, "Right. That's what I thought." Claudia shrugged and gave him a compassionate smile.

Hunting Valley, Ohio

Ahmed Karam was a busy man, and his Gulfstream G280 had become a second home. Certified for steep-approach operations and able to navigate short runways and high-altitude airports in low-visibility conditions, it was the ideal craft for his commutes between cities in the U.S., Guadalajara, Bogotá, Beirut, and coastal towns in West Africa.

Between trips, the respites he enjoyed most were those at his home on County Line Road in the exclusive village of Hunting

Valley in northeast Ohio. His twenty-two thousand square foot stone and timber mansion was hidden among the trees on his fifteen-acre property. It afforded him the solitude and privacy people of his stature cherished. Families who had become wealthy over several generations as owners of Cleveland's many successful banks and manufacturing businesses chose Hunting Valley as the home for their sprawling equestrian estates. It was where they enjoyed the discreet lifestyle favored by old money, which suited Ahmed perfectly. He had purchased the property through the executor of his trust, an established Wall Street financier with Ivy League credentials, so no one in the elite enclave could have stonewalled his purchase if they had taken issue with his Middle Eastern heritage. Ahmed had a dark complexion with refined features, making him appear more Greek than Arabic. His salt and pepper hair was cut short and impeccably trimmed, as was his beard. Typically seen in Saville Road suits, bespoke shoes, and Brioni ties, he could easily be taken for a conservative London banker. The muscular build of his youth had softened around his tall frame, and he was now borderline overweight. But he carried himself like a proud soldier and spoke fluent English and Spanish with only the hint of an accent. By all appearances, Ahmed was a refined and respectable man.

It was a cool, overcast morning as Ahmed enjoyed his tea on the south veranda overlooking the pool. Three deer were grazing where the manicured lawn met the tree line, and a flock of Canadian geese had adopted the large pond as their summer home. It was a setting that would have been fitting in Jackson Hole or Sun Valley. As he sipped his tea and savored the tranquility, he thought: *Alhamdulillah—Praise be to Allah. I live a truly blessed life.*

His young Lebanese houseman, tall and lean, with an immaculate beard and hair pulled up in a bun, stepped outside and said softly, "Sorry for the interruption, Mr. Karam, but there is something you should see." Ahmed and his houseman, Elias, went to the adjacent office, where a bank of screens mounted on the oak-paneled wall displayed a live feed from the property's eight security cameras. "Top left monitor, sir, outside the front gate."

There was a 20-foot apron connecting the driveway to the road. Barely within view of the camera, they could see the fronts of three black Chevy SUVs, unmarked, with two men in each, speaking into radios. "How long have they been there, Elias?"

"They pulled up about three minutes ago."

Seconds later, the vehicle's passenger door closest to the gate opened, and a large man stepped out wearing a black Kevlar vest marked "FBI" on the back. He went to the driver's window of the second vehicle and appeared to be having a heated discussion when a man from the third vehicle joined him.

"Do we have audio on the front camera?" Ahmed asked. Elias took the remote control and activated the volume icon on the screen. "Turn it up. I can hardly hear them."

"That's all we can get, sir, they are too far from the gate."

"Is the audio being recorded on the video feed?"

"Yes. We can enhance it on replay."

All three men returned to their vehicles, drove through the apron to make a U-turn, and sped off.

Within minutes, Elias accessed the security footage and played it through a central console with enhanced volume control. The voices came through loud and clear.

"No. We abort," said the man from the first vehicle.

"That can't be right," said the man in the second. "Our intel is dead on, this is the home, and our target is inside."

"I have orders," said the first. "From the top, in Washington. I'll get the details when we return to base, and then I'll fill you in. For now, orders are orders. We abort."

With an expressionless face, Ahmed turned calmly to Elias and said, "Phone the pilot and have my plane ready in two hours. We're leaving for Bogotá."

Birmingham, Michigan

Kip and Claudia finished their sandwiches from the local deli and returned to their desks. Adam rarely ate lunch and was glued to his screens.

"I need to leave at two today. My parents are landing at the FBO in Pontiac around two-thirty," Kip said as he tossed the bags into the trash. Ascend Aviation in Pontiac was the Fixed Base Operator that serviced the private jet the Reynolds had been chartering for their frequent trips to the Mayo Clinic in Rochester, Minnesota. Patty had convinced Dudley that if they were ever going to spend money on private jets, this was the time. If Dudley did not see the value in using their wealth to guarantee comfort for his wife on her multiple flights to and from Rochester, she told him he could begin his search for the next Mrs. Reynolds. After their third round-trip in the Citation Excel, Dudley conceded it was the only way to travel and agreed never to fly commercially again.

"Your parents could have bought a jet for what they've paid in charter fees over the past year," Claudia teased. "I'm so glad this will be one of the last trips for a while."

"We all have our fingers crossed," Kip said. "It was a real blow when the cancer returned after Mother's lumpectomy. Even after a year, I don't understand how that disease works. The doctors at Mayo were confident the chemo treatments had reduced the tumors enough that the lumpectomy would be all she needed. When she got the news in June that she would need a double mastectomy, she was relieved and joked about how much she is going to enjoy her new 'girls'—she says they will make her feel young again."

"Feel young again? My god, your mother's only, what, forty-something?"

"Fifty-five. The Botox helps a lot. But my dad has been a wreck through all this, and according to Mother, the trips to Mayo I couldn't accompany her on were a nightmare. Dad's drinking has become a real problem. He's starting earlier in the day and is really of no help to her after lunchtime."

"I'm sorry to hear that. I know this has taken a toll on you as well. It's great that you could go with her on so many of the trips. It's helped her a lot, and you've grown close as a family."

"I'm glad too. The five weeks she was there for the radiation treatments were almost too much for my dad to handle. Their executive suite at the Kahler Grand Hotel was adjoined to the clinic and provided all the comforts Mother needed, but if I hadn't been there for the first two weeks, I don't know what would have happened. Dad was a mess."

Adam was at his desk when the email came in from his contact at the CIA. He sat at Kip and Claudia's workstation and shared the news. "I've just heard from our client, and as a result of our work, they've accomplished their goals and declared the project a success. They asked me to extend their congratulations to my team. So, congratulations. It's time for high-fives all around, The Three Musketeers have scored a victory: mission accomplished. This guarantees future work with this client and other groups in Washington who are now familiar with CSG and our abilities."

"So, the raid was a success?" Claudia asked. "They've arrested Ahmed Karam, apprehended his computers, and have what they need to shut his operations down?"

"Well, not exactly," Adam said. "The FBI was stationed in front of Karam's home in Hunting Valley about an hour ago, ready to advance, when they got a last-minute order from Washington to stand down."

"Washington is a big place," Kip said. "Which agency told the FBI to stand down, and why?"

"It wasn't an agency. Senior officials at the State Department worked with Obama's national security team."

Before Adam could continue, Kip said, "That makes no sense. Why would they want the raid to be aborted?"

"Well," Adam said, "Here's the story. In the years following the 9/11 attacks, the DEA initiated an effort to bring together the intelligence, law enforcement, and military communities in the fight against narcoterrorism and money laundering linked to terrorist organizations. The DEA established the Counter-Narcoterrorism Operations Center in Chantilly, Virginia, just outside of DC, and named their activities 'Project Cassandra.' In 2006, they launched what they called Operation Titan and, for the next two years, conducted a joint investigation with Colombian authorities into a global money-laundering and drug-trafficking alliance between Latin American traffickers and Lebanese operatives. The case investigators deployed 370 wiretaps and monitored 700 thousand conversations, leading to 130 arrests and the seizure of $23 million. That created a significant vacuum in their Colombian operations, and the agents knew someone had stepped in as the new kingpin in Colombia. Until now, they didn't know who it was. Identifying him is what we were hired for."

"Got it," Kip said. "But that doesn't explain why Obama's national security team would shut down the FBI raid. I mean, they had him, right?"

"Yes. Claudia's surveillance of the five men running the charities gave us the first connection to Karam. It took months to link any financial transactions between them, because the cryptocurrency they have been using is a relatively new vehicle for laundering money. But we finally made some connections thanks to Claude's expertise in cryptology and her experience at the NSA. Once we began tracking Karam's Gulfstream and could pinpoint his whereabouts, we confirmed he would be at his home in Ohio this morning."

"Adam, I don't want to be petulant, but I already know all that. I wrote the client briefs while that was unfolding. That still doesn't explain the aborted raid. Or am I missing something?"

"Patience is all you're missing," Adam said. "I'm getting to it. When Obama came into office in 2009, he inherited the wars in Iraq and Afghanistan. He wanted to begin shifting intelligence and military resources from the Middle East to Southeast Asia, where he saw China's expansion of activities as a growing threat to global security. This is your area of expertise, Kip."

Kip raised his chin and eyebrows, offering his most patient look.

Adam continued, "The administration's biggest obstacle to getting the U.S. disengaged from the Middle East is Iran and its proxies, Hizbullah being its largest and most organized. Obama's State Department is carefully laying the groundwork to negotiate a nuclear deal with Iran that will limit, or even halt, its enrichment of uranium for use in nuclear warheads. Once that is secured, the U.S. can gradually end its two wars and leave behind a greatly reduced threat from Iran's aggression in the Middle East. Obama's national security team has warned that further crackdowns against Hizbullah might destabilize Lebanon now that they are part of its ruling government. That could alienate Iran at what Obama sees as the critical early stages of talks."

"I'm with you so far," Kip said.

"Obama appointed Lisa Monaco as his counterterrorism and homeland security advisor in January. She has been advising

Obama's team that further crackdowns against Hizbullah could result in retaliatory terrorist actions against the U.S. and further destabilize Lebanon and the prospects of a deal with Iran. Senior officials at the State Department and National Security Council have been shutting down, derailing, or delaying Hizbullah-related cases without explanation. That has become the established internal policy of the Obama administration, which is why our client's raid was aborted."

"But the good news is, we've demonstrated our credibility to our client," Claudia said. "We've shown we can deliver on what we've been hired to do."

Adam laughed and said, "That's right, Musketeers. Onward and upwards. One for all…"

"And all for one!" chimed Claudia and Kip.

Bogotá, Colombia

Elias accompanied Ahmed on many of his trips and was busy preparing his boss's supper as the Gulfstream crossed over Cuba on their five-hour flight to Bogotá. Ahmed had configured his plane with four seats in the front of the cabin—two on each side, facing each other—and two smaller seats against the rear wall, across from the banquette where he enjoyed quick naps on his longer journeys. Ahmed was seated at the front and working from the pull-down table.

"Would you like a drink with your dinner, sir?" Elias asked.

"No, thank you. But I would like a glass of the 2006 Pétrus Bordeaux. I need to make a call before I eat, so please wait on the food."

It was only 6:30 on Wednesday morning in Guangzhou, but Ahmed knew his associate would take his call. Ahmed was an important client. Ahmed needed information before he arrived in Bogotá, and he had been waiting to phone after the FBI's visit that morning. Li Chen was Ahmed's associate at Guangzhou Manufacturing and would have answers to his questions.

Chen was awake when he saw Ahmed's name on his cell phone. "Good morning, Mr. Karam. I mean, good evening. Everything okay?"

"Thank you for taking my call so early. Mr. Li, I have more questions about the eight containers seized in Oakland last year. You said the containers were diverted to the Foster & Young vessel at the last minute, leaving two days early to avoid bad weather. The tropical storm, Sanba, was one of the largest of the decade, and it had already started to form when our vessel left port. It seems every ship at the Hong Kong port was at risk of being delayed in transit that week. Strangely, your logistics people thought there was an advantage to shipping our containers early. When we followed up with Menzer, the original shipper, their logistics manager said he had made the change at their client's request, Guangzhou Manufacturing. Did your company make that request?"

Chen waited a moment before answering. He remembered his call to Kenny Shiu after the containers had been seized, and he had instructed him to say the change was made in the best interest of Karam's company. He understood why Karam would be suspicious and agreed that something was wrong. "That is what I was told. Our man inside Menzer is the senior logistics manager, who has worked with us for many years. I have no reason to think he would lie to me."

"I now have reason to believe that Mr. Shiu may have lied. He may be working for one of my competitors in the U.S. People can be tempted to do dishonest things if a sufficient bribe is offered and if they believe they will not be caught. My company is ready to begin placing orders with you again, and I need to be sure our distribution network is solid from end to end. That begins with your company. What is its new name?"

"Pearl River Industries, at the same address. Only the registered business owners have changed. Beijing has provided their names to us. I am still the managing director."

"Good. That gives me confidence about things on your side and mine. We have new distribution partners in some important markets and plan to increase the quantity of our orders after a few test shipments. But before we resume purchasing, I must ensure things are in order at your port. I want two of my associates to leave tonight for Hong Kong and meet with your man at Menzer, in private. Can you please give me his name and address? My men will arrive on the afternoon of the fifth and will meet with him after he leaves work. Please do not let him know, in case he has reason to avoid such a meeting. Agreed?"

"Yes, Mr. Karam. Agreed. His name is Kenny Shiu, 126 Caldecott Hill, in Kowloon. Do you want a phone number?"

"No need, just give me a description. My men will find him."

Birmingham, Michigan

Rhonda had become Sophia's closest friend and confidant over the years. They were relaxing with a glass of pinot grigio in Sophia's living room and discussing new interior design trends when Rhonda changed the conversation. "Sophia, you seem a bit down tonight. Withdrawn. Is everything okay?"

"You know me too well. Yes, I'm struggling with something at work and could use some advice. In the ten years I've been counseling grieving families, I have always found it easy to make a connection with them, especially the mothers who have lost a child or their husband. It takes a while with each one, but I always find something to get hold of and use as a common thread to link us. I think I can do that because my empathy is unconditional."

"That's why you are so good at what you do. You truly care and can relate to what they are going through on a very personal level. You've told me many times you sometimes feel guilty because it seems you are getting more from the counseling sessions than your clients are."

"But things are different with the woman I am counseling now, and I am ashamed to say why."

"Because of the guilt feelings?"

"No, I think I have finally come to terms with those. This is different. I am having trouble connecting with my client because she is Muslim. Rhonda, I know this sounds horrible, but whenever she talks about the tragic death of her husband, also a Muslim, all I can envision are the faces of the terrorists who murdered Conrad. I can't summon up feelings of empathy for him. It's as if my subconscious is still seeking retribution against the Muslims who killed Conrad, even though I know I am prejudicing an entire group of people who are as kind and loving as anyone else. But because of that, I'm unable to relate to my client in the same way I have with others. I've had three sessions with her, and I can tell she is having trouble getting comfortable with me and trusting me fully. I don't know how to get through this."

"I know you must protect her confidentiality, but since I don't know who your client is, can you tell me how her husband died?"

"That's part of what makes this so hard. Their family was sitting at a sidewalk café in Dearborn in July. Their two children went inside to get ice cream, and my client realized they had no money, so she got up to follow them in. Just as she stepped through the door, an anti-Muslim fanatic swerved his car off the road and crashed into the patio. A dozen people were seriously injured, and three people died before making it to the emergency room: a mother, her six-year-old son, and my client's husband. Rhonda, this poor woman watched her husband be savagely murdered in front of her children, just as I had. If anyone can understand the trauma she experienced and the monumental challenge it is to live with that every day, taking care of not only her own needs but also those of her two children, I am that person. I'm trained and experienced in how to counsel her, but I'm holding something back. I'm not giving her one hundred percent, and I'm afraid she can tell. Part of me thinks I should ask her to see a different counselor, but I would never forgive myself for giving up on her like that. What should I do?"

"Keep going. You understand your challenge, and I think you know the solution. You need to see your client as a fellow human being who is suffering and take yourself out of the equation. You still have work to do to let go of your anger toward the men who murdered Conrad, and that includes getting past your association of all Muslim men with those terrorists. You know intellectually that it is a minority of Islamists who adhere to radical beliefs about destroying Western societies. Your brain tries to make things comprehensible by identifying a place to direct your anger and finding someone to blame. Don't fight that, accept it for how the mind copes and keep looking to your client and figuring out *her* needs, independent of yours. Then you will do the right thing. You said when you began studying this field that you wanted to help others as a way to help yourself. This is part of that journey, and I think it's a path worth taking."

"Thanks for that, Rhonda. I knew talking to you would help."

"I love you, girlfriend. Any time."

They heard the garage door close and turned to see Claudia coming in from the kitchen, sporting a bright smile.

"Hi, *Mamá*. Hi, Rhonda. You two look all cozy with your feet up, wine glasses in hand," Claudia said.

"We're enjoying a nice chat and catching up," Sophia said. "You're home late for a Tuesday. Long day at work?"

"Actually, no. Our team wrapped up the project we've been working on for the past two years, and the client is pleased with our results. Adam is certain we will get new projects from them and other organizations they work with. Custom Solutions Group is a real success now, and Adam is thrilled, as far as anyone can tell with Adam. So, we closed up shop shortly after three and left for the day. Adam was leaving for wherever he goes when he isn't working, and Kip and I went for a walk through the parks and around the lake. I'm going upstairs to freshen up and then leaving to meet Kip for dinner at the Hyde Park Grill."

"Well, congratulations, *mi cielo*. Get a glass and have a seat, we'll toast your team's success. Adam said he would be stopping by to install new updates on my laptop, so perhaps he can join us."

"Maybe on my way out. I've got to go up and change," Claudia said as she headed toward the stairs.

Rhonda could not contain her curiosity and said, "Is it just me, Sophia, or is Claudia becoming enthralled with Kip? Her face lights up whenever she says his name, and her eyes sparkle. Do you think things are getting serious with their relationship? You know, that they are becoming more than just great friends?"

"Oh, I hope so, Rhonda. I hope so. Claudia shared with me how terrified she is of falling in love with a man and then losing him. Conrad loved Claudia deeply, but that is the only experience she's had of being loved by a man. It makes sense that she is unable to trust that she won't be devastated again by losing a man's love. My heart has been aching for her every day. I pray she might finally be able to conquer her fear. I adore Kip and would give anything to have him as my son-in-law. He already feels like part of the family."

Ten minutes later, Adam turned the key to the front door and walked through the foyer wearing denim jeans, a navy polo shirt, and tan construction boots—not his customary look. As he turned toward the living room, Claudia swept down the steps and, with extended arms, said, "We're not at work now, *mon frère*, so like it or not, I'm giving you a hug. I am so proud of how you led our team to victory on this project!"

Claudia stepped back from the hug and said, "Did you change your cologne? I could swear you smell like 'horse.'"

"And you smell like fresh flowers. Got a date?"

"Nope. I'm just meeting Kip for dinner, he agrees we have something to celebrate. He said he has everything he needs to begin writing an article about the Asian link between South American drug cartels and Middle East terrorist networks. He even has a contact at *The Atlantic* who is interested in publishing it."

Claudia said her goodbyes and left through the kitchen. Adam turned to Sophia and Rhonda and said confidently, "She will marry that man. Just watch."

Bogotá, Colombia

The Gulfstream rolled to a stop in front of the private air terminal at El Dorado International Airport shortly before eight p.m. Ahmed's black Yukon Denali and two Colombian-based associates, Alejandro and Sebastian, waited planeside.

"Elias, these men will not come to the house with us. They will be traveling on the flights you just booked. Please drive us to the departures terminal for Emirates to let them out, and then we will go to the house."

"Yes, sir," Elias said as he opened the large golf umbrella. It was typical subtropical weather for a September evening in Bogotá, with clouds hovering above the Andean plateau and depositing a steady, warm rain. Elias thought about his home village in Lebanon, where it would be hot and dry. *I miss my family and country, but Mr. Karam is a fair man, gives me a good life, and sends my family money to ensure they have enough.* Alhamdulillah—*Praise be to Allah.* It was Elias's way of alleviating his guilt for abetting his boss's underworld business dealings.

Both men stepped out of the Yukon to greet Ahmed, and he signaled for them to get in the backseat. He sat up front with Elias and turned around to say, "Your flight to Dubai departs at ten-thirty, and you will pick up your tickets at the counter. The flight from there to Hong Kong is also on Emirates, and you will arrive at three-forty-five Hong Kong time on Thursday afternoon. That gives you time to clear immigration and customs before meeting with Mr. Shiu. Hong Kong does not require visas for Colombian citizens, so you will pass through quickly. Here is his address. Take a taxi to his home and wait in the park directly across the street from his condominium building. He will come from the Lai Chi Kok subway station shortly after seven. I have been assured he will be wearing a lightweight navy nylon jacket with the white Menzer logo front and back, and he will be carrying a vinyl letter carrier with the Menzer logo. He is a proud company man, and this has been his uniform for twenty years. Do whatever is needed to get the truth. If he is double-crossing our supplier and working with one of our competitors, he will pay the price for his betrayal. But we will leave that to our friends in Guangzhou."

Ahmed's home in Bogotá was a quarter of the size of his mansion in Hunting Valley, but it was equally elegant. Built high above the valley, the house was split into two levels, with the living areas on the top floor and the sleeping quarters, sauna, and indoor pool on the lower level. The modern architecture was a combination of stones—granite, marble, and grey brick—with various woods on the walls, floors, and ceiling. The most outstanding features were the floor-to-ceiling glass panes, framed in black stainless steel, offering sweeping views of the valley below.

Reaching his residence involved a two-mile drive up a winding road through a heavily wooded area dotted with gated entrances to homes that sat back from the road and out of view. It was an exclusive enclave for Bogotá's wealthiest residents, and each estate was guarded like a military encampment. Gaining entrance involved an identity check by armed guards who inspected the interior and trunk areas for weapons, while bomb-sniffing dogs circled the vehicles and men with mirrored wands scanned the undersides. After four decades of conflict between the Colombian government and the FARC, even the very wealthy were not safe. Over 20 thousand people had been kidnapped and ransomed by FARC forces as a way to fund their operations. Rich people like Ahmed could afford to live in these heavily secured enclaves, but the rest of Colombia's citizens could not.

Ahmed was greeted by his live-in housekeeper and cook, Mariana, a robust woman with greying hair tied in a bun and a face with more wrinkles than a woman in her 40s should have. Living in Ahmed's luxurious home provided Mariana with an escape from the poverty most people in Colombia endured. Still, she missed being with her family, often for days at a time. Ahmed paid her well in exchange for her pledge never to disclose the business discussions she would overhear when serving guests or tidying rooms where he worked. It was an arrangement that worked well for them both, and Mariana had looked after the home for 20 years.

"Would you like something to eat tonight, *señor* Karam?"

"No, thank you, Mariana. I am going to relax in my den before going to bed. Please bring me a cognac, the Delamain." As he settled into his chair in front of the fireplace, Ahmed saw the sprawling city below and thought: *There is so much poverty for so many people, a fate they cannot escape. Yet, from where I sit, I see only beauty in the sparkling lights and the expansive hilltops beyond the valley. Allah chooses who will enjoy such a life as mine. I am one of his chosen—an entitled one.* Alhamdulillah.

Thursday, the 5th

Hong Kong Special Administrative Region of the People's Republic of China

The day's rain had finally stopped when Kenny Shiu emerged from the subway. A light fog was blanketing his neighborhood, making the evening's humidity all the more oppressive. He debated stopping at the corner shop to pick up dinner but decided to go home and relax with a cold beer. It had been a busy day at the docks, and he still had some emails to respond to. He would go out later and eat a proper dinner in a restaurant.

After collecting his things from the lobby mailbox, Kenny punched his security code into the keypad when two unfamiliar men entered the glass entryway. He sensed something was wrong: these men were not Asian, and after 20 years of living here, he recognized most residents.

Sebastian, the taller, dark-complexioned man with black hair and a mustache, spoke first. "Good evening, Mr. Shiu. Did you have a productive day at the docks? Shame about all the rain." Kenny surmised from the man's accented English and Hispanic looks that he was most likely from South America, causing the hair on the back of his neck to stand on end.

The shorter man, Alejandro, wore a red baseball cap and black-framed glasses. He had his hands in the pockets of his navy windbreaker and opened the front just enough to expose the knife holstered to his hip. Anything could be acquired at the local markets if one knew where to shop. Glancing sideways at the security camera in the corner of the ceiling, he said, "Let's go outside and talk about your day. We want to learn some things about your work."

Kenny knew all about the underbelly of the drug trade he was clandestinely enabling, but he had never come face to face with any of its players. The game had just encroached on his home turf, and he was terrified. Rendered speechless, Kenny nodded as they opened the door to step outside. When there was a break in the traffic, the three men crossed the street and walked into the park, still busy with commuters and shoppers. Sebastian put his hand on Kenny's shoulder and leaned closer to say, "You would be foolish to call out or try to run. My friend is very quick with his hands and is quite skilled at carving. It would be a shame if you were to lose any fingers tonight. Answer our questions, and we'll be on our way. Then you can tell Mr. Li all about our chat. He'll be interested in knowing how things went." Hearing Li's name sent shivers down Kenny's spine.

They stopped in front of a bench about two hundred feet inside the wooded path, and Sebastian said, "No need to sit, Mr. Shiu. This won't take long. We only have one question. Did you mistakenly share information with anyone in the U.S., perhaps with someone who has contacts at their DEA or Customs and Border Patrol in Oakland? You are aware that eight of our clients' containers did not make it to their destination last year, and we cannot figure out how the authorities in Oakland knew our shipment had been diverted at the last minute. Only you, Mr. Shiu, could have known about the change, so only you could have leaked that information. Of course, it would be extremely dangerous for you to do something like that. Double-crossing Mr. Li would have grave consequences, but sometimes men make bad decisions when offered handsome bribes or promised a more lucrative career path. Was that the case, Mr. Shiu? Is that what you've done? You can answer honestly. We would not hurt you too badly right here, too many people around. Punishment would come directly from our mutual boss and his friends."

Kenny's brain raced to find an answer. If he disclosed that he had been duped by the alleged Steve Norris, or Kilpatrick Reynolds, he would be exposed as a fool, losing both face and his job. Mr. Li obviously had reason to disbelieve his excuse about a typhoon being the reason the shipment to Oakland was diverted, so repeating the lie would not work. Unable to reply without stammering, Kenny said, "I would never betray Mr. Li. I have worked with him for many years, and he has always been good to me. I am a loyal man, and he knows it. But I think I know who it might have been if someone tipped off the authorities in Oakland. The problem is, this man left Hong Kong last year."

"I'm sure you can be quite resourceful, Mr. Shiu, having been in this line of work for so long. We need you to give us his name and tell us how we can locate him. He didn't find his way to you and your docks without some local assistance. There are many questions to be answered by this man, so you can understand how important it is that when talking to your local contacts, nobody tips off the tipster that our boss wants to meet with him. If that should happen, this meeting of ours will soon be nothing but a fond memory. I'd hate to think what would come next for you. Don't delay, Mr. Shiu, we need your information before we fly out on the weekend. We will meet you here at nine a.m. on Saturday. That gives you an entire day to do your job. Have a nice evening, Mr. Shiu."

White Sulphur Springs, West Virginia

Glenda wrapped up a hectic day at the resort, and although exhausted, she stuck to her plan and swung by her house to pick up the German chocolate cake she had baked for Ryan's 30th birthday. He had declined her invitation to a party at the house, saying he would rather spend the evening at home with Jenny than risk another blow-up with his father. Ryan rarely went to his parents' house these days, as most visits ended in an argument between Hank and Ryan. Hank would say Ryan looked dragged down, Ryan would say he was tired from work, Hank would suggest Ryan drink less and knock off taking the pain pills, Ryan would accuse him of calling the kettle black, and Ryan would storm out. Glenda wondered how long it would be before the two came to blows.

Glenda arrived at Jenny's shortly before six, and Jenny told her that Ryan had stopped at The Rusty Nail after work to have a quick drink with friends. Glenda placed the cake on the kitchen counter and waited a moment before saying, "Jenny, dear, I hope I ain't out of line sayin' this, but Ryan's behavior these days concerns me. I thought gettin' that job at the resort might help set him straight, you know, have him pull back on the drinkin' every day. I know you're doin' all you can to help him, but he seems, I don't know, addicted to his bad habits. I'm worried about him and wonder if there's anythin' I can do to help."

Jenny said, "Do you have a few minutes to talk? I have something important to tell you."

"Of course, dear. What is it?"

"Ryan and I thought it might be best to move away for a bit, you know, go somewhere to get a fresh start. I know how much you love him and how hard it would be to see us go, but it wouldn't be forever, just long enough to get himself right in a new environment, meet new people, see new things, get a good job. I don't mean to be disrespectful, Glenda, but I also think Ryan needs to get away from his father. Don't be upset with me, but I think Hank and Ryan are like water and oil. No matter how hard we try to help, they just aren't going to mix. Not until something changes."

Glenda dropped her head and took a deep breath. "As hard as it would be for me if you two was to leave, I have to say, it is probably the best thing. Both those men have ferocious tempers, each for their own reasons, and when two angry men are put in a room together, it never ends good. And with them, it's harder cause they're kin. And you know what they say: 'You can choose your friends, but you can't choose your family.' They're stuck with each other, and I don't see how they will sort this out if somethin' don't change. It breaks my heart watchin' the two men I love most tryin' to let go of all that anger they still got from their time growin' up."

"Did Hank have it rough as a kid?"

"Oh, honey, it is almost too sad to talk about." Glenda was momentarily lost in her thoughts and then said, "But I'm gonna tell you so you can understand all that's goin' on." Glenda closed her eyes, took another deep breath, and began her story.

"Hank was seven years old when his father was drafted into that war in Vietnam. It was 1965, and he was 27. No sooner did he get deployed when his squadron got ambushed in the jungle. Twenty men was killed, including Hank's father. Hank's brother was nine, and the family lived in Whitwell, Tennessee. His father had worked at the Grundy Coal Mines. Their mother could never hold a job because of her struggles with drugs—heroin, I think—and they was dirt poor. When she heard her

husband had been killed, she went off the deep end and died of a drug overdose just two weeks later. Hank's grandma did her best to raise the two boys, but she was single. Her husband had ran out on her after losin' his job as a long-haul trucker—and they only got by on handouts from friends and family. Because both parents were dead, the VA's survivor's benefits never come through. Hank's mother barely made ends meet, and they never lived in the same place for more than a few months, so Hank never got proper schoolin'. When he turned 15, he dropped out, and usin' his brother's driver's license—it said he was seventeen—Hank got a job at the mines. And then the good Lord intervened. Right after Thanksgivin' in 1981, Hank got fed up with workin' the mines. He quit his job, moved here to live with his brother, and looked for different work. And do you know, on December eighth, durin' the night shift, there was 56 men in the mine, and one of 'em lit a cigarette and exploded the methane collected down there. Thirteen men died, and had somethin' not told Hank to quit when he did, he would have been workin' that night too. Praise God, he had left."

Jenny brushed a tear aside and said, "My God, Glenda. No wonder Hank struggles with his emotions, losing both parents at such a young age and being moved about so much. Those are horrible things for a child to deal with."

"I know it must seem to you like Hank is always angry with Ryan, but truth be told, he's not angry. He loves his children more than anythin' on this earth. What he is, though, is scared, scared they won't be strong enough to deal with whatever life sends their way. That's why he put all that pressure on Ryan as a boy to be strong, to stand up for himself, to always win and never lose. It's because he wanted Ryan to have a better life than he had. But what scares Hank most is the drugs. He saw what they did to his mother, and he's terrified they may take Ryan from him, too. Hank loves his kids, sweetie, he would give his life for them."

Jenny walked toward Glenda and opened her arms for a hug. "Does Ryan know this?"

Glenda stepped into Jenny's embrace and said, "No, dear. Hank asked me never to tell the children. He says he don't want nobody feelin' sorry for him, least not his own kids. It's a matter of pride for him, showin' everyone that even when times is hard, he is strong. He says nobody needs to know about the past. Only the future matters."

"I can see why you stick by his side. He's a good man, Glenda, and you are a very strong woman. Thanks for letting me know all this. It helps a lot."

Friday, the 6th

Hong Kong Special Administrative Region of the People's Republic of China

The steady patter of rain on the car's roof irritated Kenny. He and his associate from Menzer, Tommy Chao, had been sitting in their parked car for almost an hour. It was easy enough to find a home address for Steve Norris after visiting his Facebook page. How foolish, Kenny thought, for Steve to post a picture of himself in front of his apartment block. A quick online search confirmed the address and included an apartment number: 502. They were about to meet the real Steve Norris, and Kenny had no way of knowing what they might encounter when they did. He had asked Tommy to accompany him in case Mr. Norris offered any resistance. Tommy had spent two decades serving as the strong man for groups like Li Chen's. The hole where his ear should have been and the scar along his neck were a testament to his resilience.

Shortly before 8:30, lights came on inside a small apartment on the fifth floor. Although they had not seen a Caucasian man enter the building, it had been the only activity on that floor during the past hour, so Kenny decided to take a chance. He and Tommy entered the lobby and pretended to be looking for something in Kenny's satchel, making conversation about the weather. Two minutes later, an older woman carrying groceries walked in, and both men stepped to the side to let her in. As the door closed, Kenny stuck his foot to hold it open and feigned typing a security code into the pad. They waited for the next elevator, each of them pulling on a pair of surgical gloves as they proceeded to the fifth floor.

What they did not know was that Steve had been living for the past year with his girlfriend, Susan Wang. Susan was expecting Steve to come home any minute, as he had stopped on their way from dinner to fill a prescription. When she heard the knock, she assumed Steve had forgotten his key and opened the door without looking to see who it was.

"Sorry, you must have the wrong apartment," Susan said.

"Does Steve Norris live here?" Kenny asked.

"Yes, but he's not expecting anyone. Can I help you?"

Kenny pushed Susan into the apartment without answering, and Tommy shut the door behind them. "I don't believe you can," Kenny said. "We need information from Mr. Norris that only he can provide."

Knowing this was not a friendly visit and anxious to get the intimidating men to leave, Susan tried to placate them. "I am his fiancée and can provide you with any information Steve might have. Tell me what you need to know and then leave before I call the police." Susan hoped the line at the pharmacy was short and that Steve would arrive while she stalled for time.

"Well, perhaps you *can* help. Has your fiancé ever mentioned the name Kilpatrick Reynolds? He may be a work associate of Steve's."

Susan immediately knew the purpose of their visit. "No. He has never mentioned the name. I'm afraid I can't help you. Now leave before I scream for help."

Tommy reached into his jacket pocket and pulled out a wadded sock and a roll of duct tape. "Please don't make me silence you, miss. This doesn't need to be difficult. Just tell us the truth, and we'll be on our way."

Kenny said, "You are lying. Mr. Reynolds visited me last year at my work, but he was lying as well. He said he was Steve Norris from the Hong Kong Trade Development Council and wanted to interview me. We learned Mr. Reynolds owned the Sunny Luck Trading Company here in Hong Kong, but we believe he has closed the business and returned to his home in the United States. We would like to know how to get in contact with him. We have some unfinished business to settle."

After learning Kip's alias had been broken, Susan had put her fears to rest. After a year, she assumed the incident had unfolded without any problems. Kip had said she would only hear from him if he felt she was in danger of being associated with the con. Apparently, his silence was not an assurance of that. To protect Steve, Susan said, "Steve had nothing to do with this. I was the one who set up the interview for Mr. Reynolds. He never said why he wanted the interview, but he believed he would only be granted one if an organization like the Trade Development Council requested it. So, I called on Steve's behalf and set it up. That's all I know."

"And what is your name?" Kenny asked.

"Susan."

"Well, Susan, you obviously know how to contact Mr. Reynolds. So, give us his information, and we will be on our way. No need for us to bother your fiancé."

"I've lost touch with Mr. Reynolds. When he returned to the States, he changed his email address and phone number, and I haven't spoken with him since."

Kenny saw a laptop on the kitchen counter and said, "Is that your laptop, Susan?"

"Yes."

"Good. Let's try a little experiment. Open your email and search for 'Kilpatrick Reynolds'; perhaps something from the past will appear."

Susan was terrified. She hadn't cleared her files in over a year. "We only communicated by phone, and only a few times. I don't remember any emails."

"Well, that's the beauty of our digital age. There's no need to remember anything, the software does that for us. Now be a good girl and type in his name."

The result was worse than she feared. The email read:

> *Tuesday, September 7, 2012 at 15:32*
> *SWang@hku.hk.edu*
> *To: Kip Reynolds*
> *All set. Your interview is at 4 p.m. Go to the main*
> *reception on Mai Ching Rd and ask for Kenny Shiu.*
> *He's expecting you. Good luck.*

"And look at that," Kenny said. "Technology really is our friend. With your memory now jogged, you can go ahead and give me 'Kip' Reynolds' phone number. I've had enough of the lying. To make sure you aren't experiencing another memory lapse, why don't you give me your phone, and I'll see for myself if you have his number?"

Susan felt a wave of panic when she realized Kip had phoned her on his new cell as soon as he returned to the States, and she had put his number into her contacts. She was unable to speak.

"Give me your phone, Susan. We are done playing games." His piercing look told her Kenny was out of patience, and Tommy was beginning to extend the roll of tape.

Kenny glanced at the table in the small breakfast nook and saw an iPhone. He removed his right glove and opened Susan's contacts list, finding Kip's name among the many listed under 'K.' Searching the call history, he saw one from Kip dated September 18, 2012, the day after Kip returned to Birmingham and was given a new phone. Kip had misunderstood Adam when he said to stop sending texts from his old phone and stop making any calls. He thought Adam had meant only from that phone. Kip had been too embarrassed to admit he had called Susan from the new phone and decided all would be well as long as he made no more calls to her.

Kenny slid Susan's phone into his jacket and gave Tommy a nod. Tommy came up from behind Susan, pushed one of the four straight-backed kitchen chairs into the back of her knees, and pushed her shoulders down. Before she could yell, Kenny came from the front and inserted his own balled-up sock into her mouth. Tommy pulled her arms back, and Kenny held her while Tommy bound her wrists with duct tape. Tommy then wrapped the tape around her torso, strapping her to the chair, and said to Kenny, "This is not what we expected, and we still have Mr. Norris to deal with, but this woman is an accomplice and needs to be taken care of as well."

Kenny and Tommy turned when they heard the click of a key in the front door and saw a man resembling Kip Reynolds walk in: Steve Norris. Kenny bolted toward Steve and wrestled his arms behind his back. With Susan immobilized, Tommy approached Steve and stuffed a wadded sock into his mouth. Kenny and Tommy bound Steve to a kitchen chair as they had done with Susan. Kenny turned to Tommy and said, "Today must be our lucky day. Only two people in this city know what happened to our special shipment last year, and here they are, in the same room. Now that we have what we need to find their associate, Mr. Reynolds, we can wrap things up and assure our boss that we have eliminated the source of his problems."

Susan and Steve locked eyes, sharing looks of terrified anticipation. Would these men simply take her phone and leave them to struggle free while they made their escape? The answer came in less than a minute. Kenny and Tommy hadn't anticipated Susan being in the apartment, their plan had only included dealing with Steve. Tommy had already taken the clear plastic bag from his jacket when Kenny realized they would now need two. He scanned the room and spotted a thick plastic shopping bag on the kitchen counter for toting glass bottles to and from the markets. It would have to do. As Kenny emptied the bag, Tommy snapped his own through the air, billowing it full, and lifted it above Steve's head. Susan began struggling violently as she watched Tommy drop the bag over Steve's head and start wrapping the tape around his neck. Kenny held the back of Susan's chair to keep it from tipping and then covered her head with his bag. After three tight turns of the tape around Steve's neck, Tommy cut it with a pocketknife and stepped toward Susan to do the same. Kenny and Tommy held down the chairs until the thrashing slowed, and after another minute, their victims' suffocated bodies went limp, and the room went silent.

After waiting another minute, Kenny said, "I think Mr. Li will be pleased. We've done a thorough job of cleaning up any mess our friend from America may have made. We can deliver the iPhone to our out-of-town visitors tomorrow morning, and then rest assured they will handle everything else Stateside. Our work is done here. Time for a nice cold beer."

Bogotá, Colombia

It was one o'clock in the afternoon at the El Chato Bistró off of Calle 65 in central Bogotá. Ahmed Karam was seated at a table at the back of the elegant restaurant. He spoke quietly with an associate, a dark-skinned, overweight man with slicked-back hair, a narrow nose, and perfect white teeth that glowed in the dimly lit corner. His gold jewelry suggested wealth.

Ahmed said, "So, Miguel, our supplier in Guangzhou has restarted operations, and our shipping arrangements with Menzer at the Hong Kong port are still in place. I need an idea of the quantities you plan to order for your new network. Have you made all the changes?"

"Yes. It looks like our friends from Mexico relocated their operations to Raleigh after we 'removed' their distributor in Charleston. We have been able to expand operations through our hub in Knoxville. We recruited one of the Mexicans' previous dealers from West Virginia, Tobias Furth, and we are delivering product to him through that hub."

"That is our fruit and vegetable wholesaler, correct?"

"Yes."

"Will we continue to deliver sporting goods and other 'supplies' from China to the youth center near Knoxville, as before? We must keep our local factory well stocked," Ahmed said.

"Yes, sir. No changes there."

"Except the Chinese manufacturer is now doing business as Pearl River Industries," Ahmed said. "Otherwise, it is business as usual with shipments from Hong Kong coming through the California ports and the containers being delivered by truck."

A waiter approached as Ahmed's phone rang, and Ahmed signaled him to go away. "Good morning, Mr. Shiu. It is quite early for you. Are you phoning with good news at one in the morning?"

"Good afternoon, Mr. Karam. I have the name and phone number of the individual who identified and tracked our shipment last year. His name is Kilpatrick Reynolds, and he has left Hong Kong and moved back to the U.S., where he is now based. He goes by the name Kip. I am meeting your associates this morning before they return to Bogotá, and I am giving them a phone with his contact information in it. Please be assured that we secured the phone without leaving any witnesses behind, a nice, clean job."

Ahmed said, "Very nice work, Mr. Shiu. I am meeting with someone now who can help us locate this man in the U.S. Once we do, we will take it from there. We look forward to continuing our business with you. I'll be in touch."

Ahmed waved the waiter over and turned to Miguel. "Do you know the name, Kip Reynolds?"

"No. That name is not familiar. Should I know him?"

"No. But once you locate him, we will get to know him well. If he works for a competitor, I fear Mr. Reynolds will soon be unemployed." Both men grinned with pleasure at the prospect of exacting revenge on the group they believed had taken out their operations on that rainy night near the Charleston rail yards.

Saturday, the 7th

Bloomfield Hills, Michigan

The Bloomfield Hills Country Club was built in 1909, with its main clubhouse in the antebellum style, framed with white columns, wrap-around lattice balconies on both floors, and sweeping views of the golf course's 18th hole. Dudley's grandparents were some of the first members, and Dudley had spent his boyhood playing golf there with his father and friends. Before launching into the world of polo and spending most of his time at the stables, Kip was there for swimming and tennis during the summers and joined his parents for lunches and dinners throughout the year. Patty had long ago tired of the club's menu choices, but her lack of culinary skills and a roster full of social events precluded her from cooking at home, so eating at the club was convenient. Although Dudley was fond of good scotch, exceptional cuisine was never a priority, and he settled for whatever was put in front of him, hamburgers and fries being a favorite.

Patty had invited Kip and Claudia to join them for lunch, and with temperatures in the 90s, she opted for a table in the paneled room adjacent to the outdoor terrace with views of the golf course. Patty stood from her leather captain's chair to greet them, and after exchanging air kisses, she commented on Claudia's tasteful cotton sundress and the French braid in her hair. Kip wore a powder blue polo shirt with khaki slacks, his club uniform.

Claudia extended her hand and said, "Thank you so much for the invitation, Mrs. Reynolds. It's the perfect day to be inside. Hopefully, the heat wave will break soon. Will Mr. Reynolds be joining us?"

"Yes, dear. He's changing from golf and will be right up."

With her brightest smile, Claudia said, "You are the picture of health, Mrs. Reynolds. It's hard to believe you had been so ill."

Patty had recently been diagnosed as cancer-free, and her hair was now a full six inches long. Vanity required her to still wear a platinum blond wig, stylishly secured with a black velvet headband and pulled back in its customary ponytail with a pearl-studded clip. Patty had not regained the last ten pounds she had lost through recovery, and her diamond and sapphire bracelet occasionally slipped off her wrist. Claudia saw Patty catching the bracelet as she sat down and said, "I have always admired your bracelet, Mrs. Reynolds. I'm so glad you can still wear it, it seems quite special to you."

"How observant, it *is* special. Dudley gave it to me on our 10th anniversary after discovering it at a jeweler's in Birmingham. I badgered him to buy it until he caved. It was right after his father passed away, when we moved into our home, and I said if we were going to go broke taking care of that behemoth of a house, then I wanted to enjoy my last gift of jewelry." Patty's laugh told Claudia the comment was her way of expressing appreciation for Dudley's generosity. The bracelet had been very expensive.

Dudley arrived in the dining room and stopped by the bar to order his drink. Kip and Claudia stood as he approached the table and noticed that the small ducks Dudley typically sported on his trousers had been moved to his woven belt: yellow ducks on a green background that matched his pants. His polo shirt was a bright yellow and featured the Club's logo on the pocket.

"It's nice to see you again, Claudia. Kip tells us you've all been busy at work and have just completed a big assignment. Congratulations. It sounds like you both will enjoy our upcoming vacation."

"I'm thrilled to be coming along. Thank you for inviting me," Claudia said. "And I'm looking forward to meeting Bradley's fiancée. It's great they can join us."

Patty said, "Everything is set for our arrival on the 13th. I phoned the Greenbrier this morning, and they confirmed we could get three of their lovely cottages, all next to each other. They each have two bedrooms with private baths, so we should be more than comfortable. Mr. Reynolds' friends from Pinehurst will also be there, but they are staying in the main building. The cottages were booked out when they finally made reservations. Typical for Dudley's friends, always waiting until the last minute."

"And you have the flights confirmed as well?" Dudley asked.

"Of course I do. Since there are six of us, I chartered the Citation Sovereign. Bradley and the girl fly into the Detroit airport on the evening of the 12th and will stay with us that night. Kip, dear, will you pick up Claudia the next morning and drive yourselves to Pontiac?"

"Sure thing, Mom. And thanks again for planning this and including Claudia and my little brother's fiancée. What did you say her name is?"

"Gold Digger, I suspect. Sorry, just my gut feeling. Anyhow, I hope Bradley knows what he's doing. He's a sitting duck for women like her," Patty said with a sneer.

"Should we just call her Goldie? Or maybe, Diggs?" Kip asked.

"Just kidding, son. Dudley, what's her name?"

Dudley was preoccupied with tasting his drink and hadn't heard Patty.

"Dudley! Her name? The girl's name?"

"The server? I think it's Melanie. Why? Did you want to order?"

"Oh, for heaven's sake," Patty said. "You are impossible."

Kip reached under the table for Claudia's hand and squeezed it as he addressed his mother. "It should be a great time. Thanks again for including us." A wave of excitement passed through Claudia's body at the touch of Kip's hand, and she hoped this trip would be the first step on a romantic journey through a long future together.

Tuesday, the 9ᵗʰ

Birmingham, Michigan

The swooshing of car tires on the wet pavement below Adam's apartment was relaxing. There had been a steady rain all afternoon, and the smells of summer were coming in through the open sliding door leading to the small balcony. Adam had stepped out an hour earlier and said he would be back by four, leaving Kip and Claudia engrossed in their laptop screens as they wrapped up work for the day. Kip was clearing out his spam folder and emptying the trash in preparation for their trip to the Greenbrier on Friday morning. It would be an opportunity to shift gears, relax, and spend quality time with Claudia and his family. He did not want any open items to deal with. There was plenty to celebrate between his mother's recovery and their success at work.

Curious to know how things were going with Susan Wang in Hong Kong, Kip had set up a Google alert for any posts made to the University of Hong Kong's website about their Foreign Studies programs. He wanted to know if Susan was scheduled for any lectures or had perhaps published an article.

Kip was moving quickly through his emails and clicking the delete button with gusto until he saw the subject line, "Dr. Wang Lecture Cancelled." He clicked it open and read the short announcement.

> *It is with sorrow that we announce the cancelation*
> *of Dr. Wang's September 16 lecture on 'The Future*
> *of Sino-Japanese Trade Relations.' We were*

advised today of Dr. Wang's untimely passing and wish to join our academic community in expressing condolences to her family and friends.

The sudden wail of sirens on the street below jangled Kip's nerves as he re-read the email. He tried to block out the noise as the shock settled in: Susan was dead. *Had she been ill?* They hadn't communicated in almost a year, and although they had become friendly during the two years Kip lived in Hong Kong, she would not have considered him a close friend. Perhaps she had been sick and did not think to reach out and let him know. But the wrenching feeling in his gut told him it was probably not a coincidence that Susan had died immediately after the raid on Ahmed's home. He propped his elbows on the desk and buried his face in his palms. *How could Ahmed have possibly linked Susan to the raid?* As more emergency vehicles barreled past the building, Kip slipped his palms to his ears to dampen the sound of a firetruck's blasting horn. *Even though my alias as Steve Norris had been broken, how could Ahmed have made the connection between Susan and Steve?* Kip let out a deep breath with a long sigh. *Did Susan die because of me, because I asked her for help? Is this my fault?*

Claudia looked across their desks and could see that Kip was distressed. She got up and stepped onto the balcony, looking north on Woodward Avenue to see what was happening. Sliding the door closed as she walked back in, she said, "Why is it that whenever it rains, people become idiots and forget how to drive? Two cars have spun around and are crumpled in the middle of the road, with a third lying on its side. Dozens of cars are stopped behind the wreck, and the ambulances can't get through. This won't get cleared up for some time. Good thing we can take the back streets home."

Kip raised his head, and through squinted eyes rapidly filling with tears, he told Claudia about the email. Unable to make out his words above the drone of the sirens, she walked to his side and asked him to repeat them. As Kip shared his remorse at the possibility he had brought about this tragedy, Claudia slid Adam's chair over to Kip's side of the desk and sat in front of him. She took his hands and said, "Kip, we have no way of knowing what happened. I understand your concern about being responsible, but until we have answers, you can't jump to conclusions."

The ding of the elevator's bell announced Adam's arrival before entering the apartment, his hair soaked and jacket dripping. "Glad I took the back streets, it's a real mess on Woodward. What's with all the sirens?" He saw the distraught looks on their faces and fell silent as he waited for someone to speak. Claudia wanted to spare Kip the pain of telling Adam about Susan's death, so she gave him the news.

Kip was staring off in a daze, and Claudia lifted his hands, inviting him to stand. She put her arms around him and leaned to his ear, "We'll get to the truth, don't worry, and regardless of what we find, you have us to support you. Remember, one for all and all for one."

Adam walked over and put a hand on each of their shoulders. "I'll get to the bottom of this, and regardless of what I find, remember: we are getting retribution against terrorists who've murdered innocent people and destroyed the lives of those who love them. Rest assured, if they took Susan's life, Ahmed and the people he works with will eventually have their downfall, and we are doing our part to ensure that. This isn't over yet. There's more work to be done."

Claudia looked at Kip and then back at Adam. "Should we cancel our trip to the Greenbrier so we can stay and help?"

"No. I'll need a few days to access the Hong Kong Hospital Authority databases to see if Susan had ever been admitted. I'll also try to get into the Hong Kong Police Force records. And although it may not be filed yet, I'll scan for a death certificate at the General Register Office. I can do all that while you're away, and we can figure out our next steps once you're back. I'm afraid it will take a while. That's a lot of databases to hack into."

Kip said, "I'm going to head home and try to get my brain around this. I'll pick you up in the morning as planned, Claude. Mom scheduled the plane for ten, so I'll see you around nine-thirty."

"Did you drive here?" she asked.

"No. It was sunny when I left this morning, so I walked."

"So did I. Adam, can you give Kip a lift home?"

"Sure. Give me a minute to change my shirt."

Kip stuffed his laptop into its case and said, "Thanks, Adam. I'm good. I'll take the umbrella. It's a light rain now, and I could use the air. I've got a lot to process."

Claudia hugged Kip and told him to call her if he needed to talk. As soon as Kip walked out, Claudia asked Adam, "How do you know the names of the agencies and offices in Hong Kong where the records are kept? You were pretty specific."

"I monitor all our phone records and had seen that Kip placed a quick call to Susan the day after he returned from Hong Kong. It was the first call he made on his new phone. I immediately reminded Kip he was not to phone Susan, and without admitting he already had, he promised he would not call. It was a lie by omission. I trusted Kip would not phone her again, so I let it go. However, understanding the danger Susan was in, I started checking some of the police databases to see if there were any incidents involving either Susan, her boyfriend, or even Kenny. I haven't checked in since the attempted raid at Ahmed's, and until now, I had no need to look at hospital records or death certificates. I'll be honest, Sis, I have a bad feeling about this. Really bad."

Thursday, the 12th

Mapledale, West Virginia

Ryan's weekday landscaping job at the Greenbrier was going well, and Jenny made sure he never missed a day. It was a challenge after a night of drinking, especially if he took pain pills to help him sleep. He suffered the adverse effects the next morning from combining alcohol with pain pills: tiredness, irritability, and mood swings. However, he drank less often, and Jenny saw it as a sign of progress when Ryan asked if he could join her at night and share her bed. He was gradually coming out of what had been a drug-induced lethargy, one that had suppressed his libido and rendered him physically incapable of making love to her. At least now, they were intimate in every way, giving Jenny a ray of hope that Ryan might eventually get well.

Even with his health improving, the past year had been more stressful than any he had known, including the one following his train accident. Two months after Tobias slaughtered Roy and Ryan had gone through the anguish of burying him in the backyard, things became more complicated. Tobias reappeared at their home in November and had a confrontation with Ryan, which Jenny had witnessed.

> *"I'm going to make this real easy for you both,"*
> *Tobias had said. "My business got hurt badly after*
> *that incident by the railyards, but I'm doing good*
> *with it now. Our friend Ryan here would be in a*
> *bunch of trouble if the folks with law enforcement*
> *found out he has been part of my operating network.*
> *So, every couple of weeks, Ryan will hop in his van*
> *and make a trip to Knoxville for me, like I asked him*

to before. You can see it was a bad decision to say no to me when I asked for your help. It's a real shame what happened to your little dog. So, to make sure nothing else bad happens around here, I will ask one more time for you to do me these small favors. You'll make a nice bit of pocket change for your troubles, and nobody will know that you've been helping a felon for all these years. Nobody finds out, and nobody gets hurt. See how easy that is? All you both need to do is say 'yes,' and it will be business as usual."

Knowing that Tobias's threats were genuine, and seeing no alternatives, Jenny and Ryan had agreed to work with him until they could figure out a plan to move out of the state. Shortly after the railyard incident, Jenny had told Ryan about following him to Charleston. He had been furious, not because he felt Jenny was stalking him, but because she had risked being harmed. They both understood how dangerous their situation had become and knew something had to change. Maybe go to Scottsdale and live near her sister, Jenny thought. There would be plenty of work there, and they would get a clean break from Tobias's world of drugs and dealing. That might be the best way to help Ryan recover from his addictions and escape from the scenes of his childhood trauma with Hank.

Jenny had a seven o'clock appointment with a patient this evening, and Ryan decided to stop at The Rusty Nail on his way home from an exhausting day at the resort. The parking lot was especially full for a Thursday night, and to park, Ryan had to wedge his van between two pickups scattered on the lawn. He walked into the usual assault of sounds and smells and ordered his first beer at the bar. Before it arrived, he felt a hand drop on his shoulder and detected the stale odor of Drakkar Noir, Tobias's cologne.

"I was hoping I might find you here," Tobias said. "Let's you and me step out back and have a quick chat. There's some accounting work to handle."

Ryan knew what Tobias wanted to talk about. "I'll join you in a few. Just ordered a beer."

"No, you'll come with me now. If this goes well, I'll buy you a beer after we talk. If it doesn't, you'll be wanting something much stronger for the pain."

They were the only people standing in the back, and even with the loud voices and jukebox inside, things went quiet as soon as the door closed behind them. All Ryan heard was the croaking of frogs by the creek and the pounding of his heart.

"It's time for you to settle up on your debt," Tobias said. "Seems your habit with the oxy and weed has run up a sizeable bill over the past year. Five grand, give or take a few hundred. I don't like being treated like a bank, so it's time to pay up. First off, you will still be making two runs a month to Knoxville, but the next few will be on the house. Let's call it 'volunteer work.' That should take care of the interest. But you still owe me five K, and I want it paid back in full by the end of this month. You and your sweet girlfriend look to be hard workers, and I believe her daddy is a doctor, so I'm sure you can come up with the money between you both. And I'm not asking for it, I'm demanding it. But don't worry if you can't get it all by then, I have a backup plan. I'll just bet your girl's daddy holds a big ole life insurance policy, you know, should anything untimely happen to him. I'm guessing there would be plenty of money coming her way if the insurance company should need to payout."

In an instant, Ryan lunged at Tobias and knocked him to the ground. Both men were rolling on the sharp gravel, exchanging blows, when Tobias's assistant, a large man built like a bear, jumped out of a black Yukon parked behind the building. Ryan was on top of Tobias, ready to drive a fist into his face, when the man ran up from behind and placed the barrel of his pistol directly on Ryan's neck. "This ends now, little man. Get up."

They each got up slowly, Tobias struggling to catch his breath and Ryan resisting the urge to reach for the gun.

"Nice to see you, Mickey," Tobias said. "My instincts were right. Ryan here decided to get stupid and put up a fight. Terrible idea, Mr. Jackson. You aren't playing in the Little Leagues anymore, friend. Let's not have your doggie's unfortunate accident be for nothing. Have it be his gift to you and your girl, his life instead of yours. Now get out of here, and don't let me see you until you have all the money. This is the last warning you'll get." As Ryan walked away, Tobias called out, "And it looks like I owe you a beer. See you soon."

A car had parked directly behind Ryan's van, and he could not back out. The driver had gone inside, but a teenage boy was in the passenger seat with the window open.

Ryan called to him, "Hey! I gotta go. Someone needs to move your car."

"My mom's gone in to haul my dad out. She won't be too long unless he kicks up a fuss again."

Ryan got into his van to wait and resisted the urge to slam his fists into the steering wheel. With his adrenaline pumped, thoughts raced through his head.

> *I've screwed everythin' up big time. If Jenny don't leave me because of this, then she's crazy. Dad is right. I am just a loser, a big-time loser who don't deserve a good woman like Jenny. And I was gonna take her to dinner next week, wearin' the suit I just*

bought at the Goodwill, and ask her to marry me. If she goes to live by her sister in Scottsdale, no way she's takin' me with her now. I promised I'd get help with my drinkin' and stuff once we got out of here, and then I could get a good job and make decent money for a house. Guess I'll never have my own kids and a normal, quiet life. If Jenny can't love me, ain't nobody who can."

A razor-thin woman in short shorts and a tank top came around the corner and shoved her overweight husband into the backseat of her car. After a loud exchange of words, she started the engine and drove off. Ryan backed out and began his drive home, dreading explaining everything to Jenny.

Jenny saw the scratches on Ryan's face and arms as soon as he walked in.

"Oh, Ryan, what's happened? You're hurt."

Apprehensive about letting Jenny know the peril he had put them in, Ryan said, "I need to get cleaned up. I'll tell you later."

Seeing that Ryan was rattled, Jenny let it go and said, "I'll get some soap and water to clean out those cuts and then put some Neosporin on them once you've showered."

Without looking at her, Ryan nodded and went to the refrigerator, took a beer, and went to their bedroom, where he downed two of the oxycodone tablets stashed in his dresser. It was time to retreat to that dark place in his mind, his inner cave where the demons lived, and escape from another devastating day.

Friday, the 13th

White Sulphur Springs, West Virginia

The Reynolds' flight from the private airport in Pontiac to Greenbrier Valley took just over an hour. Dudley had enjoyed his first scotch of the day while relaxing with a *New York Times* in the front of the cabin. Drinking at ten a.m. was early even for him, but his wife's recovery from cancer and his son's wedding engagement were perfect excuses to imbibe. Bradley and Skyler, the fiancé whose name Patty could not remember, had left their seats after take-off and settled onto the banquette at the rear of the cabin. Bradley's mop of sun-streaked hair and his Billabong long-sleeve T-shirt confirmed his status as a card-carrying California surfer boy. Skyler's tight-fitting dress, knock-off Louis Vuitton handbag, and long, messy hair confirmed Patty's opinion that Skyler was low class and in it for the money. Patty disapproved of the giggling and cuddling they were engaging in, but when Kip caught the disdain on her face, he gestured that she should let them both be and mouthed the words, 'puppy love.' Claudia was seated next to Kip in the center of the cabin and had to suppress her desire to take his hand as they talked about his plans for publishing the article he was writing. As far as Kip's parents knew, their relationship was nothing more than a close friendship, and until they announced otherwise, they would continue to act as such. They both intended to change the status of their friendship this week. They would need to decide on their sleeping arrangements, separate bedrooms or one? Without exchanging words, they each knew they shared the same desire. It was time.

A car and driver from the hotel drove plane-side and loaded their luggage and Dudley's golf clubs into the van. They arrived 25 minutes later under the grand portico of the Greenbrier Resort. The long drive along the winding entrance brought back memories to Kip of his trip there five years prior and his fight with Ryan at The Rusty Nail. Kip understood why the image of him hugging Jenny had evoked such anger in his friend, and he regretted never having reached out to set the record straight. Kip had hoped that the affection Jenny showed toward Ryan had endured and that she would be able to help him get well. In Kip's heart, he cared deeply about what Ryan's future would hold and was sorry he had only added to his troubles.

The private cottages at the Greenbrier Resort ran parallel to the walkways leading from the main hotel down to the swimming pool, tennis courts, and golf club. They were single-floor, colonial-style buildings with covered front porches set 20 feet from the paths and nestled among trees. On the morning the Reynolds party moved into their three cottages, Ryan happened to be working at the bottom of the hill below the cottage at the far end, the one Dudley and Patty had chosen. Kip and Claudia were next door, with Bradly and Skyler at the other end of the three-cottage cluster. Ryan was raking a garden bed when he saw six guests exiting the horse-drawn carriage that had brought them to their cottages. It took a second look to realize who the guests were. It had been 13 years since meeting the Reynolds family at Bradley's birthday party, but in a flash, he recognized Kip, and like the first time he had laid eyes upon Claudia, he gasped at the sight of her. She had blossomed into the stunning young woman everyone had said she would become. He was transfixed.

Only after Kip began instructing the bellman where to take the bags did Ryan break his stare and crouch to stay out of sight. Memories from the Riding Club came to mind, her warm smiles when she thanked him for helping with Chester, the compliments she gave for a job well done, and the cold drinks she brought him from home on hot summer days. Ryan now felt foolish having thought Claudia might have been showing something more than kindness toward him, that her gestures might have been a form of affection. He knew his place, and it was not in a world where he was in any way attractive to Claudia as a boyfriend might be. At the time, her kindness had given him an inkling of false hope. However, he could see now that Jenny was his perfect partner: kind, caring, and able to love him despite his many struggles. At that moment, he fully appreciated how blessed he was to have Jenny in his life and to be in a place where they both fit in.

The bellman finished unloading the bags, and Ryan's attention was diverted to Patty and Dudley, walking up the steps to their cottage. The sunlight reflected off the brilliant diamonds in Patty's anniversary bracelet. Ryan thought: *That thing's got to be worth a small fortune, surely enough to pawn and pay back Tobias with.*

Ryan decided to discreetly continue his work near the cottages while he devised a plan to steal the bracelet. He knew he could not take it from her if he found her alone, that would no doubt land him in jail. There had to be another way. And then the answer presented itself.

Bradley and Skyler walked over to Kip and Claudia's door and knocked. They came right out, and the four walked to the third cottage where Patty and Dudley were closing the door to leave. Ryan was standing beside an old oak tree, out of their line of sight, but he could see them. What he did not see was the diamond bracelet on Patty's arm. Then, he heard what he needed to know to devise his plan.

Patty said, "Hurry up, Dudley. Your tee time is in 15 minutes, and you don't know yet if your golf clubs have been taken to the Clubhouse. My spa appointment isn't until one thirty, so I'm going to get a coffee in the café. I should get back at the same time as you.

I booked a full afternoon of services, and I'll need a nap before dinner. See you around five."

"We'll be hanging out at the pool all afternoon," Bradley said. "See ya later."

"Claude and I are going down to the tennis courts for a quick game and then taking the three-mile hike around the golf course. We should be back in plenty of time for dinner. Are we in the formal dining room tonight? Jacket and tie?"

"No, dear, that's tomorrow night," Patty said. "It's Italian tonight, at The Forum, seven o'clock. We can all meet at the lounge at six-thirty for a drink."

As they said their goodbyes, Ryan looked again and confirmed Patty was not wearing the bracelet. This was his chance. All he had to do was finish raking the garden and head for the main building. Glenda had worked a half day in the housekeeping department, and Ryan knew her pass key to all the rooms would be inside her locker. He had gone into her locker many times to borrow a few dollars from her purse, and she had given him the combination. It would take less than fifteen minutes to slip into the Reynolds' cottage and find the bracelet. There were no other staff in the area, and nobody would find it odd to see Ryan walking around the building. He had no qualms about stealing jewelry from Kip's mother; the family had wealth beyond his imagination. He would steal the bracelet and pray for God's forgiveness, He should understand that Ryan was doing what was needed to fix the problem with Tobias and keep Jenny safe. Nothing else mattered, and he trusted God would understand and judge him fairly.

Saturday, the 14th

Mountain View Gun and Pawn was on the main strip running through White Sulphur Springs and opened at ten. The bell tinkling above the door announced Ryan's arrival and summoned the portly, white-bearded proprietor from the back. The faded embroidery on his denim shirt pocket read, 'Warren.' Ryan pulled the bracelet from his windbreaker and said, "How much will you give me for this? It's genuine."

"Sure it is," said Warren sarcastically. "They always is."

"For real, man. It is."

Warren held it for a moment and bounced it in his hand to gauge the weight. He said, "Give me a minute. I'll be right back." He returned from the workroom and said, "Boy, where did you get this from? We don't take no stolen goods here, and there's no way you come by this honestly. I don't need no details, but I can't take this unless you tell me it weren't stolen."

"Got it from my aunt over in Asheville. She was married to the mayor but had no kids, so she gave it to me when she died. Said in her will, I should use it to take some courses at the community college and get a decent job for my future."

Warren was not going to tell his customer that the retail value of the bracelet was close to $40 thousand, and he did not believe a word of Ryan's story. But business was business, and this would make Warren a lot of money. "Fine piece of jewelry your auntie left you. I respect a man who wants to better himself, goin' to college and all, so I'm gonna give you thirty-eight hundred dollars for it. I'll probably lose on the deal if you don't come back for it, but I'll take the risk."

Ryan could tell by Warren's tone that there was no need to haggle. He also knew Jenny had some money saved and hoped she would have the twelve hundred dollars to pay Tobias the full five thousand. He took the cash and drove to Tobias's storage lockers to make his first payment. Tobias told Ryan he appreciated the down payment, but made it clear the balance was due at the end of the month and that Ryan would still be making his run to Knoxville that night.

Ryan was deep in thought on the short drive home. *One more run tonight, and if Jenny has the rest of the money, we'll be headin' out to Scottsdale at the end of the month to plan our move and finally get away from all this.* He could already envision the cactus in the desert, a small home near the suburbs, a rock garden in front, palm trees in the back, and a child's bike on the porch. A world without Tobias in it.

Jenny had become angry and scared after learning about Ryan's run-in with Tobias and his threat to harm them and her father. But she accepted the harsh reality of going to the police and the risk of being implicated in Tobias's illegal drug racket. Doing the right thing and turning him in would only hurt them. The best solution was to leave their families behind and start a new life in another state. She resolved to forgive Ryan for getting himself in debt because of his drug use, knowing her love for him would give her the strength to help him find his way to sobriety, God willing.

Ryan backed his van into the loading dock at Wooddale Produce Wholesalers at nine-thirty that night. It was an old warehouse on the outskirts of Knoxville that had served numerous wholesalers over the decades, none of whom could stay in business for more than a few years. As Ryan opened the doors, the dock manager walked to the back of the van and said, "Evenin'. We got a dozen cartons tonight, three each of tomatoes, onions, cukes, and squash. Give us fifteen minutes, and you'll be on your way. Oh, and our boss wants you to give this envelope to Tobias. Tell him it's from Miguel." Ryan stuffed the envelope into his windbreaker and climbed into the van.

It was a short drive from the warehouse back to Route 81, and Ryan settled in for the four-hour drive home. It was his third trip to Knoxville, and he knew the roads well. Passing through the Cumberland Mountains kept him alert, even though he was tired after a long and stressful day. But tonight, there seemed to be a problem with the van. After an hour of riding the brakes on the downhill turns, Ryan could tell they were getting soft, requiring frequent pumping to decelerate properly. Over the past month, he had noticed tiny puddles of brake fluid under the van after being parked overnight. He suspected a small leak and kept a quart of fluid in the van if it needed topping up. The blue roadside sign announced an exit ahead for the Tri-Cities Parkway with a Wendy's restaurant near the freeway. Concentrating on the brakes and focusing on navigating the challenging road, he did not notice the Ram pickup that had been following him. Ryan pulled into the Wendy's parking lot, topped up the brake fluid, and decided to use the restroom and buy a sandwich. When he came out, he would check under the van to see if any more fluid had leaked.

The two men in the pickup followed Ryan inside, glad he went down the hallway to the restroom. It was ten o'clock, and all the customers were using the drive-through, so the inside was empty except for the three of them and a few employees.

As Ryan walked toward the urinals, each man grabbed him by the arm, and the larger man, with a tattooed neck and a crooked nose, put his hand over Ryan's mouth and said, "You'll need to hold it, I'm afraid. We're goin' outside."

The other man was much smaller but equally intimidating, sticking the end of what Ryan assumed to be a pistol into his rib. "Nice and quiet," he said. "No fuss."

A door at the end of the hallway led to an exit, and the two men walked Ryan out to the parking lot behind the kitchen. The smaller man looked around to make sure there were no surveillance cameras and gave his associate a nod, who produced a roll of duct tape and gagged Ryan. The larger man held on to Ryan and kept him still while the other reached into Ryan's back pocket and took the van keys. He said, "Okay," as he stepped back from Ryan, and his associate pulled Ryan backward over his extended leg, sending him to the ground. As soon as he landed, Ryan saw the smaller man remove the pistol from his jacket and take aim. There was a sudden click and a swooshing sound as the door to the restaurant opened, and two workers carrying bags of trash emerged. They stopped when they saw the armed man look at them, then at his associate, and shake his head 'no,' gesturing with his head toward the parking lot beside the building.

The two men fled around the building, and the smaller one got into Ryan's van while the other took his place in the pickup. They left the parking lot a minute later and went to the freeway. They drove east, away from Knoxville. After ten minutes, they pulled into the apron of a sandy ramp used by runaway trucks to stop their out-of-control vehicles on steep downhill stretches. They transferred the produce cartons from the van into the back of their truck, shifted the van into neutral, rolled it to the edge of the hillside, and pushed it into the ravine below. The van rolled over twice and, without igniting, landed on its roof with its wheels slowly spinning, marking the end of the road for Ryan's piece-of-shit van.

When the men left Wendy's lot, Ryan got up and began removing the duct tape. The workers went to Ryan and asked him if he was okay. He said he was, thanked them, and declined their offer to phone the police. "No need to call. I know these guys. They said I owe them money, but I don't. I'll turn them in tomorrow morning.

They won't get far."

One of the workers said, "How will you get home?"

"I'll call my girlfriend to come get me. I'm all good, thanks."

All he could do now was phone Jenny and pray, once again, that she would be understanding about what had happened and stick with him until they were able to escape their living hell.

Sunday, the 15th

3:00 a.m.

Ryan had walked to the LaQuinta Inn next door to Wendy's and booked a room for his short stay. Jenny arrived four hours later, and they were home by seven. Ryan had fallen asleep in the car after explaining what had happened, and they dreaded thinking about what kind of trouble they would be in when Tobias learned about the theft. Ryan had told Tobias he would come to the storage lockers at 10:00 with the delivery, so after two hours of sleep at home, he gave Jenny a long hug and left in her car to face the music.

10:00 a.m.

Ryan was shocked at Tobias's reaction when he pulled up without the van. The door to one of his storage units was open, and Tobias was relaxing in a canvas lawn chair inside, sipping coffee from a Styrofoam cup and eating a pastry from its plastic wrapper. Tobias smiled as Ryan walked toward him, but it was not a friendly smile, it was menacing.

"Well, good morning, sunshine," Tobias said. "Glad you could make it. Good thing your girlfriend could lend you her car, it would have been a long walk. Did you forget something? Like, my boxes?"

Ryan could not interpret Tobias's demeanor and was speechless.

Tobias took a moment to enjoy staring at Ryan's confused face and said, "Shame about your van. That's gonna set you back a good chunk of change. New cars ain't cheap. But I wonder what we're going to do about them stolen boxes."

Tobias had no intention of letting Ryan know the full value of the drugs. The six one-gallon Ziplock bags held 12,000 oxy pills each, with a street value of $20 per pill. The hundred pounds of crystal meth, divided into ten packages, were worth about one million. Tobias was on the hook for a shipment worth more than three million dollars on the street, a million of which he needed to pay to the cartel.

"I'm sure you can imagine how upset my people will be if I can't pay them quickly for the shipment," Tobias said. "Because of you and your carelessness, I can't do that. Which means we both have a very serious problem."

Earlier that morning, Tobias received a phone call from his brother-in-law, Eddie, in Asheville. He had divorced Tobias's sister the previous year, and shortly after, he began buying drugs from a Mexican cartel known as *El Outro*, the gang whose distributor had been shot dead at the railyards in Charleston. Eddie was now buying from one of *El Outro's* new distributors in Asheville.

Eddie had said, "Toby, my group got a large shipment of high-quality product this morning that my boss says 'fell off the back of a truck' last night, and they need to move it fast. You interested?"

"Where did it come from?"

"My guy didn't say, but a friend in Raleigh who works with me said the Mexicans hijacked a van leaving Knoxville last night and hit the jackpot." Tobias instantly knew that the stolen drugs were meant to be *his* jackpot. The Mexicans were seeking retribution for the killing of their man in Charleston and the theft of their drugs.

Wanting nothing to do with the war that would now break out

between the cartels, Tobias said, "Thanks for asking, Eddie, but I'm a bit overstocked. I'm gonna pass."

Tobias knew that the Knoxville operation was run by a cartel out of Bogotá and managed by a man named Miguel, the man Ahmed had assigned to locate Kip Reynolds. Unbeknownst to Ryan, he was about to hand Tobias an envelope with a description and artist's rendering of their suspect. Thanks to Adam's many precautions, they hadn't been able to find any photos of Kip online, and they had so far been unable to trace his phone number to an address. Knowing that Tobias used to buy from the Mexican cartel, Miguel asked him and anyone who had worked with them if they knew who Kip was.

Surprised that Tobias already knew what had happened, Ryan said, "I didn't do nothin' wrong, man. I was ambushed. I had no way to know them two guys was following me."

"There's a lot you don't notice. I might even say you're careless. But I notice everything, like how you miraculously came up with almost four grand in less than a day. That struck me as odd, getting a hold of that much money so fast, and it got me to wondering. Maybe you've been skimming off some of the product you've been picking up for me and selling it on the side, you know, usin' ole Tobias as a bank to finance your own little business."

"I swear, I've never stolen a thing from you! Honest, you gotta believe me." Ryan was telling the truth and tried to think of what he could do to convince Tobias.

"And why should I believe a low-life like you? A guy who would do anything to keep the drugs coming to support his habit? You've broken the cardinal rule in this business: don't use the products you handle. It never goes well, and you're proof of that. I think I've got bigger problems with you than I thought." Tobias paused, squinted, and said quietly, "Maybe it's time to end our relationship. That girl of yours sure is gonna miss you."

Panicked by the threat, Ryan blurted, "I stole somethin' real expensive from some rich folks and pawned it. That's where I got the cash."

"Well, well, now we get to the truth. Those folks must be very rich. Pawnbrokers pay shit nothing for things, so whatever you stole was worth a whole bunch of money. What did you steal, and where did you steal it from?"

"Some jewelry from a family stayin' at the resort. I know them from when I lived up north. They're from Michigan."

"How rich are they?"

"Stinkin' rich. Family made a fortune doin' somethin' in the car business. They're like, multi-millionaires."

"Are they still at the resort?"

"Yeah. I heard my friend tell the luggage guy they're leavin' on Tuesday."

"Your friend?"

"Oh, yeah. Their son, Kip. I knew him real good, until we had a big fight. We don't talk no more."

Within seconds, Tobias had an idea. A family with a fortune would be willing to pay a sizeable ransom for the return of their kidnapped son. Tobias knew of cases where wealthy families had paid as much as a million dollars for the release of a family member, and a million dollars would solve his problem with the cartel. Tobias decided to let Ryan go and take some time to figure out a plan.

"Tell you what," Tobias said. "You go home to get some beauty rest, and I'll stop by in an hour or so with a few ideas about how we can make things right between us. Tell your girlfriend I was very understanding about what happened and how sorry I was that you both had to go through such a terrible thing. Then, stay home until I get there. You hear me? Stay home."

"Yeah. I hear you."

"Good. Now get the hell out of here, loser."

Tobias took the last swig of his gas station coffee and opened the envelope from Ryan. Miguel had given him a heads-up about its contents, but he had not told Tobias the name of the man they were looking for. The face in the drawings was unfamiliar to Tobias, but he was startled when he saw the name 'Kip Reynolds' written below one of the artists' renderings. *Kip?* Tobias had only heard that name once, five minutes ago, from Ryan. What were the odds it was Kip Reynolds? The odds were good, he decided, especially if this man was working for the Mexicans. If they were seeking retribution for the killing of their distributor at the railyards, and Ryan had said anything to his friend Kip about his pickup from the Colombians in Knoxville, the Mexicans would have known where and when to strike. Tobias thought that could explain why the Colombians wanted to find Kip. Tobias was too low on the Colombian cartel's totem pole to know about Kip's role in having their containers seized, the actual reason they wanted to find him. Even without all the facts, Tobias felt the pieces fit together, and it was clear to him what he needed to do: abduct Kip Reynolds and turn him over to Miguel's people so they could extract a million dollars from his family. Tobias grinned at the prospect of absolving his financial debt to Miguel while elevating his stature with the cartel by delivering Kip Reynolds. It seemed too good to be true.

Miguel answered Tobias's call an hour later and, after receiving the news, put him on hold while he phoned his boss in Bogotá, Ahmed Karam. Three minutes later, Miguel hung up and continued his call with Tobias. "Our boss is quite pleased with the news and will come from Bogotá this evening to handle things himself. His plane will arrive at the Greenbrier Valley Airport sometime this evening, depending on how long it takes with the immigration and customs officers in Miami. But you must have Mr. Reynolds in your custody by then and bring him to the airport. The boss will take things from there. Understood?"

"Understood. Will you be there?" Tobias asked.

"No. The boss is quite pleased with this development and would like to thank you personally for your good work. I do not need to attend. Drive to the security gate at the private terminal and tell the agent you are meeting the incoming flight with tail number 7TA—seven-Tango-Alpha. Say you are picking up the passenger for his stay at the resort. They will show you where to park while you await the plane's arrival. Once the Gulfstream is parked, drive plane side and wait for instructions."

"I'll be there," Tobias said, and then he got to work on the details of his plan.

11:45 a.m.

Tobias pulled into Jenny's driveway and was pleased Ryan had done as instructed. He and Jenny were waiting in the living room. Tobias helped himself to a seat on the sofa and said, "Does your friend, Kip, suspect that it was you who may have stolen his mother's jewelry?"

"Nope," Ryan said. "Nobody seen me there. I was workin' by their cottages and stay hid while they was movin' into their rooms. I snuck in after they all left and got out fast."

"So your friend does not know you were there?"

"Nope."

"Good. There might be a way your friend and his rich family can help us solve our financial problem. Millionaires can be quite resourceful when they need to be. I want to talk to your friend and suggest a way for him to help us. I'm certain I can convince him it is in his best interest and his family's best interest to work with us on finding a solution. Here's what I need you to do. You'll drive to the resort now and hang out around their rooms. At some point, you are bound to see your friend. Act surprised when you see him and say how good it is to run into him. Let him know you work there so he won't be suspicious."

"He ain't gonna believe I'm glad to see him. We didn't exactly part on good terms. I threatened to kill him at The Rusty Nail when I saw him hittin' on Jenny."

Jenny shot Ryan a look of disapproval. She had long ago explained to him what had actually happened that night.

"You did, huh?' Tobias said. "Well, you will have to do some fine acting and convince him you're ready to let bygones be bygones. How long ago was that?"

"'Bout five years."

"Well, a lot can happen in five years. You'll have to make him believe you. Invite him here for dinner tonight. Tell him you will pick him up around 5:45 and bring him to the house. Don't tell him anyone else will be here. And no need to cook dinner, young lady, your guest won't be staying long."

"Guests," Ryan said. "He's got a girlfriend. Pretty sure he won't come without her."

"Not ideal, but we'll deal with it. Now get going. You might be in time to catch him on his way to lunch. Don't screw up. Remember, your lives depend on it."

12:20 p.m.

Tobias was right. Just as Ryan walked from the employee parking lot to the cottages, Kip and Claudia turned onto the path leading to the poolside bistró and walked straight toward him. The skies were partly cloudy, and the sun broke through, shining directly into Claudia's eyes when she thought she recognized Ryan. "Kip, is that Ryan walking toward us? I can't make out the face."

Ryan's silhouette and way of walking were unmistakable to Kip, and he said, "My God, Claude. That's him." He took her hand and quickened their pace, waving to Ryan as they approached. "Well, as I live and breathe. Ryan Jackson, how's it going? You remember Claudia, don't you?"

Ryan's throat tensed, and even after five years, the anger from their fight at the bar rekindled as he thought, *Of course, I remember Claudia, do you think I'm stupid?* But knowing he was on a mission, he controlled himself and said, "Sure. Hey Claudia. I work here now, my dad's the grounds manager and got me a job landscapin'. I thought I seen you the other day, but I had to keep movin'. Guess I was right, it *was* you." And then, gathering all the self-control he could, said, "It's great to see you guys. A lot's happened since you were here before, Kip. Sorry about everything. I wasn't doin' good back then, havin' some troubles after my accident. Didn't mean anything I said. Jenny and I are a couple now, livin' together at her house, and she told me what really happened that night. My bad."

"All is forgiven, mate. You're looking good, Jenny must be treating you right," Kip said.

"I'll bet she's a lovely woman," Claudia said. "I'd enjoy meeting her sometime, but we leave Tuesday morning."

Ryan seized the opportunity. "Jenny's home now, makin' somethin' in the crockpot for dinner. Won't be fancy or nothin', but she's a great cook and always makes plenty. How 'bout you guys come over for dinner? She loves company."

Claudia said, "Do you want to call her and ask if it's okay? We'd love to come, wouldn't we, Kip?"

Before Kip could answer, Ryan said, "I'm sure it's fine. Our neighbors were gonna come over, but their kid's sick, so they canceled this morning. Jenny was all set for company." Ryan noticed how easy it was to lie, and it bothered him. For all his faults, he knew he was an honest man. If lying and deceiving had now become a part of who he was, he felt it was too high a price to pay for being unable to conquer his addictions and end up in a situation like this. He was selling out the man who had befriended him when he moved to Pontiac, when he needed help, which disturbed him deeply. But reality set in. *This is life and death for me and Jenny*, he thought. *Who cares what happens to me? It's Jenny I care about. I'll do anything to protect her. Anything, including this.*

Kip said to Claudia, "The family is having dinner tonight at the hotel's steakhouse. I'll let Mother know we won't be joining them. We'll all be together for the send-off dinner tomorrow, so I'm sure it will be fine."

"Jenny and me live just ten minutes down the road. I'll pick you guys up at the valet stand at 5:45 if that works for you," Ryan said, hardly believing this had all unfolded so easily.

"Great," Kip said. "Looking forward to it. Does Jenny like chocolate? There's a great candy shop here, I'll bring truffles."

"Sure," Ryan said, having no idea what truffles were. "See you then."

As Kip and Claudia continued their walk toward the pool, a strange combination of feelings came over Ryan: relief, satisfaction, and sadness. He realized that as soon as Jenny had told him Kip was not hitting on her that night, he had regretted fighting with Kip. He missed his friendship. He had often thought about phoning Kip and apologizing, but each time he did, he became anxious, drank a few beers, and took a pain pill. Numbing himself was his only way of dealing with difficult emotions. As he watched them walk away, Ryan thought, *I've got to find a way to straighten my brain out. Jenny says that with God's help, I can. It's time to put my trust in them both and find out, as soon as this is over.*

4:00 p.m.

Kip and Claudia ate lunch at the bistró and then enjoyed a few hours by the pool. The sky was clouding over, so they turned in their towels and started back to their cottage. Kip said, "Head on back without me, Claude. Mom and Dad should still be at the golf club. I'll let them know we won't be joining them for dinner."

Perfect, Claudia thought. *I'll have the room to myself and can finally call Adam.*

Claudia sat on the bed and phoned without changing from her bathing suit and robe. Adam saw it was her and picked up right away. After exchanging hellos and a minute of chit-chat, Adam asked how her trip with Kip's family was going. Claudia said, "Well, I think they is takin' quite a shine to this here mountain girl. I'm settlin' right into these here parts and talkin' like the locals." Then she heard a familiar sound in the background and said, "Adam, where are you? Did I hear a horse snorting?"

Unwilling to disclose his location, Adam darted into a quiet room and shut the door. "Must have been my chortle. You've got quite the sense of humor, Daisy Duke. What's up?"

Claudia took a deep breath, closed her eyes, and said, "Adam, I think this is it, what I've been waiting for since the day I met Kip. He and I slept in our own rooms on the night we arrived, but last night, we cuddled on the sofa for hours, and it was awkward saying goodnight and separating when it was time for bed. In every other way, we are living like lovers. I've been the one holding back, terrified I'd be destroyed if I ever lost Kip, but Adam, it's time. It's time I let go of my fears and let Kip know how much I love him. I just need to say that out loud and to hear you say I'm making the right decision. You've always looked out for me, and I know you will tell me if I'm making a mistake."

Without missing a beat, Adam said, "As long as you use protection, you won't be making a mistake."

Claudia knew it was Adam's quirky way of confirming it was the right decision. "Thank you, Dr. Kinzler. You're the best."

"I know."

Claudia could feel his smile. Then she said, "Have you gotten any information about Susan Wang?"

"Yes, and it's worse than I feared. Police records show that Susan had been living with Steve Norris, and they were both murdered on the night of the sixth, suffocated. Their bodies weren't found until the next day. There was nothing suspicious on the lobby's CCT cameras and no signs of a forcible break-in. The police have no suspects and no motive, but it was noted as 'a mob-style killing' with no evidence left at the crime scene. This was a planned hit. It's good you're flying home on Tuesday, best not to be away while we figure this out."

"I'm not going to tell Kip tonight. I'll let you tell him once we're home. He'll have a lot of questions for you. I'll have him bring us straight to the office after we land. We should get there in the early afternoon."

"Are you staying in tonight?"

"Actually, no. Remember the young man who used to work at the Riding Club, Kip's friend, Ryan?"

"Nope. Never met him."

"Maybe not. Kip's friend lives near the resort, and they've caught up with each other after almost five years. We're going to his house for dinner with him and his girlfriend. Kip met her years ago when he was here with his family. We won't be back late."

"I have no reason to think you guys are in any danger down there, you flew privately and would be hard to track, but be careful. We don't know the full scope of what we're dealing with, but we can be certain things will get worse before they get better."

"I'm on full alert, *mon frére. Bonsoir.*" Claudia hung up and was lost in her thoughts when Kip walked in and saw the concerned look on her face.

"Everything okay? You look worried."

Electing to play the actress role, she smiled and said, "Other than being unable to decide what to wear tonight, everything is peachy."

Kip chuckled and said, "I wouldn't worry too much about it. Whatever you choose, we'll be overdressed. I'm pretty sure this evening is going to be very casual."

5:15 p.m.

Mickey Fines had been working with Tobias for several years. Although they were distant cousins, they did not get to know each other until they spent a year together at the Charleston Work Release Center following unrelated arrests for drug possession. A squat, bald man, with more tattoo ink than skin showing through on his torso and arms, Mickey was well-suited to provide Tobias muscle when the job demanded it. One look at the man stopped people in their tracks. He was happy to accompany Tobias on his visit to Ryan and Jenny's home that afternoon. He liked this kind of job, intimidation was his specialty.

When Ryan let them in, Jenny knew they were in trouble. Mickey's face was stone-like when Tobias introduced him as 'his associate,' after which Mickey found his way to the living room armchair and sat down. Ryan and Jenny stood in the entranceway, speechless, until Tobias said, "Be on your way now to pick up your friends. Mickey and I will keep Jenny company until you get back, real nice and cozy in the living room here. If you had any thoughts of trying something cute, now would be the time to say goodbye to Jenny for the last time. Bring your friends here and act like nothing is going on. Introduce me as your neighbor. I'll take it from there. And be back by six, we're on a tight schedule."

"For what?" Ryan asked.

"Just be back by six. Jenny and I will be sitting on the porch, waiting for you."

5:45 p.m.

Kip and Claudia were waiting under the Greenbrier's grand portico when Ryan pulled up in Jenny's blue Prius, a gift from her father when he celebrated his retirement and upgraded to a Lexus. Kip inquired about Ryan's family, asked how he came to be working at the resort and confirmed how glad they both were to be spending the evening together. Rain was settling in as they pulled into Jenny's driveway, and there was a quiet rumbling of thunder behind the mountain ridge as daylight faded into the evening. Ryan and Claudia sat up front, and Ryan felt a chill as he stepped out of the car and looked at Jenny on the porch, seated beside Tobias, now clad in black. Claudia's eyes went first to the Yukon parked in the driveway, and then to the man on the porch. Her gut told her something was wrong.

Kip waved to Jenny, wondering who the man next to her was. He thought it was odd that Roy was not in the yard to greet them. Then he realized Roy would have been about 13 years old and asked Ryan, "Do you still have your good buddy Roy to pal around with, or did old age finally take him to the great dog park in the sky?"

Tobias heard Kip's question and jumped up. "You guys are right on time. Jenny and I were just chewing the fat here. Looks like we got some rain coming in, so let's head inside."

Ryan said hesitantly, "This is our neighbor from next door. Turns out his kid is okay, so he's gonna join us."

Claudia's radar was sending out an alarm. This all felt like a set-up, and the troubled look on Jenny's face seemed to validate her suspicion. As the others walked inside, Claudia trailed a few steps behind and sent a text to Adam:

> *trouble here can't talk now if I send SOS, get help*
> *no address track my phone*

Tobias held the door as the others walked in. As they turned toward the living room, he shut the door behind them and pulled a Glock pistol from his jacket. They stopped in their tracks at the sight of Mickey on the sofa. Mickey stood while lifting a gun from his lap, and a clap of thunder behind the house caused Jenny to stifle a scream.

"No need to be afraid if everyone behaves and does as they're told. Sit down, you two, on the sofa," Tobias said, waving his gun at Ryan and Jenny, "and both of you, in the chairs. My friend Mickey here can act as ugly as he looks, so don't provoke him. Now, sit quietly while I step outside and make a call. Then, we can discuss what I need everyone to do. Looks like there won't be any dinner after all. Sorry."

Claudia wanted to send an SOS text to Adam but knew better than to try with Mickey keeping guard. She was seated with her back to the window and could hear Tobias talking on the porch behind her, only able to catch the odd words: "We have him… girlfriend… Okay, ten o'clock…which airport…only twenty minutes away… yes, her as well… see you then, Mr. Karam… my pleasure."

Tobias returned and stood at the living room door, gesturing to Mickey that he wanted to talk to him. As Mickey was leaving the room, Claudia discreetly typed into the phone on her lap: *sos-karam-10 pm greenbrier airport*

When she hit 'send,' Tobias looked past Mickey and saw

Claudia with her phone. "Take their phones," he barked at Mickey. Looking at the others, he said, "I'll hold onto those. We might need Mr. Reynolds to make a call to his parents tonight, depending on what the boss decides. I'm happy to tell you, Mr. Reynolds, that you'll be meeting him later. He has some business to discuss with you. In the meantime, let's all relax for a few hours while we await his arrival. If I'm not mistaken, it's time for *Jeopardy*. Why don't one of you turn on the TV while Mickey and I sit in the dining room and plan our get-together with the boss? It might be a long night. I hope you all got a late lunch."

6:30 p.m.

Birmingham, Michigan

Adam deciphered Claudia's message, and he jumped into action without knowing why Ahmed Karam would be arriving in Greenbrier County at 10:00. His investigative work for the CIA had identified Ahmed's Gulfstream with the tail number 7TA, so using the FlightAware website, he located Ahmed's plane en route from Bogotá to Miami. Adam knew that any overseas flight landing in the U.S. would need to clear immigration and customs. Given the Greenbrier Valley Airport's small size, they would not have officers on-site, requiring an initial landing in Miami. That meant Adam had about three hours to get to the Greenbrier Valley Airport if he wanted to arrive before Ahmed and put a stop to his plans.

"Hello, Mrs. Reynolds, this is Adam Kinzler. Thanks for taking my call."

"Oh, hello, Adam. We were just leaving for dinner. I didn't see a name when your call came in, but I recognized the area code from home, so I picked up. Are you trying to reach Kip? Is his phone not working?"

"Actually, it's you I want to talk to. There's no need to be concerned, but I must get to White Sulphur Springs right away. As in, immediately. Do you know where Kip and my sister went for dinner?"

"Well, no. Not exactly. Somewhere nearby, at a friend's house, someone Kip knew from home. Why?"

Adam had already activated the GPS tracking device on Claudia's phone and saw that she was two miles south of the resort, just off Main Street. "I'm afraid I don't have details, but I received a message from Claudia saying her friends were in trouble and that she urgently needed my help. She's unable to call for the police, so I suspect they are being held somewhere against their will. I can locate them once I am there, but I need to get there now. Mrs. Reynolds, can you contact NetJets to see if they can make a plane available to bring me down? I can be at the Detroit airport in less than an hour."

"Adam, I need to sit down. What you've just said is terrifying. Give me a moment."

Adam heard Patty calling across the room. "Dudley, wake up. There's an emergency, and I need your help. Dudley!"

"Oh, for heaven's sake," Patty said to Adam. "My husband is passed out in the chair and is useless. I will see if I can get you a plane, but what on earth is going on? You're scaring me."

"Mrs. Reynolds, I will be honest. I don't know exactly what is going on, but I have enough information to know that Kip and Claudia are okay and will not be hurt if I can get there in time. Please trust me. There is nothing you can do right now to help. I believe I can make things right once I'm there."

"Yes, of course, I'll call and phone you right back."

Patty's hands trembled as she scrolled through the roster of previous calls and became frustrated when she could not identify any with her contact at NetJets. She walked over to Dudley's crumpled body and shook his shoulders. "Dudley! Wake up, for God's sake. I need your help."

Dudley opened his eyes and mumbled, "I have to lie down. Too many scotches this afternoon," and collapsed onto the bed after three wobbly steps across the room. He was out cold.

After a few deep breaths and another attempt, Patty found the last call with the NetJets concierge in her roster and reached her on the second ring. The company could have a CJ5 aircraft staged at the Detroit Metropolitan Airport in ninety minutes, at eight p.m. Patty phoned Adam to give him the tail number of the plane and reminded him he would need to present a government-issued ID when he arrived at the reception lobby of the private terminal. Adam did the math and calculated that he should land at the Greenbrier Valley Airport shortly before 9:30, depending on the weather. He had checked the flight conditions while Patty was booking the jet and was concerned about storm activity in West Virginia. The front passing through Greenbrier County was due to clear the area by 8:00, but weather in the mountains was unpredictable, and another front was spreading south from Ohio and east from Tennessee. This was a rare instance when Adam crossed his fingers and wished for the one thing he knew someone should never count on: good luck. But that is what he would need if he were going to intercept the drug kingpin who was financing the kind of terrorists who had killed their father. It was time for retribution, and Adam would welcome all the luck he could get.

8:45 p.m.

White Sulphur Springs, West Virginia

The last two hours felt like an eternity. Claudia fought to block out the din of canned applause on the TV game shows and the barrage of commercials telling her to buy Tide detergent, Crest toothpaste, and Liberty Mutual insurance. She was concentrating on solving her own puzzle. After Ahmed Karam had linked Kip to the diversion and seizure of his containers from China, how could he possibly have connected Kip to Ryan? It was pure coincidence that they were staying at the Greenbrier and that Kip had run into Ryan after five years with no contact between them. It only made sense that somehow, this man, Tobias, and his associate were the conduit connecting them all. If so, then their abduction had to be related to the drug trade, and these men had to be involved locally, with Ryan and with Ahmed. Even without solving the entire puzzle, Claudia knew their situation was dire and that no interaction with Ahmed would end well. She prayed Adam had been able to deduce enough from her short text to somehow prevent the meeting from happening.

Kip, however, was missing one big piece of the puzzle. Jenny had told him when they first met that Ryan was using drugs and engaging in some illicit activity that was putting money in his pocket. It was easy enough to see the connection between Ryan and the two men, they fit every stereotype for drug dealers and had no doubt been supplying Ryan. Kip did not know that Tobias had been working for Ahmed's cartel and that tonight's dinner was a set-up to bring them to him.

Ryan had less information about what was happening than anyone. He had no idea why Tobias's boss would want to meet with Kip. He couldn't imagine how they would know him. The gravity of the situation had to be profound. Otherwise, why would Tobias and

Mickey be holding them at gunpoint? Tobias did business in a dangerous world, and guns were undoubtedly a part of it, but why did they need them here if all they wanted was for Kip to meet his boss and talk? And what would they talk about? Underscoring Ryan's confusion was the pervasive sadness stemming from his betrayal of the man who had been such a good friend. Lying, deceiving, betraying—Ryan hated who he had become. He was compelled to confirm his vow. After this ordeal, he would ask for the help he desperately needed to become sober and live with Jenny as a married couple, with a decent job, and hopefully, a yard full of kids.

Tobias and Mickey had been huddled in the dining room for the past hour. Jenny got up and called to them, "Can we please order a pizza? We're all starved."

"No. And sit back down," Tobias said.

"I need to use the restroom. It's down the hall."

"Sorry. You'll have to hold it. Things are about to get started."

Tobias followed her to the living room and said, "Ryan, any chance a poor boy like you owns a suit jacket?"

Ryan had used his last paycheck to buy a dark navy sports coat to wear out to dinner next week when he would surprise Jenny with his marriage proposal. "Yeah, I got one."

Jenny gave Ryan a surprised look.

"Mickey," Tobias said, pointing his gun toward the hallway, "Go back and get the jacket. Shouldn't be hard to find among all the rags he wears. It's time to leave for the airport. Boss just texted from the plane. He's due in at ten."

9:00 p.m.

After pulling the tight-fitting sports jacket over his black t-shirt, Tobias said, "OK, Mr. Reynolds, let's go meet the boss." He pointed to Claudia and said, "And he will especially enjoy meeting you, the boss has a real fondness for beautiful women." Kip's blood pressure was quickly rising, paining him to feel so helpless.

"Mickey will stay here and look after your friends. Don't worry, you'll be in good hands. And speaking of hands, both of you clasp your hands together in front of your waists." Tobias nodded to Mickey, who pulled a handful of zip ties from his jacket and bound their hands.

Tobias sneered as he poked the barrel of his gun into Kip's side and opened the door to go outside while Mickey took Ryan and Jenny into the living room. Tobias opened the doors on the passenger side of the Yukon and motioned for Claudia to get in the front and Kip in the back. A flash of lightning illuminated the car as Tobias pulled out of the driveway, and he could see the look of terror on his passengers' faces. The wiper blades' steady rhythm, the rooftop's pelting rain, and the seat belt sign's repetitive dinging sounded a persistent warning that they were in danger. Kip had no idea where they were going, and Claudia could not tell him they were about to come face-to-face with Ahmed. He would find out soon enough.

9:15 p.m.

"If I don't go to the bathroom, I will burst. I swear, I'll pee right here," Jenny said to Mickey. Mickey, who had yet to speak, waved the gun toward the hall and nodded.

Jenny knew she only had a minute to devise a plan. If she could create a distraction and get Mickey to leave the living room, Ryan would stand a chance of getting out of the house and going for help. It would be dangerous, but it seemed like the only option. Jenny saw the scented candle she kept on the windowsill and the Bic lighter beside it. Then the idea hit her. She rolled up the hand towel beside the sink, held the lighter at the bottom corner, and set it on fire. The flame began creeping up the towel within seconds, and thick grey smoke billowed to the ceiling. Once a small cloud had formed, she walked toward the door and opened it six inches, holding the burning towel at the top of the opening. As soon as the smoke escaped, the smoke detector in the hallway released its piercing alarm, and Mickey bolted from his chair, running toward the bathroom.

Ryan lunged at Mickey's legs as he passed before him and tackled him to the ground. Jenny dropped the towel, ran toward the living room, and used the full momentum from her dash to drive her foot into Mickey's face. The immediate gushing of blood told her she had broken his nose. She had also knocked him out. Ryan saw the zip ties sticking out of Mickey's pocket and took them. He quickly tied Mickey's wrists together, then his ankles, and told Jenny to slide Mickey's torso forward while he pulled his legs to his arms and bound them together.

Ryan snatched the gun and was ready to get up when Jenny cried, "This son-of-a-bitch deserves worse," at which point she cocked her right leg back to deliver another blow to Mickey's head. Her other foot was standing on the bloodied wood floor and slipped from under her. She fell to the left and put out her arm to break the fall. It happened too fast for Ryan to catch her, and the scream she let out when she hit the floor told him she was injured. He helped her up and told her to put her right arm around his shoulder as he helped her to the car. The deafening screech from the smoke detector stopped as they walked out the door, casting an eerie silence over the yard. All they could hear was the TV din with another advertisement for Glade Air Freshener.

9:25 p.m.

Lewisburg, West Virginia

Tobias stopped the black Yukon in front of the security gate at the tarmac entrance. The rain was letting up, and a thin fog hung over the airport. The lights along the runway shimmered like diamonds. The rotating light on top of the control tower and the hum of an idling propeller reminded Kip of the departure scene at the end of *Casa Blanca*, except in this scene, they were waiting for a plane's arrival.

Tobias lowered his window to talk with the guard. "We're here to meet 7-Tango-Alpha, picking up guests to take to the Greenbrier."

"Head over to the side of the tarmac, next to the terminal. You can drive over to the plane once the door is opened."

As he raised the window and the security gate slid open, Tobias chuckled and said, "Now, that was easy. I like easy. I like it a lot."

9:30 p.m.

Mapledale, West Virginia

Ryan's parents lived ten minutes from Jenny's house, and he saw the lights on as they pulled into the driveway. He helped Jenny up to the front door and walked right in.

"And who the hell comes into a man's house without knockin'?" Hank said as he stood from the sofa. He had come home late from work and was still dressed in his khaki pants and a short-sleeved uniform shirt. "A rude and inconsiderate person, that's who."

Glenda got up from her recliner and said, "Jenny, dear, are you hurt? Why are you holding onto Ryan like that? You're as white as a sheet. Come sit down."

Ryan helped Jenny onto the sofa and said, "Dad, we got trouble, big trouble, and I need your help. We gotta head to the airport in your pickup and get there before ten." When Ryan heard Tobias say his boss would be at the airport at 10:00, he knew the Greenbrier Valley Airport was the only one that was that close.

"What kind of trouble?" Hank asked.

"You remember my friend Kip from the Riding Club and the girl whose daddy got killed in that plane on 9/11, Claudia? Well, they was here stayin' at the resort and came by tonight for dinner. We were ambushed by two thugs who tied 'em up, shoved 'em into a car, and took off to meet a plane comin' into the airport. These are bad men, Dad, evil men. I've got to get my friends away before they're put in that plane."

Hank could tell by the looks on their faces how serious the situation was, and Ryan's passionate plea for help revealed a side of him that Hank had not seen before. During the past five years, Hank had only known Ryan to be lethargic, disinterested, and despondent. Now, he was looking at a man on a mission—energized, focused, and passionate about doing the right thing for his friends. In that moment, Hank's feelings of disappointment about his son abated and were replaced with a sense of pride and respect. Ryan was doing the right thing for his friends and appeared willing to do whatever was needed to save them. Ryan was turning to Hank for help for the first time, and Hank was more than eager to provide it.

"Glenda, take care of Jenny while we head over there." Hank reached under the sofa, pulled out his 308 Winchester, and nodded toward the door. He sped out of the driveway, leaving a spray of gravel in his wake. Turning to Ryan, he said, "Don't worry, son, we've got this. We'll do whatever it takes to rescue your friends, just you and me. Seems a good time for us to mend our bridges and partner up to do some good for a change. What you're doin' for your friends is what any good man would do, and I can see now, you got everythin' it takes to be that kind of a man. I'm proud of you, son. Now, let's go kick some ass."

Ryan sat stunned, hearing his father's words of praise for the first time. He thought, *Maybe God does care about me after all. Maybe people can change.*

Altitude: 20,000 feet

Adam's flight was 50 miles from the Greenbrier Regional Airport, and he had just finished telling Patty that she and Dudley should stay in their cottage and wait for his call to tell them that everything was okay with Kip and Claudia. Patty told Adam that Mr. Reynolds had finally woken up and was a nervous wreck, insisting that he head to the hotel and wait in the bar. Adam made Patty promise to keep Dudley in the room and suggested they call room service for whatever Dudley needed. Patty declared her husband to be useless and told Adam that what Mr. Reynolds really needed was a new wife.

The pilot activated the cabin speaker and announced, "Sir, we have some stormy weather moving through Greenbrier that should clear in about ten minutes, but we'll need to circle up here until it does." Adam hoped that Ahmed's flight had not landed before the storm came through. All he needed was a ten-minute head start. The clock was ticking.

9:45 p.m.

As they sped through town on their way to Interstate 64, a direct route to the airport, Ryan told Hank what had transpired that evening. Hank was glad he had spent the extra money to install an oversized grille guard on his F-250 truck. These were the exact conditions, slick roads and low visibility, where a deer running into the road could cause significant damage to a vehicle. The rain had turned into a drizzle, and intermittent flashes of lightning illuminated the clouds above the mountain ridges. Hank needed to keep both hands on the wheel and concentrate on the road. "Ryan, get on the phone and call the police. If those men are armed, this is a job for law enforcement."

"Then you gotta give me your phone, they took mine."

"Jesus, they took your phone? Here."

It took the 911 dispatcher several minutes of questioning to ascertain that this was a kidnapping situation with armed suspects and that an ambulance might be required. She explained that the emergency team was tending to a car wreck on the east side of town and that the officers would need at least 25 minutes to get to the airport. The dispatcher then advised Ryan to stay back and wait for the team to arrive.

"The hell we will," Hank said. "We're 15 minutes away, and we're goin' in, no matter what."

9:50 p.m.

Lewisburg, West Virginia

The storms passed through, and Adam's flight was cleared to land. A ground attendant assisted with opening the plane door, and Adam jogged toward the entrance to the reception area. Pretending to walk down the hall to the restroom, he slipped out the side door and stood beside the building, looking out at the tarmac. His was the only plane there, so he guessed he had arrived before Ahmed, but a black Yukon idling at the end of the building looked suspicious. The darkened windows kept him from seeing the passengers, but his instincts told him the car had something to do with Ahmed's arrival. He had checked his phone tracker during the flight, and the GPS had placed Claudia's phone at the airport. She was most likely in the car. Then he heard the distant drone of jet engines and saw the flashing lights on the wingtips of the approaching aircraft. *This must be him*, Adam thought. *Time to meet our man.*

10:00 p.m.

The Gulfstream rolled to a stop 50 feet from the terminal, and the attendant walked over to block the tires. The pilots had advised the tower that they had refueled in Miami and would turn around and depart after dropping off their passengers. The co-pilot exited the cockpit and activated the button to lower the cabin door. As he returned to the cockpit, he heard the pilot say to the tower, "How long is our window?" The next storm was rolling in, and the air traffic controller had informed them of an imminent ground hold.

As soon as the cabin door touched the tarmac, Tobias drove parallel to the Gulfstream and stopped at the foot of the stairs. He opened both doors on the passenger side and said to Claudia and Kip, "Keep your hands close to your waist and walk slowly up the steps. Don't do anything to draw attention."

Standing at the rear of the cabin was the tall and elegant figure of Ahmed Karam, impeccably attired in a white linen shirt, a burgundy cashmere cardigan draped over his shoulders, and tapered black slacks. He reeked of wealth. But when he graciously gestured for his guests to be seated on the banquette, the glare in his eyes betrayed his kindly demeanor. He was determined to find out who Kip was working for, and as a bonus, he would weigh the risk of demanding a hefty ransom for Kip's release. That would be decided once he had his information. Everything depended on his hostages' willingness to cooperate.

After they were seated, Ahmed walked to the front of the cabin, and Tobias indicated he had something to tell him. Leaning forward so as not to be overheard, Tobias said quietly, "I have been phoning my associate for the last half hour, but he doesn't answer. He has friends of these two detained at the girl's house. Something must be wrong, and I think I should go back."

Ahmed reached into his briefcase and removed his sleek, chrome-plated Colt 1911 pistol. "I'm sure everything here will be fine. Go back to the house and let me know what you find."

"Sure thing, sir. Oh, and here are their phones, in case Mr. Reynolds needs to call his parents for something." *Like a million dollars*, he thought. "The flip phone belongs to their friend, Mr. Jackson. You won't be needing that, and come to think of it, neither will he." Tobias's smile was pure evil, and he had intended for Kip and Claudia to see it.

Adam watched from the side of the building as Tobias drove back to the security gate and waited for it to open. As soon as it closed behind him and Tobias drove off, Adam confidently walked to the offside of the plane so he would appear to the tower as if conducting an inspection. He then knelt underneath the fuselage, listening to ascertain what was unfolding inside. The pilots were preoccupied with their navigation screens and planning their return flight to Bogotá. The ground attendant had gone inside the terminal, and Adam's approach went unseen.

As Tobias drove around the corner to exit the airport grounds, he was blinded by the oncoming headlights of a pickup truck speeding toward him. He had to swerve right to miss hitting it, and the reflection of the Yukon's lights off the chrome grille forced him to squint. Torn between turning back to see if the truck was going to the private terminal and getting to the house to find out what had happened to Mickey, he opted for the latter. The truck would have to get past security, giving Ahmed time to react before anyone could get to his hostages.

Ryan yelled, "Dad, that was the guy who's got my friends! We're too late, I can see the plane from here, and the lights are on inside." As soon as Ryan said the last word, a single lightning bolt struck the ground beyond the runway, dancing back and forth as the blackened skies began dropping a deluge of rain. It was a bad omen.

When they were 30 yards from the security gate, driving along a straight approach, Hank put both hands on the wheel as he hit the accelerator and cried, "Hold on, son, we're goin' in!" The F-250's grille guard smashed into the wire mesh gate and ripped it off its rollers, sending it flying to the side. Five seconds later, they were stopped in front of the plane. Hank killed the engine, and they jumped out of the cab.

Adam leaped from under the plane and drew his Sig Sauer Luger, not knowing if the men were friends or foes. Hank swung his rifle onto his left shoulder and pointed it toward the plane door, while Ryan crouched in the shooting position and took aim at Adam. Rain pelted their faces, and none of them could identify the other. It was a standoff.

Ahmed heard the gate crash and knew there was trouble. He rose from his seat facing the banquette and pulled Claudia's arms, forcing her toward the door. He stood atop the stairs with the gun barrel against her temple and looked toward Hank and Ryan. A lightning flash illuminated the tarmac, and Ahmed spotted Adam to the left of the steps, about five paces back, standing with his legs apart and ready to fire.

When the clap of thunder subsided, Ahmed called out, "Drop your guns, or she dies!" Another flash of lightning and Adam could see the look on Ahmed's face: he was dead serious. Adam bent down and slid his gun in front of him, waiting for Hank and Ryan to do the same. Ryan lowered his pistol, but Hank was steadfast and kept his eye on the scope.

Adam yelled to Hank, "He's not bluffing. Drop your rifle, that's my sister. I know about this man, he'll kill her."

As Hank slowly lowered the rifle to his left side, Ahmed pushed Claudia into the cabin with a force that knocked her down and then stepped back into the doorway. He turned to the right and, with both hands on the pistol, sent a bullet straight through Hank's right shoulder. The rifle fell when Hank clutched at his chest, and he stood rigid for a moment before sinking to the ground. The bullet had passed through his chest, but the bleeding was profuse, and Hank was dazed. Ryan bent down to roll him onto his back, terrified he might not be breathing, and he heard Hank say through labored breaths, "Get up and back away. Do as I say!"

Ahmed had left the plane and was walking to pick up Adam's gun when a shot was fired from the side of the pickup. Hank had gathered what strength he had, rolled onto his left side, and without pausing to use his scope, shot a .308 mm bullet straight through the right side of Ahmed's head. Adam was standing ten feet from Ahmed and witnessed the left side of his head explode into a spray of blood and brain as the bullet exited the skull. It was more than fitting that when Ahmed was struck, the sky lit up with a multi-pronged bolt of lightning that spanned the horizon, accompanied by a clap of thunder announcing the end of the downpour.

The sound of approaching sirens was getting louder, and just as

Adam was entering the plane, three police cars and an ambulance turned the corner and drove onto the tarmac. One of the pilots helped Claudia stand while the other went to Kip, and Adam was able to cut the zip ties with the Swiss Army knife he had never been without.

Claudia hugged Adam quickly and said, "I guess you never know when you'll need a good knife."

"Nope," Adam said, "You never know. "

Kip cracked a smile and shook his head.

"Now, you two stay in here until I come back."

The tarmac had become a sea of flashing emergency lights, and a soft mist began rising from the hot pavement. With guns drawn, one policeman approached Hank and Ryan, while another stood above Ahmed's decimated body and stared in disbelief. The third officer walked toward the plane and met Adam as he descended the steps, signaling everything was okay. Kip and Claudia stood behind Adam at the top of the steps, embraced each other, and shared an emotional kiss.

The medics rolled Hank onto a stretcher, raised it to full height, and started toward the open back door of the ambulance. Ryan walked beside the stretcher and leaned down to Hank. "You're a hero, Dad. A real hero. I'm proud of you."

Hank tilted his head and looked into Ryan's eyes. "And I'm proud of you, son. I'm sorry for all the times I called you a loser, or worse, but those days are over. Now it's time to get us both fixed up, most likely with a bunch of drugs for me, but most definitely without any for you. We got two mighty fine women waiting for us at home, and even though they won't admit it, they need us. We gotta get ourselves right for them and for our friends." Both men shared a compassionate smile that was a first for each of them.

"I promise, Dad, with my hand to God, I'm gonna get help." As they lifted the stretcher into the ambulance, Ryan raised his hand and called out, "I love you, Dad. See ya at the hospital."

EPILOGUE

2014

Friday night's dream,
On Saturday told,
Is sure to come true,
Be it never so old.

— MOTHER GOOSE

CHAPTER 18

Full Circle

SEPTEMBER 2014

Friday, the 19th

Palm Beach, Florida

Patty and Dudley sat under a white umbrella on the outdoor dining patio at the Breakers Hotel. The iconic Italian Renaissance-style resort was on a 140-acre oceanfront property featuring Beaux-Arts architecture, soaring frescoed ceilings, lush tropical gardens, and an opulent lobby inspired by Italian palaces. It was Patty's version of heaven on earth. Having quickly sold their mansion to a star player with the Detroit Lions, her wish to live in Palm Beach was now fulfilled, and their membership at the exclusive Breakers Ocean Club granted her a lifestyle she had always desired. The summer was ending, along with the heat and humidity the season brings to the Florida tropics, and the Reynolds were enjoying the light ocean breeze. Two months after moving into their three-bedroom condominium at One North Breakers Row, a highly coveted address in Palm Beach, Dudley settled into his routine of morning golf, lunch by the ocean, and dinner at one of the many restaurants in town. Patty was enjoying her new circle of society ladies and relished their introductions to the movers and shakers in the town's robust philanthropic community.

An attractive Hispanic waiter in a pale blue polo shirt and khaki shorts approached the table and said, "Another club soda and cranberry, Mr. Reynolds?"

"Yes, please. And two limes this time." Patty looked at Dudley and was delighted to see her newly sober husband with his neatly trimmed hair and frameless glasses, and struggled to remember how much he used to embarrass her in public. Immediately upon returning to Bloomfield Hills from the Greenbrier last year, Dudley sought treatment from a psychiatrist specialized in treating addiction. He began a course of psychotherapy that included the use of Naltrexone to help eliminate alcohol cravings. As soon as their move to Palm Beach was complete, Patty helped Dudley connect to a local Alcoholics Anonymous group, and he was now attending two weekly meetings. Although he still embraced his eclectic taste in clothes, minus the quirky hats, in every regard, he was a new man: bright-eyed, energetic, and taking joy in the simplest of things. Patty was thrilled. After decades of struggling to resurrect the romantic attraction that had brought them together, those feelings were rekindled, and Patty was again in love with her husband.

Patty extended her right arm, straightened her fingers, and said, "I don't know what I would do if Kip hadn't been able to retrieve this bracelet. He never did say if they caught the thief. I still can't believe Kip had to pay the pawnbroker to get it back. What a racket that is. But I have it now and will continue to treasure it forever, my dear, just as I will you."

They looked across the terrace and saw Bradley striding beside the pool and heading for their table. At his side was a striking blonde woman who looked to be in her mid-twenties, wearing a breezy white cotton sundress with a tiny polka dot print and carrying a beige, quilted clutch with the classic Chanel logo embossed in gold on the flap. Patty said, "Thank heavens Bradley came to his senses and stopped seeing that horrid gold digger. What was her name: Tyler?"

"Skyler," Dudley said. "Jessica is definitely more to your liking. Oh, I'm sorry, I meant, more to *Brad's* liking."

Patty smiled at Dudley as she stood to wave and signal them over. "Thank goodness for that. I could not have tolerated that other girl as our daughter-in-law. Bradley has chosen well, Jessica is delightful."

With the advent of becoming a married man at the age of 28, Bradley had transitioned from his youthful surfer dude persona to that of an adult college student. Without his ponytail or customary T-shirts, shorts, and sandals, the new office casual look he had adopted would help him fit right in on the University of California, San Diego's campus. Having declared a major in marine biology, he was looking forward to his future career studying the ocean habitat for the aquatic life he had shared it with over the past eight years. Jessica was his undergraduate professor when he began his studies last year. After the fourth day in her class, they started dating and became engaged at the end of August.

As soon as Bradley and Jessica were seated and had ordered iced teas, Kip and Claudia came up from behind.

"Ah, there you are. I wondered if you would be joining us," Dudley said.

Kip kissed Patty on the cheek and said hello to the others. "We stayed at the museum longer than we planned. But just as you promised, Dad, we found the photograph taken in 1901 of your great-grandfather standing with Henry Flagler in front of this hotel. Did you know that the hotel used to be called The Palm Beach Inn until Flagler expanded it in 1901 and named it The Breakers?"

"Yes, dear," Patty said. "It was the first hotel in southern Florida built on the oceanfront, and guests who stayed at his other hotel, built alongside the Lake Worth Lagoon, began requesting rooms at the hotel 'over by the breakers'; hence, the name."

Dudley looked at Claudia and said, "Henry Flagler was John D. Rockefeller's business partner and a co-owner of the Standard Oil Company. He also owned several railroads and built the lines from the north down to Florida."

Patty said, "Flagler wanted this to be 'A New American Riviera.' He built Whitehall Estate as a home for himself and his new wife, and now it's the Flagler Museum. I'm sure you learned all about that on your visit."

Claudia laughed and said, "To be honest, Mrs. Reynolds, I was so busy looking at the grandeur of the architecture and all the beautiful furnishings that I didn't stop to read much."

"No matter," Dudley said. "There are some things you might find interesting that aren't written about there."

Patty and Kip exchanged smiles, knowing what was to follow.

"My great-grandfather worked with Flagler in New York, and his son, my grandfather, began working for Standard Oil in 1918 when he was 25. Until then, Standard Oil mostly sold kerosene for heating and lighting, and gasoline was a byproduct they discarded when the oil was refined. With the advent of Henry Ford's automobile, there was suddenly a huge demand for gasoline, and the oil business grew exponentially. My grandfather moved to Michigan to assist Standard Oil with their R&D work for the automobile companies. He quickly saw an opportunity to manufacture components used in the final assembly of cars and started his own company, Reynolds Industries. His son, my father, joined the family company right out of college. He took over the operations when my grandfather retired and ran it until 1968, when he sold it to the

Japanese. And here we sit, possibly in the same location my great-grandfather may have enjoyed a drink with old man Flagler."

Patty clasped his forearm, smiled broadly, and said, "Yes, dear, he very well may have. So, with that thought, let's toast our sons and their beautiful fiancés."

Dudley rose and lifted his glass. "To my cherished sons and their precious brides-to-be. May you all know the happiness I have found with my bride of 35 years. Here's to an even brighter future for the Reynolds family and its newest members."

"And not to be a meddling mother-in-law, but I'd like to say how much we're looking forward to welcoming the next generation of Reynolds."

"Don't scare them off, Mom," Kip said lovingly. "They haven't gone down the aisle yet."

"And speaking of that, have you and Claudia set a date for your wedding?" Patty asked.

"Not yet," Kip said as he took Claudia's hand. "Once we have, you will be among the first to know. Everyone might want time to catch their breath after Brad and Jessica tie the knot in May. So, most likely in the fall."

Lunch finished with three slices of key lime pie shared between the six of them, and after coffee was served, Patty said, "Kip, what time do you and Claudia fly out?"

"Our flight boards at five-thirty, so we had best get going. Our bags are in the rental car, so no need to go back to the condo."

They walked through the covered colonnade on their way to the valet stand, each couple holding hands and swinging their arms. Kip left the group to hand his claim stub to the attendant, and Dudley walked up to put his arm around his shoulder.

"Son, I want you to know how proud I am. You've taken the bull by the horns and established yourself as a successful journalist. You have a brilliant career ahead of you. I realize now that I was never able to face reality, it was too confronting, but you were right. I've never held an actual job, and if it weren't for your mother, I would probably still be drinking my life away. It may be too late for me to launch a career now, but you have your whole life ahead of you to make a real difference in this world. Getting your article published in *The Atlantic* is a huge first step toward that. You have become your own man, and nothing could make me prouder."

"That means a lot, Dad. Thanks. And don't undersell yourself. Battling an alcohol addiction is a lifetime job, maybe an unconventional one, but a job, nonetheless. You are off to a great start, and I have full faith you will live a long, healthy life. You've got Mom by your side, and I have Claudia. Seems to me we are pretty darned lucky."

"Believe me, son, luck has nothing to do with it. We are truly blessed."

Sunday, the 14th

Birmingham, Michigan

Claudia stepped over two boxes in the center of the living room and scanned the stacks of cartons lining the walls of the other rooms. She could not decide who had moved in with more things: she or Kip. The furniture they had ordered through Sophia's newly opened design studio would arrive at the end of the month, the window treatments and lighting fixtures a few weeks after that. Claudia knew the two-floor condo would be spectacular given her mother's incredible flair for design, and she was pleased she and Kip could agree on a contemporary style with warm earth tones and soft lines.

Their new home was across from Shain Park in the city's center and only two blocks from Sophia's townhouse on Brown Street. She was a regular visitor and promised to create a home worthy of a magazine spread. They had no doubt she would.

Kip was at the kitchen island checking emails he may have missed over the weekend. Claudia had just arrived home from a morning at the stables and was still wearing her riding clothes when she joined him.

"How was your ride?" Kip asked.

"Perfect, just perfect. With all the spunk he still has, it's hard to believe Chester's 18 years old now. People at the stables say that as fit as he is, he's sure to have several more good years of riding left in him."

"Let's be honest, Claude. If the Riding Club had not agreed to sell him to you, there's a good chance they would have continued using him as a lesson horse with multiple riders every week. It wouldn't have been long before he went lame."

"Well, now he's mine, and all he has to do is go out on the trails a few times a week to get some exercise and then spend his days grazing in the pasture with his buds. He's enjoying a cushy retirement with all the pampering I give him."

"That horse is a Godsend for you, and he deserves it. After all that happened last year, you needed a way to de-stress. Reconnecting with horses seemed the perfect way, and now we can see that it has been."

Intending to be sarcastic, Claudia said, "Right. There's nothing like having a pistol held to your head while looking over a tarmac and seeing two other shooters aiming to kill. When Ahmed's gun fired, I was certain that was the end of us. But here we are, and once we know Tobias and Mickey are locked up for good, we can go to bed at night assured that justice has been served and that the whole ordeal will finally be over."

Claudia sat at the island across from Kip and opened her laptop. She logged into the FBI's secure database, where she had access to information about open cases. "It looks like Tobias and Mickey's trial is coming up in three weeks. The FBI confirmed last week they have enough evidence that you and I won't need to testify in court, our depositions should do for now. We just need to be available if the trial unfolds and we are called in. Either way, between the kidnapping and federal drug trafficking charges, those two are going to be put away for a long, long time."

"As rewarding as that is, it still feels like only a drop in the ocean, given the global scale of the drug trafficking problem. But I'm glad justice is being done, even if only for these two criminals."

"Do you know 'The Tale of the Starfish'?" Claudia asked as she walked to him.

"The story about the little girl on the beach who came across hundreds of stranded starfish, and although she couldn't save them all, she began throwing some back, one at a time?"

"Yes, and she made a difference for each starfish, even though she couldn't save them all. We made a difference, Kip, and now others can be inspired to join in our crusade. Your article will be a catalyst for that."

"You're right, Claude, we did make a difference, and now we have the rest of our lives to build upon that."

"Yes," she said, wrapping her arms around him and kissing his forehead, "The rest of our lives."

Sunday, the 21st

Bloomfield Hills, Michigan

The far end of the indoor riding arena at the Bloomfield Riding Club had been permanently sectioned off to provide a dedicated home for the Northern Detroit Therapeutic Riding Center. Natalie Alazar, known to everyone as Talia, was the executive director of its hippotherapy program. She managed equine-assisted activities for local youth with various emotional and physical disabilities. Her team members taught horseback riding and general horsemanship skills that enhanced their participants' cognitive, physical, social, and emotional well-being. Programs like hers were growing in popularity worldwide, and after only three years, Talia's was considered among the best.

Talia stepped into the arena as the Sunday morning session was wrapping up. Of Ethiopian heritage, her complexion was dark almond with a healthy glow, making her look younger than her 30 years. Her shoulder-length, tightly-curled black hair was parted in the center, framing a strong face with high cheekbones and a sculpted jaw. She exuded confidence, yet she had a warmth that softened her commanding, take-charge demeanor when interacting with her team. Talia was the heartbeat that drove the program, and everyone loved her, especially her head volunteer, Adam Kinzler.

Adam stood atop a wooden platform, six feet wide, 15 feet long, and elevated three feet above the floor of the riding arena. It was accessed by a ramp on either side and two steps leading up from the back. Adam stood in his white polo shirt with the riding center's logo on the front pocket, waiting for Mr. Buttons and his rider to approach the platform. Mr. Buttons was a medium-sized palomino gelding who had been at this job for seven years. He had previously enjoyed an illustrious career as a barrel-racing horse for a young lady who had won multiple state championships on him. Known in horse circles as a 'Steady-Eddy,' and declared to be 'bombproof,' Mr. Buttons was the quietest and most sure-footed of all the horses in the program. He was used for special students with multiple disabilities. He could always be counted on to take care of his riders and ensure their safety. His rider today was a ten-year-old African American boy named Nathan who had been born with spina bifida and lived with a form of autism that had kept him non-verbal throughout his life. Every horseback riding session allowed Nathan to leave the confines of his wheelchair and experience the physical sensation of movement. At the same time, the neural pathways in his spine were stimulated in a way that otherwise would be impossible. Nathan's sessions were on Wednesday afternoons and Sunday mornings, and Adam was always there to assist.

During his sessions, Mr. Buttons was led around the arena with one staff member at his head and a therapist on each side to hold Nathan's legs in place and secure his balance. Nathan could hold one rein in each hand and practiced cueing Mr. Buttons to walk forward, turn in each direction, and halt. Some days were more challenging than others, but every session ended with Nathan sitting taller in the saddle and grinning from ear to ear.

With the help of his ground assistants, Nathan brought Mr. Buttons to a halt alongside the platform. Adam lifted him from the saddle with a hand on each hip and eased him into the wheelchair waiting on the side. Nathan's mother left work to attend every session, and she was walking up the steps to congratulate him for another brilliant ride. As she approached the wheelchair, Mr. Buttons turned his head toward Nathan, indicating he was looking for the apple slices he expected after each ride. Adam placed a slice in Nathan's hand, and what happened next was one of the miracles that participants in the program prayed for. Nathan laid his palm open to offer the apple, and after Mr. Buttons gently wiggled his warm lips on his hand to take the treat, Nathan placed his palm on his horse's soft nostril, leaned forward, and whispered: "Thank you." Along with everyone else, Adam's eyes teared up, knowing that Nathan's life was forever changed.

Once the participants and horses had left the arena, Adam and Talia walked into the barn with their arms around each other's waists. Their relationship was not a secret, and it was clear to everyone on Talia's team that they were meant to be together, often quoting from *Forrest Gump*: "Talia and Adam, they go together like peas and carrots." They had met 18 months ago when Adam learned the Center was looking for volunteers. Being only a 15-minute bike ride from his condo, he went to the Center to observe their work. Much to his dismay, he had to concede that some horses *did* enjoy their jobs, contrary to what he had debated with Claudia as teens, and that these horses enjoyed the important job of changing lives. His heart went out to these youths who were working so hard to overcome their challenges, and he immediately signed up to volunteer. He had only gotten around to telling Claudia after he celebrated his first anniversary and was awarded "Volunteer of the Year."

Talia stopped in the barn aisle and said to Adam, "We'd better get moving, or we'll arrive at the Christening smelling like a horse. It starts at eleven."

"No worries, I have a change of clothes in the car. Do you need to run home first?"

"Nope. Same."

As they walked toward the tack room to change, they saw the silhouette of the property manager walking toward them with his brown-and-white Jack Russell terrier trotting ahead. He whistled to his dog and said, "Don't run too far ahead now, Alphie. We're just going to check the water buckets and make sure they're full before we leave. And with your bad luck, that little tabby cat may sneak out from around a corner and take another swipe at your nose."

"We'll see you at the church, Ryan," Adam said. "It's a big day, and we don't want to be late. Shouldn't you be on your way home to pick up Jenny?"

"Her mom said she would bring them to the church early so they could settle in. I'm just finishing up here, and then I'll grab a shower upstairs."

Adam marveled at how much Ryan's grammar had improved after only two semesters of English at the community college. Once Ryan and Jenny had walked down the aisle at the Unitarian Church of Greenbrier last October, everyone said that marrying Jenny was the smartest thing Ryan had ever done. She was good for him in many ways, and giving him the confidence to enroll in college was just one of them. But partnering with him to achieve sobriety was their most significant victory. The sight of Hank lying in his blood on the tarmac cemented into Ryan's mind his vow to seek help and become sober. It was his addictions that had almost cost Hank his life and had put Jenny's in jeopardy. Had it not been for Hank and Adam's brave intervention, Ahmed may have succeeded in kidnapping both Kip and Claudia. Ryan realized that Claudia had lost her father due to an act of terrorism, and he had almost lost his father to a bullet fired by a man who financed those acts. He could not imagine living with himself if anything had happened to them, all because he had been unable to conquer his addictions. Jenny persuaded him to meet with the pastor at their church, who led Ryan to the local Alcoholics Anonymous chapter and the sponsor who supported him. Jenny and Ryan were now active church members, and Ryan was about to celebrate his first full year of sobriety.

Ryan and Jenny wanted to start a new life, and after Hank

recovered from his bullet wound, they announced they were ready to move from West Virginia. Kip had explained to his parents that Ryan believed he was inviting Kip and Claudia to dinner at his home so an associate of Tobias could discuss business with Kip. Kip informed them that Ryan had no idea it was a set-up for their kidnapping. After Kip revealed how Ryan and Hank had risked their lives to rescue them, the Reynolds expressed their gratitude by gifting Ryan and Jenny a small home on the outskirts of Bloomfield Hills. When Adam learned that the Bloomfield Riding Club was looking for a new property manager, he mentioned it to Claudia. She told Adam about the Jackson family's time in Michigan, Hank's job at the Club, and Ryan's experience as a teenager assisting with stable management. Adam referred Ryan to Talia, who passed his name along to the Club's managing director. Considering Ryan's work history at the renowned Greenbrier Resort and a glowing referral from the Reynolds, Ryan was hired.

Ryan reached down to pick up Alphie and heard the familiar hiss of water escaping from a hose in the shower stall. "Hold on, boy, give me a minute." Ryan guessed the nozzle on that hose had been replaced a hundred times over the years, and he chuckled when he thought back to the day Kip had first brought it to his attention. He reflected on how their lives had evolved over the years and raised his head to give thanks for their many blessings. The first words of a hymn they sang in church came to mind and brought a smile of contentment to his face.

> *"God moves in a mysterious way,*
> *His wonders to perform;*
> *He plants his footsteps in the sea,*
> *And rides upon the storm."*

Birmingham, Michigan

Sophia and her friend Rhonda had spent the morning in the kitchen preparing Mediterranean-style tapas for the gathering after church. With Claudia and Kip still moving into their new condo, Sophia was delighted to host the Christening party. She shuddered to think of what might have happened without Hank, Ryan, and Jenny rescuing Claudia and Kip. Organizing the celebration of their newborn's future was the least she could do to show her gratitude.

When the back door opened, Sophia was sliding a loaf of focaccia bread into the oven. A tall man in his early 50s walked into the kitchen and tapped the screen on his Fitbit. "I did it: three miles, 35 minutes, fifty-eight hundred steps, and three hundred calories burned. I'll be down to 175 by the end of the month." With a satisfied grin, he asked, "When do we eat? It smells amazing!"

Malik Barzani was granted refugee status at the end of 2007 after serving three years as an interpreter for the U.S. government in Iraq. After returning from a two-week campaign with U.S. soldiers, Malik learned that insurgents, who viewed him as a traitor, had raided his home and killed his wife and two teenage children. Their bodies were buried the following day in a local cemetery. Malik remained at their graveside for a week, praying for their souls, taking no food, and sleeping in the open on a straw mat. Unable to work, he returned to his office at the U.S. Embassy in Baghdad and submitted his request for asylum in the United States. He was resettled in Dearborn, known for its large Muslim population, and informed that there would be a job available for him translating government documents when he was ready to resume work. Last winter, Sophia struggled to remove the ice from her windshield after leaving work, and Malik approached her car with his scraper to help. The attraction was immediate, and Malik invited Sophia to join him across the street for a coffee while her car warmed up. After six months of dating, Malik moved into Sophia's townhouse.

Sophia turned from the oven to put her arms around Malik's neck and gave him a quick kiss. "The church service finishes at 12:30, so hurry up and shower. We'll eat as soon as they arrive. You can have an apple to tie you over, only 95 calories. I think you can afford it."

As Malik headed upstairs, Rhonda said, "It's hard to believe it's only been a year since you began tackling your insecurities around counseling a Muslim client. Sophia, your resolve to conquer any obstacle is inspiring. Malik loves you very much, and you deserve a good man to partner with. I think that's what Conrad would want for you. You have a chance to be happy in a long-term relationship again, and Malik deserves a woman like you who can understand the pain of losing his family. It also doesn't hurt that he is so easy on the eyes!"

"I love him in every possible way, Rhonda. I have so many blessings. Now I have Claudia and Kip's wedding to look forward to, and if I'm reading the signs right, Adam and Talia might also be walking down the aisle someday soon. I can't wait to see Ryan and Jenny's baby, it will get me excited about having grandchildren of my own."

The first car arrived and parked in front of the townhouse. It was Ryan, Jenny, and their two-month-old son, Jeremiah, named after Ryan's grandpa. They struggled to unload the many totes laden with diapers, formula bottles, blankets, rattles, and wipes, and Jenny said to Ryan, "Oh, honey, did you have to bring the guitar as well? I think we have enough to carry."

"Oh yes, I promised Kip that Jerry would enjoy his first concert today. Kip insisted."

"Perfect," Jenny said, "A Christening and a concert all on the same day."

Hank and Glenda pulled behind them and jumped out to lend a hand. As Ryan waited for Jenny to unbuckle Jeremiah from the car seat, he playfully patted Hank's stomach and said, "I got so used to seeing you with that old spare tire around your belly, I have to look twice to make sure it's you."

Glenda said, "It's amazing what happens when a man quits drinkin' as much as your daddy used to. Them beer calories sure add up."

"I was up to eight cans a night. Can't say I miss that. One or two after work does me just fine now. But the weekend trips I've been makin' here to work on the renovations to you all's home sure has burned up a lot of calories."

Ryan said, "Jenny and me, I mean, Jenny and I, really appreciate all the work you've done for us these past six months. It's like we have a brand-new house. You and me make good work partners now that we finally get along," Ryan said with a mischievous smile.

"I guess it took a bullet in the chest to bring me to my senses. You are a good man. The only thing that got in my way of seein' it all these years was my own thick skull. I can see now why your grandpa threatened to put a bullet through it if I didn't change my ways."

Glenda put her arm around Hank's shoulder and said, "Anyhow, now you're fit as a fiddle and ready to settle into your new role as Grandpa."

Jenny's parents were the last to arrive, and the group went to the front door to receive a hero's welcome, as if attending a Christening had been an epic voyage. Hugs were exchanged, Malik joined them, and everyone settled in. Sophia said, "We should go ahead and start eating before the food gets cold. Adam texted, and they'll be here shortly, unless he gets stopped again speeding through town in his new BMW."

After an hour of everyone milling about with plates of food and glasses of sparkling grape juice, Kip said to the group, "I think we should head to the living room now. Ryan has a little surprise for us all. Hank and Glenda want to be on the road before it gets too late, they have an eight-hour drive ahead of them."

Both sets of grandparents sat on the L-shaped sofa with Jenny and Jeremiah in the middle, while Kip and Claudia settled onto the oversized ottoman in front. Adam and Talia claimed the loveseat, holding hands and looking the part of lovers, while Sophia and Malik stood with Rhonda under the archway. Ryan perched himself on the edge of a wingback chair beside the fireplace and rested on his knee the Gibson guitar Jeremiah's great-grandfather had gifted him 20 years prior. He was still wearing his navy blue blazer from church, and with his newly-fashioned haircut and clean complexion, he could have passed as a stand-in for Glen Campbell.

Everyone sat in quiet anticipation while Ryan adjusted his fingers on the strings, eager to hear Jeremiah's proud papa fill the room with song. The introductory chords to Lee Ann Womack's country hit, *I Hope You Dance*, rang familiar, and when Ryan's alto voice, with its silky vibrato tones, began wafting through the room, goosebumps raised, and spines tingled. Hearing Ryan's heartfelt ode to his newborn son was a magical experience they would never forget.

When the last notes had faded, the room went silent as friends and family wiped their tears and let out their breath. Hank started the applause, and the others enthusiastically joined in. Jeremiah approved through a quiet groan that quickly escalated to a full-blown cry. Ryan stood to go to his son, and Hank got up to go to his. Hank put his arms around Ryan, gave him a hug and a pat on his back, then stepped back to place his hands on Ryan's shoulders. With a fatherly smile, he said, "Don't you ever stop playin' that guitar and singin' them sweet songs of yours, or you're gonna have me to answer to."

"Yes, sir," Ryan said with a quick salute. "Count on it."

The group began shifting to make their way out when Talia leaned toward Adam and whispered in his ear. Adam nodded and said, "Hey, everybody, one more thing before you leave. We didn't want to steal Jeremiah's spotlight, but since you are all here, Talia and I have an announcement to make. We're engaged."

Even Jeremiah went quiet as the news settled in, but the silence was broken when Sophia turned to Rhonda and her face exploded with joy. "*Querido Dios del cielo, gracias!* God has answered all my prayers!"

Claudia beamed and said, "I hate to tell you, *mon frére*, but even without an engagement ring on her finger, you weren't fooling anyone. We knew it was only a matter of time."

Talia took Adam's hand and said, "Older cultures in Ethiopia don't exchange rings for an engagement, they throw a big party for their family and friends. We are planning a trip to my hometown right after New Year's. We call Christmas Genna, and it's celebrated on January seventh. That's when we'll have the party. We don't dare go before then. Fasting for 43 days before Genna is our tradition. We want no part of that. We'll be here in December to enjoy every bite of Sophia's holiday cooking."

"I'll get you so fat, your family won't recognize you," Sophia said.

Talia laughed and said, "Now, that would be something. A fat Ethiopian!"

Ryan and Jenny were huddled over Jeremiah when Adam said, "I have a special request for our wedding celebration. I propose we have the ceremony at Christ Church Cranbrook, and Ryan, I would like you to provide the music. Given what you just showed us, I can't think of anyone I'd rather have."

Ryan looked up, beaming. "You're on."

"Well, if that's the case, then I have a crazy idea," Kip said. "Why don't we join forces and have a double wedding?"

The couples exchanged puzzled looks, and it took a moment for the idea to settle in. Claudia broke the silence. "That would be awesome!"

Adam said, "It's not the craziest idea I've ever heard. I like it. Talia?"

"It would be a blast," she said, "And your mom could wrap all her creative design ideas around one big event. Pretty efficient, if you ask me."

Kip smiled at Claudia and said, "There's no way an event like this can happen without my mother having a big, no, huge, role in the planning." He looked to Sophia. "Do you think you could survive being partnered with Patty for that? She lives for organizing social events and will tell you that no one can plan a better one than she can."

"Rest assured," Sophia said, "We will be the dynamic duo of wedding planners. I'd love it!"

Claudia said to Adam, "Have you and Talia set a date?"

"Not yet, but we'll have one set before we leave for Ethiopia. The family will want to know. And how about you, Claude? Do you guys have a date?"

"Well, we don't have the exact weekend, but we were thinking maybe come September."

Adam looked at Talia and said, "Well then, September it is. It seems about as good a month as any."

And as if reading the others' minds, Kip, Claudia, and Adam chimed in unison, "All for one, and one for all!"

Talia and Sophia exchanged looks and shrugged. Talia said, "It must be an inside joke."

"And we are on the outside," Sophia said. "Welcome to the family."

THE END

ACKNOWLEDGEMENTS

They say it takes a village to accomplish some things. In the case of this novel, it took only a small group of talented friends.

Tony—The inspiration for Adam Kinzler's character and a driving force in creating the storyline. Thanks for sorting out the technical details and helping me get the facts right.

Mary—Head of my cheerleading squad and a never-ending source of inspiration. Thank you for reading each chapter as I completed it, and for all your time reviewing the final draft.

Linda—Editor extraordinaire and a pleasure to work with. Thank you for your diligent work and invaluable input. You brought clarity and richness to the story that made it much better than it would have been.